RNF

D1381624

Debra Webb ... Y
bestselling author of more than one hundred novels,
including those in reader-favorite series Faces of Evil,
the Colby Agency and the Shades of Death. With more
than four million books sold in numerous languages
and countries, Debra's love of storytelling goes back
to childhood on a farm in Alabama. Visit Debra at
www.debrawebb.com.

Jenna Kernan has penned over two dozen novels and
received two RITA® Award nominations. Jenna is every
bit as adventurous as her heroines. Her hobbies include
recreational gold prospecting, scuba diving and gem
hunting. Jenna grew up in the Catskills and currently
lives in the Hudson Valley in New York State with her
husband. Follow Jenna on Twitter, @jennakernan, on
Facebook or at www.jennakernan.com.

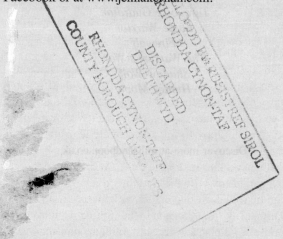

SIN AND BONE

DEBRA WEBB

BLACK ROCK GUARDIAN

JENNA KERNAN

MILLS & BOON

First Published in Great Britain 2018
by Mills & Boon, an imprint of HarperCollins*Publishers*
1 London Bridge Street, London, SE1 9GF

Sin and Bone © 2018 Debra Webb
Black Rock Guardian © 2018 Jeannette H. Monaco

ISBN: 978-0-263-26577-4

39-0618

MIX
Paper from
responsible sources
FSC® C007454

This book is produced from independently certified FSC™
paper to ensure responsible forest management.

For more information visit: www.harpercollins.co.uk/green

Printed and bound in Spain
by CPI, Barcelona

SIN AND BONE

DEBRA WEBB

This book is dedicated to Chicago, one of my favorite cities and the home of the Colby Agency!

Chapter One

The Edge Emergency Department, Chicago
Monday, June 4, 5:30 p.m.

Dr. Devon Pierce listened as administrators from more than a dozen hospitals in metropolitan areas across the nation bemoaned the increasing difficulty of maintaining emergency departments. Once the opening discussion concluded, Devon was the featured speaker.

He rarely agreed to speak to committees and groups, even in a teleconference, which was the case today. His participation required only that he sit in his office and speak to the monitor on his desk. He much preferred to remain focused on his work at the Edge. There were times, however, when his participation in the world of research and development was required in order to push his lagging colleagues toward the most advanced medical technologies. Emergency treatment centers like the Edge were the future of emergency medicine. There was no better state-of-the-art facility.

Devon had set his career as a practicing physician aside and spent six years developing the concept for the center's prototype before opening it in his hometown of Chicago. The success of the past year provided significant evidence that his beliefs about the future of emergency rooms were correct. This would be his legacy to the work he loved.

The subject of cost reared its inevitable and unpleasant head in the ongoing discussion as it always did. How could a person measure the worth of saving a human life? He said as much to those listening eagerly for a comment from him. All involved were aware, perhaps to varying degrees, just how much his dedication to his work had cost him. He'd long ago stopped keeping account. His work required what it required. There were no other factors or concerns to weigh.

Half an hour later, Devon had scarcely uttered his closing remarks when the door to his office opened. Patricia Ezell, his secretary, silently moved to his desk. She passed him a note, probably not containing the sort of news he wanted if her worried expression was any indicator, and it generally was.

You're needed in the OR stat.

"I'm afraid I won't be able to take any questions. Duty calls." Devon severed his connection to the conference and stood. "What's going on?" he asked as he closed a single button on his suit jacket.

Patricia shook her head. "Dr. Reagan rushed a patient into surgery in OR 1. He says he needs you there."

Ice hardened in Devon's veins. "Reagan is well aware that I don't—"

"He has the surgery under control, Dr. Pierce. It's…" Patricia took a deep breath. "The patient was unconscious when the paramedics brought her in. Her driver's license identifies her as Cara Pierce."

A spear of pain arrowed through Devon, making him hesitate. He closed his laptop. "Few of us have a name so unique that it's not shared with others." There were likely numerous Cara Pierces in the country. Chicago was a large city. Of course there would be other people with the same name as his late wife. This should be no surprise to the highly trained and, frankly, brilliant members of his staff.

"One of the registration specialists browsed the contacts list in her cell phone and called the number listed as Husband."

Devon hesitated once more, this time at the door. His secretary's reluctance to provide whatever other details she had at her disposal was growing increasingly tedious. "Is her husband en route?"

Patricia cleared her throat. "Based on the number in her contacts list, her husband is already here. The number is *yours*." She held out his cell phone. "I took the call."

Devon stared at the thin, sleek device in her hand. He'd left his cell with Patricia for the duration of the teleconference. He hated the distracting vibration of an incoming call when he was trying to run a teleconference. Normally he would have turned it off and that would have been it, but he was expecting an important work call—one that he would pause his teleconference to take if necessary. So he'd assigned Patricia cell phone duty with instructions to interrupt him only if that call came in, or if there was a life-and-death situation.

He reached for it now.

"Thank you, Patricia. Ask the paramedic who brought her in to drop by my office when he has a break."

The walk from his office in the admin wing to the surgery unit took all of two minutes. One of the finely tuned features of the Edge design was ensuring that each wing of the emergency department was never more than two to three minutes away from anything else. A great deal of planning had gone into the round design of the building with the care initiation front and center and the less urgent care units spanning into different wings around the circle. Straight through the very center, the rear portion of the design contained the more urgent services, imaging and surgery. Every square foot of the facility was designed for optimum efficiency. Each member of staff was carefully chosen and represented the very best in their field.

As he neared the surgery suite, he considered what his secretary had told him about the patient. The mere idea was absurd. There'd been a mistake. A mix-up of some sort.

Cara.

His wife was dead. He'd buried her six years and five months ago.

Devon moved into the observation area where all three operating rooms could be viewed. He touched the keypad and the black tint of the glass that made up the top half of the wall all the way around the observation area cleared, allowing him to see inside and those in the OR to see him. Two of the rooms were empty. One held Cara Pierce.

The patient's hair was covered with the usual generic cap, preventing him from distinguishing the color. Most of her face was obscured by the oxygen mask. He turned on the audio in OR 1.

"Evening, Dr. Pierce," Reagan said without glancing up, his hands moving in swift, perfectly orchestrated movements that were all too familiar to Devon.

"Dr. Reagan." Devon's fingers twitched as he

watched the finely choreographed dance around the patient. His life had revolved around saving lives for so long that his entire body was finely tuned into that instinctive rhythm.

"Splenic rupture. Concussion but no bleeding that we've found." Reagan remained focused on the video screen as he manipulated the laparoscopic instruments to resect and suture the damaged organ. "She'll be a little bruised and unhappy about the small surgical scars we'll leave behind but, otherwise, she should be as good as new before you know it."

Five or ten seconds elapsed before Devon could respond or move to go. "Watch for intracranial hemorrhaging." He switched off the audio, darkened the glass once more and walked away.

A weight, one that he had not felt in years, settled on his chest. His wife had died of intracranial hemorrhaging. There had been no one to save her and his efforts had been too little too late. The old ache twisted inside him.

But this woman—who shared Cara's name—was not his wife.

Devon drew in a deep breath and returned to his office. Patricia glanced up at him as he passed her desk but he said nothing. With his office door closed, he moved to the window overlooking the meticulously manicured grounds surrounding the facility. Trees and shrubs were precisely placed amid the expanse of asphalt, lending a welcoming, pleasing appearance. He'd insisted on extensive research for design purposes. What aspects would make the family members of patients feel more at home? What could be done to set a soothing tone for patients? A patient's outlook and sense of well-being and safety were immensely important to healing.

Devon stared at nothing in particular for a long while. When his mind and pulse rate had calmed sufficiently, he settled behind his desk. A couple of clicks of the keyboard opened the patient portal. He pulled up the chart for the Caucasian female he'd observed in surgery. He surveyed the injuries listed as well as the paramedic's comments. The kinds of injuries she had suffered were alarmingly similar to those his late wife had suffered in the car accident that had taken her life.

Pierce, Cara Reese, thirty-seven. Her address was listed as the Lake Bluff residence Devon had built for his late wife more than a decade ago...the house he had inhabited *alone* for the past six-plus years.

He scrolled down the file to a copy of her driver's license.

His breath trapped in his lungs.

Blond hair, blue eyes. Height five-six, weight one-ten. Date of birth, November 10—all the statistics matched the ones that would have been found on Cara's license. But it was the photo that proved the most shocking of all. Silky blond hair brushed her shoulders. Mischief sparkled in her eyes.

The woman in the photo was Cara. His Cara.

Devon was on his feet before his brain registered that he had pushed up from his chair. The DMV photo was the same one from the last time his wife renewed her license eight years ago. As if that September morning had happened only yesterday, he recalled vividly when she realized her driver's license had expired. She'd been so busy planning another trip before the holidays were upon them she'd completely forgotten. He'd teased her relentlessly.

His chest screamed for oxygen, forcing him to draw in a tight breath. The name could certainly be chalked up to pure coincidence. Even the physical characteristics and the shared birthday. The photo...that was an entirely different story.

A rap on his door pulled him back to the present. Devon reluctantly shifted his attention there. Why wasn't Patricia handling visitors? He needed time to untangle this startling mystery. At the sound of another knock, he called, "Come in."

The door opened and a young man stuck his head inside. "You wanted to see me, Dr. Pierce?"

Devon didn't recognize the face but the uniform was as familiar as his own reflection, maybe more so since he hadn't scrutinized himself in a mirror in years. More than six, to be exact. The contrasting navy trousers and light blue shirt marked his visitor as a member of the Elite Ambulance service. The identifying badge above the breast pocket confirmed Devon's assessment. *The paramedic.*

"You brought in the female patient from the automobile accident?"

He nodded. "My partner and I. Yes, sir. It appeared to be a one-car accident on the Kennedy Expressway near Division. It was the strangest thing."

Devon gestured to the pair of chairs in front of his desk and the young man took a seat. The badge clipped onto his pocket sported the name Warren Eckert. "Strange in what way, Mr. Eckert?"

Devon lowered into his own chair as Eckert spoke. "Nobody witnessed the accident. There was a sizable dent on the front driver's-side fender, but nothing to suggest an accident capable of causing the kind of injuries the patient sustained."

"What kind of vehicle was she driving?"

"A brand-new Lexus. Black. Fully loaded." Eckert whistled, long and low. "Sharp car for sure."

Cara had driven a Lexus. Devon had bought it for her on her last birthday before she died.

"Do you recall seeing anything in the vehicle besides your patient? Luggage perhaps, or a briefcase?"

Eckert shook his head. "I don't remember. Sorry."

"What about the officers investigating the scene?" Obviously the police had been there, probably before Eckert arrived.

"Joe Telly was the only cop on the scene. He called us before he called backup."

"The woman was not conscious when you arrived?"

"No, sir."

"Was she able to speak to the officer before your arrival?" Devon's instincts were humming. How had a woman involved in such a seemingly minor accident been injured so severely?

"She was unconscious when Telly pulled over to check on her."

"How would you describe the woman?" Devon thought about the photo on the driver's license. "I'm sure you concluded an approximate age and such."

The other man nodded. "Blond hair, blue eyes. Medium height. Kind of thin. Midthirties, I'd say."

"Well dressed?" Her clothes had been removed before surgery and very little of her body had been visible on the operating table.

Eckert nodded slowly. "She was wearing a dress. A

short black one. Like she might have been headed to a party or dinner out or something. Not the kind of out-fit you'd wear to work unless you're a hostess in an up-scale restaurant or something like that."

"Thank you, Mr. Eckert." Devon stood. "I appreci-ate your time."

"Do you know her?"

The rumor had already made the rounds. "No. I'm afraid I don't."

When the paramedic had exited the office, Devon pulled up the record on this Cara Pierce…this woman who could not be his wife.

Preliminary tox screen showed no drugs. And yet if there was no intracranial hemorrhaging, why had she still been unconscious when she arrived at the ER? Re-maining unconscious for an extended period generally indicated a serious injury, illness or drug use.

Devon picked up his cell phone and made the call he should have made weeks ago. When she answered, he dived straight into what needed to be said without pre-amble. "Victoria, I was mistaken. I will require your services after all."

His old friend Victoria Colby-Camp agreed to have her investigator meet him at his residence at eight to-night.

Devon ended the call and tossed his phone onto his desk. Last month, someone had left him an ominous message right here in his office. At first, he'd been de-termined to have the Colby Agency look into the issue. It wasn't every day that someone who knew how to best his security system dropped by his office and left such a bold message.

I know what you did.

But then he'd decided to drop it. Why stir up his painful past? He knew what he had done. Why allow anyone else to delve into that unpleasant territory?

If the man who'd left him that message was trying to reach him again, he'd certainly prompted Devon's attention this time.

What better way to send a message than to resurrect the dead?

Chapter Two

Isabella Lytle was surprised when the gate to the Pierce property opened without her having to buzz the enigmatic owner for admittance. Instead, the instant her car nosed up to the entrance, the towering iron gates parted and opened wide for her.

She rolled up the long drive, coming to a stop in front of the palatial home. Bella shook her head. She never liked to judge anyone, but Dr. Devon Pierce grated on her somehow. She'd never met the man in person but she had studied his background until she knew it by heart. Victoria had first assigned Bella his case one month ago, but then Dr. Pierce had decided he didn't need the agency's assistance after all.

That should have been the end of it.

But it wasn't.

Even before this latest call for assistance, Bella had not been able to stop attempting to dissect the man. What made him who he was? What event or events in his childhood and then as an adult had narrowed his focus to a singular purpose—his work? What secrets did he keep? The man had secrets, Bella had no doubt.

The many photos she'd discovered of him on Google sucked her into his world. She knew the clothes he wore, the way he held himself. In recent years, he'd attended endless fund-raisers seeking support for his development of the emergency department of the future. Urbane and sophisticated was the best way to describe his style and the way he carried himself. Beautiful women with money flocked to him as if he were the most eligible bachelor in Chicago, which he probably was. On top of everything else, he was intensely handsome and mysterious.

That was the part that kept reeling her in.

She closed her eyes and gave her head a little shake. Her need to figure him out had become a bit of an obsession.

She forced the thoughts away as her gaze swept over the mansion that would be more suited for a royal estate in England. Who needed twenty-six thousand square feet of living space? A six-car garage? Not to mention an ostentatious fountain perched right in the middle of the parking courtyard. Her eyes rolled upward as she climbed out of her practical sedan. No one. Especially not a man who lived alone. Maybe he was attached to it since he'd lived here with his wife. The estate was an hour's drive from his work in the city. Was this his way of escaping the twelve-to sixteen-hour days?

Was this his hiding place?

Five acres loaded with lots of trees and lush landscaping backed up to Lake Michigan. The main part of the house was large enough but then it winged off on both sides, extending along the manicured grounds, eventually connecting to triple-car garages on either side of the drive, creating a sort of fortress. The iron-and-brick fence was at least twelve feet high and stretched as far as the eye could see, disappearing into the dense woods.

"Lovely." She made the assessment grudgingly with a heavy dose of reluctance. The house was undeniably, extravagantly attractive. Really, it was. She shouldered her bag and shoved her car door shut as she sent a final glance back at the massive gates that had already closed. Dusk had settled, awakening the discreet and well-placed landscape lighting. Did he have the interior lights on timers as well? Every light in the house appeared to be spilling through the windows to greet her.

"I'd hate to pay your electric bill, Dr. Pierce."

She exhaled a big breath and decided she'd dawdled long enough. The cobblestone was damp beneath her shoes from the early-evening rain. Three steps up and she was at the front door.

Victoria, her employer, had sensed Bella's strong reaction to this client. Bella had assured Victoria that she could handle Devon Pierce. The real question in Bella's mind was whether or not Pierce could handle her. To do her job, she would need his cooperation. Not in a million years could she see him cooperating on the necessary level. He was accustomed to being in control...of keeping his secrets. Pierce was a man who preferred doing things his way.

As brilliant as he was, he couldn't be the best at everything. If that was possible, he wouldn't need the Colby Agency's help now.

A part of her—one she intended no one to ever see— wanted him submissive on every level. Chasing away the notion and bracing for the icy glower for which he was known, she pressed the doorbell, listened as it chimed through the house. The door opened and she stared at the man from her numerous Google searches. To her dismay, he was even hotter in person than he was on the computer screen.

She stood under his scrutiny and felt her temper rising. His gaze roved over her, head to toe and back. She'd taken great care with what she chose to wear tonight. A navy skirt, the hem landing just above her knees, and the matching jacket. Her favorite silk shell with its high neckline in the same dark blue color. She never wore heels. At five-nine, she'd always preferred flats. A good pair of shoes with rubber soles and sturdy straps had served her well.

Deep inside she fully comprehended that she would need every part of her professional armor to protect her from his dark lure. She was well aware that her obsession with him hovered on a very narrow ledge. One wrong move and she would slip.

Even as the warning echoed in her brain, her gaze swept over his handsome face. Square jaw darkened by the stubble of a day's beard growth, dark blue eyes analyzing her even as she did the same. He wore a tailored charcoal suit, probably silk. A paler gray shirt peeked from between the lapels of the jacket. He had dispensed with his tie and left a couple of buttons undone. The platinum cuff links remained nestled at the center of his perfectly folded French cuffs. Bella suspected this was as relaxed as he allowed himself to be in front of company.

"Ms. Lytle." He opened the door wider in invitation.

She concentrated her attention on the details of his home rather than on the man. This was the one aspect of Dr. Devon Pierce that remained private. Though there had been plenty of photos of the exterior of the home on the internet, there was none of the interior.

Black and white marble flowed across the floor in a diamond pattern. The walls as well as the ornate trim were coated in an old-world white paint, the aged matte finish an elegant contrast to the glossy floors. A chandelier drenched in crystal hung twelve or so feet overhead. The rich, ornate mahogany table to the left and the cushioned gray bench to the right lent a warm hue to the boundless canvas of sleek black and white.

"I have coffee waiting," he announced.

She nodded. "Lead the way, Doctor."

The large entry hall flowed straight ahead. Some twenty or so feet from the front door, the hall parted to the right and left. On each side, a grand staircase led up to the second level. A wide door beneath the staircase on the right provided a glimpse of the kitchen—opulent wood cabinetry, acres of sleek granite and an expansive wall of windows. The double doors to her far left were closed. A library or his office, she supposed.

Moving straight ahead, the entry hall progressed into a truly stunning great room. The whitewashed walls soared to a vaulted ceiling, complete with rustic wood beams that looked as though they might have held up a bridge somewhere in the Mediterranean in another century. The stone fireplace was huge. The marble floors of the entry hall had given way to gleaming hardwood. The furnishings were upholstered in sophisticated burgundies and golds. To soften the hard surfaces, a classic Persian rug was spread over the center of the room, the burgundy and gold yarn so muted it had surely been washed out by decades of wear in a castle somewhere.

Whatever charm the man lacked in demeanor had

been infused into his home. The place was utterly breathtaking. Massive and yet somehow intimate. Nothing like the cool, distant man.

Two sofas faced each other in the center of the room. The silver coffee service sat on the cocktail table between them. As Bella settled onto the edge of one of the sofas, she shifted her gaze and full attention to him. Not an easy feat with so many striking pieces of art she'd only just noticed on the walls.

"Please, have a seat," he said, his voice as terse as it had been when he answered the door. "Do you take cream or sugar?"

"Black is fine, thank you."

She wondered if there were half a dozen housekeepers and a couple of cooks hidden somewhere in the house. God only knew how many gardeners the property required. She glanced around. Surely a member of staff lurked about someplace. She couldn't imagine Devon Pierce using his skilled surgeon's hands to perform such a menial task as preparing coffee.

Former surgeon, she amended. Though his license and hospital privileges and credentials remained in place, he did not routinely practice medicine.

He placed a cup and saucer in front of her, the rich black coffee steaming. Vintage china, she noted. His wife must have been a collector. He poured himself a cup and sat down on the sofa opposite her.

"Victoria tells me you're very good at solving mysteries." He sipped his coffee.

"I'm very good at seeing the details others often miss." The coffee warmed her. From the moment she'd stepped into the house, she'd felt cold. *Liar.* Meeting the man she'd been cyberstalking had sent her temperature rising. *Foolish.* "I spent seven years with the Alabama Bureau of Investigation. I never failed to solve the case I was assigned."

He seemed to consider her answer for a time, his eyes probing hers as if he intended to confirm every word by looking directly inside her soul.

"You graduated from the prestigious University of Alabama with a psych undergraduate degree and a master's in criminal justice," he continued. "Two years as a victim counselor with Birmingham PD and the FBI wanted you but you chose the ABI over the better opportunity."

There it was. That arrogance she instinctively understood would be a part of his personality. She had zero tolerance for it. "The FBI isn't better, Dr. Pierce. It's merely larger with a broader jurisdiction. The work I did for the ABI was immensely important. Had I chosen the FBI, I would have spent a great deal of time working toward the opportunity to be a field investigator. Instead, I went straight to the work that I wanted to do—solving crime in the field."

He set his coffee aside. "I appreciate a stellar résumé, Ms. Lytle, and yours is quite good. But I always look at the person behind the credentials. The heart of the person begins with their roots."

For the first time since she was eighteen, Bella felt the heat of shame rush along her nerve endings. The idea that this man held that much power over her further flustered her. "Not everyone is born into the perfect scenario for who and what they want to become, Dr. Pierce. Some of us had to fight our way out of where we were before we could reach where we wanted to be."

"Your father murdered your mother when you were

ten and your thirteen-year-old sister shot and killed him in self-defense," he stated as if she had said nothing at all. "According to the police reports, he was coming at you next and your sister protected you." He studied her a long moment. "The reports also said that the two of you couldn't keep your stories straight. In the end, you seemed to agree with whatever your older sister said."

The blast of a shotgun echoed in Bella's brain followed by screaming…so much screaming. She gathered every ounce of self-control she possessed to prevent her hands from shaking when she carefully set the cup and saucer on the table. "That's right." She held his gaze without flinching. "My father was an alcoholic with a mean streak a mile wide. It would have served my mother far better if she had blown his head off long before he decided to wash his hands of the three of us. My sister was forced to protect us when our mother failed."

Unfortunately, their mother had been weak. Bella blinked once, twice. So weak.

He stared at her for a long time. Pierce was forty-five, ten years her senior, but he didn't look more than forty. His dark brown hair was thick and trimmed in a distinguished yet fashionable style. A few strands of gray had invaded the lush color at his temples. Blue eyes, the color of the sea. Chiseled jaw with a nose that was ever so slightly off center, probably from the car accident when his wife was fatally injured. He'd suffered a broken nose, a fractured jaw and collarbone as well as a gash in the head. Despite his rigorous work schedule, he kept his tall, lean body in excellent condition. She imagined the female nurses and doctors on his staff spent plenty of time discussing the handsome administrator. Particularly since he was single.

Sadly his personality reportedly left a great deal to
be desired.

"You narrowly avoided foster care," he went on with
his well-prepared monologue of her early history, "but
an estranged aunt, your mother's sister, came forward to
whisk the two of you to Mobile. At sixteen, your sister
dropped out of high school and took a job at a local hair
salon. She married and had three children by the time
she was twenty. If I counted accurately, she's on husband number five now. You didn't appear very happy in
school either. The school counselor documented bruises
on several occasions. She listed you as withdrawn and
lacking the ability to make friends. Child services were
called to your home on more than one occasion."

The shame faded and fury took its place, igniting
a blaze that rushed through her veins. "My aunt had
rigid religious and disciplinarian views. As for the other,
most children go through times in school when making
friends is difficult."

Bella had nothing else to say about that part of her
life. Her aunt hadn't really been the problem. It was her
husband. Bella was fairly confident he got off on beating her and her sister. The slightest infraction required
a trip to the woodshed. After her sister left, Bella had
tolerated his beatings for a couple more years. Eventually, she'd had enough and she'd got her hands on the
ax and threatened to kill him the same way she and her
sister had killed their mean-ass daddy. From that point
forward, they'd had an agreement of sorts. He didn't
touch her and she didn't cut off his head in his sleep.
He never touched her again.

Funny how the tendency to choose the wrong kind of
man seemed to run in families sometimes. Her mother,

Sin and Bone

her aunt and then her sister. The three looked right over a nice guy and went for the jerk every time.

Bella never intended to allow a man to rule her. *Never.* If Dr. Pierce was under the impression that his extensive knowledge of her past would somehow put her off, he was mistaken. Her past wasn't something she cared to discuss and, frankly, it still embarrassed her to some degree, but this man would need a lot more than humiliating backstory to undermine her determination or her confidence.

Pierce stared at her for a full minute before he spoke again. "My wife died six years and five months ago. My hands were inside her body when her heart stopped beating. I did everything humanly possible to stop the hemorrhaging but I couldn't. She died on the operating table in a hospital that didn't have the proper equipment or the necessary staff. The only surgeon within an hour of the hospital couldn't get there fast enough because of the record-breaking snowstorm that had hit the area. I was the only chance she had of surviving and I failed. I have no idea why someone would use her to rattle me now, but that's precisely what happened today."

Victoria had briefed Bella on the incident. According to her employer's second conversation with Pierce today, he'd examined today's patient after she was placed in the ICU. She had blond hair and pale blue eyes, like his late wife. Similar build. But she was, of course, not his wife. Her face was different though there were definite similarities. Shoe size was wrong. Her fingers weren't as long as Mrs. Pierce's had been.

Not that there had ever been any question. The point was that someone had gone to a great deal of trouble to find a woman who, on first look, greatly resembled Cara Pierce.

"You were able to speak with her." It wasn't a question. Victoria had told Bella as much. She simply wanted to watch his reaction as he answered.

"Briefly. She claimed not to know her name or mine. She couldn't say where her home was or what had happened to her."

"Which could be as a result of her injuries," Bella suggested.

"It's possible but doubtful, in my opinion. There are also certain drugs that can produce the same effect. We're running new screens for those substances."

"Did you tell the police?" Bella knew he had not. She'd spoken to a contact at Chicago PD and nothing else had come in about the accident. As far as the police knew, the woman hit the guardrail. The accident was her fault. No alcohol in her blood. She would survive and the only property damage was her own.

"No, I haven't spoken to the police about the matter." He crossed his arms over his chest in a classic defense gesture. "Since the situation is obviously very personal, I intend to conduct my own investigation first."

Bella wasn't surprised. He wasn't the sort of man to turn over control of something so extremely personal unless he had no other choice. "You do realize that legally you have an obligation to inform the police about the patient's situation."

Another of those long staring sessions came next. Finally, he said, "I do and I will, when I'm ready."

"This is your dime, Dr. Pierce, so we'll play your way until I am compelled to take a different tactic. If at any time I feel the woman in that hospital room is vulnerable to the situation in some way, I will go to the police myself."

"I've assigned security to her room," he said, his tone flat. "She's completely safe."

"As long as we're clear on that point."

"We're quite clear, Ms. Lytle."

She straightened her back, squared her shoulders. "Is there anything else you should tell me before we begin?"

He shook his head, the move so slight she would not have noticed had she not been watching him so closely. "Nothing at all."

Something else Bella had learned during ten years of investigative work, seven at the ABI and three with the Colby Agency, was that when a man could look you straight in the eye and lie without a single tell, he was dangerous.

"Tell me about your enemies, Dr. Pierce."

"When I first began the development phase of the Edge, two years before my wife was killed, I had a couple of partners. Jack Hayman and Richard Sutter. Both eventually fell off the project." One corner of his mouth lifted as if he might smile. "Jack knew basically nothing about what I was doing. He simply wanted to invest part of his vast fortune in something useful."

"What about Richard Sutter?"

Pierce lifted one shoulder in a negligible shrug. "Our parting was less than amiable. He filed several lawsuits but all were dismissed as frivolous."

"Less than amiable" was a vast understatement. "He suffered tremendous financial losses when the two of you severed your business relationship."

A single nod. "Our visions for the project turned out

to be vastly different. Severing the relationship was his choice, not mine."

Bella held back the laugh that tickled her throat but she couldn't completely hide the smile. "My assessment of those events is that you left him no other choice."

He stood. "There are always choices, Ms. Lytle. Perhaps limited, but choices nonetheless. I think I'll have something stronger than the coffee. Would you like a drink?"

"The coffee is fine."

She watched as he crossed the room, then opened a cabinet that revealed a bar lined with mirrors and glass shelves. He reached for a bottle of bourbon and poured a significant serving into a glass. His every move was measured, elegant, like the suit he wore.

Bella had read many articles about Pierce before tragedy sent his life on a different path. She'd even watched a couple of television interviews. Dr. Devon Pierce had been a real Chicago hero at Rush University Medical Center. He'd smiled often in the interviews. He'd spoken like a man determined to help others... determined to do good. He and two partners were developing a new kind of ER model. He had been a man with a mission. A happy man.

This was not the same man. He'd resigned from his position as head of surgery at Rush. He'd become completely obsessed with his mission to create a better ER. He'd withdrawn from society beyond the necessary appearances at fund-raisers. But he had completed his mission. His prototype, the Edge, was an unparalleled emergency department dedicated to his late wife.

When he'd taken his seat once more, she asked, "Assuming his goal is to ruin you or perhaps worse, do you believe Mr. Sutter would go to these extremes to have his vengeance?"

"Richard is an extremely intelligent man with vast resources. He certainly possesses the means to carry out such an elaborately planned plot, but I would prefer to think not. Yet here we are." He sipped his drink.

Bella watched him savor the taste that lingered on his lips. Her throat parched and she had to look away. "You knew the man—like a brother, you claimed in one of the interviews I watched. Would he want to simply damage your reputation? Or is he capable of far worse?"

That blue gaze trapped hers once more. "Powerful men rarely have set boundaries, Ms. Lytle."

She didn't have to ask if he fell into that same category. "Would he overstep the bounds of the law? Risk criminal charges and perhaps jail time?" As Pierce pointed out, setting up a woman who resembled his wife, complete with similar physical injuries, and delivering her in such a way as was done today was not a small thing. And certainly not one that was legal under any circumstances.

"I believe that may be the case."

"Was a lack of resources why he didn't come after you before? Five years is quite a while to wait for revenge." Sutter and Pierce had broken their partnership five years ago. Sutter had seemingly fallen off the face of the earth until about eighteen months ago. Bella had tracked his return back that far. He stayed out of the public eye these days.

"His resources took a hit when our association ended but he was far from devastated financially," Pierce explained. "It was likely the failed legal steps and the cancer that kept him from making a move like this before.

Rumor is he found a private hospital in some country not burdened by the FDA's restraints to seek treatment. I have no idea how long he was out of the country."

A near-death experience like surviving cancer often changed a person's priorities. It was possible that survival had sent Sutter on his own mission. "This might be the most important question I ask you tonight, Dr. Pierce," she warned. "Does Sutter have a legitimate reason to want revenge?" She waited, watched his face, his eyes.

One, two, three seconds elapsed. He downed another sip of bourbon. "Yes."

"All right." Bella appreciated that it hadn't been necessary to drag that answer out of him. More than that, she was grateful he answered honestly. "Does he have some sort of information or evidence that could hurt you?" After all, the message left in Pierce's office had been pretty clear: *I know what you did.*

"Professionally, no."

"What about personally?" Bella waited, suddenly unable to breathe.

He finished off the bourbon before meeting her gaze. "He believes I killed my wife."

There was an answer she hadn't expected. "Does he have tangible evidence or probable cause to believe you wanted your wife dead?"

Bella was certain her heart didn't beat while she waited for him to answer.

"Have you ever loved something so much you would do anything to possess it and, once it was yours, to keep it?"

His words were spoken so softly, she'd had to strain to hear. As for his question, if she was completely honest she would confess that she felt exactly that way about her work. Her career defined her. There was nothing else. Her sister and she rarely talked, never visited each other. Basically she had no family. No real love life. Her career—her professional reputation—was everything. She would do anything within the law to keep it.

"I suppose so," she said at last.

"I loved my wife, Ms. Lytle." His fingers tightened on the empty glass. "More than anything. I thought giving her everything her heart desired was enough, but it wasn't. She wanted more and I didn't see that until it was too late."

"She turned to someone else," Bella supplied. It happened to career-focused—obsessed—people all the time.

He placed his glass on the table next to the deserted coffee. "She did indeed."

"What did you do about that?" The urge to feel sympathy for him hit her harder than it should have.

"Nothing. I ignored it. Hoped it would go away."

An odd answer for a man who prided himself on keeping his life in perfect order. "Was Sutter the other party involved?"

He turned his palms up. "I have no idea. She took that secret with her to her grave."

The idea that Sutter remained Pierce's partner for a while after her death seemed to negate that possibility. "You never hired a private investigator to look into her extracurricular activities?"

"I did not." He cleared his throat. "I had no desire to confirm my suspicions. I loved her. As I said, I hoped if the worst was true that it would pass."

As heartfelt as his answer sounded, Pierce was the

sort of man who generally kept tabs on all aspects of his world. Why would he ignore some part he believed to be out of sync, or worse, out of his control completely?

"How did you come to learn that Sutter suspected you killed your wife?" A good deal of time passed before the two ended their partnership. If Sutter truly believed such a thing, why wouldn't he have brought it up sooner? Weeks or months after Cara Pierce died? Particularly if there was a possibility he had been in love with her.

"Perhaps he thought if he stayed close to me that I would eventually confess to him or that he would find some sort of evidence." He stared at the glass as if weighing the prospect of having a second drink. "I really have no idea what he was thinking. Or why he thought it."

"Did he know you were aware of your wife's affair?"

"I assume he did. He would likely see that as a motive for me wanting her dead. Frankly, there is nothing else his message could have meant."

"But your wife died in a hospital after a car crash. What's his theory about how you murdered her under the circumstances?"

Bella had read the reports. The accident was caused by a horrendous snowstorm. As he said before, the nearest hospital was not adequately equipped. There was no one to do the surgery his wife needed. There was only Devon Pierce and he'd had a broken collarbone, a gash in his head requiring twenty stitches, a broken nose and a fractured jaw. He'd refused to allow them to see to his injuries until his wife was stabilized. When no one could help her, he'd tried. He'd just completed the repair to her ruptured spleen when the bleeding in her brain sent the situation spiraling out of control. According to their statements, the medical staff at the hospital had all agreed: there was nothing else Dr. Pierce or anyone on-site could have done.

Nothing to indicate foul play.

Pierce stood again. "I have no answer for that question. I can only presume Sutter has lost his mind. If you have no other questions, I have work to do."

His sixteen-to twenty-hour-a-day work schedule was something else she'd read about the man. "I'll meet you at your office first thing in the morning," she said as she pushed to her feet.

"I'm usually there by seven."

"I'll be there as well," she fired back without hesitation.

They didn't speak as they walked side by side to the front door. Bella's mind kept going back to the seemingly unfounded idea that anyone could think he murdered his wife. Nothing she had read suggested outbursts or trouble handling his temper. She'd investigated her share of domestic violence cases and he didn't fit the profile. The wife, on the other hand, fit the profile of spoiled rich wife perfectly. Not that Bella had discovered anything overly negative about her, but she had a penchant for spending and self-indulgence.

At the door, she couldn't leave without asking again. "This makes no sense. The person coordinating this threat to you, whether Sutter or someone else, is smart." She waited until he met her gaze. "He must have some reason to believe there was foul play on your part." And some reason to think resurrecting Devon Pierce's dead wife would somehow drive him to drastic measures.

There had been an investigation into his conduct as

a physician in the situation. Standard procedure. But the extenuating circumstances warranted the steps he had taken that night.

The eyes that had scrutinized her so intently before abruptly looked away. "We made the trip to see her family once a year, so I had been there numerous times. I was aware of the meager health-care services available in the area." He shrugged. "Perhaps he believes I chose a sedan at the rental car agency rather than an SUV equipped with four-wheel drive and then took that particular road in the storm for the very purpose of ensuring an accident. It was the most treacherous, curvy and hilly. But it was also the shortest route. It felt like the right decision at the time."

"Did you choose the sedan?"

He stared at her now. "There were no SUVs available. They'd all been taken. It was either the car or wait for an SUV to be returned. Which, given the weather, could have been hours or days. I'm not a patient man, Ms. Lytle."

She sensed that he wanted to shake her with his seemingly blunt self-incrimination. "Were the two of you arguing when the accident occurred?"

"Yes." His face tightened. "She wanted me to turn around. I refused. We were almost there. Going back wasn't an option. The road behind us was worse than what lay ahead of us."

Bella still couldn't see it. "Causing an accident is too risky. You couldn't have known her injuries would be any more life-threatening than your own."

"Unless I gave her head a couple of extra bashes against the window to ensure there was sufficient damage and then waited." His gaze narrowed as if he were remembering. "I seem to recall at least two different accounts of what time our car was noticed. The police pressured me for a bit about the timing of my call for help."

Her heart beat faster with his every word. She wanted to argue that he was only trying to make her uncertain of her own conclusions, but there was something in his eyes as he looked at her now...something that dared her to ignore his words.

He shrugged. "In retrospect, I suppose it was the perfect plan for getting away with murder. No murder weapon to prove I planned the act. No evidence at all to suggest anything but an accident. And the coup de grâce—half a dozen witnesses watched my frantic efforts to save my wife in that operating room."

Bella adjusted the strap of her bag on her shoulder. "Thank you for your time, Dr. Pierce. Good night."

She walked out without looking back. He closed the door behind her without saying more.

Whatever he was hiding, it wasn't murder. She would bet her career on that assessment.

Dr. Devon Pierce was a man of contradictions. Warm to his patients. Cold to the outside world. Pretentious and direct...and yet Bella saw an undercurrent of vulnerability and grief.

It was the latter that pulled at her defenses.

She needed to solve this case quickly...or risk falling under Devon Pierce's enigmatic spell.

If she hadn't already.

Chapter Three

Ms. Lytle had been waiting at his office door when he arrived at seven that morning.

Devon had warned her that he had work to do before they proceeded with the investigation. He refused to allow this diversion to distract him. The medical world was watching, scrutinizing every aspect of this facility's performance. The slightest slip could create a major setback. The Edge and all it represented for the future of emergency medicine were far too important to allow anything to get in the way of forward progress.

He had provided Ms. Lytle with the assistant administrator's office. The position was as yet unfilled, so the office was vacant. He was here sixteen or more hours most days and never far away the rest of the time. Perhaps at a later time, he would view the need for an assistant differently. For now, Patricia represented the only assistant he required. In fact, he'd already discussed with her the possibility of upgrading her position from secretary to personal assistant. She had been with him for ten years, first as his secretary at Rush and then during the development stage of the Edge. Patricia had never once let him down.

She had been most unhappy with Ms. Lytle's request for an interview with her this morning. Now, forty-five minutes later, the private investigator had returned to her desk and so far hadn't said a single word to Devon. He stared at the woman seated across from him now. "Patricia Ezell is above reproach. If you insulted her in some way, I would require that you apologize immediately."

A smile lifted Isabella Lytle's inordinately lush lips. At their initial meeting last night, he'd at first thought she wore lipstick but he recognized now that she didn't. Her lips were naturally a deep crimson, full and wide.

"I asked the hard questions, yes, but if Ms. Ezell took offense at any of those questions, that's unfortunate. They were all crucial. The people closest to you represent the greatest danger. Whether by design or accident, they make you vulnerable merely because they have your confidence."

His first instinct was to argue the point but he chose to let it go. She'd already interviewed Patricia. Not another living soul knew him so well. The entire staff at the Edge had been made aware that Ms. Lytle was to be treated with respect and given complete access. "Since there is no one else to interview, what is your agenda for the day?"

He had not expected that she would stay so close. He didn't know what he had expected. Having her study his every move was disconcerting.

Today she wore all black. Black slacks, black jacket, black sweater that hugged her throat. All that was visible of her pale skin was her face and hands. Her dark hair, as dark as the clothes she wore, had been arranged in a French twist. She might have appeared stern or harsh if not for her expressive brown eyes and that voluptuous mouth. There was a kindness, a gentleness about her eyes. Yet she emanated a firm, steady strength that warned she was far from soft.

"Actually, I'd like to interview the woman the police identified as your wife."

A new thread of unease filtered through him. He'd stopped by the woman's—a Jane Doe, for all intents and purposes—room this morning. She'd still been asleep. Security remained at her door 24/7. Until someone claimed her and took her away, he intended to keep her close and protected.

"Very well."

As they exited his office, he noticed that Patricia did not so much as spare a glance toward Ms. Lytle. He would speak to her as soon as this interview was over.

Ms. Lytle walked slightly in front of him. Her stride was confident, determined. His research showed that she was not married, had never been married. No children. Isabella Lytle lived alone on Armitage Avenue in the Lincoln Park area. No previous engagements. No long-term boyfriends or girlfriends.

Before he could quash the thought, he wondered about the woman. Were her most intimate needs kept hidden? A dirty secret she wanted no one to know? His gaze moved down her shapely backside. Or perhaps she was like him—work was her only true companion. Anything else was an afterthought.

They moved around the circular corridor until they reached the quarantine unit. The Edge did not keep patients more than twenty-four hours unless it was necessary to quarantine them until proper care could be arranged. There were overnight beds in the behavioral and senior units, but all other patients were either treated and released or transported to nearby hospitals. The Edge was not intended as anything other than an emergency care facility. Since the woman's true identity had not been determined, there was no next of kin to take her home and no medical necessity to prompt a transfer.

He would, however, need to turn the situation over to the police soon. No matter that she was an impostor and clearly connected to some criminal activity, he could not keep holding her as if she were a prisoner. As some point, the entire matter would need to be turned over to the police.

But not until he was satisfied.

A quick nod to the security guard outside the room and the man took a break. Devon rapped twice on the door before opening it for Ms. Lytle to enter ahead of him. The woman listed as Cara Pierce was awake. She turned in surprise or perhaps in fear as they entered the room.

"Good morning." Ms. Lytle approached her bedside and introduced herself. "I'm Investigator Isabella Lytle and I have a few questions for you."

The woman frowned and then winced. "I don't remember anything." She glanced at Devon. "I've already told you that."

Devon had reviewed her chart this morning. She'd slept well. Had consumed a good portion of her breakfast. Vitals were good. The general symptoms associated with splenic rupture were all but gone. Vision was within normal range. No light-headedness or shock.

Beyond the confusion about her identity, all appeared to be well.

Then again, mere confusion rarely included a driver's license and vehicle registration in the wrong name. Obviously the woman was working with someone. Frankly, her brain injury was hardly significant enough to have caused any serious confusion or amnesia. Now that she was stable, there was no reason she shouldn't be able to tell the truth. No other drugs had been found in the follow-up toxicology. Of course, there were a number of drugs that dissipated too quickly to be caught in a tox screen.

"Let's talk about who you are," Ms. Lytle suggested to the woman in the bed. "What is your name?"

The pretend Cara blinked, then looked away. "I don't know."

Ms. Lytle set her bag on the floor and reached inside. She removed a plastic bag somewhat larger than a typical sandwich bag. With her hand inside the bag, she used it like a glove to pick up the plastic cup on the patient's overbed table. Then she pulled the plastic over the cup, successfully bagging it.

With a quick smile at the other woman, Ms. Lytle said, "The police might be able to track down your identity through your fingerprints."

Big blue eyes stared first at Ms. Lytle and then at Devon. "Is that legal?" she asked him. "For her to come into my room and take my fingerprints like that?" She knotted her fingers together. "I haven't done anything wrong."

"Don't you want to know who you are?" Devon braced his hands on the footboard of the bed. "You may have a husband or family worried about you."

She stared directly at him, her blue eyes pooled with tears. Fear, whether real or simulated, glistened there. "You're certain I'm not your wife?"

"No. You are not my wife."

Ms. Lytle placed the commandeered cup into her bag and retrieved a pad and pen. "Why don't we start with whatever you remember before arriving at the ER?"

The woman blinked, stared for a long moment at Ms. Lytle. "I don't remember anything."

Ms. Lytle nodded. "All right, then. We'll see what the police can find. If there are any outstanding warrants or investigations related to your fingerprints, they will discuss those issues directly with you. I wish you a speedy recovery."

The woman, looking decidedly pale against the white sheets, bit her bottom lip as if to hold back whatever words wanted to pop out of her. Ms. Lytle picked up her bag and turned toward the door before hesitating. She studied the other woman for half a minute before she spoke. "You do realize that if someone hired you to pretend to be Cara Pierce that you're a loose end?"

The pretender's eyes grew wider. "I don't understand what you mean."

"When that person—the person who hired you—is finished with whatever game he's playing, you will be an unnecessary risk. We—" she gestured to Devon "—can help you, but we're not going to waste resources on an uncooperative witness."

A frown furrowed across her brow. "Witness?"

Ms. Lytle nodded. "That's what you are. Someone has committed a crime. You obviously know who that someone is, so that makes you a witness, perhaps an accessory. If you willingly participated in that crime, then you'll be charged accordingly—unless you cooperate, in which case the DA might offer you immunity."

"So," she said slowly, "you're a cop."

Isabella Lytle had introduced herself as an investigator. Devon hadn't considered it at the time but the move was an ingenious one.

"Investigator Lytle," he said, saving her the lie, "has been assigned to your case. If you cooperate, she may be able to help you avoid legal charges."

Silence thickened for several seconds before the woman blurted, "I didn't know he was going to try to kill me or I would never have gone along with this crazy scheme." She looked from Devon to Ms. Lytle, her fingers knotted in the sheet. "I thought it was a game."

Ms. Lytle asked, "The man who hired you, do you know his name?"

She shook her head and then winced. Her head no doubt still ached. "He never told me his name. He offered me five thousand dollars and promised there was a bonus if I didn't screw up."

Ms. Lytle reached for her pad and pen once more. "Can you describe the man to me?"

She blew out a big breath, and her blond bangs fluttered. "You're not going to believe this but it was dark in the room where we met. He wouldn't let me turn on the lights. He told me what he wanted, gave me a thousand bucks up front and walked out. Next thing I knew, I was snagged from my regular corner. I don't remember anything after that until I woke up here."

"You're a prostitute, is that correct?" Outrage burst inside Devon. The idea that whoever had done this had taken advantage of someone so vulnerable made him all the angrier.

"A girl's gotta make a living somehow." She straightened the sheet at her waist. Smoothed the wrinkles her nervous fingers had created.

"Where did you and this man meet?" Ms. Lytle asked.

"Over on East Ontario." She fidgeted with the edge of the sheet some more. "A car picked me up and took me to that real fancy hotel over on Michigan Avenue." Her lips trembled into a small smile. "I was thinking that was going to be my lucky day. You know, a big tipper."

"Which hotel?" Ms. Lytle asked.

When the woman had given the name and address of the hotel, Devon demanded, "What can you tell me about his voice? Deep? Did he sound older or younger?"

"Not really so deep. He sounded older than me for sure." She moistened her lips. "His voice was kind of gravelly like he'd spent a lot of years smoking."

"What exactly did he ask you to do?" Devon demanded. He realized he'd taken over the interview but it was his prerogative. Ms. Lytle worked for him, after all. This outrageous situation was about him! Fury twisted sharply inside him.

"He said all I had to do was pretend to be someone else for a day. Easy money. Big money." She shrugged one thin shoulder. "I didn't know I'd be getting hurt and almost die."

"What's your name?" Ms. Lytle asked before Devon could launch his next question.

"Audrey." She stared at her manicured fingernails, anywhere but at the woman questioning her. "Audrey Maynard."

"Audrey," Ms. Lytle began, "you said the hotel room

was dark. Did you get any sense of his height or how big or small he was?"

She started to move her head but winced. "Not really. He was sitting in a chair. I could sort of make out his form against the cream-colored chair. He wore dark clothes. He wasn't a big guy. Thin and medium height, I guess."

"Did he wear cologne?"

She thought about that question for a moment. "Yes. Something expensive. I think it was that Clive something or other. I only smelled it a couple other times— once when I was part of a group of girls who attended this secret party with a bunch of really rich guys. The stuff costs like thousands of dollars."

"Clive Christian," Devon said. The woman in the bed as well as Ms. Lytle turned to stare at him. He was well acquainted with the cologne she meant.

"That's it." She pointed at him. "And you. You wear it. I smelled it when you checked on me this morning."

"Did you keep any of the money he gave you?" Ms. Lytle asked. "What was the money in? A bag? A box?"

"It was in a bag. The shiny pink kind like you get from that fancy lingerie place. But I threw it away."

"What did you do with the money?" Ms. Lytle prodded.

"I paid my mother's rent. She was behind. She's sick. Emphysema." She sighed. "It's bad."

Ms. Lytle asked, "Did he contact you again after that?"

"He just said he'd send his car after me when he was ready."

"When did the car come for you?"

"Yesterday morning. It was waiting outside my mother's place when I walked out the door."

"Tell us about the car." Ms. Lytle prepared to jot down the information.

"Black. One of those big sedans you see hauling rich people around but not a limo."

"What about the license plate? Did you see it?" Devon asked.

"No. I'd had a rough night. I was pretty out of it."

"Did you see the driver?" Ms. Lytle inquired before Devon could.

"Yeah. He was white. Midtwenties maybe. Black hair, cut short. Not exactly cute. He looked, you know, indifferent. Wore a black suit. He told me I was to go with him the way I agreed. After I got in the car, he didn't say a word."

"Where did he take you?"

"Damen Silos. He just put me out and drove off. I was still staring after him when someone grabbed me from behind." She frowned. "Wait. Maybe I did see part of the license plate." She called off two numbers. "There were some numbers and then a TX. That's all I can remember."

"Thank you," Ms. Lytle said. "We may have more questions later."

"When will I be able to go home? I'm sure my mom is worried about me. I'm all she's got."

Ms. Lytle looked to Devon.

"Leave the contact information with Ms. Lytle and we'll see that your mother is informed of your where-abouts."

He walked out of the room. The guard resumed his position next to the door as Devon moved away. How many people knew the cologne he wore? The description of the man who'd hired her was insufficient but there was enough to further convince Devon with whom he was dealing. His former partner Richard Sutter.

Ms. Lytle hurried from the room to catch up with him. "It's time to call in the police, Dr. Pierce. I don't believe she's telling us the whole truth."

When he stalled, she glanced back at the room and the guard stationed there before meeting his impatient glare. "I know when a witness is lying, and for whatever reason, the woman in that room lied with every breath."

He had come to the same conclusion. When he continued to stare in the direction of the room without responding to Ms. Lytle's suggestion, she went on, "At the very least, I should get this cup to a friend of mine who can run the prints. We need to confirm who she is. She has rights and we're walking all over those rights by not bringing in the proper authorities."

His attention shifted to her, fury whipping through him. "I am well aware of the patient's rights, Ms. Lytle."

"Then you know we have to do something to protect her. I spent far too many years as a cop to ignore the situation. The man who hired her will not want her talking. Victoria and the Colby Agency have a reputation for high standards. I'm not about to let Victoria or the agency down."

"I'm not asking you to let anyone down." He started walking toward his office once more. "She has protection at her door and we're going to do something right now."

She hurried to keep up with his long strides. Though she was five-nine and in excellent physical condition, he stood at six-two and was quite fit himself. He had the advantage physically. He forced away thoughts of testing her physical endurance in all sorts of ways.

As they reached his office, she managed to get ahead of him and to block the door. "Where exactly are we going?"

He reached for patience. "To see the car. Any personal effects may still be in the vehicle. I'd like to see those and the registration."

"Makes sense." She stepped away from the door. "But I'm driving."

C&C Towing, Noon

GEORGE TALBOT, her friend in Chicago's Crime Scene Processing Unit, had promised to get results on the prints back to her ASAP. For the moment, she had let Pierce off the hook about reporting to PD what they had learned from the woman who had pretended to be his wife. But as soon as they'd had a look at any personal effects in the vehicle, the call would be made. The TX Maynard had told them about meant the car was a taxi or other chauffeured vehicle. If they could track down the vehicle and the driver, they might learn who'd hired him.

"This is it." The tow-truck driver had escorted them into the storage yard, down the fifth row and seven cars over to where the Lexus was parked. "Damage isn't so bad. We have a repair service if you want her fixed. We're happy to fax an estimate to your insurance company."

"I'll let you know," Pierce said. "At the moment, I'd like to gather my wife's belongings."

The lie rolled off his tongue without the first flinch or glance away from the man in the summer-weight coveralls. Bella had barely slept last night for mulling over their conversation in his home. Devon Pierce had the poker face down to a science. It was nearly impossible to determine what was truth and what was not. Worse, there was something about him that pulled at her. Certainly not his immense charm, she mused. Something deeper...something darker.

Perhaps a darkness similar to the one that lived inside her—a distrust of others so deep and profound that it muddied any personal feelings she might hope to ever develop. Who was she kidding? She had decided long ago that a personal life was too complicated. Work was far easier.

"All rightie, then." The driver tossed the keys to Pierce. "Drop them by on your way out. We don't release the keys or the vehicle until the bill is settled."

Pierce gave him a nod.

When the driver had headed back to his office, Pierce reached for the driver's-side door. Bella stopped him with a hand on his arm. "This car is evidence."

"Be that as it may, I'm having a look in the car." His tone warned there would be no discussion on the subject.

She reached into her bag and dug up a couple of pairs of latex gloves. She passed a pair to him.

He shot her a look. "The fact that you carry gloves around in your bag could be construed as—"

"I'm a private investigator. The last thing I ever want to do is render a piece of evidence unusable in court."

She'd seen more than her share of bumbling detectives do exactly that and the perp ended up getting off on a technicality. Not happening on her watch.

While he settled behind the steering wheel, Bella opened the door to the back seat and had a look there.

The small black clutch Maynard—or whoever she was—had with her was brought to the hospital. It had contained the driver's license, lip gloss and a small round makeup mirror. One black high heel lay on the back floorboard. No overnight bag. No trash or spare change. The car looked and smelled brand-new.

"Have a look at this."

Bella withdrew her upper body from the back seat and moved to the driver's door. He held documents he'd taken from the glove box.

"The car was bought—if I'm reading this correctly— yesterday." He passed the paperwork to her. "There's nothing else here except one black shoe."

"The other one is in the back seat." She skimmed the pages. It appeared Cara Pierce had bought the car from the local Lexus dealership yesterday morning. She passed the papers back to him. "Did you check the console between the seats?"

"It's empty."

He peered up at her, blue eyes dark with fury. His lean jaw was taut with that same anger. Someone was using his painful past to get to him. But what was the endgame? That was the part Bella couldn't yet see. Were they trying to discredit him professionally or destroy him personally? The rage in his eyes turned to something even more fierce…something desperate and urgent, something hungry. Bella abruptly realized how close she was standing to him.

Her ability to breathe vanished. "Well." She stumbled back a step from the vee made by the open door of the car. "Let's check the trunk."

He pressed the button on the dash and a *pop* confirmed the trunk had opened. Bella headed that way with Pierce close behind. She struggled to dispel the hum of uncertainty and something like need inside her. The foolish reaction was surely related to her utter inability to sleep last night.

The trunk was empty save a single sheet of lined paper with words scribbled frantically across it. The page looked as if it had been ripped from a notebook. Blood was smeared across the center of it.

Pierce snatched up the page and stared at it.

"Don't touch anything," she warned again. Then she surveyed the trunk once more. Another spot of crimson at the edge of the carpeting snagged her attention. She lifted the carpeting that covered the spare tire area and she stopped.

Blood.

Lots of blood.

Pierce leaned in close, his face far too near to hers. "Ms. Lytle, I believe it's time to call the police now."

Chapter Four

The Edge, 1:55 p.m.

For the second time today, Bella found herself walking briskly to keep up with Pierce's hurried strides. She had to admit, seeing the half dozen Chicago PD cruisers out front was enough to have anyone rushing to see what was going on.

Once the call was made, he'd refused to wait at the tow lot until the police arrived. Bella had almost refused to bring him back and then he'd reached for his cell to order a car. She'd had no choice. As much as she'd felt that legally speaking they needed to wait for the police to take possession of the Lexus, she had known she could not allow Pierce out of her sight. He was at the edge—no pun intended.

Whatever had been on that page—he'd thrust it into his jacket pocket too quickly for her to get so much as a glimpse—it had shaken him. The paper was evidence and he'd taken it from the scene. He'd put her in an untenable position. Yet her first responsibility was to the client. She couldn't say for a certainty that the paper he'd taken was significant evidence—which would present the one situation in which her obligation to him slipped out of first place. Basically until she knew what was on that page, she needed to focus on protecting the client.

From himself as much as any other threat.

They reached the quarantine unit and the door to Maynard's room was open. The guard was no longer at the door. Bella glanced at Pierce and his face was clouded with that same anger she'd been watching darken his eyes since their conversation with his pretend wife hours ago.

A uniformed Chicago PD officer and two men in suits—detectives, she surmised—were crowded around Maynard's bed.

"What's going on here?" Pierce demanded.

"Dr. Pierce," one of the suits said, "glad you're finally here."

The suit glanced at Bella. "Detective Corwin," he said, then gestured to the other suit. "Detective Hodge."

He didn't introduce the uniform, but his name, Laurence, was on his name tag anyway.

"Investigator Isabella Lytle." She thrust out her hand. "The Colby Agency."

"We have a situation," Corwin said.

"Your patient—" Hodge checked his notes "—Cara Pierce."

"That is not her name," Pierce snapped.

Bella started to speak but Hodge cut her off. "She called 911 and reported that you, Dr. Pierce, had kidnapped her and held her hostage for two months until she escaped yesterday. That running from you is the reason she had the accident. She said you were holding her here at the hospital as well and that she had to get away so she could hide from you."

"What?" Pierce demanded. "We spoke to her—Audrey Maynard—just this morning. She claimed to have been paid by some person she couldn't name or identify to pretend to be my deceased wife. The man who hired her also orchestrated her accident so that she would be brought here. Ask her for yourself."

The suits and the uniform stepped away from the bed. It was empty.

Bella's instincts rocketed to the next level. "How long has she been gone?"

"The call came in to dispatch around noon," Corwin said. "We've been here maybe half an hour." He shifted his gaze to Pierce. "Waiting for you."

"Where's the guard who was stationed at her door?" Pierce demanded.

"We've interviewed him," said Corwin, who seemed to be the lead detective. "He's headed downtown, where we'll question him some more."

"What did the guard say happened?" Bella asked before Pierce could make another demand.

"He says she came to the door demanding a phone. When he refused to provide her with one, she took off down the hall. She snatched a cell phone off the counter at the nurses' station. When we got here," Corwin went on, "she was gone. We've got uniforms crawling all over this place."

Bella held up her hands when Pierce would have bellowed something not in the least helpful. "Take your time, gentlemen. Interview every member of staff if necessary. Ms. Maynard was not a prisoner here. The guard was for her protection since we couldn't determine if there was a further threat to her life. Considering the way she was brought here, we were concerned.

As for her sudden disappearance, she can't have gotten far in her physical condition."

"Hold up." Corwin shook his head. "What does all that mean?"

"Why don't we take this discussion to my office?" Pierce suggested. "We'll explain everything."

Corwin instructed Laurence to wait at the abandoned room. He and Hodge followed Bella and Pierce to his office. Patricia glanced up as Pierce warned that he didn't want to be disturbed. She ignored Bella altogether. Apparently she was still unhappy about the questions Bella had asked. There was no help for that.

Once the two detectives were settled in front of Pierce's desk and Bella had taken a seat at a small conference table, Pierce explained the events that had taken place since Maynard's arrival in the ER. He walked them through his interview that morning and the information about the car's license plate and the hotel where she'd met the man who'd hired her. Occasionally he looked to Bella for confirmation. When he reached the part where they looked at the car Maynard had been driving, he allowed Bella to take over.

"The interior of the car appeared fine," she said. "According to the paperwork in the glove box, it was only purchased yesterday. The one troubling issue we noted was the blood in the trunk."

The relief on Pierce's face when she didn't mention the page he'd tucked into his jacket was palpable. *Protect the client.*

"Ms. Lytle," Hodge said, "the dealership reported that car stolen. We got the call just a little while ago."

"Then the paperwork was forged," Pierce said. "To

prevent the officers who responded to the accident from becoming suspicious."

Corwin nodded. "Evidently. We're well aware of who you are, Dr. Pierce. Your work in the community is well noted and our captain warned us to keep the gloves on for this one. The way I hear it, the mayor himself is a personal friend of yours."

"Dr. Pierce wants the truth," Bella interceded. "He wants you to investigate this situation to the best of your ability. A woman was brought to him posing as his deceased wife. Clearly, someone is attempting to besmirch his name and to cause him great personal pain."

"Since we can't question the woman you claim is Audrey Maynard," Corwin began, "we're going to need your full cooperation, Dr. Pierce."

When Pierce would have spoken, Bella held up a hand for him to wait. "Before we proceed, Dr. Pierce has a right to proper counsel, particularly in an unknown situation like this one. If your assertions are accurate, Ms. Maynard and whoever hired her are attempting to frame Dr. Pierce in a very serious crime. Kidnapping is a very grave crime."

Corwin heaved a breath. "First, this is not an assertion. You can listen to the 911 call for yourself. The woman made the statement. She gave the name Layla Devereux."

"That may be her street name," Bella argued. "I'm confident if you take her prints from the cell phone she used or from the room, you'll find that her name is Audrey Maynard." Her friend had sent a text confirming the name and a couple of arrests for solicitation. Bella had the address listed as her home but, under the circumstances, she wasn't giving up that information.

She wouldn't compromise the identity of her lab contact—or herself—by telling them she'd already found the information before reporting the crime. These two could figure it out for themselves.

"We have a two-man forensic team en route as we speak," Hodge assured her.

"Don't waste your time investigating me, Detective," Pierce said. "The man who hired this woman, who seriously injured her, is the person you should be looking for. If my associate, Ms. Lytle, and I are correct in our conclusions, Ms. Maynard is very likely in danger. The man behind this, whatever it is, will want to ensure nothing and no one leads back to him."

"Let's talk about your enemies," Corwin suggested.

While Pierce spoke, Bella sent a text to her Colby Agency backup. She wanted someone at the address listed as Maynard's residence just in case she showed up there. Bella sent him a pic she'd snapped of Maynard in the room this morning.

Pierce went through the same paces with the detectives that Bella had put him through last night. The sooner they satisfied the detectives, the sooner they would be on their way.

When enough questions had been asked and answered, Bella took advantage of a pause and asked, "Where did Ms. Maynard claim Dr. Pierce had been holding her these last two months? And how did she escape in a brand-new stolen Lexus with another woman's driver's license in her bag?"

She felt confident the detectives could see the absurdity of the scenario the same as she. Pierce spent sixteen or more hours a day here. He'd said as much and had the staff and security footage to back it up. He'd already asked his security specialist to pull up the feed for all exterior doors and the parking lot to show Maynard's exit. If someone picked her up, maybe the license plate would be captured on the video. Or, at the very least, the make and model of the vehicle.

Corwin looked to Pierce. "She says you kept her in your home. The clothes, the ID with your dead wife's name were things you forced her to use. Furthermore, she said you have a red room and that's where you kept her as your private sex slave."

When Pierce stared blankly at him, Hodge tacked on, "You know, like that movie, *Fifty Shades*."

When Pierce didn't appear able to find his voice, Bella argued, "It sounds as if she did a lot of talking on that call for a woman who wanted out of here for fear that her captor or one of his hirelings would return at any moment."

Pierce glanced at her, a glimmer of appreciation in his gaze.

Corwin nodded. "Definitely. I'm with you. Sounds like a setup." He pressed his lips together and made a noncommittal sound. "But then there's the issue of those rumors that lingered after your wife died."

Bella looked from Corwin to Pierce. His face had closed. No more anger, no more gratitude or uncertainty. The poker face was back. "What are you implying, Detective?"

"The doc knows," Corwin said to Bella rather than respond to Pierce's demand. "When his wife died, there were rumors that he wanted her dead."

Bella rose from her chair before she realized she intended to do so. "Thank you, Detectives. Dr. Pierce has been through quite enough for today. I'm certain you'll let him know if you have additional questions."

Corwin looked from her to Pierce. "Is that the way you want to play this, Doc?"

Pierce removed a business card from the center drawer of his desk and handed it to Corwin. "Contact my attorney if you have more questions."

The two detectives stood. "If you've got nothing to hide, you needn't be concerned." As he turned away, Corwin paused to survey Bella from head to toe and back. "Be careful, Investigator Lytle. You might find yourself strapped to a leather bed."

When the two had exited the door, Bella closed it. She looked directly at Pierce. "I'm going to assume none of what they're suggesting is true."

Pierce said nothing.

"You know they're going to get a warrant."

Pierce's cool composure slipped, but only for a moment. "A warrant wasn't mentioned. I doubt they'd go to those extremes just yet."

Bella struggled to keep from rolling her eyes. "They aren't going to give you the heads-up—they'll want to catch you off guard. They don't want to risk you hiding or disposing of evidence before they get there. But you can bet a warrant is coming. If they search your house, will they find anything incriminating?"

"Nothing that will connect me to any of this."

His tone was flat, his face giving nothing away.

"Have you ever met Audrey Maynard before?"

"No."

She already knew he had nothing to do with his wife's death, so she wasn't even going there. "Do you have a so-called red room?"

"How is that relevant?"

A spark of anger was back in his eyes.

Holy hell. "When they search your home—and they will—anything that lends credibility to her story will throw up warning signs and warrant further investigation."

She tried to focus on her job instead of Pierce's so-called red room. Suddenly, the short-sleeved silk sweater she'd chosen to wear today felt too thick though it was thin and gauzy. Perspiration rose on her skin. The urge to peel off her jacket was nearly overwhelming. Of all the things she expected to learn about Dr. Devon Pierce during this investigation, his taste for kink wasn't one of them. She blinked away the images of his lean body, naked save leather handcuffs. She drew in a harsh breath, willed her mind to stop conjuring those erotic mental pictures. "I need you to be open and honest with me, Dr. Pierce. It's the only way I can help you."

"What they will find," he said, forcing her attention back to him, "is personal and irrelevant to this investigation."

Liar.

She closed her eyes and shook her head. "Our time is short. I hope your status in the community and the powerful people with whom you are associated will slow their efforts to get a warrant. That said, I doubt those two will stop until they persuade one judge or the other to sign the warrant. But we'll worry about crossing that bridge when it's in front of us. For now, we're going to visit Audrey Maynard's mother."

A frown furrowed his handsome brow. "You believe she'll talk to us or are you hoping her daughter will be hiding there?"

Bella wanted to believe Devon Pierce was as honest as he was handsome. As much as she hated to admit it, she wasn't immune to his mysterious pull. But her instincts warned her he wasn't being completely truthful. There was more to the story. "I do believe we can gain some amount of cooperation. As for Audrey, it's possible she would risk going to a known location. I suppose it depends on just how scared she is." She grabbed her bag and headed for the door. "Let's go."

The sooner she was out of this office and focused on the investigation, the sooner she could clear her head of the images the detectives' accusations against Pierce had elicited.

His bare skin draped in leather and chains flashed full-size in her mind.

You are in trouble here, Bella.

Deep trouble.

South Bishop Street, 5:00 p.m.

THE MORGAN PARK neighborhood was an old one with plenty of historic bungalows to prove its age. Some parts were undergoing gentrification and others were less fortunate. The small brick bungalow belonging to Olivia Maynard landed somewhere in the middle with its sagging roof begging for attention and picket fence in need of paint while meticulously groomed shrubs and vibrant blooming flowers filled the yard. On the front porch, an array of eclectic pots overflowed with more flowers. A swing and a rocking chair welcomed visitors while at the same time clashing with the iron bars on the windows and the triple dead bolts on the door.

Bella knocked on the door. If they were lucky, they

had got here before the police and would have the information they needed before their arrival. She wanted to hear the mother's take on the daughter before her opinion was colored by reality. Pierce stood so close to her that she felt too hot again in her chosen wardrobe. She resisted the urge to step away from him.

Was his closeness an attempt to intimidate her?

No answer at the door. She knocked again and waited, absently rubbing her knuckles. Would Audrey have dared to take off on her own? Had she chosen to completely ignore the warning about being a loose end? Bella hated the idea of her ending up dead. She wouldn't have been the first prostitute to get caught up in a game that led to her demise.

Whoever had hired her to pretend to be Pierce's wife clearly was not playing games.

The shade on the door drew back far enough for someone to peek out. One by one, the dead bolts were released and the door swung open a couple of inches.

"If you're selling something, including religion, I'm not interested." The woman had blond hair, though her gray roots were starting to show, and blue eyes. Her face was an older version of her daughter's.

Definitely Audrey's mother.

"Mrs. Maynard?"

The woman looked at Bella and said, "If you're cops, Audrey's not here. I haven't seen her for a couple of days."

At least part of that statement was good news.

"Mrs. Maynard, my name is Isabella Lytle and this is my associate, Dr. Devon Pierce. We're here about Audrey."

Her face fell, and fear crept into her eyes. "Is she all right?"

"Please," Bella urged, "may we come inside?"

The door opened wide in invitation and Bella breathed a sigh of relief. Inside, her eyes quickly adjusted to the dim interior. A lamp sat on a table flanked by two chairs. On the far wall was a small box-style television perched on a long narrow table loaded with framed photographs. Across the small room to Bella's left was a well-loved sofa. A throw and a couple of pillows were tucked at one end. The part in the curtains allowed a strip of sunlight to cut across the worn wood floor.

Hands wringing together, Ms. Maynard sat down in the chair closest to the television set. She reached for the oxygen concentrator on the table next to her chair. She put the nasal cannula in place, draped the lines over her ears and inhaled deeply. She closed her eyes and seemed to relax a little.

When she'd opened her eyes, Pierce asked, speaking for the first time, "When was the last time you saw your daughter?"

"Sunday night, I think. She was gone the next morning before I woke up." She shrugged her thin shoulders. "I suppose she could have left in the middle of the night, but she was here when I went to bed Sunday night."

This was really good news. The mother's statement directly contradicted the daughter's assertion against Pierce. Audrey Maynard left her home either late Sunday night or early Monday morning and showed up in the ER on Monday evening. Dr. Pierce's whereabouts, other than the few hours before seven Tuesday morning, could be verified.

Bella pulled the photo she'd taken of Audrey on screen and showed it to Mrs. Maynard. "Is this your daughter?"

Her face crumpled. "Yes. Oh my Lord, is she hurt?"

"She was in an accident," Pierce explained, "but we took care of her injuries."

"So she's all right?" The older woman looked from Pierce to Bella and back.

"She was when we last saw her," Bella explained. "She left the hospital this afternoon and we're concerned for her safety. We believe she may be involved with a dangerous man."

Her mother shook her head. "I knew something was wrong when she paid my house payment for the next two months." She sighed. "This place should have been paid for years ago but I've had to borrow the money for upkeep every now and then. I guess I'll be making payments for the rest of my days."

"We want to help your daughter, Mrs. Maynard," Pierce said. "If she was in trouble, where might she go?"

"She's got lots of friends that do…" She shrugged. "…what she does. But they probably wouldn't tell you a thing if you asked them."

Bella drew a business card from her bag and gave it to Mrs. Maynard. "The police will be visiting you as well, probably today. Tell them anything at all you can remember about whatever your daughter said to you in the past few days. Any friends who might know where she is. Any place she might hide."

She stared at the card for a moment, then asked, "You're a private investigator?"

"Yes, ma'am. I want to find your daughter before anyone who might want to hurt her does."

The lines on the woman's face deepened. "You talk to her friends. They might talk to you since you're not a cop. You can find them over on East Ontario. But if they think you're a cop, they won't say a word. I know those girls." She looked Bella directly in the eyes. "I used to be one of them. They don't trust cops and they're always looking for the customer that will give them a way out."

Bella turned to a fresh page in her notebook. "Can you give me names, descriptions of some of her friends?" Otherwise finding them would be like searching for a needle in a haystack. Bella needed a starting place.

Mrs. Maynard got up, taking her portable oxygen supplier with her, and went to the table where the television sat. She picked up a framed photograph and brought it to Bella. "She printed that from a picture she took with her phone. She said that way I know who her friends really are." She pointed to the redhead in the photo. "That's Jasmine. The brunette is Talia and the other blonde is Miranda. They've been friends for a good long while now. They're the best chance you've got at getting the truth."

"Thank you, Mrs. Maynard." Bella snapped a pic of the photo with her cell and then stood. Pierce followed her lead. "We'll do all we can to find her," she assured the lady.

As they left, Bella warned Mrs. Maynard to keep her doors and windows locked and her phone close. She urged the woman not to allow anyone inside unless he or she showed proper credentials. Audrey likely didn't realize she'd put her mother in a perilous position as well. Sometimes people just didn't think.

Once she and Pierce were in her car, Pierce asked, "What now?"

"Now we find her friends and see if they'll talk to us." Bella thought about that for a moment. "Actually, I'm reasonably certain they would talk to you before they would me."

He stared at her. She kept her attention on the street but she could feel that blue gaze boring a hole into her.

"Whatever's necessary."

Bella glanced at him. He stared forward. If the man had a so-called red room, he shouldn't have any trouble approaching and charming a few ladies of the night.

The drive to Audrey Maynard's territory took just over twenty minutes. It didn't take long to spot the blonde and the redhead. Bella pulled to the curb on the opposite side of the street from the ladies.

She looked to her passenger. "Good luck."

He stared at her for a long moment and then got out. Bella watched as he closed the center button on his elegant suit, then squared his shoulders and strode across the street. The two women immediately started to smile and wave at him.

Bella couldn't hear the conversation but she could easily imagine how it was going down just watching the back-and-forth. The redhead, Jasmine, hugged his arm and leaned in close. He stared down at her upturned face for a moment and a spear of something hot cut through Bella.

Not jealousy, she told herself.

She shook it off and watched as he spoke, smiled and allowed the women to hang on him like he was Santa and they had waited all year for a chance to tell him what they wanted for Christmas. The blonde, Miranda, trailed her fingers up his back and into his silky hair. Bella had to look away for a moment.

"Don't be ridiculous," she muttered. Shaking her head, she forced her attention back across the street. The longer the women stroked him and leaned into him, the more uncomfortable she grew. She squirmed in her seat, her fingers tightening on the steering wheel.

Finally, when Pierce broke from the two, she was able to draw in a breath.

He returned to the car and settled into the passenger seat.

"Did you learn anything?" Her voice sounded too high to her own ears.

Pierce turned to her. He frowned. "What's wrong?"

Bella started to ask what he meant but then she caught a glimpse of herself in the rearview mirror. Her face was flushed.

"I'm fine. Did you find out where Audrey might be?"

Before he answered, he reached into his pocket and retrieved his cell. He glanced at the screen, touched the accept-call button and said, "Pierce."

Bella struggled to gather her composure while he listened to his caller. She relaxed her shoulders, took three deep breaths and loosened her grip on the steering wheel. Being so attracted to her client that she couldn't focus on the task at hand wouldn't do. It was out of character for her, and she didn't intend to let it become a part of her character now—no matter how ridiculously alluring Devon Pierce was.

Pierce thanked the caller and put his phone away. He turned to Bella. "That was Detective Corwin."

Bella braced for bad news. She did not want to hear that Audrey Maynard was dead. She thought of the worried mother they'd just visited who had likely introduced her daughter to the life.

"Have they found her?" She held her breath.

Pierce gave his head a shake. "No. But they did find a mechanic from the Lexus dealership. He'd been shot with a .32. Apparently the blood in the trunk of the stolen car was his. I'm guessing he was their way into the dealership for the vehicle."

Dread trickled through her. "Please tell me you don't own a .32."

"I don't."

Thank God. Bella started the car. Whether Pierce realized it or not, they were in trouble. The case just went from potential kidnapping and sexual abuse to murder.

And Dr. Devon Pierce was the only real person of interest.

Before heading to his home, they stopped by the hotel where Audrey Maynard had said she met with the man who hired her. The hotel refused to give out any information or to share security video footage without a warrant.

Maybe the police would have better luck.

Chapter Five

Arbor Drive, Lake Bluff, 7:48 p.m.

When they arrived at his home, Devon would have preferred to go inside alone. To have peace and quiet in which to consider the moving parts of this nightmare until he could put the pieces together and come up with some sort of logic.

If Richard was behind this insanity, and he must be, why now? Why involve Cara?

The answer echoed inside him. Because Richard understood. He knew without doubt that resurrecting the circumstances around his late wife's death was the only way to truly do harm to Devon. The nasty rumors of murder had died down not long after the funeral. But that didn't mean stirring them up wouldn't damage his reputation—and his industry-changing work at the Edge.

Ms. Lytle parked between the fountain and the front door. She shut off the engine and turned to him. "We need to talk and I expect total honesty."

He met her gaze in the fading car interior lights. "We haven't talked enough?"

His brain needed to shut down. He wasn't sure he

could trust himself to make proper decisions or to hold a civil discourse at this point. To bring *this* here—to bring *her* here again—was too much.

"I don't think you fully grasp the weight of the situation. Someone is framing you and they're doing a hell of a good job. It's imperative that we stay ahead of this. By morning, the police could show up with a warrant. It's only logical that reporters will follow. We need to be prepared."

"Very well." He reached for the door. "We'll talk."

He'd wanted to return to the Edge to pick up his car but she'd insisted that she would be chauffeuring him everywhere until this nightmare was over. He thought the suggestion was ludicrous and yet here they were. He had other vehicles at his disposal. If he decided to dismiss her, other transportation was not an issue.

He trudged up the steps and to the front door. A few seconds later, they were inside. He locked the door behind them and reset the alarm out of habit. "Would you like a drink?"

Devon intended to have several. He rarely allowed himself more than one but tonight was different. Tonight he needed...*more*.

"No, thank you." She hesitated a moment then added, "You should eat first."

She stood several feet away and still she felt too close. A few strands of her dark hair had come loose and fallen around her face, softening her all-business appearance.

"My kitchen is at your disposal if you're hungry." The craving roaring inside him right now would not be satisfied with anything in that kitchen.

He made it to the bar and had reached for the bottle

of Scotch he reserved for celebrations. This was certainly no celebration but he didn't care. He downed a substantial serving of the smoky, dry whiskey. Then he closed his eyes and willed himself to relax.

"What's on the page you stuffed into your pocket besides blood?"

He reluctantly opened his eyes and met her impatient stare. "It's a page from my late wife's private journal."

She looked surprised. No more so than he.

"How did someone get their hands on a page from her journal?"

He poured himself another drink. "That is an answer I would sincerely like to know myself." He lifted the glass to his lips but her hand on his arm stopped him from turning up the bottom as he'd intended.

"I need your head on straight for the rest of the questions I have."

He stared at her for a moment, the glass mere centimeters from his mouth, her fingers somehow searing his skin through his clothing. "Trust me, Ms. Lytle, this is merely a bracer." He searched her dark eyes. "In fact, I'm certain you will prefer me without the fierce edge I'm experiencing at the moment."

Her hand fell away. He downed the drink.

When he'd savored the promised relief for a moment, he set the glass aside and turned to her. "Ask what you will. I'm all yours."

Had the last part been a Freudian slip? She stared at him as if she wondered the same.

"We can talk while we eat," she announced before turning and walking away.

He watched the determined strides, the sway of her hips, her back as straight as a ballerina's. That she had entered his private world troubled him immensely. This—he looked around the room—small sliver of his existence was intensely personal. The rest of his world was work. At work, he was in control, untouchable, respected. Here he was alone, desperate, needy. He kept the two worlds completely separate.

Isabella Lytle did not belong in this part.

He licked the lingering taste of Scotch from his lips. He couldn't deny his attraction to her. The challenge she represented intrigued him. Never had he seen a woman handle herself the way Bella Lytle did. She wasn't easily intimidated and her mind was quicksilver sharp. A part of him desired to throw caution to the wind and discover the woman underneath that professional facade. But no matter how much he craved her…no matter how much he wanted to take her completely apart, that would be a mistake.

He was well aware why he was suddenly so fascinated by this woman he hardly knew. The hunger for a physical outlet kept his mind away from the ugly past that had abruptly come back to haunt him.

In no hurry, he moved toward the kitchen. As he neared, he heard cabinet doors closing, dinnerware settling onto stone. When he entered the room, she stood at the open door of the refrigerator browsing the shelves. His house manager ensured the kitchen was stocked, providing numerous options. Usually he prepared dinner for himself each night, though recently he'd had no appetite.

She didn't inquire as to what he wanted to eat. Instead she prepared two small plates with cheese, fruit and cold cuts. To occupy himself, he went to the pantry and grabbed a box of crackers. She took the box and arranged the crackers next to the rest and then passed a plate to him.

Another trip to the refrigerator and she returned with two bottles of water. He reached into a drawer and retrieved linen napkins. They sat at the island and ate in silence. He forced himself to chew and then swallow. She was right about the alcohol. She was right about the rest as well. By morning, the police would be at his doorstep. He had to prepare.

She wanted him to tell her everything…to open himself up to her.

He caught himself staring at her and looked away. Whatever questions she had, she should ask them. Anything would be better than his preoccupation with her lips sliding across the tines of the fork or resting against the mouth of the water bottle. His control was slipping away quickly and he loathed the desperation clawing at him.

Not since Cara had anyone got under his skin quite like the beautiful and elusive Ms. Lytle.

"You had questions?" His tone was sharper than he'd intended.

She dabbed the napkin to her lips, and he stared at the place she had touched. Her lips were far too lush, too deeply colored. He licked his own, the urge to taste hers building deep inside him.

"Your wife kept a journal. Was there a particular reason she kept a record of her feelings while you were married or was this something she'd always done?"

He tossed his napkin atop his plate. He'd forced himself to eat a few bites but he couldn't stomach any more. "We were married for five years. I had no idea she kept a journal until shortly before her death."

"You discovered it and didn't like what you found?"

Her dark eyes probed his, looking for signs of untruths. She was very, very good at spotting those. He'd recognized her intense stares for what they were: a silent interrogation. Underneath her scrutiny, he felt his desire for her rise.

He wasn't used to being unsettled by a woman—or anyone else, for that matter. And the sensation made him want to unsettle her back.

"That's correct."

"Was this around the time of the accident?"

"Of course." He gave his head a slight shake. "Would the story be even half as titillating had I not made the discovery on the precipice of such a tragedy?"

"This is not fiction, Dr. Pierce," she chastised.

"Certainly not." He looked away for a moment. "I found her journal the day before we left for Binghamton, New York, her hometown. It was too late to change our plans. Her family was expecting us." He shrugged. "I suppose I was still in denial."

"You fought about it?"

"We fought, yes." The voices from that evening whispered through his mind, her ranting at him at the top of her lungs. Tears streaming down her beautiful face. His deeper voice, simmering with rage and threats of an ugly divorce, of leaving her with nothing. She threw her perfume bottle at him. He'd dodged and the elegant glass had smashed against the hearth of the fireplace in their room.

"Did you threaten her in any way?"

There was the tiniest glimmer of sadness in her eyes now. Or perhaps it was sympathy. Of all the things she had to offer, her sympathy was not what he wanted.

"I never threatened my wife with anything other than a divorce."

She tilted her head and stared at him. "The journal contained something inflammatory enough to make you consider a divorce? Did you have a prenuptial agreement?"

"I had suspected she was having an affair for some time. As I told you before, I hoped it would pass. But the journal made it clear that would not be the case." He exhaled a big breath. "And no, there was no prenuptial agreement."

Ms. Lytle slipped from her seat and took her plate to the sink. She folded her napkin and left it on the counter. While he did the same, she said, "Do you still have the journal?"

"Yes." He braced his hands on the counter, his back to her. He knew it was only a matter of time before she asked to see it.

He felt raw, exposed, and he hated it. He was unused to being tipped off center, which this investigation had done. He wanted to rage against the unfairness of it. Unfortunately, the only outlet he had was Bella Lytle, who was off-limits. A professional contact only.

So why was he drawn to her in such a primal way? Why did he want to unsettle the coolheaded investigator as he'd been unsettled?

"What secrets did you discover?"

"The journal intimately detailed the affair that had been going on for six months."

"With your partner?"

Devon faced her then. "I didn't believe so at the time. Though the entries in her journal were quite explicit, she never named her coconspirator."

"Where is it?"

"I keep it in my bedside table."

Dismay claimed her face. "You're serious."

It wasn't a question. She recognized the truth.

"It reminds me every day not to trust anyone with my deepest, darkest secrets."

She shook her head. "Please tell me you haven't read it a thousand times."

"Only once." He stared at his hands, fingers spread on the cool surface of the granite countertop. "When I found it, I read all the way through."

"Why punish yourself that way?"

He met her gaze, saw the disapproval there. "Because I deserved to be punished if all that she felt was true."

She looked away first. "What significance did the final entry have? The one someone left for you in the trunk of a stolen car with a pool of blood."

He reached into his pocket for the crumpled page. He slapped it down on the sleek countertop, the crimson smear on the page a shocking contrast to the cool whites, browns and grays of the granite.

She picked up the page that had been torn loose from the rest. Part of the lower half had been left attached to the binding as if the page had been ripped away in a rush. Ms. Lytle didn't have to recite the words aloud. Devon knew them by heart.

He will kill me rather than risk anyone knowing the truth.

When her gaze rested on his once more, she asked, "What made her believe you would rather see her dead than to allow the truth to be told?"

He shook his head. "I have no idea. I asked what the hell she meant and her only response was that I didn't understand. She said I could never understand. That everything wasn't about me."

Apparently, his wife had been right. The final months of their marriage may not have been about him at all. Didn't mean he wasn't still left to pick up the pieces.

"What truth is she referring to?"

Devon gave the only answer he could. "I have no idea."

Whether she believed him or not, he couldn't say. She shrugged, stared at the page. "We should put this in a bag. Any prints or other evidence left behind are likely contaminated already, but we should preserve whatever possible." Her gaze settled onto his. "I'd like to see the journal."

There it was. Another breach of his carefully constructed existence.

His first instinct was to refuse her request. What difference could the autobiography of his wife's infidelity make now? But he understood that he was too close to this to see things clearly. Perhaps he couldn't see how beyond proving motive the journal might serve the investigation.

"Very well. I'll get it for you."

"I should have a look around your home as well." She glanced across the kitchen. "If there is anything else incriminating that the police might find when they execute their search, I need to see it first."

RATHER THAN ANSWER, Pierce only regarded her for one long moment. He wanted to deny her request; Bella could see that certainty in his eyes. Self-preservation, she suspected, kept him from doing so.

She was prepared to remind him of the agency's

strict confidentiality policy and stellar investigator-client reputation when he said, "We'll take the grand tour, then."

Bella followed him through the first-floor rooms. A dining table that seated eighteen spanned the eclectic European dining room. Two powder rooms and a smoking room. The double doors she'd first noticed at the other end of the entry hall did lead to his study. The walls, bookshelves and desk were a rich mahogany. The shelves were lined with medical journals. Framed awards and achievements filled one wall. There were no photos of family. His parents were deceased and he had no other close relatives, according to the background material provided by the agency and her research.

She surveyed the lovely artwork on the walls as they climbed the east staircase. One by one, he showed her through the upper-floor wings of the house. So far she'd counted nine bedrooms, twelve baths and eighteen fireplaces. Every room was exquisitely decorated and utterly *empty* of any sign of a human touch beyond the decor.

From the windows that faced the back of the property, she saw the lights playing on Lake Michigan. She wondered if he and his wife had ever considered filling this home with children, or if it had only been a showplace to impress friends and associates. As far as Bella could see, it had become nothing more than a mausoleum. A large empty hotel where he spent his nights.

His suite was the last one they entered. The room was large, the decor at once elegant and comfortable. He walked to his side of the enormous bed and reached into the second drawer of his night table. The leather-bound journal wasn't large, about six by nine inches. He handed it to her.

"Have you always kept it here, in your bedroom?"

"Yes." He glanced around the room as if looking for somewhere to settle his attention.

"When did you notice the page missing?"

"I didn't know it was missing until we found it in the trunk of that car."

Bella measured the weight of the book. It weighed hardly anything and yet it had destroyed a marriage. "When is the last time you recall opening it?"

"The one and only time I've opened it. The day before we left for New York."

She left him standing near the bed as she walked through the closet. There were two actually. One on either side of the massive bath. The white closet was empty. Not even a speck of dust littered the shelves. He'd had all her things removed. The mahogany closet was filled with expensive suits and shoes. Ties were folded and displayed in glass cases. Neatly pressed shirts in dozens of colors hung in well-ordered rows. The room smelled of leather and that expensive cologne he wore.

She returned to the bedroom. He waited at the door, his tall frame blocking her exit from the closet.

"Have you seen all you need to see?"

Did he really expect her to forget what Detective Corwin had said? "I need to see *everything*. The room Corwin mentioned is not exempt. I suspect it will be named specifically in the warrant."

"As you wish."

This time, they descended the west-side staircase. He led the way along the back downstairs hall where the laundry room and mudroom were located. A door half-way between the two opened onto a small landing. A less ornate staircase descended into the basement level, though nothing about the space looked like a basement.

The stairs ended in a large game room. A pool table stood in the center. A bar wrapped around one corner of the space. The biggest television she'd ever seen in her life hung on one wall. The wraparound seating area created the perfect conversation spot. Another fireplace. Another bathroom.

And a final door.

He took his wallet from his trousers and removed a key from its hiding place. He opened the door and pushed it inward, then turned on the lights.

The first thing she noticed was the seemingly end-less amount of black. The walls were black; the floor and ceiling were black. All appeared to be leather. A bed—or something in the shape of a bed—was the sin-gle red element, also leather. She moved around the room. A row of shelves displayed an abundance of sex toys, whips and the like, some objects not readily iden-tifiable. Every imaginable kind of condom filled a glass fishbowl.

Her heart started to pound harder and harder. A re-freshment center claimed a few feet against the wall. The glass door of the fridge revealed wine coolers, beer, colas and bottled water. Opposite the bed, a steel bar hung horizontally, maybe eight feet from the floor. Chains hung from the bar. Padded handcuffs dangled on the ends of the chains.

Before she could stop her runaway imagination, she pictured Devon Pierce shackled there. Naked, of course. His lean body taut in expectation of the whip's sting.

Her nipples hardened and an ache throbbed between her thighs.

She should not be here.

He waited at the door, watching her, assessing her reaction.

Could he see how aroused she was?

She turned on him. "Do you bring women here regularly?"

"How is that relevant, Ms. Lytle?"

"Ms. Maynard accused you of holding her here. For two months. Can anyone else refute that accusation? Someone you brought here for an evening of entertainment in the past few weeks?" Even as she asked the questions, her throat grew so dry she could hardly speak. Her pulse was racing. Her skin was on fire.

She needed out of this room.

"I haven't brought anyone here recently." He took a step in her direction. "Perhaps a month ago." Another couple of feet disappeared between them.

"That would be within the two-month time frame. Do you have contact information for her? She may be needed as a witness if Mrs. Maynard's testimony about Audrey's whereabouts doesn't suffice."

"The sorts of women I bring here don't provide contact information."

He was standing right next to her now, staring down at her as if she were his partner for the evening.

"You shouldn't be afraid of your desire, Isabella," he said in a low voice that made her wonder what he saw in her expression.

She blinked. "Bella," she corrected. "My friends call me Bella."

"Bella." He licked his lips when he said her name as if tasting it. "It suits you."

She said nothing. She couldn't. Her skin was flushed. Her state of agitation was obvious.

He reached up, traced a finger along her cheek. She shivered. "You are very beautiful, Bella."

"Is that what you tell them when you bring them here?" A flash of anger melted into anticipation. "Every woman wants to be called beautiful. Is that what you do for the women you bring home? Make them feel special, wanted, sexy?"

His hand flattened on her chest, the tips of his fingers tracing the collar of her blouse. Her body throbbed at his firm touch.

His fingers trailed more softly against the hollow of her throat. "Is that how you feel, Bella? Special? Sexy?"

She tried not to shiver but his words, the sound of his voice, made her ache with want. "Maybe a little."

His hand moved lower, slipping inside her jacket, closing around her breast. Her breath caught. He squeezed. Pleasure shot through her.

She lifted her chin in defiance of her own weakness. "I should go."

He moved in closer. The fingers of his left hand closed around the nape of her neck, threaded into her hair, loosening the pins holding it. His right hand squeezed her breast harder then slid down to her waist and slid around to the small of her back. He pulled her against his body. She felt every hard ridge and angle of him.

Slowly, so very slowly, he lowered his face to hers. Their lips brushed. She gasped. Sought someplace for her hands. No. No. She couldn't touch him… If she touched him now, the battle would be over.

As if he'd abruptly realized his mistake, he stepped away from her. She swayed, struggled to regain her equilibrium.

"You should stay here tonight. Her journal doesn't leave this house. Choose whatever guest room you like."

Were his attempts to put her off balance some endeavor to push her away from this ultra-personal part of the investigation? Did he somehow believe he could prevent her from dissecting this facet of his history? No way. In fact, it was her turn to put him off balance.

"I'll take this room."

He hesitated at the door but didn't look back. Oh yes, direct hit. When he'd gone, she removed her jacket and folded it like a pillow on the enormous red leather bed. She toed off her shoes and relaxed onto the overly firm surface. She opened the journal of Cara Pierce and started to read.

An hour and many pages later, she came to the first entry that changed dramatically in tone.

I shouldn't have allowed myself to be seduced. Or perhaps I was the one doing the seducing. We were both equally surprised. We spent hours together, never leaving the rumpled sheets of the bed. My adventurous lover learned every part of me. Every secret place that longed for more than I ever hoped for. This was the most sexually demanding and beautiful encounter of my life.

I want more.

Bella closed the journal and laid it aside. She stood and walked around the room. She paused at the shelves and studied the various bondage items. Ropes, handcuffs, collars. She fingered a leather riding crop. Blindfolds, vibrators, clamps. She moved to the steel bar at the other end of the room. The chains and padded cuffs dangling from the bar again had her imagining Pierce restrained there. Would he want his playmate to use that riding crop to torture him or would she be on her knees in front of him?

Need pulsed deep inside her. Though Cara Pierce clearly had not been speaking of her husband in that journal passage, Bella had imagined him doing those things to her. Her hand went to her breast, to the one he had squeezed so tightly. Her nipples remained as hard as stone.

She wasn't a prude. She'd played a few sex games, but nothing on this level.

It was late. She should get some sleep. She lay down on the red leather bed once more. She stared at the ceiling, only then noticing the mirror. She touched her breast again, thought of his hand there and then sliding lower. She closed her eyes and thought of him kissing every part of her, exploring every hot, shivery inch. Bringing her to release over and over with nothing more than his skilled hands and those incredible lips. She rolled onto her side and bit down on her lower lip to hold back her cries when desire rippled through her.

She drifted off to sleep while images of him spooned against her, kissing her all over, followed her into her dreams.

Chapter Six

Wednesday, June 6, 6:05 a.m.

He was trying to distract her.

Bella finger-combed her hair, then arranged it into her preferred twist and pinned it into place. She smoothed her sweater and slipped into her jacket. He distracted her because he didn't want to answer those hard, personal questions.

She stepped back into the room with its massive red leather bed. She was glad the space had included an en suite bath. Though the stainless-steel garden tub had given her pause, she supposed it was as much a design statement as a place to indulge in sexual activity.

She stared at the red leather bed as she exited the bath. Before she could stem the flow, a stream of images—all involving Devon Pierce naked—filled her mind. With a shake of her head, she opened the journal and read through a few more entries. Cara was meeting her lover at least once a week, most often twice. The interludes were intensely erotic.

My lover flogged me today. It was my first experience with sexual torture. No one has ever touched me that way. I was secured facedown on the bed with my arms and legs spread wide. The whip didn't break the skin but created red welts everywhere it touched. I cried out, the tears stinging my eyes as the leather stung my skin. Then my lover licked and kissed every red mark on my body, soothing and suckling until I was dizzy with desire. I don't dare write of the other things. All I can say is that I have never experienced a full body orgasm until today. It went on and on and I can't get enough.

Bella shivered as she closed the journal and tucked it into her bag. No matter how much Devon Pierce wanted to believe a warrant wasn't coming, Bella knew better. It was a matter of time before the cavalry came calling. For that reason, despite his edict that the journal was not to leave the house, it was going with her.

She fingered the inflammatory volume in her bag while she considered the ramifications of withholding evidence, but decided that this wasn't exactly evidence—not for Audrey Maynard's allegations of kidnapping, anyway, which was what the cops were investigating. The police did not need to know about the journal. The affair Cara Pierce was involved in would prove motive for her husband for a death that had already been investigated and deemed an accident. At this point, there was no need to stir up trouble on that front. Having it turned into a murder investigation all these years later wouldn't help anyone.

Speaking of Dr. Pierce, Bella found him in the kitchen pouring himself a coffee. He wore a navy suit today with an equally dark blue shirt, the fabric no doubt the finest available, like the rest of his wardrobe. The jacket hung on the back of a chair at the small breakfast table perched in the large bay window. She placed her bag on the floor next to a stool that stood at the counter. The decision not to bring up last night's incident was an easy one to make.

"Good morning." She reached for a mug.

He shifted his attention to her, the French-press carafe in his hand. "Good morning." He filled her cup without her having to ask. "I won't inquire as to how you slept. That room was not designed for comfort."

"Surprisingly well." She inhaled deeply of the bold flavored coffee. Whether it was the blend or the French press, it smelled incredible. She tasted it and moaned before she could stop herself. "You're very good with coffee, Dr. Pierce."

"I'm very good with many things, Ms. Lytle."

She studied his handsome face. She knew this whole investigation was torture for him. A man so private suddenly forced to reveal his deepest desires wasn't going to handle it with grace. He was going to deflect and strike out. He knew he had got to her last night and he hoped to use his new discovery to keep her off balance. Not happening. "I'm confident you are. I thought we had dispensed with the formalities. Call me Bella."

"Bella." He said her name as if tasting wine and attempting to dissect the flavor.

"After my grandmother." She sipped the delicious coffee and shifted her focus to the news on the television across the room. "I hope I haven't caused you to be late this morning." He'd told her that his usual workday began around seven.

"I sometimes work from my office here." He set his cup aside.

She really needed to go by her place and pick up a change of clothes. The shower had been refreshing but her clothes were heavy with yesterday's tension.

"Did the journal provide any insights that might help you solve the case?"

The question was one he genuinely wanted an answer to, she knew this, but the tone of his question was caustic, indifferent. He wanted to appear uncaring, but the good doctor was not quite as adept at lying about this particular subject as he would obviously prefer her to believe.

"Not yet. I have a ways to go."

The tension along his jawline warned that he was not pleased with her reading those so very private entries.

"Your wife must have been a very selfish woman."

Bella had done her research. Rather than spend some of her time and efforts to charitable pursuits, Cara Pierce traveled extensively while her husband devoted himself entirely to his work. She wore extravagant clothes and jewelry and she refused to have children. That was something Bella had learned in the journal. Pierce—Devon—wanted children. His wife adamantly did not. She bemoaned the idea of ruining her body with stretch marks.

How had he fallen in love with a woman who held so little in common with him?

"She traveled all the time while you worked," she added for clarification.

"Perhaps she was merely lonely. I was not a very attentive husband."

The doorbell rang before she could argue with his reasoning.

Devon picked up a remote and changed the channel on the small television mounted near the refrigerator. The image on the screen was of his front door and the parking enclave. Several cars besides her own sat around the center fountain. Detectives Corwin and Hodge stood at the door, a couple of uniforms and what looked like a crime scene team behind them.

"So it begins," Pierce muttered.

Bella set her cup aside and followed him through the house. "Where's your housekeeper?"

"My house manager and her staff have the week off."

"You gave everyone the same week off?" she asked as they walked across the glossy marble and headed for the door.

"She oversees the cleaning staff and the landscaping team. It's best that they vacation at the same time."

She got it now. If the rest of the staff was off at the same time as the manager, he didn't have to interact with them.

They reached the door just as another chime of the bell echoed through the vast hall. "I'll handle this," she said, hoping he would acquiesce to her offer.

He gestured to the door and stepped back. She understood how detectives analyzed their persons of interest. Corwin and Hodge would be scrutinizing his every word, his every look. They made it their mission to understand how to get under his skin. How to prod responses. Pierce would be far better served to not give them any more ammunition.

Bella opened the door and flashed the detectives a smile. "Good morning, gentlemen." She opened the door wide as she stepped back. "Please come in."

Corwin thrust the warrant at Pierce without bothering to say good morning or even hello. From the dark circles under his eyes and the rumpled suit, he'd likely been working all night. Bella remembered well the nec-

essary hours required to investigate a case like this one.
No one wanted more bodies piling up.

One of the uniforms stayed outside the door while
the other came inside. The team of forensic techs spilled
in next. Hodge hooked a thumb toward them. "They'll
be here for a while."

Bella nodded. "As long as nothing is damaged and
every single thing they touch is put back exactly as it
was, you won't get any trouble from us."

Corwin strolled over to her, close enough to whisper
his question. "Isn't that the same suit you were wearing yesterday?"

Bella looked him up and down, and when she responded, she didn't whisper. "That's funny—I was just
thinking the same thing about those khaki trousers and
the tweed jacket you're wearing. With the white shirt
it's a little more difficult to say, but there is the matter
of all those wrinkles."

The other detective's lips quirked with the need to
smile.

Moving on to business, Bella filled in the two detectives as to what Maynard's mother had to say, including the part about her daughter being home recently.
If she'd been held hostage by Pierce for the past two
months as she'd claimed, it was unlikely that he'd allow
her to go home for visits.

"Any news on Audrey Maynard's whereabouts?"
Pierce asked, his tone sharp, impatient.

Hodge shrugged. "Nothing. It's like she dropped off
the planet."

"Or got dead," Corwin countered. He looked from
Bella to Pierce and back. "I'm presuming the two of
you were together last night."

"That's correct," Bella said without hesitation. "We worked late. Rather than drive an hour home, it was more reasonable that I stay here."

The techs fanned out, taking the upstairs rooms first. Corwin shifted his attention to Pierce. The doctor was six or more inches taller than either of the detectives, so looking up was necessary. "Hodge and I would like to see the red room."

"I think you've watched too many movies, gentlemen." Pierce indicated they should follow him. "What I have is an adult game room."

Bella suspected the room wasn't about games or even sexual pleasure; the space was about punishment. She kept those thoughts to herself. Who was she to cast the first stone? God knew she had plenty of her own hang-ups.

En route, Bella gathered her bag. She didn't want one of the techs poking into her things, particularly the journal. Cara Pierce's private notes about her life were not something these guys needed to see just yet. Not until Bella had something to neutralize the advantage the glaring motive the woman's words appeared to provide.

While Corwin and Hodge were examining the numerous sex toys, Bella pulled Pierce aside and warned him that this could take all day, maybe longer. If he wanted her to stay and go through the house with the detectives, she would gladly do so. At this point, however, her instincts were leaning toward sticking to him.

So far, the trouble that had shown up at his doorstep was designed to create issues for him, but that scenario could change quickly. If the person behind this obvious setup felt his ultimate goal was not being accomplished quickly enough, he could make an attempt on Pierce's life. At least one person had lost his life so far.

Pierce apparently felt the same. He called in the house manager's chief assistant to stay with the house while the police did what they had to do. During the drive into the city, Bella had a captive audience for a little more than an hour. She decided now was as good a time as any to bring up her concerns about his private staff.

"I'm sure you vet your staff very carefully," she began, "but your wife's journal was kept in your bedside table. There was a page torn from it. I have to say that it's very likely you have an employee who is willing to take money in exchange for access to your home, or at least to the things inside your home."

"I am aware that scenario is swiftly becoming one I cannot deny." His voice was grim. "My security system is not one easily breached. If the system had been tampered with, audio or video altered, I would know it. The page was either given to my former partner, or he was allowed into my home after the security system had been turned off."

Bella merged onto the interstate. "You're convinced, then, that it's Sutter."

"I can think of no one else who knew me well enough to know my weaknesses. Jack Hayman never showed any interest in my personal life. Even now, he spends most of his time on a beach somewhere surrounded by exotic women. I doubt he would go to all this trouble for any reason."

If Hayman was ruled out and it was Sutter who had the affair with Pierce's wife, he likely knew all his secrets. Cara would have shared plenty with her lover.

"Did you have the adult game room before she died?" Traffic was already crazy heavy. Those who lived in the suburbs were winding their way into the city, their automobiles lined up bumper to bumper.

"No. That came after."

She thought of the things his late wife had said in her journal. Clearly her secret lover was playing those same sorts of games with her. "Were you and your wife intimate in that way?"

"Are you asking me if we played games? Used pleasure enhancements?"

Heat flushed her skin, making her want to squirm in her seat. She was a professional investigator who'd asked any number of personal questions throughout her career. She'd heard it all, from all kinds of people. It took a hell of a lot more than sexual kink to knock her off balance.

And yet that was exactly what Dr. Devon Pierce and his ridiculously sexy adult game room had done.

As uncomfortable as asking made her, she needed to know—to understand the dynamics between them. Didn't she?

"Did you?"

"No. I was very busy and preoccupied. I'm certain she considered our sex life quite boring."

After the way he'd touched Bella last night, she doubted sex with Pierce would be boring by any definition of the word. "You were married for five years before the accident. Surely there was a time when the two of you were happy."

The silence was so thick it was difficult to breathe. She adjusted her grip on the steering wheel, stared at the rows of taillights in front of her. The decision to have this conversation now suddenly felt incredibly awkward. Pretending that last night hadn't happened felt like the right thing to do when she'd got up this morning. In spite of that decision, there was no way around talking about sex.

"We were happy at first. She became jealous of my work. Felt neglected. Rightfully so." He sighed and stared out the window. "I'm not sure anything I could have done differently would have mattered, but I will always wonder."

Bella allowed the silence to settle between them.

They'd just taken the exit for downtown when he answered a call on his cell. "I'm almost there," he said to the caller. When he'd put his phone away, he surveyed the traffic. "A bus loaded with children headed to a dance competition crashed on the expressway. Most of the injured are en route to the Edge."

Even as he said the words, a half dozen ambulances seemed to appear out of nowhere, sirens blaring.

By the time they reached the parking area, the ambulances were already lined up at the emergency entrance. Bella pulled as close to the area as possible. "Go," she said. "I'll park and catch up with you inside."

She watched until Pierce was safely inside. She parked her car and hurried to the ER's entrance. Gurneys were rushing in with patients while others were rushing out to retrieve more. Children were wailing. Mothers were crying. Keeping her attention on their faces rather than their bloody bodies, Bella hurried to the registration desk.

"What can I do to help?"

The two registration specialists glanced at her. The

older of the two evidently recognized her as a friend of Dr. Pierce's.

"We've got six adults, including the bus driver, here who were with the children," said the older woman, Patsy, according to her name tag. "But we'll have a whole lot more showing up. There're sixteen children. The parents of the others will be arriving any minute. If you can keep them calm until we get the paperwork done, that would be great."

Bella nodded. "I can do that."

As Patsy said, a dozen or more cars descended on the ER parking lot in the half hour that followed. Frantic parents were not easily placated. One of the mothers who had been on the bus and who was uninjured helped with passing along information about whose child was where. Some were at imaging; others were in treatment rooms. Thankfully only two had injuries serious enough to warrant surgery.

One by one, the parents were reunited with their children in treatment rooms or in the ER lobby if they had been released.

When everyone appeared settled, Bella walked through the double doors into the corridor beyond the triage area. She passed the nurses' station. As she approached Treatment Room Six, she heard Pierce's voice.

The door opened and a nurse walked out. She smiled at Bella and left the door partially open. A girl—six or seven years old, Bella guessed—sat on the exam table. Her left eye was swollen and swiftly turning colors. There was a bandage on her right leg. The mother stood on the opposite side of her, her worried face showing her struggle to keep up with what Pierce was saying.

"Bethany is going to be fine, but the images show a small linear skull fracture."

The mother covered her mouth with her hands. "Oh my God." Tears flowed down her cheeks.

"There's no shift or movement in the bones—that's a very good thing. Most likely we can simply monitor her overnight and send her home."

The mother's hands came away from her mouth, rested at her throat. "So she'll be okay."

"Absolutely. But," he said carefully, "because I'm not one to take chances with the life of such a precious little girl—" he smiled down at the child "—we're going to transfer her over to Rush Medical Center for the night. The nurse is taking care of the arrangements now."

The worry was back. The mother's face paled. "Something is wrong."

The little girl looked from her mother to Pierce and back. "Mommy?"

"This is just to make me feel better, Mrs. Jamison, I assure you. If on the outside chance Bethany needs any additional treatment, she will be in the best hospital this city has. I'm quite certain that's not going to happen, but I would feel better if she was there. I think you'll both rest better tonight at Rush."

"All right. My husband is on the way. Can we wait to be moved until he's here?"

"Of course." Pierce held out his hand to the little girl. She shook it with all her might. "You are a very brave little girl, Bethany. Your mother and father should be very proud."

The little girl grinned and the mother thanked him profusely. Before he could get away, she grabbed him and hugged him fiercely.

When at last the relieved mother released him, he walked out of the room. When he saw Bella, surprise flashed in his eyes. Bella smiled. "I had no idea you had such a way with children."

"I'm only an ogre with beautiful women."

Bella laughed. She had a feeling Dr. Devon Pierce was no monster at all. The problem was all those secrets he'd been keeping for so long. They tended to weigh a person down, darken their spirit. "You would make a very good father."

"No." He captured her eyes with his own, his gaze hard. "I wouldn't."

Stinging from his pointed rebuke, she shadowed him as he moved through the ER ensuring all was under control. Their next stop was in the surgery unit, where he checked on the two patients now in recovery. Both were doing well and would be moving on to Rush for admission.

As they walked toward his office, Bella paused and waited for him to meet her gaze. "It's time we tracked down your old partners and found out what they've been up to."

"If nothing else," he said, looking away, "you'll learn that my wife wasn't the only person who felt cheated by me."

As long as they learned which one felt cheated badly enough to seek revenge, Bella could deal with the rest. The sooner this case was solved, the less likely she was to cross the line she had brushed far too closely last night.

Chapter Seven

Chicago Police Department, 1:00 p.m.

Detective Corwin had called. He'd asked Devon to come downtown at his earliest convenience.

"They found something."

Bella's words reverberated inside him as she sent him a pointed glance before turning back to maneuvering through Chicago traffic. She'd insisted on driving. He'd agreed without protest. He wasn't entirely sure he could trust his ability to focus at this time. Not to mention his car was at home. The woman who'd pretended to be his wife remained missing, unless they had found her body and that was the reason for this command appearance.

"We really should call your attorney," she repeated. She'd made this statement twice already.

"I'll call my attorney if I need him."

Too many people were aware of his weaknesses and secrets already. He detested the idea that the woman driving had learned the most private part of him. His ability to experience pleasure came only with pain. He could only imagine how many more people would be involved before this was over.

"You holding up okay?"

If he didn't say something, she would continue prodding at him. "Why wouldn't I be? The police believe I'm a murderer, perhaps a repeat offender if Maynard is not found alive. I see no readily available avenue for refuting their insinuations."

He chose not to discuss the subject of how Ms. Lytle must see him. She was attracted to him; that was evident. As much as he would like to learn every part of her, he would be far more pleased if she respected his accomplishments. Whatever else he was beyond the creator of the Edge was of little value.

Hadn't his own wife proved as much? He was unable to please her...unable to make her happy in any way.

"You know, you could have stood by your position that they call your attorney with further questions."

"I might as well get it over with," he confessed. "Otherwise, they'll believe my lack of cooperation is yet further proof that I'm guilty." He'd considered this at length during the long sleepless hours last night. He had nothing to hide—at least nothing related to criminal activity.

Bella parked on the street near their destination. "What they believe is irrelevant." She turned to face him. "All that matters is what they can prove."

They emerged from her sedan simultaneously. "What do you believe?"

She met his gaze over the car. "I believe someone is trying very hard to make you look guilty. Let's not give them any help."

She'd avoided his question. Perhaps her avoidance was an answer in itself.

Inside the precinct, they were escorted to a small conference room and offered water or soft drinks. He declined and she did as well. They didn't speak while they waited. Devon felt confident the detectives were listening in hopes of gleaning some tidbit that would support their case. Ten minutes, then fifteen passed. The delay was another tactic designed to make him restless, to heighten his anxiety.

Rather than allow their attempts to get under his skin to take root, he thought of all the children who'd been injured this morning and how exhilarated he'd felt caring for them.

He missed that part of his work. The patients. Although his accomplishments were designed to ensure a higher patient survival rate in the ER setting, he couldn't deny missing the hands-on part of medicine. He thought of the volunteer work one of his nurses, Eva Bowman, did at a free clinic. Maybe he should consider an option such as that one.

His thoughts drifted from helping others to self-indulgence. Touching Bella hadn't been his plan last night. He'd reluctantly showed her what she wanted to see but then he saw her expression. She'd been affected, aroused—not repulsed as he would have imagined. Suddenly, he'd found himself lost in the smell of her, aching at the sight of her. The room was not for his pleasure and yet he'd taken great pleasure standing in the space and merely touching her.

For that he deserved to be punished severely.

When Corwin entered, Hodge came in right behind him. Both carried paper cups filled with steaming coffee from the corner shop. Now they were merely trying to make him angry. *Let's waste the doctor's time while we go for coffee.* Devon wasn't falling for it. The two detectives had unquestionably been observing their prey while someone else strolled to the corner coffee shop. Another game. Nothing more.

"We had to call out another team," Corwin said as he sat down. "That's a big house you've got, Dr. Pierce."

Devon said nothing in response.

"Did you finish?" Bella demanded. "I certainly hope you left things the way you found them."

Hodge shrugged. "We do our best."

"Why are we here?" she demanded.

Corwin sipped his coffee, then leaned back in his chair. "I know I said this before, but I swear you act more like an attorney than an ex-cop. If I hadn't reviewed your record personally, I would have my doubts."

"You were a good cop," Hodge said.

"Are we going somewhere with this?" She looked from one to the other. "Dr. Pierce has a medical facility to oversee. A medical facility that's an integral part of this community. I'm certain there are people far higher up the food chain than the two of you who understand the importance of his work."

The two shared a look of feigned disbelief. "I guess we better get on with it," Corwin said.

"Yeah," Hodge agreed. "We wouldn't want the mayor or anyone important giving us any grief."

"You know," Corwin added, speaking to Bella, "you're only in here because the doctor insisted."

"Perhaps you'd rather deal with my attorney," Devon suggested.

Corwin shut his mouth on the subject. Still, he had that look. The one that said they had something. Whatever they had found, it was significant. The two were far too cocky to believe otherwise. Devon knew Bella had the journal, not that he was happy about her taking it out of his house. As it turned out, the move was a smart one. Anything else the police could have found was no doubt planted.

Bella was right about something else as well. He had a traitor on his staff. There was no way around that conclusion.

"First," Corwin began, "we found blood in the pocket of one of your suit jackets."

Hell. The journal page. Some of the blood on it must have still been transferable.

"You're aware we opened the trunk and found the blood," Devon offered.

"So you touched the blood?" Corwin argued.

"He's a doctor," Bella put in. "A physician's instinct would be to check to see where the blood was coming from and whether or not it was still warm and pliable."

Devon resisted the urge to stare at her. She hadn't lied, exactly, but she'd skirted all around it.

Corwin nodded. "You see, Hodge. I told you he'd have an explanation for why the blood was in his pocket."

Hodge bobbed his head up and down. "He's smart. I'll give him that."

"Gentlemen," Bella said, interrupting their back-and-forth, "why don't we move on to why you asked Dr. Pierce here? Just this morning, there was a terrible bus crash on the expressway. I'm sure you heard about it. The Edge was inundated with the victims of that crash. Dr. Pierce doesn't have time for guessing games."

Bravo. Devon resisted the urge to smile.

"We found this." Corwin nodded and Hodge placed a large envelope on the table. Corwin removed the items inside. A woman's purse. A prescription bottle. A hairbrush sporting several blond hairs. And, finally, a strip of three photos—the kind from one of those photo booths one might see in a mall. All carefully packaged in clear plastic bags and labeled as evidence.

Devon didn't have to pick up the prescription bottle to know to whom it belonged. Images of Audrey Maynard stared at him from the photo strip.

"Audrey Maynard has never been in my home." Devon looked from Hodge to Corwin. "Until she showed up at the ER, I had never heard her name or met her."

"You're sticking by your story that this is a setup," Corwin offered, skepticism heavy in his tone.

"Detective," Bella countered, "do you really have to ask? Considering I was once a cop, you must know that I was well aware you would be coming with a warrant. Dr. Pierce and I had more than ample time to ensure nothing incriminating or inflammatory would be found at his home. Why would he leave a crucial piece of evidence for you to find? This entire situation is swiftly turning into a circus."

Corwin stared directly at Devon. "If you're being framed, Dr. Pierce, help us understand who would do such a thing. We're operating in the dark beyond what evidence you see and all of it points to you. If you're innocent, then give us a different direction to go in."

"We have no choice but to follow the evidence," Hodge reminded Bella. "Any cop knows that."

"Jack Hayman," Devon said, ignoring Bella's glance when he supplied the name. "He was my partner for several years. We parted under less-than-amicable terms. I can think of no one else who would go to these extents."

"What about a former patient?" Corwin asked. "Haven't you ever lost a patient or left one unsatisfied?"

"I've never left a patient unsatisfied, Detective." Devon reined in his frustration. "The only patient I've ever lost—"

"Was your wife," Corwin said for him. "Does your late wife have any family members who might feel you were responsible for her death? A brother? Father? Anyone?"

"Father, mother, a brother and two sisters," Devon said. "They still invite me to holiday gatherings. I doubt one of them has suddenly decided I did something wrong and somehow contributed to Cara's death."

Bella stared at him in surprise but she quickly recovered. "Is there anything else?" she asked the detectives. "If not, I see no reason for Dr. Pierce to be detained further. He has answered your questions and has nothing further to add."

"Maynard's mother confirmed her daughter was at home on several occasions the past few weeks, so her accusations against you do appear to be unfounded. But we're far from done with this, Dr. Pierce." Corwin stood. "We're turning this city upside down looking for Maynard. If we can find her alive, maybe she can shed some light on what's really going on. Meanwhile, we'll look up this Jack Hayman character, your former partner."

"Thank you." Devon glanced at the items on the table as he followed Bella from the room.

The likelihood that Maynard was still alive grew slimmer every day that she remained missing. It wasn't necessary to be a cop to recognize that sad statistic. The person who had planned this elaborate game had taken great care to perfectly cover all possibilities.

But perfection was an unattainable goal. There would be a mistake somewhere. All Devon had to do was find it.

They were in the car before Bella spoke. "You never mentioned that her family still contacts you."

"You didn't ask." He fastened his seat belt. "I didn't see how that information was relevant."

She eased the car into traffic. "As long as you're certain they're not holding you accountable for her death, then it's not."

"I'm certain."

"Why did you give them Hayman's name when it's more likely Sutter they should be trying to find?"

"Because I want to speak to Sutter first. I'm counting on you to recognize if he's lying."

She met his gaze for a second. "Where can we find him?"

"We'll start with his wife."

Mariah Sutter always seemed to have a soft spot for Devon, at least until Cara died. She distanced herself from him afterward. She could very well refuse to speak to him at all. He supposed it would depend upon how angry she was with Richard today. The two had a volatile relationship.

Perhaps if he told her that he suspected Richard of having an affair with Cara she would spill her guts. But then she would tell the police when they inevitably interviewed her.

Then they would have a motive that, to their way of thinking, had been festering for years.

Clark Street, 4:00 p.m.

SHOEHORNED BETWEEN FORMER industrial landmarks that were now stunning homes, the Sutter residence was a sleek Asian-inspired showplace. The outdoors was beautifully incorporated into the indoor living space, complete with a rooftop deck and unparalleled views of the city's skyline.

Bella decided that despite Sutter's failed partnership with Pierce, the man had done exceedingly well financially. The house alone had to be worth north of twelve million. She could only imagine the value of the artwork and the furnishings.

Why would a man with all *this* to lose risk carrying out a plot like the one plaguing Pierce? Was revenge for a professional and perhaps personal grievance several years in the past really worth such an enormous sacrifice?

Mariah Sutter breezed into the expansive entertaining area in a floor-length gauzy white covering that gave her an air of floating. The sheer fabric did little to conceal a minuscule gold bathing suit beneath. Sutter was fifty but her body looked like that of a twenty-year-old.

"Devon!" She held her hands out to him as she approached. "What a delight to see you."

He took her hands, leaned in and kissed her cheek. "The pleasure is always mine."

The older woman looked to Bella. "And who is this?" She beamed a smile at Devon. "Have you finally decided to stop living like a hermit?"

Bella blushed. She hated the reaction but she'd been cursed with the response since she was a child.

"Mariah Sutter, this is Isabella Lytle, my associate. We're working on a new project." He smiled at Bella and her blush deepened.

"Nice to meet you, Mrs. Sutter."

"Hmm. She's far too attractive for a mere associate. And so polite." Mariah sighed. "Please sit down and visit for a while. It's been ages. Would you like a refreshment?"

"Water would be nice," Bella said when Mariah's gaze rested on her.

"The same for me."

The words had no more been uttered than a man wearing only a tight-fitting swimsuit walked in carrying a tray of glasses filled with ice water and decorated with wedges of lime.

When they had been served, he left the room, his gaze lingering on Mariah as he walked away.

"The proverbial pool boy," she said with a laugh. "I do adore surrounding myself with attractive humans."

"Mariah," Devon said, "I would like a meeting with Richard. Is he in town?"

"He's in Wimbledon. He has a niece who's playing. He wanted me to go but, frankly, I can't tolerate the girl's mother. She is such a pretentious bitch."

"How long has he been in the London area?"

Bella let Devon handle the questions this time. Anything she asked would no doubt be viewed as suspicious.

Mariah appeared to consider the question. "A week now, I think. He won't return for another two. I'm sure he'll pop over to Wentworth for a few rounds of golf. You know Richard—he likes to take advantage of every opportunity to put something in a hole."

Bella felt another blush climbing her throat.

Mariah laughed. "I do believe I've embarrassed your associate, Devon."

Bella smiled. "Not at all. Are you a golfer as well?"

"Good heavens, no. I prefer shopping." Her gaze lingered on Bella. "For all sorts of beautiful things."

Bella had the distinct impression the older woman was flirting with her.

"If you would," Devon said, drawing Mariah's attention to him, "let Richard know I need a conference call. Nothing too time-consuming. Only a few minutes of his time."

"I hope he hasn't filed another of those ridiculous lawsuits." She rolled her eyes. "The man is admittedly a very bad sport. I say let bygones be bygones. I never liked losing a good friend over something as trivial as money."

"I noticed the Lexus in your courtyard," Bella said. "I've considered trying one. Have you been pleased with yours?"

"I have no complaints. Really, transportation is Richard's department. He brings them home and I drive them."

"I suppose the dealership has a good service department." Bella watched the other woman closely as she waited for an answer.

"We have someone who picks the vehicles up when they need servicing. They always bring a replacement. Like clockwork."

Bella made a decision. She reached for her cell and pulled up the picture of Audrey Maynard. "Have you ever met this woman?"

Mariah reached for a pair of cheaters on the table

next to her chair. She slipped on the narrow gold frames and peered at the photo.

"Oh yes. I think she's one of Richard's assistants. Or at least, that's what he called her. My guess is she was one of his flings. He does so love the young things." Mariah frowned and then looked to Devon. "I never noticed how much she looks like Cara." She turned back to Bella. "Why do you ask? Is she involved with something my husband should know about?"

"She may be," Devon said. "She's missing and the police are searching for her."

"The police? Whatever for?"

"A number of charges," Bella said before he could. "It's imperative we find her."

"When I can get in touch with Richard, I'll let him know."

"Mariah, has Richard spoken recently about seeking revenge against me? As much as I appreciate your graciousness today, we both know Richard despises me."

"You think Richard has something to do with whatever she's doing."

"I think someone is trying to make me believe that," he allowed. "If that's the case, Richard may be vulnerable as well."

"I wish I could say Richard would never do such a thing, but I can't." Mariah shook her head. "He isn't the same since the two of you ended your partnership. The cancer only made him more bitter. I don't know him anymore, and in truth, I spend as little time with him as possible."

Devon thanked her for her time and she walked them to the door. Outside, the sound of the infinity pool trickling over its edge accompanied them to the street. Bella walked around her car, checking the tires and the hood. She looked underneath for any leaked fluids.

When they were in the car and driving away, he asked, "You're concerned that someone might be following us?"

"If no one is following us, then the person framing you is a fool, and we both know that's not the case." She hadn't spotted a tail but she had that feeling, that hair-raising prickle that warned something was off.

"We should visit your house manager." Bella merged into traffic.

"If she's home. She took the week off. She may be visiting her sister in Rockford."

"Maybe we'll get lucky and she's relaxing at home."

Mapleton Avenue, Oak Park, 6:20 p.m.

THE USUAL FORTY-FIVE-MINUTE drive to the Oak Park neighborhood took well over an hour in evening rush-hour traffic. On the way, Bella questioned him about Mariah. Did she seem her usual self? Did anything she said set off warning bells? Did she and Richard have an open marriage?

Mariah had seemed the same as always. Light-hearted, friendly, open. Devon had suspected that Richard and Mariah had affairs whenever they chose. But they were always discreet. The only part that had set off warning bells was the one lie he knew for a certainty that she had told him. She had said that Richard was in Wimbledon for the tournament and that was wrong. This year, the games didn't begin until the end of the month. It was possible Richard had told her this lie, assuming she wouldn't bother to verify it, allowing her to believe he would be out of the country to cover his activities.

"Victoria has a contact who can determine whether Richard left the country," Bella said, "assuming he used his own passport. It will take some time, but we can verify that aspect of what his wife said."

"I will be deeply indebted to Victoria for her help." There were few people he trusted as much as he did Victoria Colby-Camp.

"Apparently Richard's financial losses weren't as significant after your partnership dissolved as I assumed."

She spared him a glance as she parked in front of the small home of Devon's house manager, Mrs. Harper. Devon released his seat belt and reached for the door. "I'm confident he considered slipping from a billionaire to a mere millionaire quite tragic."

Bella laughed. He liked the sound of it. "I guess so."

Mrs. Harper's home was a classic early-twentieth-century Craftsman wrapped in tan stucco. The windows and trim were highlighted by green and terra-cotta. The lawn was neat and the flowerpots on the front steps overflowed with blooms.

Bella climbed the steps in front of him. He found himself again admiring her backside. He wondered if it felt as firm as it looked. His fingers itched to test those well-toned muscles.

She knocked on the door. Inside, the sound of a television gave him hope that perhaps his house manager was home. A minute or so passed and Bella knocked again.

Mrs. Harper rarely took a vacation. He generally had to insist. At seventy, she shouldn't push herself so hard. When he'd hired her as head housekeeper, he'd quickly noticed how very good she was at ensuring the entire property was kept in order. If not for her—since Cara had no interest in such things—he would have had his hands full monitoring what the rest of his staff was doing and what was needed. He quickly spotted her organizing ability and offered her the position of house manager over the entire estate. She had refused, insisting she was not qualified. He'd persevered and she'd finally accepted the position and a sizable raise in salary. Last year he'd given her a new SUV as a token of his appreciation. Each year, he gave her something. She was invaluable to him.

Worry edged into his thoughts. If she was home, why didn't she come to the door? Something moved in the front window.

Bella had spotted the movement as well. They both stared at a cat walking along the table that sat in front of the window. At first, Devon thought the white cat had a crimson streak in its fur, but on a closer look, it wasn't a stripe. It was blood. Part of the fur had matted and dried to a darker, rustier red.

Devon grabbed the doorknob and twisted. Locked. He slammed against the wood, using his shoulder like a battering ram. Another hard shove and the door popped open. Inside, the coppery smell of blood and the stench of death were thick in the air. The cat squalled and rocketed across the room.

Bella drew a gun from her bag. Devon stared at the unexpected move. He hadn't realized she had a weapon.

"Call 911."

He withdrew his cell and made the call as he followed her into the kitchen. Gertrude Harper lay in the middle of the room on the beige tile floor, blood pooled around her torso. A large knife protruded from the center of her chest.

"Don't get in the blood," Bella warned. "I'll check the rest of the house."

There was no need to check her pulse. The blood had coagulated. Judging by the condition of her body, the bloating and the bloody foam that had leaked from her mouth and nose, she had likely been dead for at least three days, possibly longer since the air-conditioning was set to a rather low temperature.

He backed away from the body and the pool of blood. He saw no indication of a struggle. The back door was locked, the area around the lock undamaged. He moved back to the front door and noted the same beyond the splintering around the lock that had occurred when he broke in. Whoever had come into her home and murdered her had been allowed inside. No breaking and entering. No struggle.

She had known her killer.

The cat peeked from under the table. Mrs. Harper always talked about her cats. She'd had several at any given time during most of her life but she was down to one now. Casper. The ghost, she had called him.

How long had it been since he'd eaten?

Devon searched the cabinets until he found the cat food. He emptied a small can into a saucer and placed it on the floor. He wasn't sure where the water bowl was, so he made a new one using a cereal bowl.

Watching the cat devour the food, he suddenly felt very tired. Devon sat down on the floor next to the cat and leaned against the cabinet. Mrs. Harper was a kind, hardworking woman who certainly did not deserve such a violent death. She had grandchildren, a son…a bloody cat.

Bella came back into the room. She looked at him for a moment, then crouched down nearby. "The rest of the house is clean and orderly. I can't see that anything was disturbed." She put her arm over her mouth to block the smell. "We should probably wait outside." She searched his face. "You okay?"

"Of course." He stood. Decided the cat needed another helping, checked the water bowl and then he joined Bella on the front porch.

"I'm assuming Mrs. Harper had the codes to your security system. Keys to your house."

"Yes. She had full access to everything except my personal computer."

"This is how Maynard's belongings got into your house," Bella said. "It's how she knew about the room. You need to call a locksmith and your security company right now."

Feeling wearier than he had in a very long time, Devon made the call. He'd hoped that maybe someone who worked at his home under Mrs. Harper's supervision had caused the breach.

The sound of sirens in the distance sickened him.

Maybe he deserved all of this but Mrs. Harper didn't…the dead mechanic didn't.

Why didn't Richard or whoever the hell wanted something from him just do whatever necessary to take it?

Why all the games?

Why now?

Chapter Eight

Evergreen Avenue, 8:30 p.m.

The Old Town neighborhood had grabbed Bella's heart the first time she strolled along the tree-lined narrow streets with its Victorian buildings and brick alleyways. She'd actually stumbled over the house on Evergreen completely by accident. The historic architecture and classic brick had been exactly what she wanted. Three bedrooms, three baths and an office. Perfect. Plenty of room if her sister and the children ever wanted to visit.

Bella wasn't holding her breath on that one but she could always dream. She and her sister had lost touch after she basically abandoned Bella and then, years later, refused any sort of help financially rather than drifting from one jerk of a husband to the next.

The price of a house in this neighborhood had been difficult to swallow but Bella was frugal in other areas. Her car was not a luxury model. She shopped sale racks at her favorite department stores. Her furniture was an eclectic collection of what she'd already owned and revitalized with unique flea-market finds. It felt like home. She was happy here.

Devon Pierce stood in the center of her small living

room and surveyed the decor. His expression didn't show approval or distaste. Her whole house would fit into his west-side parking garage with lots of room to spare. Whatever he thought of her home, she refused to be nervous. This was *her*. She neither needed nor wanted to impress him.

Well, maybe just a little.

"I'll be right back," she said.

He nodded, his attention captured by the framed photographs on her mantel.

She rushed up the stairs to her bedroom. Poking her head into the closet, she dragged her leather overnight bag from the top shelf. She'd had the well-broken-in bag since she graduated high school. Her favorite teacher had bought it for her. The woman had assured Bella that she would go far and she had made her promise to believe in herself.

"So far, so good." Not once since she'd left for college had Bella doubted her ability to rise above where she'd come from. She was more than capable of going as far as she chose, and she refused to believe otherwise. The Colby Agency had given her the opportunity to fulfill herself professionally on many levels. Chicago provided a fresh start with no one to look at her and wonder how she survived, much less thrived.

Until Devon Pierce. He hadn't hidden his surprise in regard to what he'd learned about her past. To her surprise, she had not been intimidated at all by his questions. Impatient, less than thrilled, but not daunted in any way.

All she needed right now were a few things for the next couple of days. She left her overnight bag on the bed while she selected the clothes she needed to pack.

Conservative tops, slacks and a couple of lightweight dress jackets. She tossed in her favorite sleepwear. A spare pair of shoes, underthings and her cosmetics bag. She kept a cosmetics bag packed for just this sort of occasion. Often, an assignment would mean travel. Better to be prepared ahead of time than to snatch up items and ultimately forget something like her favorite moisturizer or dental floss.

On second thought, she stuffed the book she'd been reading into the mix and grabbed a box of rounds for her Ruger. The last thing any Colby investigator ever wanted was to have to use a weapon, but sometimes it was necessary. This case was growing more and more volatile. Getting caught unprepared was the other last thing any investigator wanted.

She hefted the leather bag and looked around the room just to be sure she hadn't forgotten anything. "Phone charger." She collected the one from her bedside table and tucked it into her bag. She'd been using the one in the car but it was a hassle to remember to plug her phone in whenever she slid behind the wheel.

Downstairs, Pierce had wandered through the dining room and into the kitchen. She left her bag by the front door and joined him.

"It's not so fancy but it makes me happy."

A rare smile tilted his lips. "It's very homey."

She nodded, not certain whether that was a compliment or an insult. "Thanks."

"There's an abundance of color and a lot of—" he shrugged "—*things*, but it feels inviting and calm somehow."

So maybe it was a compliment. "I feel calm when I'm here."

"You're ready to go?"

"I am."

When they reached the living room, he paused by the fireplace. "May I ask you a question?"

Since he appeared to be taken with the photograph of her and her sister when they were kids—eight and eleven—she imagined the question would be about that night. The one where the only world she'd ever known had vanished down a dark hole.

"Sure."

"Have you ever wished you could go back and change the past? Somehow make it turn out differently?"

The sadness in his eyes tugged at something deep inside her. "There are some things that can't be changed," she confessed. "If given the chance, would I try to save my mother's life in a do-over? No question. Would it have changed the tragedy that was our childhoods? Probably not. My mother, as much as I loved her, was a selfish woman incapable of taking care of herself, much less two daughters. She would have moved on to another no-good man and the cycle would have started over again."

He turned away from the photo. "Is that why you've never married? You're afraid of choosing the wrong man?"

Fire rushed up her cheeks. "I'm not afraid of making the wrong choice, no. I've just never met a man I cared to allow to have that much power over my life. I like making my own decisions and not being forced to cater to someone else's needs."

He looked at her for so long she felt that blush move over her entire body.

"You don't want to be ruled."

She laughed. "Therein lies the problem. I have a boss at work. She respects me. I respect her. I don't need a boss at home. I've yet to see a relationship where the woman doesn't feel *ruled* to some degree. No offense. I just don't feel like I need a full-time man to fulfill me."

"You're a very intelligent woman, Isabella Lytle. But your past rules you whether you realize it or not. Two strong, confident people can have a relationship where mutual respect is a key element, if they choose."

"My past may rule me, Dr. Pierce, but at least I learned from it. Your wife cheated on you. Obviously she didn't respect you nearly as much as you believed."

One eyebrow reared up a little higher than the other. "Perhaps not."

Bella felt like an ass for making such a hurtful assessment. Well, hell.

He'd already put her bag in the back seat and settled into the passenger seat by the time she locked up and descended the front steps. She checked the street and moved around to the driver's side.

As soon as she'd pulled out onto the street, she apologized. "I shouldn't have made such a hateful remark. I was wrong. I have no idea what you and your wife felt about each other. I've never been married. I have no right to judge. The truth is, I rarely do beyond making assessments and conclusions about a case. I was being defensive and that was wrong of me. You have every right to think what you will."

"No apology necessary, Ms. Lytle. What you said is correct. Furthermore, had I respected my wife as I should have, I would have been there for her. She wouldn't have felt the need to seek comfort elsewhere."

Arbor Drive, Lake Bluff, 11:40 p.m.

BELLA ACCEPTED A room a few doors down the hall from his this time. She had no desire to sleep on that rock-hard leather bed again.

Then again, it wasn't designed for sleep.

She shook off the notion and stepped out of the shower. Step by step, she went through her nightly ritual. Blow-dried her hair, checked her cuticles and nails, dabbed on a little moisturizer. It felt good to slip on her preferred sleepwear—lounge pants and a T-shirt. Riffling through her bag in search of her lip moisturizer, she came across the journal. Seated on the bed, she opened it to the last entry she'd read.

Devon hadn't talked about the woman who'd been murdered, Mrs. Harper. She'd worked for him for a very long time. Bella was certain he must feel some pain at her death, particularly such a violent one. But he'd said nothing. Yet he'd sat on the floor of her bloody kitchen and attended to her cat.

She wasn't sure she would ever understand Devon Pierce.

Or his wife.

Bella turned her attention back to the journal.

Devon made love to me tonight. I tried. I really tried to feel what I should feel. His body is strong and beautiful. He loves me, I know he does. But there are things I will never give him. Children. My heart. He deserves more. For tonight, I allow him to do with my body what he will. He lavishes my skin with his mouth...his hands, and he fills me full. Still, I feel nothing. He is not the lover I want...the one I love.

The idea that he had read that entry made Bella feel

ill. This was the woman he'd loved, married and wanted as the mother of his children. The one with whom he had intended to spend the rest of his life. Was this the reason he kept his personal relationships as impersonal as possible now?

Like you, Bella. Pierce had struck a nerve. How would she ever trust anyone after what she'd lived through with her parents, her aunt and uncle and then her sister? How could she dare trust anyone on that level? She had made up her mind long ago that no one would ever possess that kind of control over her life.

Never.

Her stomach grumbled. She groaned. Pierce had offered to prepare dinner but she'd begged off. She'd spent nearly every minute of the past twenty hours with him. She needed some space. She checked the clock. It was nearly midnight. Surely he'd gone to bed by now.

She had to eat. Taking a fortifying breath, she opened the door and stepped into the long hall. No need to take her weapon. He'd set the security system with its new passcode. The locks had been changed. For now, they were secure. His bedroom door was closed. Hadn't it been open when she passed earlier?

Taking her time, she descended the stairs. As much as she loved her little house, she had to admit that this place was breathtaking. She really liked the old-world look and the gorgeous furnishings. Too big, though. Way too big. A dozen children wouldn't be enough to fill all the empty space.

She made it down the stairs without running into him.

So far, so good.

The kitchen was dark. She flipped on a few lights

and went to the fridge. Her stomach rumbled some more as she perused the offerings. Since it was so late, she decided on a bagel and cream cheese. Maybe she'd have a glass of wine, too. Balancing the bagel and cheese in one hand, she grabbed the bottle of white wine with the other and pushed the door closed with her foot. She turned to place her goods on the counter and he was there, right in front of her, watching.

The bottle of wine almost slipped out of her grasp. "Jesus, you startled me."

He took the bottle from her. "I'll open it for you."

"Thanks." She managed a smile. Searched her brain for something appropriate to say. "Did you eat already?"

He kept his gaze on the bottle and flinched when she asked the question. She doubted he'd eaten anything unless whiskey counted as a food group. Still, he said, "Yes."

The cork made a little pop as he removed it. He rounded up a glass and poured. She smeared cream cheese on two bagels. When he passed the stemmed glass to her, she shoved a bagel at him. "You lied about eating."

He took the bagel. Stared at it without confirming or denying her assertion. "I keep thinking that I should have called Mrs. Harper and checked on her. I should have asked about her plans for the week." He shook his head. "But if I had, she would have assumed I didn't want her to take the time off." He sighed, the sound forlorn. "No one should die that way. Violently and alone."

Bella resisted the urge to reach out and touch him, to comfort him somehow. "You're not responsible for what her killer did. This is out of your control, Dr. Pierce. Believe it or not, you can't control everything around you."

It was that moment when she realized why he was so distant. Why he had no real personal life. Because he couldn't control it. He would deprive himself of those things before he would risk the pain that came with having less than absolute control.

She bit off a piece of the bagel and chewed, mostly to ensure the wine didn't go straight to her head. When she'd swallowed and washed it down with more of the wine, she said, "You are such a hypocrite, Dr. Pierce."

He'd taken a couple of bites from the bagel but now set it aside. "In what way, Ms. Lytle?"

"You shame me for how I refuse to engage in a lasting relationship. You analyze me, concluding that I'm afraid of making the wrong choices and ending up like the other women in my family, so I avoid relationships altogether. While you do exactly the same thing. You keep everyone you can't control at arm's length. The only people you allow anywhere near you are your employees and the women you hire to fulfill your sexual needs."

The silence that followed her monologue had her turning up the glass and emptying it. Not nearly enough. She poured herself some more. He took the bottle from her hand before she could set it aside. He drank straight from the mouth of it. Mesmerized by the defined muscles of his throat, she managed to get her own glass to her lips so she could drink.

He set the bottle aside. "You're almost right."

She swallowed a gulp of wine and laughed. "Almost? Where did I go wrong, Doctor? Because I'm not seeing it."

"I don't hire women solely for the purpose of sexual release."

She downed another gulp of wine, hoped it would calm her pounding heart. Or maybe just make her light-headed enough not to care how her foolish body reacted to him.

"I hire them to punish me."

She finished off the wine, set her glass aside. She must have heard him wrong. "I don't understand."

He reached for her hand. "Come. I'll show you."

She should have resisted. She should have simply said no.

She should have gone back to her room.

But she did none of those things.

She allowed him to lead her along that endless corridor and then down the stairs…to the *room*. His fingers held loosely to hers. Pulling away would have been easy. But she didn't.

The lights were dim except for two spaces, the bed and the horizontal bar where the handcuffs hung from chains.

He'd already shed his jacket and tie. Now he unbuttoned his dark blue shirt. The color, she only now realized, made his eyes more the color of the sea. Her pulse stumbled. "What're you doing?"

She felt dizzy. The wine, she told herself. *So not smart, Bella.*

He cast the shirt aside. Her throat tightened at the sight of his bare, broad shoulders and the exquisite way they crowned a beautifully sculpted chest and then tapered into a lean waist. His ribbed abdomen spoke of rigorous workouts. *Punishment.* The realization came so suddenly she swayed.

He walked over to the dangling cuffs and thrust his hands into them. He pulled downward and the cuffs locked, securing around his wrists with a succinct snap. He looked at her, a gleam of vulnerability in his eyes. "Pick up the whip."

"What?" Only then did she notice the coiled leather waiting near him like a snake ready to stride. She shook her head, aware enough to know the almost-hidden note of desperation in his voice wasn't from sexual need. "No."

"You're afraid." He kept his blue eyes steady on her. "You don't need to be afraid, Bella."

The way he said her name made her shiver, made the nerves all over her body tingle.

"I'm not afraid." Well, maybe she was. She was afraid because heat was roaring through her now. She was on fire. She was tempted, so tempted, but also terrified that she would do this and like it and not be able to stop. Sex play was one thing, but taking advantage of Devon's self-loathing was something completely different.

"Do it. *Now*."

His curt tone made her jump.

Did he really think he could make her do this by snapping at her? "No."

"Then go back upstairs, little girl. This is no place for you." He looked away.

What the...? She was walking toward him before her brain had given her feet the order. She snatched up the whip that lay at his feet, the black leather tool nearly invisible against the obsidian leather floor. She walked around him.

"You're a freak. You know that, right?"

"Yes, I do know that." Those blue eyes were hooded now.

Her throat was so dry she couldn't possibly swallow.

Her hands shook and wild sensations rushed through her body. Power, urgency, need, fear… The turmoil whipped through her like a hurricane. "What is it you want me to do?"

"Six lashes."

"You're serious?"

"Do it now."

Hands still shaking, she walked around to his back. Broad, muscled and…scarred. Her breath trapped in her lungs as she instinctively moved closer. She reached out, touched his skin. He tensed, those sculpted muscles going rigid. The scars weren't deep but they were raised ever so slightly and discolored.

"Why?" The word whispered out of her.

"Because I need to feel the pain."

She moved around to face him. She stared at him for a long moment, the whip clenched tight in her hand. "No." She shook her head, her certainty mounting. "You don't *need* to feel the pain. It's just the only way you know to let go of control long enough to feel anything."

"You're a psychiatrist now, are you?"

"No, but I watched my parents torture each other my whole childhood because the pain was the only time when they felt free from the rest of the burden life had dumped on them. What you're doing to yourself is the sexual equivalent of cutting."

"You can't do it," he challenged. "You're afraid. Afraid you'll enjoy it too much. Perhaps as your mother did. Or your sister."

She threw down the whip and slapped him hard on the jaw with the flat palm of her hand.

He shook it off and smiled at her. "Do it again."

Damn him! She'd played right into his ploy. Worse,

her body hummed with need and, damn her, she *wanted* to do it again.

"Pick up the whip and show me how bad you can be, Ms. Lytle."

"No." She reached for the hem of her T-shirt. He might have her on fire for him, he might have her ready to explode with need, but he would not rule her. "If we're going to do this, we'll do it my way."

She tossed the shirt onto the floor. His gaze fixed on her breasts. She pushed her lounge pants down her legs and kicked them aside, leaving nothing but the lace panties. Lacy lingerie was her one secret indulgence. Now she waited for his reaction. For him to deny that his body could want something without the pain.

He stared at her, his nostrils flaring, chest rising and falling rapidly.

She moved toward him. When she was close enough, she reached for his fly. He drew away but she had the upper hand since there was only so far he could go. She slid the belt from its loops with a hiss of leather against silk. Then she pulled the button free, carefully lowered the zipper over his hardened body.

She dropped to her knees and removed his shoes, his socks, and then she tugged his trousers down his long legs. His briefs bulged with the desire he would have preferred to deny. He didn't want to enjoy this. She understood now. He wanted to be punished for failing his dead wife. For failing himself.

She walked around behind him, making him tense. She dragged the briefs over his tight backside and down his muscled thighs. Her body sizzled, dampened with need. She knelt down, pulled his underwear free of his ankles. Then she moved in close behind him. She kissed his back, licked the scars. So many scars. He shuddered. Her hands moved up and down his chest, over his ridged abdomen and lower to cradle his heavy cock.

He groaned as she smoothed her palm down the length of him. She kissed and kissed those scarred tracks, all the way down to the cleft of his ass. She made her way around him, kissing and smoothing her hands over his skin, touching him everywhere. And then she latched on to a nipple, sucked hard. He threw his head back and growled.

She sucked and nipped until his cock prodded so hard at her she thought she would come just standing there in front of him. She reached up, touched his face, traced his lips, threaded her fingers into his hair. He was so very handsome.

"Tell me what you want," she murmured.

He moistened his lips. "Nothing."

Fury snapped inside her. She gripped his cock and slid her palm back and forth, smoothing and tugging. "Nothing?"

He closed his eyes and shook his head. "Nothing."

She stepped back, peeled off her panties. His eyes came open and he watched as she walked toward him once more. She reached around his neck and held on while she lifted herself and wrapped her legs around his waist. She pressed downward, forcing his cock against her. The smooth, hard feel of his shaft rubbing against her wet folds took her breath. She was the one to groan this time. She held on tight to him while she rubbed up and down his length, careful not to allow him inside.

The friction, up and down, up and down the shaft of him, stroking harder and harder against her clitoris, her breasts grinding against his solid chest, had her rushing toward orgasm. So close, so close. She no longer cared what he wanted or didn't want. *She* wanted this. To feel him big and hard against her. The first crash of pleasure made her cry out. She rode it out, moving up and down, harder, faster.

And then she came.

He was panting as hard as her, his cock throbbing insistently against her damp folds. She laid her head against his shoulder and shivered with the final remnants of exquisite pleasure.

"You see." She lifted her head, put her lips close to his ear. "I'm not afraid to feel the pleasure without the pain. It's you who's afraid. Call it punishing yourself, call it whatever you like, but it's plain old fear."

His arms tensed as he jerked downward, the cuffs clicked and his hands were suddenly on her back, holding her firmly against him while he strode toward the bed. He placed her in the center of the dim spotlight and moved over her, his face a harsh mask of need.

She reached for his face to pull him into a kiss but he dodged the move. His mouth landed on her breast. He sucked so hard she felt the pull all the way to her core. Then he bit her. She yelped. He bit her again, then moved to the other breast. He sucked and gnawed at her until she undulated beneath him on the verge of coming again.

He pushed her thighs part, pressed the heel of his hand against her and applied just the right pressure. Orgasm crashed down on her.

His fingers dug deep inside her, caressing those clenching muscles. He pushed and tugged, loosening her, finding that spot inside that made her squirm with need. And then he moved onto his knees and lifted her.

She couldn't breathe, couldn't think. She was coming again, so hard, so hard. He pushed into her, going so deep she screamed with the delicious ache of it.

He moved slowly. She tried to buck her hips but he held her still. She begged him to go faster but he refused. So slow, so deep, so damned slow. Over and over, he penetrated her, fractured the walls she had built around her feelings, made her want something she could not name.

She cried out with the new waves coming, so very far away. He withdrew to the very tip and then he went in hard and deep, filling her so completely, his body covering hers, pressing her against the leather, skin to skin, his cock so deep he felt a part of her.

They came together and the orgasm went on and on.

When the waves of pleasure had receded, they lay there, sweating and panting for long minutes.

Finally his mouth founds hers and he kissed her.

As certain as she was that her body could take no more, she arched her hips and urged him to take her to that place of pure sensation again.

Chapter Nine

Thursday, June 7, 7:30 a.m.

Devon paced the floor while he waited for the news from Victoria. Bella had been on the phone with her for several minutes.

They had avoided each other since waking. He'd never slept in the room before. He'd lost count of the number of times they'd found release. Total exhaustion had prevented them from moving to his bedroom.

Or perhaps he had felt safer there, less personal.

He shook his head. Not so. Last night had felt intensely personal and incredibly intimate.

More than just sex.

He pushed the thought away and focused on the woman pacing the floor with the cell phone pressed against her delicate ear. Even now, he thought of all the ways he had tasted her—all of her. He knew every part of her, every sweet and salty and lush inch. He had been married to Cara for five years and had not known her so thoroughly, so intimately.

The call finally ended and Bella turned to him. "Richard Sutter has not left the country. Not unless he used an alternate ID."

"Richard is a man of means with extensive contacts. It's possible he left the country as someone else." Devon shook his head. "But it doesn't feel right."

Bella slipped her phone into the pocket of her sleek jacket. She wore a skirt today. It was straight and covered those luscious thighs all the way to her knees. The matching pale lavender jacket and blouse fit well, showing off her curves. The color suited her. She stood in front of the fireplace, the rough stone and rich wood a perfect backdrop for her softness. How could a woman look so soft and fragile and be as strong as he knew her to be? She had commanded his performance last night, drove him and guided him like a maestro leading a world-class orchestra.

"I know what you mean," she agreed, seeming distracted. "Why go to so much trouble to bring you down if he wasn't going to hang around and watch? Has he accomplished what he set out to do? I don't think so. What're your thoughts, Dr. Pierce?"

Dr. Pierce? He crossed the room and stood directly in front of her. "Devon," he said. "You should call me Devon."

She searched his eyes for a moment. "Are you certain that's what you want? Last night we both needed escape, but today is business. If we bring what we did outside that room, then we're starting something different. Is that your intent?"

A vise gripped his chest. Fear. He recognized his old friend. "Point taken, Ms. Lytle."

She opened that sexy mouth but his cell phone interrupted whatever she intended to say. Perhaps it was best.

The display showed a blocked call. "Pierce," he said.

"Help me."

The voice croaked across the line.

"Who is this?"

Bella's face turned questioning, so he put the call on speaker. "Hello?" he said, hoping to prompt the caller to speak again.

"Please help me."

The voice sounded familiar. "Ms. Maynard?"

Bella nodded her agreement with his assessment.

He urged, "Ms. Maynard, where are you?"

"I don't know who she is," said a male voice, taking over the call, "but she's lying on the sidewalk on Shakespeare over here in Logan Square. The old abandoned shoe warehouse. She said she needed help, so I let her use my phone. You better get somebody over here. She might not make it."

The call ended.

"Call an ambulance," Bella said as she rushed away. "I'll get my bag."

ONE HOUR AND thirty minutes later, they stood in the observation area of the surgery unit at the Edge. Devon had called for an ambulance to rush Audrey Maynard here. She'd been badly beaten in the last twenty-four hours. At present, the most pressing issue was the infection at the site of her previous surgery. Dr. Reagan had reopened the original surgical wound and would debride and clean as necessary before closing once more. Close observation and IV antibiotics would be needed until she was out of danger.

Since she was unconscious when she arrived, she had not been able to provide answers to any of the questions Devon or the police had for her. Corwin and Hodge had arrived and were waiting to speak with Devon now.

"Hopefully when she wakes up, she'll be ready to give some real answers."

Devon turned to the woman at his side. "If she can't or won't give any answers, we're exactly where we were when this whole thing started."

He tried to pinpoint what it was that had set this insanity in motion. There had been no new honors bestowed upon him. No flurry of activity in the news. Nothing unusual at all. It wasn't any sort of anniversary. Not of his wife's death or of when they married or of when his partnership with Sutter began or ended.

The week was like any other except for Audrey Maynard showing up pretending to be his wife and then the murder of his longtime house manager. Part of him wanted to deny the harsh realities. But then that would mean he would have to deny last night. His gaze lingered on Bella. He could not deny what he'd felt last night. For the first time in a very long time, he had felt true pleasure, genuine need.

And he yearned for more.

"We shouldn't keep the detectives waiting any longer."

He stared at her a moment longer. "No matter. We have nothing to tell them."

"They'll have questions. They always do."

The two detectives waited in the small lobby of the surgery unit. Devon invited them to his office, where they could speak in private. As they wound around the corridor to their destination, Bella quietly suggested a seating arrangement to him. Once in his office, he took the seat behind his desk, ushered the two detectives into the chairs in front of his desk, and like the last time, she settled at the small conference table to watch.

"Let's recap a few things," Corwin suggested.

Devon waited for him to begin. He saw no reason to give his permission. The detective was going to say and ask what he would. His comment was simply a way to kick off the conversation and, no doubt, a stab at setting a casual tone.

"The blood in your jacket pocket was a match to the dead mechanic's," Corwin announced.

Devon wasn't surprised. "If the blood in the trunk of the stolen Lexus was his, then of course it was the same as what you found in my pocket. We've established that I inadvertently touched the blood."

"The blond hair found in your house is a match to the hair found in the Lexus driver's seat and in the bed where Audrey Maynard stayed in this ER."

"Detective Corwin," Bella said, "we've already discussed how someone is framing Dr. Pierce. What can you tell us about who that person is? Have you followed up with Maynard's associates? Dr. Pierce's former partner? You must have something more than what you've regurgitated the past few minutes."

Hodge laughed and just as quickly bit his lips together. Corwin did not look amused.

"Your house manager was murdered in her own home, presumably for someone to steal the key to your home since it has not been found. And to get the passcode to your security system."

"Based on my assessment of time of death," Devon argued, "the timing is right. It's the only possible explanation."

"We're considering that avenue as well." Corwin flipped open his small notebook. "Why didn't you tell us about your other partner, Richard Sutter? The one your friend here called the feds about?"

"Mr. Sutter recently battled cancer," Devon told him truthfully. "I saw no reason to cause him unnecessary grief. There, you now know my secret."

"That doesn't explain why you wanted to know if he'd left the country," Corwin countered. "You must suspect his involvement. After all…" He flipped to another page in his notes. "…he filed suit against you three times. If you felt sorry for him, why didn't you toss him a bone and settle? He was your partner when you developed this highly sought-after facility."

Someone had done his homework and spoken to Richard's wife. The entire time she'd been smiling at Devon, she had been hiding the fact that she'd spewed the whole ugly past to the police. Or maybe they'd visited her after he and Bella dropped in. He couldn't be sure of anything anymore.

"Richard Sutter was once a great man with vision, but something happened five years ago and he became a liability. If you had done your homework as well as you believe, you would know Richard received a handsome settlement when we parted ways. The lawsuits that followed were the trivial pursuits of a man suffering from a brain tumor."

Corwin considered that news for a moment. "Is it possible Sutter still suffers from some brain issue that's causing him to go to all these lengths to frame you?"

"Anything is possible, Detective." Devon leaned back in his chair. "If Richard is involved, it's possible his wife is covering for him."

"She did tell us he was out of the country," Bella

confirmed. "It might be worthwhile to look into her activities."

Corwin stood. "I'll do that. Meanwhile…" He glanced at his partner, who was still seated. "…as soon as she's stable, we'll be moving Ms. Maynard to Rush."

"She'll need around-the-clock protection," Bella warned.

"And we'll make sure she gets it," Corwin said. "We wouldn't want to lose her again." He bopped his partner on the shoulder. Hodge shot to his feet and echoed his partner's sentiment.

"Dr. Reagan will advise you as to when the patient can be transported." Devon stood. "Good day, gentlemen."

When the door had closed, Bella moved toward him. "We have some more homework to do as well." She shifted her gaze from the closed door to him. "Assuming you can get away for a few hours."

"When it comes to this investigation, you're the boss."

Heat flared in her dark eyes but she turned away too quickly for him to read whether he'd made her angry… or hot. Just drawing in her scent set him on fire, made him hard. He wanted to lock the door and take her right here, on his desk, against the wall, on the conference table.

He couldn't remember when he had wanted a woman so much.

Not since he first saw Cara. They'd been snowed in at LaGuardia that Christmas. Rather than find a hotel as he usually would have, they'd spent the night in the airport talking. She had been on her way back to Atlanta, where she lived at the time. He'd been to a medical conference in Manhattan and was headed back to Chicago. The next morning they both decided to stay a few more days. A month later they'd got married. He had never been happier in his life. Maybe he would never understand what happened to change how she felt. Or why she'd had so many secrets that didn't include him. Slowly but surely she had killed his ability to feel.

Until now.

Isabella Lytle had ignited something inside him that he wasn't sure could ever be extinguished.

1:00 p.m.

THE REDHEAD WAS the only friend of Audrey Maynard's on the street today. Maybe it was the early hour or maybe the others were in hiding.

"I'm not sure this is such a good idea."

Bella glanced at Pierce. He stared across the street and up the block at the redhead, Jasmine, who was pictured in the photo with Audrey Maynard. She was chain-smoking and chatting it up with two men, both of whom looked like trouble.

"You had your chance," Bella said. "Now it's mine."

From the hospital, they'd stopped by her place and she'd changed clothes. Her tightest jeans and a white tank top that fit like a second skin. She wore a black lacy bra for contrast. The red thongs on her feet wouldn't be worth a flip—no pun intended—if she had to chase down a bad guy or make a run for it, but they gave her that casual look she needed for this approach. Her hair was pulled up into a high ponytail with a colorful scarf tied around it. She lowered the car's sun visor and dabbed on a little lip gloss in the mirror.

"You look like a teenager."

She laughed. "I don't know about that but I don't look like a cop and that's the point." She popped a piece of gum into her mouth.

When she reached for the door handle, he touched her arm. Her skin where his blunt-tipped fingers lay so gently against her tingled. "Be very careful."

"Don't worry." She draped the cross-body purse over her neck. Her Ruger fit perfectly into the small crescent-shaped bag. She'd already tucked her cell into her back pocket. It was just like the good old days undercover. She patted the bag. "I have backup."

He still didn't look convinced but he released her. When she emerged from the car, she felt giddy. It was a little silly that a mere touch would make her feel that way but it did. She'd awakened this morning tender and raw in the most intimate places. Her nipples hardened even now despite being sore from his ambitious attention. Thinking of how deeply he'd got inside her made her shiver. He'd wooed her into positions she'd never heard of, much less tried.

She felt him watching her as she jogged across the street. His clothes covered the scratches and teeth marks she'd left on his skin. She'd refused to use the whip on him but she'd tortured him just the same. She had explored every part of him. Tasted all of him. She licked her lips, wishing she could devour his mouth right here, right now. Last night, he had tasted of heat and that smoky rich flavor of the Scotch he preferred.

The redhead glanced at her as she approached. Bella exaggerated the sway of her hips and chomped her gum. "Hey, y'all." She deepened her Southern drawl.

The redhead looked her up and down. "I don't do chicks."

The two men sniggered.

This close, Bella could see the men's bad teeth and the sores that spoke of drug abuse. Ragged jeans and dirty shirts failed to cover the serious need for showers. Stringy hair poked from under their ball caps. The red-head, on the other hand, looked unusually clean. Skin was clear, muscles well toned. Teeth looked solid and reasonably white for a smoker.

"Not even for two Benjamins?" Bella smiled. "I got a thing for redheads."

The redhead glanced at her two friends. "Go play somewhere else. I've got business."

The two fist-bumped her and moved on.

"That your posse?" Bella asked with a disapproving stare after the two.

"You want to talk or you want to get down to business?" She shifted her weight to the other hip. "I got a room."

"I have my own room." She took the other woman's hand. "I'll take you there."

Red glanced around the block. "You smell like a cop to me."

Bella squeezed her hand. "Trust me. I'm not a cop and you're safe with me."

Red walked to the car with her. Bella opened the back door and they climbed in.

"Hey, I know you." Red looked from Pierce to Bella. "What is this?" Fear glinted in her street-wary eyes.

"We only want to talk, Jasmine," Bella assured her. "Answer our questions and you get the two hundred. That's all we want. Answers."

She exhaled a big breath. "Is this about Layla?"

"If you mean Audrey," Pierce said, "that's correct."

"Is she okay?" She turned to Bella. "She was hurt real bad. I talked to her yesterday but I haven't been able to reach her today."

"Do you know who hurt her?" Bella kept her tone firm.

Red shook her head. "It was some private gig. She was promised big money for pretending to be some guy's wife. She didn't know she was going to end up in the hospital." Jasmine blew out a big breath. "The guy almost killed her."

"What guy?"

She shrugged. "She swears she never saw his face, but I'm not so sure I believe her. Anyway, he beat her up really bad."

"She's back in the hospital," Pierce said. "She almost didn't make it this time. She's very ill."

"Damn it. I told her not to trust the bastard. Anyone who won't show his face can't be trusted. I don't care if he is rich. Rich people don't care about people like us. We're disposable. All he wanted was to use her and now she's sick and hurt. Bastard."

"What about her other friends?" Bella asked. "Would they know who the man was that hired her? Or where she's been staying?"

Jasmine shook her head. "I promised I wouldn't tell. I—"

"He's not going to stop until she's dead," Bella warned. "Whoever he is, he won't risk the possibility that Audrey remembers something about him. Please help us. For her sake. She's your friend. If you want to help her, you need to help us."

Jasmine exhaled a big breath. "After she skipped out of the hospital, she decided to lie low at Talia's place over on Loomis."

"Talia?" Bella prompted.

"Talia Loman. She lives in one of her father's rental houses. He don't have nothing to do with her but he can't bear the thought of her living on the street. I don't think she would have told Talia any more than she told me. I swear Audrey doesn't know who the guy is. She didn't even get a good look at him, but she did say he smelled real good, though. Expensive."

Bella and Pierce exchanged a look.

"Have you heard from Talia in the past couple of days?"

Jasmine shook her head.

Bella dug a Sharpie from her bag. She reached for the other woman's hand, wrote her cell number on her wrist. "If you remember anything, hear anything, let me know." She gave her the two hundred-dollar bills.

"We appreciate your help," Pierce said.

Jasmine shrugged. "'Kay."

Pierce handed her three more one-hundred-dollar bills. "Take the night off and sleep in a good hotel."

And all this time Devon Pierce tried to play it so cold. Like he had no feelings at all.

Liar.

Chapter Ten

Loomis Avenue, 2:20 p.m.

Bella beat on the door a third time.

"If she's here," Devon said, frustrated, "she's not coming to the door."

The small house was silent inside. Outside, the paint was peeling off the siding. Gutters sagged. A couple of windows were cracked, both covered with clear plastic. The grass and weeds were knee-deep. If not for the sagging ceiling-fan blades turning overhead on the small porch, Devon would swear the place was abandoned.

"We should check around back."

Devon descended the porch steps behind her. His thoughts should be focused solely on finding his old friend Richard. Instead, he focused on the way the jeans Bella wore conformed to her amazing ass. He was losing control and she was the reason.

The grass was just as deep in the back. It hadn't seen a lawn mower all season. A broken-down barbecue grill stood on the deck. A couple of abused plastic chairs and a large soup can overflowing with cigarette butts rounded out the outdoor decor.

Bella hurried up the steps and banged on the back

door. By the time Devon stood next to her, she had already checked the windows. None had curtains and the old-fashioned roller blinds were only pulled halfway down. The window in the door was divided into nine small panes and revealed a kitchen beyond. No blood on the floor, no body.

"Whatever happened," Devon suggested, "Ms. Loman has apparently gone into hiding."

Bella pulled a glove from her pocket, slipped it on and wiggled the door as she leaned hard against it. "It would appear so," she said casually, as if she weren't doing all within her power to open the door.

When it didn't budge, Devon took her by the shoulders and moved her aside. Even that harmless touch made his pulse react. He turned his back to the door and punched his jacket-clad elbow through one of the windowpanes. The old thin glass shattered.

Before he could do so, she carefully threaded her arm through the wood frame that once held the pane of glass now spread over the floor inside. Jagged pieces remained around the frame like hideous teeth, making the reach inside precarious.

Bella opened the door and stepped wide over the shattered glass. Devon followed, closing the door behind him.

"Ms. Loman?" she called. "Are you home?"

They moved slowly through the house. No smell of blood. Only the stench of cigarettes and stale beer lingered. The house was sparsely furnished. A well-worn chair and a dingy sofa in the living room. A table with mismatched chairs in the kitchen. A mattress lay on the floor in the first bedroom. No clothes in the closet.

Devon crouched down and looked more closely at

what appeared to be a crimson stain in the center of the mattress. "Maynard may have slept here."

"Looks like that's all she left behind."

The final bedroom had the mattress on the floor as well as a couple of boxes overflowing with unfolded clothes. No blood, no sign of the woman who lived here.

"Maybe she helped Maynard to the location where she was found." Bella checked the closet, riffled through the four dresses hanging from the wooden dowel. "She likely recognized that her friend was very sick but needed her away from where she lived before the police were notified."

"That's what friends are for, right?" Devon commented. Frustration tightened his gut. How the hell did these people expect to get help if they didn't report the trouble to the police?

Bella stared at him for a long moment. "Think about how the police are harassing you. How they make you feel in hopes of prompting a reaction. Imagine multiplying that a thousand times. These women are just trying to survive and most of the time they feel like no one is on their side."

"I stand corrected," he confessed. "I'll see that the broken glass in the door is repaired immediately." He withdrew his phone and sent a text to the man who took care of these sorts of issues at his own home. "Done."

Bella walked out of the room. She found the broom and a page from a newspaper and cleaned up the glass. Devon tried to help but she shooed him away.

When he would have attempted another apology, his cell vibrated. Blocked call.

He showed the screen to Bella and then answered, placing the caller on speaker. "Pierce."

"Dr. Pierce, I have information you might be interested in."

Male. Sounded young.

"What sort of information?" Pierce asked. Bella nodded her approval.

"About your wife. You meet me with, say, ten thousand in hand and I'll tell you what I know."

Bella held her phone up for him to see. She had typed: You choose the time and place.

"Four thirty," Devon said. "Lincoln Park Zoo at the seal pool."

"Be sure you bring the money."

"How will I recognize you?"

"I'll recognize you."

The caller severed the connection.

"Good choice." Bella checked the time on her phone. "I'll have my backup investigator watching. He can follow the guy from the zoo. Maybe we'll learn something more that way."

Devon waited on the deck while she locked the door with her gloved hand. "You have backup?" He shouldn't be surprised. The Colby Agency was the best of the best.

"Lacon Traynor. He's on call. If I need him, I let him know. For this, I'll need him."

"I guess we're off to the zoo."

He couldn't wait to see what his enemy had up his sleeve this time.

Lincoln Park Zoo, 4:30 p.m.

THE CROWD WAS THICK.

Bella wished now that Pierce had chosen some other location. There were way too many children here for her comfort. Traynor had sent her a text with a selfie of his location. He was just down a few yards in the front row. She and Pierce had claimed front-row seats as well. Some people chose to stand as the training and the feeding of the seals started.

What she really wished was that he had allowed her to call Detective Corwin. The stakes in this case had grown way too dicey. This man they were meeting was guilty at the very least of extortion and perhaps far worse. At least two people related to this case were dead and another was gravely injured. Bella didn't like this. She didn't like it at all. But Pierce had insisted on doing this his way.

The children cheered and applauded as the seals clapped and barked for treats. A man in jeans, a khaki shirt and blue ball cap wandered over and sat down next to Pierce. Bella watched him from the corner of her eye. He had dark brown hair, and his eyes were concealed with sunglasses. The stubble on his chin could be a fashion statement or an indication of desperation. Judging by how wrinkled his shirt was, she concluded the latter. The money their mystery man had requested was in a bag they'd picked up in one of the shops. A T-shirt sporting the Lincoln Park Zoo logo concealed the bales of cash. The bag sat on the ground between them. Both she and Pierce wore zoo caps and sunglasses.

"I wasn't sure you'd really come," the man said without looking at Pierce or at her.

"I'm here and I have what you asked for. You have my undivided attention, so speak."

"Richard is my friend," said the man. He appeared to be in his early thirties. "We've been friends since I interned for him eight years ago. I'm worried about him."

Bella had done a great deal of digging into Richard Sutter. He had a medical degree but he had spent most of his career in high finance and in the development of cutting-edge medical technology. His friend was likely in one of those same fields if he'd interned for the man.

"Why would you be worried about him?" Pierce asked. "And why would it be worth anything to me?"

"Because I…" The younger man turned his face away for a moment. Then he said, "Trust me, you'll find what I have to say worth your time and your money."

"Does his wife know about the two of you?"

Bella cringed behind her sunglasses. Pierce should refrain from trying to piss the guy off until he said what he had to say.

"Probably," the guy confessed. "Richard and Mariah do their own thing. Their marriage is that way."

"Does that include sleeping with my late wife?"

Pierce's lips tightened on the words and Bella wondered if he was still in love with the woman he'd buried all those years ago. Her chest felt tight at the idea, which was ridiculous, but there it was.

"Your wife—Cara—was planning to file for divorce."

Pierce's attention cut to the other man. "How would you know this?"

He shook his head. "I didn't, but Richard did. He told me there were things you didn't know. Cara had a whole different life planned. She was only waiting for the right moment to tell you. She'd planned to do so while the two of you were in Binghamton visiting her family. Cara was not coming back to Chicago with you."

Tension simmered in waves from Pierce. Bella hoped he could keep it together to hear the guy out.

"Richard believes I learned this information and tried to harm my wife, is that it?"

Pierce's words were laced with fury.

"No." The man shook his head. "He doesn't think you had anything to do with her accident, but he's reasonably sure he knows someone who does believe you were responsible."

"Who?"

The single word was uttered so harshly that several people stared at them. Bella put a hand on his arm and gave it a squeeze.

"He tried to warn you that something big was about to happen. He left you a note in your office. Richard knew you would never listen to him, so he left that ominous note in hopes you'd begin your own investigation before all this started."

"Give me the name," Pierce demanded.

The younger man shook his head. "I can't. He wouldn't tell me. He said he had to follow up and sort out a couple of things. That was three days ago. I haven't heard from him since."

Pierce stared forward. "Then why are we here?"

"Richard said if I didn't hear from him within a certain period, I was to assume he was dead and to give you a message."

Bella's heart bumped into a faster rate.

"The only reason I asked for the money was so you'd know I had important information. I don't want the money."

His statement was a definite surprise. But Bella wasn't ready to cut him too much slack just yet.

Pierce said, "I'm listening."

"Cara was planning a new life with a new partner.

Part of that plan involved an address you should visit. You'll understand then that everything you believed about your wife before she died was a lie."

53rd Street, Hyde Park, 6:15 p.m.

THE ADDRESS THE unnamed man had provided was in the landmark Hyde Park Bank building on the penthouse floor.

Bella's associate from the agency, Traynor, had followed the self-proclaimed friend of Sutter's from the zoo. The car he was driving was a rental.

"Keep in mind," she cautioned Devon as they rode the elevator to the penthouse floor, "the elaborate setup with Maynard. This could all be part of the ongoing smoke and mirrors. Even when we see what Sutter wants us to see here, we may not have anything but more lies."

Devon had considered as much. At this point, the only person he trusted was Bella.

The doors opened into a large space with soaring ceilings and arched windows. The lobby was empty, of course. It was well after business hours. He was surprised the place wasn't locked up tight. Upholstered chairs lined three walls. A table in the center of the room held magazines and brochures. Devon didn't bother riffling through them. He walked straight to the reception desk and stared at the name on the brass plate. *Dana Jordan.* He didn't recognize the name.

"May I help you?"

Devon looked up as the woman walked up behind the desk. She'd appeared from the wide cased opening that led into the dimly lit corridor beyond the lobby.

Bella moved past him and extended her hand. She was still dressed in jeans and a tank but there was no help for that just now. They hadn't wanted to take the time for her to change. "I'm Investigator Lytle and this is Dr. Devon Pierce," she said. "We're here to speak with you about a private matter that may be related to a string of homicides."

Bravo, Bella. Devon could see the older woman's mind working even as worry claimed her face.

"As you can see, we're closed. The office is generally locked by this hour but I'm expecting a client who couldn't come in during regular hours." She glanced at her watch. "I have a few minutes. I'll try to answer any questions you have. My name is Ursula Curtis. I'm the director here." She gestured to the chairs. "Won't you have a seat?"

Bella held up one of the brochures from the table. "This is a private adoption agency."

If she had said this was Santa's workshop Devon would not have been more stunned. There had been no sign on the door other than the suite number. The magazines on the table had been run-of-the-mill women's magazines. But he hadn't bothered with the brochures.

Adoption agency.

"Yes," Ms. Curtis said. "We handle private adoptions for couples who are looking to start a family and for whatever reasons can't or opt not to have biological children."

"Several years ago," Devon said, his chest so tight he could scarcely speak, "my wife may have come to you about adoption."

Ms. Curtis looked at him, evidently picking up on

his pain. "I'm afraid our records are private. Did you come with her?"

"His wife is deceased," Bella cut in. "There are two other deaths. We believe they may be connected. Any help you can give us would be most appreciated."

Ms. Curtis drew in a sharp breath as if she'd only just realized they were talking about murder. "Your wife's name, sir?"

"Cara Pierce."

"May I see your ID?"

He showed the woman his driver's license. It annoyed the hell out of him that his hand shook.

"Let's go to my office."

He followed Ms. Curtis and Bella into the corridor. He waffled between anger and shock. Had Cara wanted a child? She'd always told him she didn't. He'd wanted children but he had acquiesced to her wishes.

How could they have lived in the same household and there be so many secrets?

In the director's office, they sat in front of her desk while she searched through file cabinets. Bella put her hand on his arm and squeezed. He couldn't look at her. What kind of man wasn't aware of his wife's most basic desires?

"Cara Pierce." Ms. Curtis withdrew a file and settled behind her desk. She opened the folder and unclipped the photo from the pages stacked neatly in the file.

The photo was of Cara. He remembered that photo. He'd taken it the year before...she died.

"She was looking for a girl baby. Under two years of age." Ms. Curtis studied the photo. She smiled. "I remember her now. She said her husband was too busy to come but he'd told her exactly what he wanted—a little girl with blond hair and blue eyes just like her. Her friend agreed."

Devon blinked. "Her friend?"

Ms. Curtis smiled. "Oh yes. She brought a friend. A woman, slightly older. Dark brown hair. The two seemed so excited. It was almost as if they were the ones looking to adopt." She blushed. "It's always nice to have supportive friends."

"What about personal information?" Bella asked. "What address did Mrs. Pierce provide?"

Devon's brain wouldn't stop playing the words over and over. *A little girl with blond hair and blue eyes...*

The address Ms. Curtis provided was not the Lake Bluff house. It was some eighty miles away in Ottawa. What the hell had Cara been doing? Had she already started a new life with someone else—someplace else—even before the accident that took her life?

"Do you remember if the friend who was with Cara was this woman?"

Devon pushed aside the tangle of questions in his brain and watched as Bella showed a photo on her cell phone to Ms. Curtis.

"Why, yes. I believe that is the woman who was with her. They appeared to be very dear friends."

Bella showed the photo to Devon before putting it away.

Mariah Sutter.

Devon thanked Ms. Curtis for her help. He couldn't get out of the building fast enough. He felt as if he were suffocating.

Once on the sidewalk, Bella said, "We should confront Mariah with this news."

"Later. Right now I want to see the house where my

wife was building her new life without bothering to tell me she was abandoning the old one."

Island Avenue, Ottawa, 8:30 p.m.

IT WAS DARK when they arrived.

Pierce had hardly said a word. Traynor had called. He'd followed the man from the zoo to an upscale loft downtown. He was watching the place until further notice. He'd also heard from Victoria's contact. Jack Hayman had been out of the country for three months. To some degree, that put him in the clear.

Bella parked a few houses away from their destination. The street and the houses weren't what she'd expected. They were small and cute, more like her house, and not at all like the mansion Cara had shared with her husband.

Pierce was already out of the car when she reached for a flashlight in the glove box. She climbed out and said, "We should be careful. The place could belong to someone else now."

He nodded with only a glance in her direction as they walked toward the small white house.

A white picket fence surrounded the house. Pierce opened the gate, the creak sounding far louder in the darkness. There was a streetlight but it was half a block away. White clapboard siding, pale green shutters and a redbrick chimney made up the exterior of the small, two-story cottage. There wasn't really a front porch, more a small stoop. The house was dark inside.

She took Devon's hand and led him around the backyard with nothing but the moonlight to guide them. The narrow backyard backed up to the river. A small seawall and an iron fence separated the two. French doors on the back patio overlooked the water. A small table and two chairs sat in the center of the patio facing a home-made fire pit. It was too dark to tell if it had been used recently without turning on the flashlight.

Devon checked the French doors and they were locked.

Bella turned to the man whose whole world was sud-denly on its ear. "We have two choices here. We can go back to Chicago and look into the owner of this prop-erty tomorrow when the offices we need to call are open for business." She took a deep breath. "Or we can break the law and go in and see what we find. I don't advise the latter. Any evidence we find would be ren-dered useless."

They were already in enough trouble for entering Mrs. Harper's home. Considering Pierce was a doctor and the possibility that Harper was gravely injured al-lowed for exigent circumstances. Not the optimal situa-tion, but justifiable. This time was different. There was absolutely nothing here to show exigent circumstances any more than there had been at the bungalow that be-longed to Maynard's friend.

"I'm going in." He reached for a chair.

She grabbed his arm. "Wait a minute. Let's see if there's an unlocked window or a hidden key before we go busting up the place." She pointed to the top of the door. "Check that ledge. Under the welcome mat and under anything else that isn't nailed down."

Bella moved from window to window. All locked or painted shut. "Damn it," she muttered.

"Found it."

She turned to see Devon putting a flowerpot back

in place. The idea that a flower with fresh blooms was growing in the pot warned that the place hadn't been deserted for any length of time. If someone was home or arrived before they were out of here, they would have a hell of a lot of explaining to do.

With those concerns ringing in her ears, she joined him at the door as he opened it and then pocketed the key. Bella reached for a wall switch and gave it a flip. A four-arm chandelier that had once been brass but had been painted white glowed to life. Streaks of gold showed behind the white, giving the metal a worn look. It hung over a table with four chairs. The table too had been whitewashed.

The kitchen and dining area overlooked the backyard and the water. The cabinets and counters were white. Small colorful touches of fuchsia, lavender and gray were scattered about. Vintage dishes and well-used cookware were stored in the cabinets along with a few canned and dry goods.

Beyond the dining side of the room was a wide cased opening that led into the living room. The fireplace was small, the brick painted white, though glimmers of the red brick still showed through.

A love seat and a couple of chairs were flanked by tables. None of the pieces were new or matched. The decor was very bohemian. Sheer, gauzy curtains in a crisp white hung on the windows.

There were no photographs anywhere. Devon moved about the room, studying decorative objects. A small wooden bird that had been painted yellow. A white ceramic dish filled with individually wrapped mints. He picked one up.

"These were her favorites. Whenever we had a party, she insisted on having a bowl of these mints."

"Let's have a look upstairs." Bella waited for him to follow.

They climbed the stairs and found two bedrooms and one bath. The first bedroom they encountered had no furniture and was painted a soft pink. White ruffled curtains hung on the windows. The next one had a standard bed with dozens of pillows atop it, with mismatched tables on either side and a long ottoman stretching across the foot of the bed.

A rock sat on one of the bedside tables. The word *happiness* had been engraved into it.

A creak drew her attention around. He had opened the closet door. He pulled on the string and the bare bulb overhead in the small closet turned on.

He touched a silky blouse, then a soft T-shirt. "These are Cara's."

A pair of sneakers lay on the floor of the closet along with an overnight bag. Bella pulled the bag out of the closet and sat down on the ottoman to see what was inside. Underthings, flip-flops and a couple more T-shirts. Bella unzipped the back pocket and found documents. She pulled them from the bag.

Petition for Dissolution of Marriage.

The divorce papers were unsigned.

Devon took the papers from her and flipped through them. The man in the ball cap had been right. Cara Pierce had been in the process of building a whole new life.

Without her husband.

"We should drive back to the city and talk to Mariah

again." Bella stood and set the overnight bag aside. "There's nothing else to be learned here."

Pierce handed the pages back to her and she put them away. She didn't bother putting the bag back into the closet.

Bella followed him across the room to the door of the en suite bath. He stood at the sink. Surveyed the array of items scattered about. A jar of moisturizer, an expensive-looking bottle of perfume. A brush. A towel covered in pink and red roses hung over the shower rod that circled the claw-foot tub.

He turned back to the door, his face impassive. "You're right. There's nothing here anymore that matters."

Cara would never be coming back here.

Bella stalled at the bottom of the stairs. She moved aside and waited until Devon had joined her in the living room.

"Look around." She crossed to the coffee table and swiped her fingers across it. "Spotless."

She walked into the kitchen and pulled open the refrigerator. Two bottles of wine. Cheese and grapes. The grapes were fresh. She checked the date on the cheese. "This expiration date is months away." She closed the door and looked at Pierce. "Someone has been here recently."

Someone who had kept every little thing exactly as it was before Cara died.

Chapter Eleven

Clark Street, Chicago, 11:00 p.m.

Mariah answered the door despite the lateness of the hour.

She smiled at Devon. "It's not a good idea to visit a woman when she's so deep into a bottle of wine and at home all alone."

Bella suspected the alone part had been thrown in because of the wine.

"It is late," he agreed, "but it would mean a great deal to me if you could give us a few more minutes of your time."

The older woman's eyebrows rose ever so slightly. "Is that humility I hear in the great Dr. Pierce's voice?"

Oh yes, she was definitely feeling the wine. "It's very important," Bella put in, hoping to prevent the frustration that claimed Devon's face from making a louder appearance. "We've discovered new details you may be able to shed some light upon."

Sadness overtook Mariah's cocky expression. "Oh."

She drew the door open wider in invitation. Then, without another word, she turned and walked deeper into the house, teetering on her high heels just the tiniest bit from the level of alcohol in her blood.

Pierce closed the door and they followed the path the lady of the house had taken. She'd already curled up on the sofa, her emerald-colored silk robe gathered around her like a queen's cloak.

"Feel free to make yourselves a drink," she offered. To Devon, she added, "You know where everything is."

He glanced at Bella and she shook her head. "Thank you," he said, "but we have a long drive ahead of us."

Mariah's eyebrows rose once more. "Really. Your associate is staying with you, then."

"My agency provides protection as well as investigative services," Bella felt compelled to explain. Even as she did so, she felt heat spread across her cheeks.

"Really." Mariah made a wry expression. "Interesting." She sipped her wine before settling her attention on Devon. "What is it you want to talk about? Cara, I presume."

He nodded. "Were you aware she was looking into adopting a child?"

A quiet knowing filled the room. All three knew the truth. There was only the matter of why. The news obviously weighed heavy on Devon Pierce. Bella felt the pain emanating from him.

No matter that his wife had been dead for more than six years and that he had reconciled himself to the reality that she'd had an affair. Finding all the rest—the visit to the adoption agency, the house on the lake and the divorce papers—was like tearing open an old wound and then rubbing broken glass into it. It cut. Deeply.

"Yes." Mariah looked away a moment. "She wanted a child but she didn't want to carry a child." She sighed. "Cara could be very selfish, as I'm sure you recall."

Devon said nothing. He waited, silent and brooding, for her to continue.

"She was an amazing woman." Mariah smiled. "You loved her." She tilted her head and studied Pierce. "I know you did. She knew this as well. But she wanted more than what you had to offer. Sometimes…" Her gaze turned distant as if she were remembering something only she knew. "Sometimes I think she wanted too much." She shrugged. "It's difficult to capture a free spirit and even harder to hold on to it for any length of time."

"Did you know about the cottage in Ottawa?"

Her philosophical expression shifted into a frown at his question. But in that brief moment before the frown took over, Bella spotted the surprise. Whatever Mariah Sutter was about to say was a lie.

"What cottage?"

She sipped her wine, careful that her gaze stayed clear of Devon's and of Bella's. She knew about the cottage. Her surprise was in hearing that he had discovered it.

"A small cottage on the water in Ottawa. Some of her things are there." He sat forward, his forearms braced against his spread thighs, hands dangling. "The place was spotless. As if she'd just walked out the door moments before we arrived."

Mariah shook her head, downed the remainder of the wine in her glass. "There must be some mistake. Cara never spoke of a secret hideaway."

"Someone knew," Devon argued. "Someone *knows*. The food in the fridge was fresh."

"You're serious." Mariah's face cleared of readable tells. "How can you be sure the place is—was—Cara's?"

"The divorce papers she had drawn up were there. Her perfume and other things were there."

"Oh my God." Mariah shook her head. "It's Richard. He must have bought the place for her. That son of a bitch."

Bella waited for Devon to respond. His body had tensed. His intent gaze focused on Mariah. "What do you mean?"

Mariah sighed. "Good God, surely you recognized that Richard was obsessed with her. He adored her. He probably bought the place for her so she could have her own space away from you. Bastard." She shook her head. "He wanted her all to himself. I guess that's where they held their secret rendezvous."

"You're saying," Bella ventured, "that you believe your husband was having an affair with Cara."

"Of course he was."

"If that's true," Bella countered, "how did the two of you remain so close? Did you not know when Cara was alive?"

"I knew." She set her empty glass aside. "By the time I realized, we were inseparable." She glanced at Devon. "You remember. We did everything together. Richard and I never had children. The two of you appeared to be following that same path." She turned to Bella then. "Our husbands were both completely absorbed in their work. We were each other's salvation."

When Mariah didn't say more, Bella prompted, "How did you remain friends after you discovered the affair?"

"How could you bear to look at her?" Devon demanded.

Mariah shrugged. "We do what we have to do. You

know the old saying—keep your friends close but your enemies closer."

"You said Audrey Maynard," Bella said, moving on, "the woman in the photo we showed you earlier, was one of Richard's assistants. How can you be sure?"

She shook her head, gave a half-hearted shrug. "I dropped by the office one day and she was there. He told me she worked for him." She laughed a self-deprecating sound. "Apparently the joke was on me. After what you just told me about this cottage and considering how much this Maynard woman looks like Cara, perhaps he's using her as a replacement. A surrogate of sorts."

Not a completely implausible scenario.

"Do you know a Kevin Unger?" Devon asked.

Traynor, Bella's backup, had called to say the man who had met them at the zoo had dropped off the rental and picked up an older-model BMW. The Beamer was registered to a Kevin Unger. Traynor had sent her a photo taken from Unger's Facebook page. Definitely the guy from the zoo.

Mariah thought about the name for a moment, then nodded. "Yes, of course. He was an intern for Richard years ago. Before Cara's death, I think. I'm not sure what became of him."

"Their relationship was purely professional?" Devon inquired.

"That was my impression but I can't say for sure," Mariah confessed. "Richard has always been very adept at keeping his personal and professional lives separate, but if you're asking me if the two could have had an affair, it's possible, yes. Richard has had many lovers, female and male."

Devon stood. Bella did as well.

"Thank you again," he said, "for your time."

Mariah dropped her feet to the floor and stood. "You really never recognized what sort of man Richard is." She laughed. "He's even worse since the cancer scare. He's rarely home. Ignores his work. I don't understand what's happening to him."

"If he comes home or calls," Devon reminded her, "I need to see him."

"I'll give him the message."

When they were in the car and driving away, Devon said, "I find it difficult to believe that I misread the man so completely."

Bella held his gaze a moment before pulling onto the street. "Maybe you didn't."

Arbor Drive, Lake Bluff
Friday, June 8, 2:00 a.m.

DEVON STARED AT the drink he'd poured.

He'd been staring at it for half an hour or more. Closing his eyes, he thought of the way the silk blouse hanging in that damned closet had smelled—like her. The perfume she'd always worn had been on the counter in the bathroom.

His wife had been starting a new life.

One that did not include him. She wanted to adopt a child. A little girl. She'd already painted the spare bedroom pink.

Devon swore and snatched up the drink. He downed the Scotch in one swallow. When he found Richard, he would have the whole truth. All these years, he had regretted on a personal level that he'd had to cut Richard out of the project. But like Jack Hayman, the fool had wanted to take shortcuts. He'd wanted to make a higher return for his investment.

The Edge was about saving lives. Of course, some amount of profit was required, but that profit must be reinvested into the facility. Men like Richard Sutter and Jack Hayman didn't have the heart for the project. Devon should have seen his error well before the situation grew ugly.

He licked his lips, hating the weakness that had permitted him to surround himself with people who would betray him.

Pushing to his feet, he reminded himself that he could not change the past. What was done was done. But he wanted—no, he needed—Richard Sutter to look him in the eye and tell him the truth.

Why the hell had he suddenly decided to torture Devon with Cara's death? What had happened in recent months? He'd dropped the last of the lawsuits three years ago. Why attempt to dig at Devon in this new way?

He thought of Mariah's words about Richard not being the same since the cancer. But he had fully recovered. Why suddenly decide to dig up all the ugliness again? Why commit murder?

Whatever he thought of Richard, he would never have believed him capable of murder. If Richard's protégé could be believed, someone else was attempting some sort of revenge against Devon. Hayman? None of it fit. If Hayman or anyone else wanted revenge against Devon for some presumed wrong, why not take it directly against him? Why go to these elaborate extremes?

He went to the bar and poured himself another Scotch.

"You're not going to find the answer in that bottle."

"Perhaps not, but at least I'll no longer care."

Whoever had set this plan in motion had killed at least one innocent person as well as the mechanic who had possibly been involved. Mrs. Harper's daughter had arrived in Chicago. Devon had assured her that he would take care of all the funeral expenses as well as the necessary cleanup at her home as soon as the police released it. Detective Corwin had allowed him to have a veterinarian pick up Casper and attend to him. The cat was unharmed. A good bath was all he'd needed. Mrs. Harper's daughter would take him home with her.

"Apparently you care more than you'd like people to know," Bella noted. "Detective Corwin told me you had called the hospital and insisted on paying for Audrey Maynard's care."

He shrugged. "I'm the reason she was injured. It was the least I could do."

"You shouldn't look at all these new discoveries and see your failure. Sometimes it doesn't matter what we do—we simply can't please the people we love the most."

He lifted the glass but hesitated before taking the drink. "I'm weary of being the topic of conversation, Ms. Lytle." He shifted to stare directly at her. "Let's talk about you. Do nightmares from your childhood wake you up at night?"

"Ms. Lytle." She laughed and gave her head a little shake. "After last night," she went on, her tone frank, her expression open, "I think we're well enough acquainted to dispense with the formalities. Besides, my friends call me Bella. We had this conversation already."

He did take a swallow of the smooth, smoky flavored

whiskey then. "Am I your friend, Bella? Fair warning—
I seem to have trouble keeping friends. They generally
run screaming or furious from our encounters."

Tendrils of her hair had fallen loose from the ponytail she'd arranged it in this morning. He liked her hair
down. Liked it up, too. His mouth felt dry, so he downed
another swallow of Scotch.

"I'd like to think that we're friends." She picked up
a glass and poured a finger of Scotch. "You're still the
client and I'm still the hired investigator, but I don't
see any reason why we can't be friends. Do you?" She
brought the glass to her lips and indulged in a small sip.

"Friends play together, don't they, Bella?"

She licked the alcohol from her bottom lip. "They
do."

He placed his glass on the counter and reached for
hers. "I would very much like to play with you now."

She downed the trace of Scotch left in her glass and
then handed it to him. "Only if I get to make the rules."

"All right."

She led the way. He followed, already growing hard
simply watching her move. She appeared so reserved
but he already knew that was just for show. He had experienced the wicked wildcat beneath all those prim
layers.

When she moved into the entry hall and started up
the stairs, he hesitated. "Where are you going?"

She glanced back. "My choice, remember?"

He had agreed to permit her to make the rules.

Upstairs, she walked into his room and turned on
the light. When he'd joined her, she closed the door and
locked it, then leaned against it.

He glanced around the room. Tension rippled through

him. He had not made love in this room in nearly seven
years. Not long after Cara was gone, he'd had her things
removed…the bed and the linens replaced. Not because
he could bring himself to hate her but because he could
not bear to see them, to touch them.

Now he settled his attention on the woman watching him all too closely. "What would you like to play?"

"Bella Says," she announced. "Sort of like Simon
Says, only different."

Anticipation strummed through him, chasing away
the doubts for the moment. "As you wish. What would
you have me do?"

"Take off your clothes."

"Not particularly original," he teased. He'd left his
jacket downstairs. He removed the cuff links, crossed
the room and dropped them onto the table next to the
bed. Then he reached for the buttons of his shirt, re-
leasing them one by one. She watched, her respiration
picking up. The rise and fall of her full breasts was mes-
merizing. He shouldered out of the shirt, allowed it to
slip down his arms and fall to the floor.

Her gaze roved over his torso. He held very still, his
arms hanging at his sides, and allowed her to look until
she had her fill.

"Everything," she clarified.

The shoes came off next. He peeled off his socks,
first one and then the other. Reaching to his waist, he
pulled the leather belt from his trousers, let it join the
shirt on the floor.

She watched his every move, her body growing restless. Watching her watch him made him want to rush
to where she stood and take her right there against the
door. Instead, he unfastened his fly and removed his

trousers. He tugged his briefs down his legs and off. His cock stood fully aroused now. His entire body strummed with need.

For a minute, she studied him, her gaze moving over his body. He waited patiently. Whatever she wanted that was his to give, he would give. So many years had passed since he had yearned to please someone the way he wanted to please her.

Finally, when he could no longer bear the anticipation, he demanded, "What now?" His voice was taut and rough. He ached to touch her.

She pushed away from the door and moved slowly toward him. When she stood directly in front of him, she reached up and removed the scarf from her hair. "On your knees."

He didn't hesitate. He lowered to his knees, his heart rocking against his sternum.

She tied the scarf around him like a blindfold. The lack of visual stimuli was like an aphrodisiac—it only made him harder.

"Stand up."

He did as she asked, hoping she would take him by the hand and lead him to the bed. He wanted to be inside her now. He wanted to taste all of her this second. He quieted the excitement building inside him and listened. She was either standing still or she'd removed the thongs so that he wouldn't hear her steps. He listened intently. The slide of fabric told him she was removing her clothes. The soft whoosh as they hit the floor, piece by piece, sent tremors rocking through his body.

She came closer. He could smell her soft skin. His breath came in short choppy bursts. His cock throbbed for her.

Her fingers slid over his back. She traced a path over his skin, lingering in places that made him groan with need. He wanted to touch her so badly. He fisted his fingers. As if she'd recognized what he wanted, she moved away. Where was she? He couldn't hear her... could no longer smell her sweet skin.

When she returned, she pulled his wrists together behind his back and tied them with a band of silk, perhaps one of his neckties. She reached up to check the blindfold and her body brushed his, the friction of her skin against his lighting a fire over every inch she touched.

He wanted to reach for her but his hands were tied. "That was rather unsportsmanlike of you." He wished he could see her.

"Tell me what gives you pleasure, Devon."

Her voice made him tremble. He gritted his teeth against the weakness. "The whip. Pain."

"Liar."

She clasped his thighs. Only then did he realize she was kneeling in front of him.

"Tell me what you want," she murmured.

He refused. What happened the other night was an anomaly. He never allowed himself the pleasure without the pain. He didn't deserve it. However much he wanted her, he didn't deserve her.

Her hot, lush lips closed over the head of his straining cock. He shuddered.

She squeezed his thighs with her soft hands while her hungry mouth drew on him, took him in deeper. Her fingers found their way to his ass and squeezed until he growled. He jerked at the restraint. Needed to touch her.

And then she stood and stepped away from him. The cool air on his heavy cock had him gasping. He felt her moving around him but she didn't touch him. Had she taken him to this edge only to leave him there, wanting, needing more?

He felt a tug on his arm and he stumbled forward. He followed the tugs. She slipped around him and released his hands. His arms fell to his sides, his fingers aching to touch her.

"On your knees," she ordered. She was in front of him again.

He dropped to his knees. Licked his lips in anticipation of a taste of her.

She grabbed two handfuls of his hair and pulled him forward. His face landed between her thighs. He feasted on her soft folds. Relished the taste of her. Wanted her to feel the same frenzy he had felt. He licked and suckled until she cried out. He used his tongue to penetrate her, to delve as deeply as possible. Slowly, he began to kiss his way up her body, but she scrambled away. He tried to follow, bumping his knee and losing his balance.

He caught up with her on the bed. Her legs were open in invitation and he moved between them and burrowed deeply into her. She was so damned hot and wet and nicely snug. She wrapped her legs around his and lifted to meet his thrusts. He wanted to see her, but the blindfold was still in place.

He leaned down, needed to kiss her. She tore the blindfold away. He blinked at the light, forced his eyes to focus so he could watch her face as she lost herself to orgasm. He closed his mouth over her breast, suckled and nibbled until she was writhing again. He moved to the next one all the while thrusting slowly in and out of her.

He dropped his head to her chest. God, he was so close...so damn close.

"Turn over," he murmured. He desperately needed to be deeper inside her. He needed her to take all of him.

"Beg," she said, her skin flush with her own need. Her breasts plump and jutting forward as if pleading for more of his attention.

"Please," he urged, "I need to be deeper inside you."

She flattened a palm against the center of his chest, held his gaze a moment as she felt his heart pounding, and then she rolled over.

"Arch your bottom for me."

She didn't move. Just lay there with that firm, rounded ass tempting him beyond all reason.

"Please, arch your bottom for me, baby," he pleaded.

With her shoulders against the bed, she lifted her bottom up to him. He nudged her urgently. He guided himself inside and he slid deep, deep into her. He groaned with the intensity of it. It felt so damned good.

Slowly, slowly, he moved inside her. Every ounce of willpower he possessed was needed to restrain his movements. In, an inch, then two, three. Deeper, deeper, until he had given her all he had to give. He felt the muscles inside her start to clench around him. He moved faster until she screamed with orgasm again. He fought to restrain his release. Just a little longer.

She suddenly scrambled away from him, leaving his pulsing cock damp and aching for release. He made a small, strangled sound at the loss of her tight heat. She got onto her knees, facing him. "I want you to look at me. To *see* me."

He kissed her face. "I see you." Kissed her eyes, her nose, her neck and shoulder. He ached so for relief that his entire body shuddered. When he could take it no longer, he grabbed her. He dropped into a sitting position and pulled her over his lap. She went down fully onto him, taking him in even deeper than before. She held him tight against her and rocked and rocked until they both screamed with release.

And then he did something he had not done in more than six years. He pulled her into his arms and held her until they lost themselves to the exhaustion.

Chapter Twelve

6:15 a.m.

Bella watched Devon sleep. The soft morning light trickled in between the slats of the shutters. Stubble darkened his square jaw. The mask of tension he wore more often than not was relaxed. Dark lashes rested against high cheekbones. Her gaze slid down, over his slightly off-center nose, to lips that had teased and tasted every part of her.

Down farther still, she noted the muscles of his neck and then the hard ridges of his chest. Her fingers itched to touch him. To slide beneath the white sheet that lay across his waist. The ferocity and desperation of his lovemaking was every bit as intense as the man himself.

A man who had been deeply wounded on multiple fronts. Betrayed by the woman he'd loved and by a friend and business partner.

Bella thought of the last journal entry she'd read and it made her ache for this man.

The need is insane. I feel addicted and I cannot resist. A moment away from my lover is like a moment without air. It leaves me gasping and desperate. We've made our decision. Our old lives are no longer rele-

vant. Now we move on to the beautiful future that is ours alone. I cannot wait to begin this new journey. Nothing...no one else matters. Only us, and our wonderful plans. Tomorrow I will tell my husband that I'm leaving. I refuse to waste another day on this empty marriage.

The words had been brutal.

Devon Pierce was a victim. Perhaps not in the criminal sense, but in a deeply personal one.

She mulled over the many journal entries she had read. It was clear Cara wanted to conceal her lover's identity. The failure to label the person as male or female seemed unreasonably cautious. It wasn't as if Richard Sutter was the only man with whom she was in contact in the city of Chicago. And if her lover was Richard, why would he send his protégé to warn Devon? Why write that message that seemed to foreshadow coming events? More important, why behave so secretively? If Richard knew the person seeking revenge against Devon, why not tell him or, if he wanted Devon to suffer for his own reasons, why get involved at all?

Unless he was covering for someone who mattered to him on some level.

Bella's heart started to pound. *Mariah Sutter.*

Devon's eyes opened and he immediately turned to her as if he'd felt her watching him. "Good morning."

"Good morning to you." She smiled. "I'm starving."

He rolled over, pressed her against the mattress. "So am I." His mouth came down on hers and he kissed her long and deep, filling her with the taste of him and instantly chasing away her hunger for anything else.

When he came up for air, she whispered, "We should talk about—"

"In a minute." He burrowed between her welcoming thighs and thrust into her.

She gasped and, despite all the places so tender from last night's hours of lovemaking, her body instantly started to move in time with his. The feel of his muscled chest rubbing against hers had her breasts hard and aching. She lifted her hips to allow his thrusts to deepen.

The rattle of her cell phone against the table next to the bed was a distant nuisance. She couldn't have stopped if her life had depended upon it. Her nails dug into his back as the pace escalated. Suddenly she was coming. She screamed with the intensity of it. He growled as he followed her over that edge.

As soon as she could think again, she dragged her cell from the table and checked the screen. Unger had left his downtown loft and Traynor was following him.

"News?"

She rolled onto her side and propped her head on his chest. "Unger is on the move. Traynor is keeping tabs on him."

His relaxed and sated expression vanished and the tension was back.

"There's something else," she said. When his gaze connected with hers, she went on, "I don't think it's Richard. In fact, I don't think he's the one who was having the affair with Cara."

"We've basically ruled out Hayman." He absently stroked her hair, his face a study in concentration. "I can't see Unger being the one."

Bella waited until he looked at her once more. "I think it's Mariah."

His raised eyebrows spoke loudly of his surprise.

"That's a hell of a leap from where we've been going with this."

"She was so precise with her thoughts on how her husband felt about Cara. Yet I heard no anger in her voice. When you mentioned the cottage, there was a glimmer of surprise but not a what-are-you-talking-about expression. She knew about the cottage. She went with Cara to the adoption agency. What man would keep the cottage so perfectly spotless and eat cheese and grapes and drink wine? I'll bet Richard is a Scotch man, like you."

"You're right. Scotch is his preferred drink. I picked up my taste for Scotch from him."

"We need to be watching Mariah."

Her cell started that incessant vibrating again. This time it was a call from Traynor. Bella answered with, "What's going on?"

"Our friend Unger lent his car to a neighbor," Traynor explained. "I followed the guy to his office, but now I'm headed back to Unger's place. I'm guessing he won't be there."

Damn it. Without eyes on Unger, they might never locate Sutter.

Clark Street, Noon

"As a detective, I suppose you spent some time on stakeouts."

Bella shifted her attention from the driveway half a block up. They hadn't spent a lot of time talking since they parked on the street that ran in front of Mariah Sutter's house. The driveway exit a few yards away was her only way in and out of the property. If she went anywhere, they would know it.

When they first arrived, Devon had called her home landline to ensure she was in the house. He'd used the excuse that he'd forgotten to ask if she'd heard from Richard. She assured him she had not. Then she'd gone on to remind him of how Richard spent hours on the golf course and in pubs when traveling in Europe. He rarely called home or checked his phone.

Like Bella, Devon wasn't buying it.

"I did my time on stakeouts." She turned back to the street. "Sometimes it was boring as hell and others it was oddly interesting."

"You're a very strong woman, Isabella Lytle." He made this statement without looking at her. "Few could have overcome a childhood such as yours and gone on to accomplish so much."

"I was lucky. I had a couple of really encouraging teachers."

"I suspect luck had very little to do with the outcome."

She turned to him. "Thank you. It wasn't always easy but I never allowed myself to believe any other outcome."

He held her gaze for a long moment. "How did you ever learn to trust again after the way your parents let you down? And your sister, she basically left you to fend for yourself."

Bella hugged herself, feeling suddenly cold. They'd turned off the engine and put the windows down. The air was still reasonably cool after the overnight low in the midfifties. Even in the hottest days of summer, the past could give her an abrupt chill that way.

"I was angry with her at first. I felt like she'd abandoned me." She shrugged. "That she should have stayed and protected me. Eventually I got over it. She killed our father to protect me. She's had to live with that and I'm certain it hasn't been easy. I can't resent her for feeling like she'd done her part. In truth, she had. He would have killed us both."

"I'm surprised you're not more angry with the world at large." He assessed her a long moment. "People seem to need to blame someone for their misfortunes."

"I had no say in what I was born into. It wasn't the world's fault. It was my parents'. They made their choices and we had to live with them. What I chose to do with my life from that point forward was no one's decision but my own. Any blame from that moment lies with me."

"I like the way you think." He smiled.

"I like the way you smile," she said before she lost her nerve. "You don't smile nearly enough." She put her hand on his and savored the texture of his skin.

"It's been a long while since I had something to smile about." He reached out and traced a gentle path on her cheek. "Despite the circumstances, I'm glad we met."

She captured his hand in hers and gave it a squeeze. "Me, too."

The moment passed and they stared forward once more. Eventually their fingers slipped apart.

"Do you feel Mariah would be capable of murder?" Bella asked. For now, they needed to remain focused on the investigation. All these confusing personal feelings would have to wait. "Two people are dead. The mechanic was shot with a small-caliber handgun and

Mrs. Harper was stabbed. Could she commit such up-close violence?"

Devon shook his head. "I wouldn't have thought so. But then I was just as certain Richard would never go that far. What about Maynard? She says she was hired by a man. Would Mariah have trusted anyone to carry out those steps or maybe there's another body waiting to be found?"

Bella nodded once. "Maynard spewed a great deal of detail, much of which was untrue."

He rubbed a hand over his clean-shaven jaw. "We can't say with complete certainty that Hayman, though out of the country, isn't the mastermind behind all this."

"As true as that is, we've found no connection to him so far. Everything seems to connect back to the Sutters."

A car parked on the street behind them. Bella watched in the rearview mirror as Lacon Traynor climbed out.

"It's Traynor." She glanced at Devon. "He must have an update he felt he needed to share in person."

Bella hit the unlock button and Traynor slid into the back seat. He was Bella's age with beach-boy blond hair and sandy-brown eyes. He hailed from Texas and she had decided you could take the man out of Texas but you couldn't take Texas out of the man. His jeans and button-up shirt were complemented with a lightweight sport jacket but there was no mistaking those boots for what they were—well-worn cowboy footwear.

"Still no sign of Unger?" She doubted finding him would be easy but she could hope.

"He's in the wind." Traynor glanced at Devon. "I had a look around inside his apartment and it appears as though he packed a hasty bag. He'd gone through drawers and left a bit of a mess. We may not be seeing the guy again."

"Devon Pierce," she said, "this is Lacon Traynor, my backup detail from the agency."

Traynor reached across the seat and shook Devon's hand. "I got a call from Ian."

Ian Michaels was at the top of the food chain at the Colby Agency. He had been with Victoria for many years. "Was he able to locate the car and driver who picked up Maynard?"

Traynor gave her a nod in the rearview mirror. "Belongs to a car service. The driver is MIA. He hasn't come to work in two days. I checked his home address. Neighbors stated they hadn't seen him in a couple of days."

Bella imagined his body would show up next but she kept the conclusion to herself. Devon was dealing with enough right now.

As if fate wanted to show her things could always be worse, Devon reached into his jacket pocket and withdrew his cell. "It's the Edge." He answered and listened for a couple of beats.

Tension coiled in Bella's stomach. She'd almost suggested that he beef up security at the facility. So far, no attempts to damage or destroy property had been made against the facility, but that could be coming. At this very moment, in fact.

"I'll be right there."

When he put the phone away, he turned to Bella. "It's Unger. He's waiting for me in my office. Patricia is concerned there's something wrong with him but he assures her he's fine, that he just needs to see me."

"I can take over here," Traynor suggested.

Bella didn't want to separate from Devon, but she needed to keep an eye on Mariah. Her instincts were screaming way too loudly for her to risk turning her back on the woman.

"I'll stay here," she countered. "You take Dr. Pierce to the Edge. I'll keep both of you posted on what's happening here."

"No." Devon shook his head. "You should be with me."

Bella felt her cheeks redden. "I'm on the right track with Mariah," she argued. "This is too important to risk letting her out of my sight. If she sees me, I can easily make up an excuse that I have more questions. If she sees Traynor, she'll be spooked."

"She has a good point," Traynor tossed in. "Lytle can take care of herself, Doc. Trust me. I've gone to hand-to-hand classes with her. She kicked my ass."

"Fine." Devon looked at her one last time before climbing out of the car.

Bella watched in the rearview mirror as they climbed into Traynor's car. Then she shifted her attention back to the home of the woman she suspected was a cold-hearted murderer.

The Edge, 1:45 p.m.

TRAYNOR PARKED IN the spot reserved for the administrator. "Those friends of yours?"

Detectives Corwin and Hodge emerged from their nondescript sedan, swaggered to the sidewalk and waited, their attention fixed on Traynor's sedan.

"The two detectives who want to pin all this on me rather than find the true perpetrator." Devon reached for the door. Ignoring the two would be futile. The sooner he allowed them to throw a few more accusations at him, the sooner he could go inside and learn what Unger had decided to share with him this time.

"Fun, fun," Traynor muttered.

"Your secretary told us you wouldn't be in today," Corwin said, his tone openly accusing as Devon approached him. "We were just about to leave."

"I hadn't planned to but when you work with emergencies you never know when your schedule will change." Devon struggled to retain his patience. Enough was enough and he'd passed *enough* a considerable time ago. "What can I do for you, gentlemen? I have matters to which I need to attend."

"Well, we have a few matters, too," Hodge said. He glanced at his partner. "You want me to tell him or you want to tell him?"

Devon resisted the urge to punch one or both.

Corwin narrowed his gaze at Traynor. "Who's your friend? What happened to the pretty one?"

"Lacon Traynor." He thrust his hand at Corwin. "The Colby Agency. My associate had an appointment. I'm standing in for her."

Corwin shook his hand. "Oh, another one of those."

Traynor gave Hodge's hand a shake as well.

Devon was ready to shake the whole lot of them.

"You had something to discuss with me?" he snapped.

Hodge frowned. "I guess we should get on with it. The doc sounds a little testy."

"Your housekeeper," Corwin began.

"House manager," Devon corrected.

"Whatever." Corwin shrugged. "We found a copy of what looks like some kind of diary or journal." He hitched his head toward the car and said to his partner, "Get the evidence."

A chill settled deep in Devon's bones. He clenched his teeth to keep the frustration from boiling out. He shouldn't be surprised that a copy of Cara's journal had shown up. The person or persons behind this insanity were pulling out all the stops.

Hodge returned with a large, clear plastic bag with a stack of white paper inside. He handed it to Devon. His late wife's gentle strokes filled the page on top. He tossed it back to the man. "This is a copy of my wife's journal. I have no idea why Mrs. Harper would have made a copy."

Corwin shrugged. "Blackmail, maybe?"

"I was not being blackmailed by Mrs. Harper or anyone else." Anger tinged his words this time. If only this were as simple as blackmail.

"Well." Corwin passed the bag back to Hodge. "Whether you are being blackmailed or not, that journal shines a whole new light on the relationship between you and your wife."

"Thing's chock-full of motive," Hodge tacked on.

Traynor stepped forward. "You planning to arrest Dr. Pierce?"

Corwin glared at the man a moment. "Nah. Not yet."

"You want to take him downtown for further questioning?"

Corwin shook his head. "Maybe later."

Traynor leaned forward, putting his face close to the other man's. "Then step aside. The doctor told you he had things to do."

The two cops backed up a couple of steps and Devon strode toward the entrance.

"I'm sure we'll have more questions for you soon, Doc," Corwin called after him.

"They're just trying to get under your skin," Traynor said, keeping stride with him. "That's how they get their kicks."

Devon gave the other man a tight nod. His frustration level was out of control at the moment. He didn't trust himself to speak.

"Dr. Pierce!" Nurse Eva Bowman rushed to meet Devon in the lobby. "You're needed in the OR now. We have a gunshot victim."

Would he never get to his office? He hoped Unger didn't tire of waiting for him and walk out.

"I'll go there now," he assured Eva. "Please tell Patricia to let the man waiting to see me know that I'll only be a few minutes more."

"The man who was in your office is in OR 2," Eva explained. "He needs immediate surgery but he refuses to be put under until he speaks to you."

Devon started striding quickly toward the surgery suite before she finished speaking. "Bring me up to speed on his condition."

"When he came into your office, Ms. Ezell wasn't aware he was injured. After he'd been waiting for a bit, she went to tell him you were en route and she spotted the blood on his shirt. He was hemodynamically stable, so we imaged him. The bullet appears to have gone right through him. The bleeding is minimal, blood pressure and respiration are reasonably stable, but Dr. Frasier wants to get in there and make sure there's no damage we're not seeing."

"Let him know I'm coming and I'll scrub in."

Eva hurried into the OR while Devon made quick

work of scrubbing and donning a sterile gown and gloves. He pushed his way through the door and moved toward the team surrounding the patient.

"His vitals are still stable, Dr. Pierce," Marissa Frasier said, "but we're wasting valuable time."

Unger tried to lift his head. A nurse rested her hand on his shoulder and he relaxed.

"Dr. Pierce," Unger said, his voice unsteady with pain. "I got into a little trouble before I could get to you." He stared up at the bright surgical lights, blinked rapidly and swallowed, the effort visible along the column of his throat. "I don't know what happened to my phone."

"Who did this?" Devon asked.

Unger swallowed again, then licked his lips. "I don't know for sure. What I do know for certain is that Richard learned the truth. He was trying to stop…" He coughed. "I think he was too late."

"Pressure is dropping," said Dr. Raiford, the anesthesiologist.

"I need to do this." Frasier looked to Devon.

He nodded. To Unger, he said, "We'll talk again when you're well."

Devon stepped out of the OR, peeled off his gloves and gown and then entered the observation area. He lowered the privacy shield and watched for a few minutes as Frasier began the exploratory. Unger was certain Richard was innocent in this despicable mess. Perhaps Bella's assessment that Mariah was the one behind all of it was on target.

He should call Bella and tell her what Unger had said. He walked out of the observation area. No. What he should do is go back to Clark Street and demand that Mariah tell him the truth.

If the woman he had known for nearly two decades was that dangerous, Bella needed backup. He should be there with Bella.

Traynor caught up with him in the corridor. "What now, Doc?"

"Take me back to join Ms. Lytle. I believe her conclusions about Mariah Sutter are far closer to the truth than we realized."

Devon hurried to his office to advise Patricia that he would be out the remainder of the day only to find Corwin and Hodge waiting for him.

"I thought of some more of those questions I needed to ask you," Corwin said. He jerked his head toward Devon's office. "Maybe we should talk in private, seeing that these things shouldn't be discussed in front of a lady."

Frustration hammering at him now, Devon gestured to his office. "Make yourselves comfortable. I'll be right there."

When the two detectives had done as he asked, he turned to Traynor. "You should go back to the stakeout with Bel—Ms. Lytle. I'll be fine here."

Traynor shook his head. "I'm afraid that's not the way it works, Doc. You're the client who needs protection. Trust me, Lytle can take care of herself."

Devon stepped in toe to toe with him. "You look like a tough guy to me, Mr. Traynor."

He shrugged without backing away a centimeter. "I've been called worse."

"Unless you leave this facility right now and provide whatever backup Ms. Lytle needs, I will have security take you there, leaving me as well as this facility unsecured."

Traynor backed off, held up his hands. "No need to get riled up, Doc. I got the message."

"Then go."

Devon turned his back on the man and walked into his office—his retreat—that felt more like a lion's den at the moment.

Chapter Thirteen

Clark Street, 2:30 p.m.

Bella closed the journal.

She'd reread all the entries related to Cara's lover. She was even more certain now that the unnamed lover was Mariah Sutter—not her husband, Richard. According to Unger, Richard was attempting to sort things out, which likely meant he suspected his wife as well.

Traynor had called and explained what happened with Unger. He'd warned Devon again that Richard had discovered the truth but that it was too late. Bella wasn't sure what that part meant. Had some aspect of Mariah's plan already been set in motion? Bella's first thought was an attack on the Edge facility. For that reason, Bella had insisted that Traynor stay right where he was and start a quiet search of the facility. Since Devon was tied up in his office with the detectives, Traynor did as she asked.

Bella couldn't see the point in Mariah going after Devon's home. He was rarely there and it meant little to him compared to his commitment to the Edge. The Edge was his baby—his entire focus. If Mariah Sutter really wanted to hurt him, she would hit him there.

Traynor was calling in another Colby investigator who specialized in explosives. He would coordinate with Chicago PD's bomb squad if he found anything suspicious or if any threats were received.

Movement in the driveway of the Sutter home drew Bella's full attention. She watched as Mariah hurried to her Lexus and climbed behind the wheel. Bella eased down in her seat as the sedan rolled out of the drive and onto the street with hardly a pause to check for traffic.

Bella gave her a moment and then eased from between the two parallel-parked cars and merged into traffic. She kept an eye on the back of Mariah's car. Bella made the same turn onto 144th Street, followed by another turn onto Halsted and then 147th.

"Where are you going, Mariah?" Bella braked and accelerated to stay with the flow of traffic while simultaneously avoiding getting any closer to the Lexus.

They moved onto the interstate ramp and Bella leaned forward as she matched her speed to the other vehicle. For the next few miles, she tried to relax. Loosened her fingers on the wheel and considered the possibilities. Maybe she was going to meet Richard. If Unger could be believed, Richard had discovered the truth, which could very well mean there was about to be a showdown between husband and wife.

Bella hoped they were on the verge of finding an ending for Devon. He deserved to be able to go on with his life. His existence since his wife's death could hardly be called living. What Bella had felt with him last night had been real. Last night had been about pleasure and need, not about pain and punishment.

The idea that they would both likely be moving on when this was over saddened her. She knew better than to get emotionally involved with a client and yet here she was, completely wrapped up in him.

Mariah merged toward I-80 West and Bella knew exactly where she was going.

The cottage.

The drive to the cottage in Ottawa was a long one. Bella had time to allow this to play out a bit before she jumped to conclusions and alerted Devon and Traynor.

Mariah's sedan settled into a lane and stayed put. Bella did the same a few cars back. Had Richard found out about the cottage as well and demanded that she meet him there? He definitely wasn't out of the country. Maybe he'd given his wife that story so he could sit back and watch what she would do with him gone. He may have had Unger following her movements.

Still, if Mariah was the one, what had made her decide to stir this pot after all these years? Her husband was the one who'd suffered through a life-threatening disease. Even that had been some time ago, nearly three years. What had occurred to tear open the old wounds and prompt her to seek revenge or whatever it was she wanted from Devon?

The Sutters certainly weren't in any financial trouble. The motive remained a mystery. And there was always a motive.

Forty minutes later, there was no longer a question about where Mariah was headed. She took the exit into Ottawa. Bella made the call. First, she tried Devon's number, but there was no answer. Then she called Traynor.

"Hey, what's going on? I couldn't reach Dr. Pierce."

"The two detectives from the PD have had him in his office for better than an hour."

A frown furrowed its way across her brow. She moved into the right lane. "Has something new happened?"

"They found a copy of his late wife's diary at the scene where the house manager was murdered."

"Damn." The journal had nothing to do with what was happening, but it cast doubt on Devon's relationship with his wife. "They're trying to rattle him in hopes of learning something they don't know."

Sometimes when the police had nowhere to go on a case, they circled around until something or someone broke. Bella doubted very seriously that Devon Pierce would be the someone who would break for them. They were wasting their time and his.

"The facility is clear so far. McAllister brought his dog. If there's anything here, we'll find it."

"Tell McAllister I owe him one." Bella was immensely grateful the Colby Agency had Ted McAllister on their team. Ted had spent years serving in the military, most of that time as an explosives expert. Both he and the dog in his unit had lost a leg and were forced to retire. The paperwork had been endless and the frustration monumental, but McAllister had managed to get permission to take the dog home with him. Polly, a German shepherd, was loved by everyone at the agency.

"I'll give Pierce's secretary a heads-up and then I'll be right behind you."

Bella caught herself when she would have urged him to stay with Devon. She was no fool. Following a suspect into a trap was always a possibility. As badly as she wanted to simultaneously prove Mariah was behind all this and to keep Devon safe, she wanted to stay alive.

"Make sure McAllister stays close."

"You got it. Be careful, Lytle. This woman, Mariah, sounds like one twisted lady."

"Will do."

Traynor was more right than he knew. If Bella had Mariah pegged accurately, she had murdered at least two people—possibly three if that driver's body showed up—and injured two others.

Mariah and Cara had been madly in love. Bella was certain of it. The two had made major plans about the future—a home, a child. They wanted it all. Cara's death had stolen that future from Mariah. But why wait nearly seven years to seek revenge against the person she blamed for stealing that future? And why not just kill Devon? Why all the games?

Bella was missing something here.

Mariah pulled into the small drive next to the cottage and emerged from her luxury car. Bella crept along hoping Mariah wouldn't look back. Bella finally drew a deep breath when the woman hurried into the house.

The vacant house for sale across the street looked like as good a place as any to hide her car. Bella pulled into the drive and eased into the carport at the rear of the small property. Once her car was out of sight, she silenced her cell, tucked it into her pocket and headed up the street.

She strolled to the third house opposite the cottage and crossed the street at the small intersection. Recalling the layout of the cottage, she decided an approach from the rear would prove the most advantageous. She darted into a backyard two houses away. The house was quiet, so hopefully no one was home.

She moved across the yard, hopped over the small white fence all the houses on this side appeared to prefer and crossed the next yard. As she reached the rickety picket fence that separated this yard from the one that was her destination, she took stock of the situation.

No voices reverberating from inside. No one passed in front of the windows.

Bella stepped over the fence and cautiously approached the rear patio. She reached the window right of the French doors first. Peeking inside, she spotted an empty kitchen. She itched to go inside but she couldn't take that risk just yet.

A door slammed loudly. Bella jumped. Had someone gone out the front door?

Glass or something on that order shattered inside. Bella held her breath and had a look through the window again.

The front door stood open. A man lay facedown in the cased opening between the kitchen and the living room. She reached for the weapon tucked at the small of her back. The man's hair was dark, peppered with gray. Could be Richard Sutter. She couldn't see his face.

A narrow river of crimson seeped from beneath him.

She had to go in.

Holding her weapon at the ready, she went to the French doors and reached for the knob. Unlocked. She eased the door open and listened.

Silence.

Slowly, she stepped into the kitchen and scanned the room.

Clear.

She moved quickly to the man on the floor. She crouched beside him, scanning the living room as she did so.

Clear.

Bella checked his carotid artery. Still alive. She

tucked her weapon into her waistband and rolled him onto his back. The knife that had entered his chest was gouged deep at an odd angle where he'd fallen against it.

Not good.

His eyes were open and his mouth worked as if he were trying to tell her something.

She reached for her cell to call for help.

Pain exploded in the back of her skull.

The agony was followed by an odd silence. The man on the floor stared up at her in defeat. Pinpricks of light sparked in front of her eyes.

And then the world went dark.

Chicago Police Department, 5:10 p.m.

DEVON PACED THE interview room. Detectives Corwin and Hodge had rushed out half an hour ago and still hadn't returned.

An hour into their questioning, the two had decided it would be best if Devon accompanied them here. At first, he'd been prepared to have them escorted out of the Edge, but then they'd told him about Maynard's revised statement.

Still, he refused to ride in the back seat of their car as if he were under arrest. Since he had ridden in this morning with Bella, he'd had to borrow his colleague Dr. Frasier's car.

He stared at his cell, willed it to ring. Why the hell hadn't he heard from Bella or from Traynor?

Something was wrong.

The door opened and the two detectives waltzed in. "Sorry for the delay," Corwin said. "We were waiting for confirmation on a couple of things."

Devon stopped his pacing and stared at the two. "Say whatever you have to say. Ask whatever you intend to ask, before I lose my patience."

In truth, he already had. He'd had to fight the urge to call his attorney. If he remained cooperative, perhaps this would be over more quickly.

Not that his cooperation had helped so far.

"Sit." Corwin gestured to a chair on Devon's side of the table as he and Hodge collapsed into the ones on their side.

Hodge shuffled through a stack of pages and handed several to his partner, keeping a few for himself.

"Ms. Maynard recanted her earlier statement and provided a new one."

Devon felt the final remnants of his patience slipping from his grasp. "You mentioned this more than an hour ago and I still have no idea how this revised statement impacts me. Why am I here?"

Corwin placed a photo on the table in front of Devon. "Do you know this man?"

Devon studied the image, then shook his head. "I don't, no. Who is he?"

"This is the missing driver," Corwin explained. "The one who picked Maynard up from her street corner and drove her to meet the person who paid her to pretend to be your wife."

Devon nodded. "I see. Did you find him?"

Hodge laughed. "Oh, we found him all right. He took a bullet right through the eye." He tapped his left eye. "It was a .32. Just like the one that killed the mechanic found in the trunk of the Lexus Maynard was driving."

Another murder. Devon's chest felt tight with the

weight of yet another death. "Do you know if it was the same weapon?"

"We're checking that now," Hodge explained. "We might not know until tomorrow, but we believe that will be the case."

Richard Sutter had a couple of weapons but Devon had no idea the caliber. It wasn't something they ever really discussed, but at some point during all the years they had known each other, the subject of weapons had come up. Richard had mentioned having one in his nightstand. He also remembered Richard mentioning that Mariah and some of her friends were taking a weapons training class. Mariah had wanted Cara to attend as well.

The urge to call Bella with this news was nearly overwhelming. She should know about this. She was watching Mariah.

He checked the time again. Something was wrong. He should have heard from her by now.

"Maynard says the driver was her boyfriend. He was the one who made the deal with the person who set all this in motion," Corwin explained. "She said that she made up the other statement because she was trying to protect her boyfriend. But now that he's dead, she spilled her guts."

"You found him first and used that to get her to talk," Devon suggested. How long had these two known about the dead driver? Or Maynard's new statement? Long enough to be running ballistics on the bullet that killed the man. Fury tightened in Devon's gut.

"Does Maynard know the person who hired her?"

Corwin shook his head. "She doesn't but she does know it was a woman."

That bad feeling he'd been ignoring swelled inside

him. "This person—this woman—hasn't left any evidence? A fingerprint? A hair? Anything?"

"Not that we've found so far," Hodge said, scanning another report.

"Is there a woman in your history," Corwin asked, "who might want revenge for some reason?"

The name burgeoned in his throat. He opened his mouth, ready to tell them all that he suspected regarding Mariah Sutter, but his cell vibrated.

He snatched it from his pocket and took the call without checking the screen. "Yes."

"This is Traynor."

Devon kept his attention on the two detectives. "I'm glad you called. Is everything in order?"

"Your ex-partner Richard Sutter is dead."

Devon stood, uncertainty raging through him. "What about Bella?"

"Her car is here at the cottage in Ottawa." Traynor hesitated a moment. "Her weapon is here, but she isn't."

"Thank you." Devon struggled to keep the fury and the fear twisting inside him from making an appearance. "I'll be there as soon as I can."

Devon ended the call and slid the phone back into his pocket, his movements as calm and relaxed as he could manage. "I have an emergency, gentlemen. I hope you'll keep me updated on your progress."

"Count on it." Corwin stood. "I kind of miss your lady friend. Where'd you say she was off to?"

"She's following up on an old friend of my late wife's."

Devon moved toward the door, the blood pounding in his ears.

"Be careful the secrets you keep, Dr. Pierce," Corwin called after him. "They can get people killed."

Chapter Fourteen

Devon made it outside without breaking into a run. He found Frasier's car and dropped behind the steering wheel. He dug for his cell, selected the contact for Mariah and then started the car.

He had merged into traffic by the time she answered. That she answered at all startled him.

"I wondered how long it would take you to call, Devon."

A searing anger blazed through him, banishing the shock. He fought hard to muster a reasonably calm voice. "What the hell are you doing, Mariah? Richard is dead. Where are you?"

Deep breath. Don't let her hear your fear.

"What? You're not even going to ask about your new friend? I saw the way you looked at her when the two of you visited my home that first time. I knew then that she was part of this, too."

A thread of sheer panic rushed through his veins. He had no idea where to go. Traynor was at the cottage. Bella wasn't there. Where would Mariah take her?

"Let's talk about this, Mariah. Tell me where to meet you. We'll work out whatever the problem is together. I'm prepared to do whatever you say."

His tone sounded reasonable, calm, though every muscle and nerve in his body strummed with bone-shattering tension.

"We're waiting for you at your home, Devon. Now, be very smart, old friend. Come alone. No police. We can settle this among ourselves, I believe. But if you force my hand, your sweet little friend will have to join Richard in hell. We both know you don't want that."

The call ended.

Devon took a breath and drove to a less busy area of the city to determine if the police were following him. He had a feeling that was the reason for the visit to the station. Otherwise the detectives could certainly have continued to interrogate him at his office. Obviously they had wanted to set up a situation and then watch his reaction. Then all they had to do was follow close behind him.

He executed a couple of turns to take him into a less traffic-heavy area. After a couple more turns, he spotted the dark sedan making all the same maneuvers. This was one time he would have preferred to be wrong.

Devon couldn't remember the last time he'd attempted to outmaneuver or outrun another vehicle. Perhaps when he was a teenager. He supposed it was never too late to determine if he possessed the necessary skills. One rapid-fire turn after the other, first right, then left, then right again, and he accelerated past a garbage truck and then veered down an alley on the left.

From there, he retraced his route via a couple of different streets and headed for the one that would take him to I-90. If he pushed the speed limit as far as he dared and still avoided being pulled over, he could make it to his house in fifty minutes.

At the next required stop, he sought and found the number for the Colby Agency. When the receptionist had transferred his call to Victoria, he explained the situation. The step was the only one he felt fully confident in taking.

"First," Victoria said, "slow down. I don't want you arriving at your home until I have people on-site."

"She warned me to come alone," he reminded his old friend. "I will not risk Bella's life by going against Mariah's demands."

"Traynor and McAllister know what they're doing, Devon," Victoria reminded him. "Sutter will not be aware they are there until they're ready for her to know."

Devon ordered his heart rate to slow. He drew in a slow, deep breath. "All right. Tell me what to do."

"I'll give you the heads-up when Traynor and McAllister are in place. Then you'll go to the house exactly as Sutter requested. Try to engage her with dialogue. People who do this have something to say. Listen. Be sympathetic. But be careful not to sound patronizing. She needs to see and feel your fear. This is real, and if she suspects that you're not worried or afraid, she'll know she's been set up."

"Very well. I'll drive the speed limit and wait for your call."

"We've got this, Devon. Keep in mind that Bella is a highly trained former detective. She knows how to take care of herself."

Devon thanked Victoria and focused on driving.

Victoria was right. Bella was more than capable. But that didn't make him feel any better about the situation. There were so many things he wanted to learn about her. For the first time in years, he wanted to feel something more than mere respect and compassion for an-other human being. He wanted a relationship with Bella.

He wanted to share a life with her for however long she would have him. He wanted to make her his.

Devon laughed out loud at the preposterous thought. Bella would be the first to tell him that she belonged to no one but herself. Whatever relationship they were able to build together, it would be one of mutual respect and admiration. Perhaps not completely. He wasn't sure she could ever feel the same fierce need for him that he felt for her. It was too early to label his feelings precisely, but they were strong.

For now, he wanted the opportunity to explore those feelings and every part of this fascinating woman.

If she was willing.

He refused to consider that one or both of them might die today.

Arbor Drive, Lake Bluff, 5:30 p.m.

BELLA'S EYES FLUTTERED OPEN. A distant ache throbbed in the back of her head. There was something she needed to remember.

Something she needed to do...

Mariah. Mariah Sutter.

Bella willed her body to sit up. The room spun and her stomach churned as if she might vomit. She scrubbed her hand across her face. Her body felt as if it belonged to someone else. What the hell was wrong with her?

She tried to clear her throat...tried to swallow. Her mouth felt dry.

Where was she? She looked around. Not the cottage. She blinked until her eyes focused on the fire-place across the room.

Devon's house.

"You're awake. Good."

Bella jerked at the sound of Mariah's voice. The throb in her head deepened and she felt ready to pass out again. As if she were watching for someone, Mariah stood by the window at the end of the room that faced the front of the property.

I need the new security code.

Bella vaguely remembered hearing the question over and over. Had she given Mariah the code? She must have. Devon had changed it after his house manager's murder. Mariah couldn't have known it otherwise. Now she remembered. The blow to her head had rattled her. She probably had a concussion considering she'd been unconscious for a bit. Mariah had disarmed her, roused her and forced her into the car she'd been driving.

Richard was dead.

Mariah had killed him.

The bitter taste in Bella's mouth made her want to gag. She suppressed the reflex. Mariah had given her something. A drug.

She squeezed her eyes shut and shook her head. The pain in her skull throbbed.

"Don't worry. I didn't give you very much. It should be almost worn off by now." Mariah strolled toward the sofa Bella had been lying on. "Liquid morphine. The pills weren't really working for me. The doctors want me to be comfortable at this stage. The past couple of days have been hell. I didn't expect the pain to become so bad so quickly."

Bella licked her lips. "You're dying," she guessed.

A weary sigh echoed from the other woman. "That's what they tell me. Frankly, until a couple of days ago, I secretly hoped they'd made a mistake. The pain is no fun, but the disease hasn't really slowed me down until lately. I swear to God, when that fool Harper tried to kill me with her damned butcher knife, I thought she might succeed. All I needed was the key and the security code to the house. Who knew she would go shopping without her list and have to come back for it. I didn't want to kill her but she left me no choice."

"Why did you do any of this?" Bella asked. The longer she could keep the woman talking and distracted, the more time she would have for shaking the effects of the drug.

"They stole everything from me," she said without hesitation. "Richard took my youth. Refused to have children. And then he had the audacity to try to seduce Cara. She came to me and cried. She was so certain it was her fault. We ended up crying together. One thing turned into another, and the next thing we knew, we were making love." She walked back to the window and stared out. "I have never loved anyone the way I loved Cara. We had everything planned. Then Richard got sick and we agreed that I should see him through that hard time." She shook her head. "That was our mistake. If we'd walked out as planned, we would have had all this time together."

Bella used the arm of the sofa and pulled to her feet. She swayed.

"When he was finally back on his feet again, Cara and I resumed our plans. Everything was arranged. She wanted to get away from Chicago for a week or so after breaking the news to Devon. I was to join her in New

York after he left. Only none of that ever happened. First, Richard found out and went ballistic. He made all sorts of threats, but we got through that one. Then there was the accident." Her voice drifted off.

"But you stayed with Richard anyway," Bella said, braced against the end of the sofa. She wasn't quite steady enough to trust herself to rush across the room and tackle the woman. Hopefully she would get there soon.

Was Mariah armed? She no doubt had Bella's weapon.

"I was too devastated to do anything else," Mariah went on, seeming to talk more to herself than to Bella. "I couldn't sleep or eat. It was as if my life had ended, too. Really, I suppose it had. The only difference was that I was still breathing. Richard and Devon started to have trouble and suddenly Richard was determined to destroy Devon's career. For a time, that was enough. Then last year, I received my own death sentence. Lung cancer. The worst kind. Something snapped inside me." She shrugged, her expression distant. "I realized that men like Richard and Devon had stolen the past as well as the future I deserved—that Cara and I deserved. And I was furious."

She stared out the window again and Bella tested her legs once more. One slow step at a time, she moved to the other sofa, just ten or so feet, but it was something. She leaned against it as she had the other sofa.

"It must have taken a great deal of planning to set up such an elaborate plan." Bella needed her talking again. "Why not just kill him? It would have been so much easier."

"Because killing him wasn't enough!" Mariah said, her voice vibrating with emotion. "You can't imagine.

Within days of learning I was dying, I started to plan. Before I killed either one of them, I wanted to make Devon suffer. To question his own sanity. And if nasty rumors about him started circulating and ruined his hospital—his *baby*—even better."

"Using the Cara look-alike was ingenious," Bella offered. "But did you have to kill the driver and the mechanic?"

"Men are so stupid." Mariah reached beneath her jacket and withdrew a .32. "The mechanic tried to back out on me after I'd paid him so handsomely. The driver, as it turns out, was Maynard's pimp boyfriend and he tried to demand more money." She laughed. "Killing them was practice. I'd never murdered anyone before. I wanted to make sure I could do it. A dress rehearsal."

"I guess Unger was lucky, then, since he survived." Bella's head had stopped spinning. The pain was worse but at least she could think clearly and stand upright without swaying.

"I had every intention of killing the little bastard. I caught him in my house. He was trying to find evidence of what I was up to for Richard. Richard had his suspicions but he couldn't prove a damned thing. The only thing he could do was stay hidden so I wouldn't kill him first. Coward."

"So now you're going to kill Devon, is that it?" Bella wished for water.

Mariah cocked her head and eyed Bella. "I can't stomach the thought of him living one day more than I do. So, yes, I'm going to kill Devon. But first, I'm going to kill you. Like Harper, I really don't want to hurt you, but I have to use whatever is at my disposal to get the job done."

Bella made a face of confusion. "What did I do? I was only hired to help him figure out what was going on. I had nothing to do with taking Cara from you or the cancer eating away at your lungs."

Mariah smiled. "You were a surprise. I wasn't worried when he hired your agency. I was confident in my plan and the steps I'd taken to cover my tracks. But when I saw the two of you together that first time, I knew I'd been given the coup de grâce. He has feelings for you. Maybe not the kind of feelings I had for Cara but something. So before I kill him, I'm going to take you away from him. He deserves to know how that feels. He should be here any moment."

Bella didn't have a lot of time. Traynor would have figured out she was in trouble and be working on some kind of backup. Apparently Mariah had given Devon their location. If Devon was smart, and Bella knew he was, he would have called Traynor or Victoria.

Mariah's plan had failed already.

As true as that most likely was, Bella understood the variables in any operation's projected outcome. Something could always go wrong and someone could end up dead. She had no weapon. She'd been drugged and the effects weren't completely worn off. The odds were not stacked in her favor.

But she'd never been a quitter and she wasn't about to start now.

"See," Mariah said with a glance out the window. "I knew he'd come alone." She sent a sinister look at Bella. "He does care about you. Otherwise he would have stayed in his office and sent the police to handle the matter."

Bella braced for making some sort of move. Devon

likely knew he was walking into a trap. If Mariah took some time to taunt him, it would give Bella more of a chance to make a move.

Mariah watched as Devon emerged from the car.

It was now or never.

Bella ran. She was barefoot, so she made it several yards before Mariah realized she had moved.

"Stop! Or I'll shoot!"

Bella darted through the cased opening and into the dining room. True to her word, Mariah fired off a shot.

Bella cut through the kitchen and raced into the entry hall just as Devon was opening the front door.

"Out!" she shouted. "Go back out!"

Devon dived for her.

They hit the floor.

Two shots exploded in the entry hall, echoing like thunder.

Bella's head was spinning again. The room tilted.

Another shot fired. This one shattered the glass in the door.

Devon scrambled to his feet and charged Mariah.

Bella scrambled onto all fours. She launched herself up and rushed to where Mariah and Devon struggled.

Mariah still had the weapon. Devon forced her hand and the .32 away from his head. The weapon fired.

Bella jerked at the sound as the bullet plowed into the plaster wall.

Traynor and McAllister barged into the room.

The next pull of the trigger was followed by a hollow sound. Mariah had fired her final round.

Traynor snatched the weapon from her hand and Devon got to his feet. McAllister subdued her with a pair of nylon cuffs. Despite knowing she'd lost and that her game was over, she ranted and railed about getting Devon one way or the other.

Bella leaned against the wall. She couldn't remember when she'd felt so tired.

"Are you all right?" Devon surveyed her as if terrified that she was gravely injured.

Bella managed a smile. "I'll live. She hit me in the head with something and then drugged me with morphine." She met his gaze. "She's dying. Lung cancer."

Mariah had lapsed into sobs. Sirens were blaring outside.

Devon demanded, "Let me have a look at you."

While the police came in and removed Mariah Sutter, Devon examined the back of Bella's head and checked her eyes and reflexes.

"I'm taking you to the Edge," he said when he'd finished. "I want a full workup. A traumatic brain injury is nothing to scoff at."

"I'm fine, really," she argued. There was no need to make a fuss.

Devon disregarded everything she said. He answered a few questions for the officer as Mariah was escorted out. He promised that he and Bella would come in tomorrow and make official statements.

"Go," Traynor said when Devon looked to him. "McAllister and I will take care of things here."

"This really isn't necessary," Bella tried again.

"Listen to the doc," Traynor ordered.

McAllister folded his beefy arms over his chest. "Don't make one of us have to carry you out of here."

Bella rolled her eyes and relented. "Fine." She turned to Devon. "Let's get this over with."

The Edge, 10:00 p.m.

DR. FRASIER STUDIED the monitor. Devon stared over her shoulder.

Bella exhaled a big breath, hoping they would hear it and realize she was waiting. When they both continued to stare at the monitor and talk quietly to one another, she said, "Well?"

"The concussion is mild," Dr. Frasier said as she turned to Bella. "You'll need someone seeing after you for a few days. If you have a headache that gets worse or any weakness, numbness or—"

"I'll be taking care of her," Devon interrupted. "I know the warning signs to watch for." To Bella, he said, "It's important that you're not alone. No driving or overexertion for at least forty-eight hours."

Bella hugged her arms around herself and the unflattering hospital gown she'd had to change into for the MRI. "Yay me."

Dr. Frasier smiled warmly. "Don't worry. Most of the time, symptoms don't linger for more than a few days. I'll write your discharge order." She left the room.

"We could take a vacation."

Bella looked up at him. "A vacation?" She held her breath. Where was he going with that?

He leaned against the table next to her, tucked a wisp of hair behind her ear with one long finger. "The business part of our relationship is over now."

"I still have to do my final report," she argued.

"I'm certain Victoria would understand if your report was delayed."

Her heart wouldn't stop pounding. She needed to think. To reason this all out. "But you have so much to do here. How can they possibly run this place without you?"

He traced the swell of her cheek. "I have complete confidence in my staff, and the truth is, I've recently realized that I need more than work."

"What is it you want to do, Dr. Pierce?"

She didn't want to read too much into this. Stressful situations—life-and-death ones in particular—often made people reach out to one another. Then, when the stressor had passed, those passions faded. She had no desire to make more of this than it was.

"I want to be with you," he said bluntly. "I want to know you—all of you. I want to begin right now. This minute."

She smiled as his lips brushed hers. "But we're in the ER."

He straightened, backed away from her. All the way to the door. He locked it.

Her heart skipped a beat. "I thought I wasn't supposed to overexert myself or something like that."

He walked the few feet back to where she sat on the exam table. Just watching him move made her pulse react. "You don't have to do anything but enjoy. Besides, I'm a doctor. I can take care of any situation that arises. Trust me."

He spread her legs and moved between them. "Aren't there rules against this behavior with a patient?" she teased.

He kissed that sensitive skin beneath her ear. "You're not *my* patient."

She shivered with the feel of his breath against the damp skin.

"I want to take you away from here." He left a kiss

along her jawline between each word. "Make love to you every day and every night for as long as you're willing."

His lips brushed her collarbone and she shook with pleasure. "As soon as I'm well enough," she countered.

He drew back. Studied her flushed face. "Of course." His hand worked its way beneath her gown and up to her bare breast. He squeezed. "How are you feeling now?"

She whimpered. "Good."

He moved on to the other breast and massaged her nipple between his fingers. Pleasure shot through her.

"Good?" he asked.

"Oh yes."

His hand slid down her rib cage, fingers reaching between her thighs, finding that damp heat that yearned for his touch. He pressed his mouth to her ear and whispered all the ways he intended to make her come as his fingers worked their magic. His free arm went around her waist, held her steady as he brought her closer and closer to orgasm. Then he gripped her tight and finished sending her over the edge.

She bit her lips together to prevent crying out with the pleasure that pulsed through her. Blindly, she reached for his fly, but he gently pushed her hands away. "Later," he murmured. "This was just a taste of all the ways I'm going to make you come apart in my arms."

She grinned. "You know what they say about payback."

"I look forward to it." He reached for the bag at the end of the table. "Now let's get you dressed so I can take you out of here."

He helped her dress. They laughed when she swayed

and kissed when they couldn't bear not to. It felt good. It felt right.

"I'm suddenly starving," she said as he slipped her shoes on her feet.

"I know a place not far from here that stays open until midnight. You good with Italian?"

"I love Italian."

When he held her hand as they walked out of the room, Bella's chest filled to bursting. It wasn't the let-me-help-you kind of touch. It was the I-want-to-hold-your-hand touch.

They spoke to the nurses and to Dr. Frasier as they left. It was as if he wanted them all to see that they were together. She liked that he didn't try to hide what he was feeling.

Outside, they walked slowly in the cool night air to his car. He'd had a driver pick up the one he'd borrowed, fill the gas tank and return it to Dr. Frasier. Traynor had told her that even before he and McAllister left the Lake Bluff house someone had been there, making the needed repairs after Mariah's shooting spree.

Devon opened her door and helped her into the car. By the time she fastened her seat belt, he was sliding behind the wheel.

"Where are we going on this vacation?" she asked, though she didn't really care. She would gladly go any-where with him.

"Where would you like to go?"

She thought about that for a moment, then turned his question on him. "Where would *you* like to go?"

He backed out of the slot and paused to look at her. "Anywhere, as long as you're there."

She laughed. "I was just thinking the same thing."

Chapter Fifteen

The Edge, Sunday, June 10, 2:00 p.m.

"You have a second-degree burn, Mr. Camp," Dr. Frasier announced.

Victoria sent Lucas a pointed look. "Told you so."

Lucas sighed, his expression downtrodden. "Yes, you did. What's the plan, Dr. Frasier?"

Dr. Frasier smiled. "It's not that bad, Mr. Camp. I'm sure you know that with a second-degree burn the damage extends a little deeper than the top layer of skin. The area is already red and sensitive but you will most likely see blistering as well. How did you say you burned yourself?"

"The barbecue grill," he confessed. "It's a biweekly ritual during the summer."

Victoria squeezed her dear husband's uninjured hand. "Only this time, someone wasn't paying attention."

As Lucas and Dr. Frasier chatted about the steps that would be taken, which weren't so bad—cleaning and applying an antibiotic and then bandaging—Victoria thought of how frightened she had been when she'd watched him reach for the veggie basket without the protection of an oven mitt. At their age, it wasn't unusual on occasion to forget where you left the keys or to forget what you walked into a room to look for, but to forget to protect your hand when you reached for a hot item and then to hang on to it until you moved it to the counter was outside the boundaries of acceptable. She would be watching her dear husband closely going forward.

Her heart ached at even the mere thought of what this could mean.

Victoria pushed away the painful idea. "I understand Devon and Bella made it safely to Saint-Tropez."

Frasier smiled. "They did."

Lucas gave her a wink. "I hear you're in charge while he's gone."

She laughed. "I am. Dr. Pierce hasn't designated a deputy administrator, so I'm it for now. Well, with Ms. Ezell's support, of course. She runs that office anyway."

Victoria knew well that there was nothing more valuable than a top-notch secretary or personal assistant. "I'm certain you'll do fine."

"Thank you." The doctor gave Lucas a pat on the shoulder. "Mr. Camp, I'll have Nurse Bowman come in and take care of you. Just keep the injured area clean. Apply an antibiotic cream once a day and keep it bandaged for a few days and you'll be as good as new before you know it."

"Thanks, Dr. Frasier."

Forty-five minutes later, they were headed home. The white bandage was stark against her husband's tanned hand.

"Lucas, I'm worried about you."

He turned to her, watched her for a while. Victoria kept her gaze on the street and traffic.

"In what way, my dear? The burn isn't so bad."

He wasn't going to like this very much. "You picked up the pan without an oven mitt and you held it for several seconds—long enough to move it—before you let go."

"Not such a smart move," he agreed. "I wasn't thinking." He reached over and patted her hand with his good one. "I assure you it was nothing more. Just an absentminded moment that I will regret for at least a week or so."

She hoped that was the case. "You haven't had any other similar moments that you haven't told me about, have you?"

"I certainly have not."

Victoria felt some amount of relief at hearing him say so. Still, her heart ached with worry.

"Do you want the truth?" he asked.

She glanced at her husband. "I not only want it, I expect it!" What sort of question was that?

"We have a rather important anniversary coming up."

Twenty years. Victoria's smile was automatic. She and Lucas had been married for almost twenty years.

"I've been planning this very special getaway. I was actually considering Saint-Tropez. I thought I would ask Bella when she returns if it was as wonderful as the rumors suggest. At any rate, I'm found out now."

"Lucas, that sounds lovely." She reached over and placed a hand on his leg. "I'd love to go to Saint-Tropez."

"You're always arranging things for others, Victoria," he said. "I wanted to do this for you—for us. I wanted it to be a surprise."

She reached for his hand and entwined her fingers with his. "It's a lovely surprise. I'm so pleased."

"I was only distracted and not paying attention." He

squeezed her fingers. "I will tell you if I ever feel there's something not quite right about any part of me."

"Is that a promise?"

"It is."

"Good." She exhaled a big breath. "I won't worry anymore, then."

This was, of course, not entirely true, but she would try.

"While you were taking care of the paperwork, Eva Bowman told me a troubling story about Dr. Frasier."

Victoria took the next turn. "So you were gossiping with your nurse," she teased.

"I certainly was. Eva is worried about Dr. Frasier. Apparently her former husband has given her trouble from time to time. He's just out of prison after a one-year stretch for felony domestic violence."

"Was Dr. Frasier the victim?"

"Unfortunately."

"Has she seen someone about a restraining order?" Not that a mere restraining order would stop the determined. But it made things simpler when the police were called.

"She has not. Eva said she'd already urged Dr. Frasier to take that step. She also gave her our number and suggested she consider calling us."

"I hope she will."

"I think I'll have Jamie do some research," Lucas said. "Find out who this guy is and where he is."

"Excellent idea. If Dr. Frasier needs us, we'll be prepared."

"Speaking of Jamie," Lucas said, "did you know she has a new boyfriend?"

"Did she tell you this?" Victoria sent him a sideways glance. She was utterly envious that he'd heard this news before she had.

"I saw it on one of her social-media pages."

Victoria frowned. "Are you monitoring our grand-daughter's accounts again?"

"I'm one of her newest friends, Lucky Luke."

Victoria laughed. "Lucky Luke?"

"Why not? I'm the luckiest man alive because you're my wife."

Victoria braked for a light and turned to him. "You are so charming, Lucas. We're both very lucky." She grinned. "What does this young man look like?"

The light changed and she rolled forward with the flow of traffic.

"Tall and handsome, of course. He's a senior at the University of Chicago."

"Have you looked into him and his family?"

"The boy's pedigree is noteworthy. I'm sure you will approve."

Victoria sighed. "Time is traveling far too fast, Lucas."

"It is." He squeezed her hand once more. "We've seen and done so much, been through so much. But, good God, what a ride."

This was true. Victoria smiled. So very true.

* * * * *

BLACK ROCK GUARDIAN

JENNA KERNAN

For Jim, always.

Chapter One

At the sound of tires crunching on the gravel drive, Ty Redhorse glanced up from beneath the hood of the '76 Cadillac Eldorado to see two cop cars pull before the open bay of his garage. His heart sank as he straightened and came to attention, as if he was still in the US Marines. The tribal police vehicles rolled to a stop. Trouble, he thought, arriving on his doorstep.

They only had six men on the Turquoise Canyon force, and two of them were here at his shop. That did not bode well, and the fact that one of them was his younger brother only made things worse. He and Jake rarely spoke and when they did it usually ended badly. But Jake had been by yesterday and Ty had been touched to see how relieved Jakey was to see him alive and well. Small wonder after what Ty had been through.

Hemi, Ty's dog, had been even happier, showing her unrestrained joy at finding him again. Jake had Hemi out searching and she tracked him, but by then he'd already made it home to the rez and to Kee, who stitched him up. Wasn't easy because he'd lost a lot of blood.

Jake cast him a worried look and glanced at Ty's shoulder as he put his unit in Park. Clearly Kee had told him about the injury. Ty inclined his chin at Jake.

The little brother Ty had helped raise, and protect

from the gang, had turned out fine. The late-day sun
of an ordinary Friday afternoon in late October gilded
Jake's skin, and the uniform gave him an air of respect-
ability. Ty smiled, unable to resist indulging in the pride
that rose in his chest at Jake inside his SUV.

The big man stepped from his police unit. That was
Jack Bear Den, the tribe's only detective, since they'd
rescinded the offer to hire detective Ava Hood. Now,
there was a woman after his heart, breaking the law to
get her niece back. Yes, her career had imploded, but
Ty would bet she didn't regret a thing.

Bear Den took charge of the most important cases on
the rez. And he was here. Ty's eyes narrowed. Not good.

"Hello, Ty," said Bear Den, extending his paw of a
hand.

Ty glanced at the rag he held, knowing he could use
it to wipe away the worst of the motor oil, but opted
against it. He accepted Jack's hand and watched as realization dawned. Bear Den's clean palm was now slick
with filthy brown motor oil. Ty's smile brightened. The
day was looking up.

"This is a surprise. You boys need an oil change?"
asked Ty.

Jack shook his head.

"Search my shop?" He motioned to the interior.

It wasn't really a joke. They'd done it before. But Ty's
days of running a chop shop were over. He had medi-
ated a position that allowed him to exist on the fringe
of the tribe's gang, the Wolf Posse, which had helped
him when no one else would. All that had changed when
each of his brothers needed his help. Getting that help
had been costly. And one, two, three, the gang had him
again. Favors did not come free.

He was caught.

Bear Den held his smile as he kept his right hand well away from his spotless clothing.

"It's clean," said Ty, indicating the Cadillac with its hood up. "Even have the paperwork."

"I believe you," said the detective. "I saw the car you restored for the chief's boy, Gus. The detailing is amazing."

Ty's eyes narrowed at the flattery.

Jake was now making his way over. He, at least, knew not to block the bay doors with his vehicle. His little brother had the look of a man who wished to be anywhere but where he was. He came to a stop two steps behind the detective, making it clear who was in charge. Ty's gaze flicked to Jake's and he read stress in his brother's wrinkled brow. Jake did not think this would go well. Ty flicked his focus back to Bear Den.

"What can I do for the boys in blue?" Ty's hand went to his forearm and he rubbed his thumb over his skin where his gang tattoo sat below the one of the marine emblem that he'd had done when in the United States Marine Corps. When he realized what he was doing, he forced his hand to his side. The grease covered most of the ink anyway.

"We're here about our missing girls," said Bear Den.

Ty knew about the missing teenagers. Suspected he knew far more than Detective Bear Den.

Police had a crime, they needed a suspect. So what crime was Jack Bear Den interested in pinning on him?

"When you getting married to that Fed, Jack?" asked Ty, changing the subject and using the detective's first name with the desired result. Bear Den's face flushed. "She's an explosives expert, right? Should make life interesting."

Bear Den did not take the bait, but he shifted from one foot to the other. Ty had him off balance.

Bear Den glanced to Jake, who stepped alongside his superior, hands on hips, as if he even had the least control of his oldest brother. Jake had two years of community college and had passed the test and joined the force right after graduation. But he'd never joined the Marine Corps or seen the kind of horrors both Ty and his youngest brother, Colt, had witnessed. Thank God.

Maybe that was why Jake felt comfortable with a gun strapped to his hip while Ty had had his fill of them in the marines.

To Jake there was right and there was wrong. That must be so comforting, not to be bothered with all those shades of gray. But who had Jake called when he realized that little white newborn he had already fallen in love with was in danger? Not the tribal police force.

"We have reason to believe that the Wolf Posse is responsible for the selection of the women that the Russian mob is targeting," said Bear Den. "Our women."

"Girls, wouldn't you say?" said Ty. "What I hear, not one is over nineteen and Maggie Kesselman's only fourteen. Right?"

Ty folded his arms, the grease on his palms sliding easily around his formidable biceps.

"You didn't deny gang involvement," said Bear Den.

"What tipped you off, Minnie Cobb attacking the health clinic, or Earle Glass trying to snatch Kacey Doka back?" Ty asked, naming the two gang members now in custody. The gang had already written them off, so no risk of revealing new information there. "Or maybe it was my big brother, Kee, helping you find that kidnapped detective on loan. What was her name? Detective Hood, right? Way I hear it, Kee has a new girlfriend and you got a new dispatcher. How does Carol Dorset feel about that?" he asked, mentioning the woman who had held the position since before Ty was born.

Bear Den scowled and his gaze shifted to Ty's injured shoulder.

Ty resisted the urge to test the stitches. Kee had put them in himself two days ago after Ty managed to make it the twenty odd miles from Antelope Lake to the rez. Once he was back on tribal land, the Feds could not touch him. So they'd sent Bear Den to rattle his cage.

Ty gave in and scratched his left shoulder. The stitches were beginning to itch.

Jake's face flushed and he pressed his lips between his teeth, clearly unhappy to be placed between his idol and his embarrassment of a brother. His worried expression, as he braced for what Ty would do next, just burned Ty up. Afraid he'd have to arrest him, probably. Ty would like to see him try.

His brother seemed to have put on weight since he'd married Lori Mott, but Ty knew he could still take him because Jake and Kee both fought fair, while he and his youngest brother, Colt, fought to win.

"So, you boys have any idea what will happen to me if one of the Wolf Posse drives by and sees two cop cars parked at my shop?" asked Ty.

"I'd imagine it would be easier to explain than if I haul your ass into the station as an accessory to kidnapping," said Bear Den.

Bear Den was talking about Ty transporting Colt's girl, Kacey, off the rez and back to her captors two and a half weeks ago. Not kidnapping, but darn close, and he was sure the tribal police would not appreciate the subtle differences. He was in serious risk of the tribe bringing charges against him, possibly turning the case over to the attorney general, and Bear Den was all for that.

"Shouldn't you be chasing the guys that blew up our dam?" asked Ty.

Bear Den's mouth quirked. "I'm multitasking. Now, you want to talk to us here or there?"

Ty faced off against the big man. He knew he could not take Bear Den in a fair fight, but he had a length of pipe just inside the open bay door. "What do you want, exactly?"

"Just some help," said Jake, standing with palms out. "These are our girls that they're taking. We want them back."

Ty had no objections to that. He just didn't want to stop breathing because of it. "What's that got to do with me?"

Bear Den took over again. His hair was growing out and it curled like a pig's tail at his temples. Ty wondered again just who had fathered this monster of a man. Certainly not Mr. Bear Den, who was big but not supersized.

"No secret you're in the Posse." Bear Den pointed to the grease-smeared tattoo of four feathers forming a *W* for wolf on Ty's forearm. The gang was an all-Native branch of the Three Kings, wore the yellow and black colors of that group and had adopted an indigenous symbol that resembled the crown worn by the Kings while representing their Native culture.

"I'm retired."

"No such thing," said Bear Den.

True enough. A better word would have been *inactive*. He knew more than he would like and less than he used to, which was still too much. And he owed favors. Way too many favors.

Ty no longer did their dirty work, but he looked the other way. Kept their cars running smoother and faster than law-enforcement vehicles and drove the occasional errand. He did what was necessary. There was just no other way to survive in a brotherhood of wolves.

"We need to know how they choose the targets, if they have targeted anyone else and where the missing are being held."

Ty could never find out that last one because the gang only snatched and delivered. They did not store the taken. That was the Kuznetsov crime family, a Russian mob that dealt in women the way a farmer deals in livestock. Buy. Sell. Breed. And they were just one of many. The outer thread of a network that stretched around the world.

"Is that all?" asked Ty, and smirked.

Bear Den's frown deepened. The man was aching to arrest him, but the tribal council had voted against turning Ty over to the Feds after the incident with Kacey Doka because her statement included that she had wished to be returned to her captors and that she accepted a ride from Ty. In other words, no coercion or capture, so not kidnapping. Ty suspected the fact that he was walking around free burned the detective's butt.

"That would do it," said Bear Den.

Ty leaned back against the grill of the Caddy and folded his arms, throwing up the first barricade. "I don't know if they have more targets. I don't know where the missing are being held and I don't know how they choose."

"But you could find out," said Jake.

Ty gave his brother a look of regret.

"Help them, like you helped me," whispered Jake as he extended his right hand, reaching out to his big brother from across a gap too wide for either of them to cross.

"You're family, Jakey. It's different." He thrust a hand into his jeans, feeling the paper with the address of the meet in his pocket. Ty rubbed the note between his thumb and index finger. "Listen, guys, I have a nice honest business here. So how about this, how about you do your job instead of asking me to do it?"

Bear Den glanced at his garage and the car beyond the Caddy.

"It's all legit, Bear Den. You can't get to me that way."

Bear Den snorted like a bull. "If they ask you for details on our investigation, could you feed them some false information?"

"They kill people for that."

Judging from his expression, that eventuality did not seem to bother the detective in the least.

"Bear Den, your police force arrested me and you did everything you could to get the tribe to turn me over to the Feds. I owe you, but not a favor."

"You threatening me?" asked the detective.

"That would be illegal. I am telling you, nicely, to piss off."

"We'd like you to meet someone," said Jake.

"Not happening."

"She's FBI," said Jake.

Ty laughed. "Oh, then let me rephrase. Not happening, ever."

Chapter Two

FBI field agent Beth Hoosay sat in the silver F-150 pickup with tribal police officer Jake Redhorse, waiting for full dark. Redhorse had parked across the highway and out of sight, but with a clear view of the roadside bar favored by bikers and Jake's older brother, Ty Redhorse. In the bed of the truck was her motorcycle, prepped and ready.

Earlier in the day, the tribal police detective, Jack Bear Den, had tried and failed to get Ty to meet with her. So they would do it the hard way.

It was beyond Beth's comprehension why the Turquoise Canyon Apache tribe's leadership had voted to keep Ty on the reservation instead of turning him over to the authorities for trial. And he was walking around free.

That was about to change, in twelve hours to be exact. Because Beth was about to meet Ty on his own turf tonight and with the advantage of him not knowing who and what she was. She had backup, but she did not intend to need it. The agents could hear everything she said and had eyes on her outside the roadside bar. Once she was inside, it would be audio only because Beth insisted that the other agents would never blend in a place like this. They'd be spotted as outsiders instantly.

She, on the other hand, had been in this joint once before when she was younger and more rebellious, after her dad had died, and she'd had the gall to date a guy who owned a bike. Worse still, he had taught her to ride. She was grateful for that much. The rest of their relationship had been less positive because it seemed to her that he'd wanted her only as an accessory to his chopper. Her mother said the bike would be the death of her and that the guy had been interested only because of her unique looks, which blended Native heritage with her father's Caribbean roots, and made her seem exotic to the son of a soybean farmer. Sometimes she just wanted to blend in. But today her looks were an asset and the reason she was here.

Beth had been handpicked for this assignment because she was Apache on her mother's side. Not Tonto Apache, like Ty Redhorse. Her Native ancestry came from the line that fought with Geronimo and lost, which was why her reservation was up in Oklahoma instead of here, where they had lost to the US Army with the help of this very tribe. She tried not to let it bother her, but many on her rez still thought the Tonto Apache were more desert people who could not even understand their language. They spoke a language that only they and God could understand.

Beth didn't care about old grudges. She cared about having a rare and shining opportunity to make a big case. The possibilities were so enthralling they made her chest ache. She wanted this, wanted the respect and acclaim that came with a bust of this importance.

Another truck pulled into the lot and a lone driver slid out and hiked up his jeans before slamming the truck door. The parking area was nearly full. They did good business on any Friday night, and tonight was no exception. Many of the men inside were just coming from work and others had no work but arrived when the bar was most crowded. She knew the establishment was most busy between five and eight and closed at midnight, except on weekends, when the place closed at two in the morning. It was approaching eight and she was beginning to worry that Ty might not show.

"He's usually here by now," said Jake. His voice sounded hopeful. "Maybe I should go in with you. It's a rough place."

"I don't need an escort, patrolman." She let him know with her tone just what she thought of his advice. Showing up with a police officer that everyone here knew was a terrible idea.

Beth had plans. She would investigate the missing women, tie their disappearances to the Kuznetsov crime family and make the kind of case that got a person noticed in the Bureau, and with that notice came the kind of posting Beth craved. Truth be told, she didn't like Oklahoma or the field office in Oklahoma City, known for the bombing of the federal building. She wanted a major posting with status in a place far away from the flat, windy plains. Unlike the army, the FBI measured rank with cases, postings and a title. So she set her sights on a major case, a major posting in a major office. The plan was to run a field office before she hit thirty-five. And Ty Redhorse could get on board or get out of her way, preferably in a small prison cell in Phoenix.

"That's him," said Jake, slumping down in his seat.

Beth smiled as Ty Redhorse roared into the dirt lot on a cream-and-coffee-colored motorcycle. The sled was a beauty, a classic Harley from the nineties, all muscle and gleaming chrome. She could not keep back her appreciation. She admired power.

Beth and Jake sat in the dark tucked up against the closed feed store across from the watering hole. Behind them, her guys sat in a van, their view blocked until Jake took off.

Ty had worked all day in his auto body shop according to surveillance. He had given no sign that his left shoulder had been recently ripped open while he was crashing through a picture window in a home in Antelope Lake. But that was the story his oldest brother, Kee, had told.

The man in question was trim and muscular and wore no helmet. He rolled to a stop right before the bar, as if he owned it, and Beth wondered if that space was reserved for him. His chopper fit perfectly between the black trucks that she knew belonged to members of the Wolf Posse, the tribe's one and only gang. Ty cut the engine, and the world went quiet. Then he planted his booted feet on both sides of his beautiful bike and rocked it to the stand as if it weighed nothing at all.

His driving gloves ended at his palms, giving her a flashing view of fingers raking through his shoulder-length black hair. He wore it blunt-cut in a traditional style so old she did not even know where it originated. The wind had done a job tousling his hair and he took a moment to set it right, raking his fingers back over his scalp. Then he threw a leg over the seat and dismounted the bike like a cowboy coming in off the range. He glanced around and looked right in their direction, gazing at them for a minute. Beside her, Jake held his breath and scooted lower in his seat.

"He can see us," whispered Officer Redhorse, more to himself, she thought, than her.

"Not unless he has night-vision goggles," she said, not whispering. He'd have to be some kind of jackrabbit to hear her from clear across the road. But she could hear him, thanks to the setup from the tech guys.

His gaze flicked away to a teen who was straddling an expensive new mountain bicycle that was, of course, black. On the boy's head sat a yellow ball cap, sideways, bill flat. He wore a new oversized black satin sports jacket. Beth made him for about thirteen because of his size. The gang colors were yellow and black, and Beth knew that recruitment started early. Ty went over to him.

"Who's that?" she asked Jake.

"Randy Tasa. Lives up in Koun'nde. He's in the ninth grade."

"Long bike ride."

"His sister, Jewell, is probably inside. She's Faras's girl."

Faras Pike was the current head of the Wolf Posse and one of the targets of her investigation.

Beth lifted the cone so she could hear them.

"Whatcha doing out here so late, Randy?" Ty asked. His voice was deeper than his brother's and held a dangerous edge.

"Deliveries."

Deliveries, my ass, thought Beth. The boy was selling weed to the customers. He was too young to get anything but a slap on the wrist, making him the perfect pusher for the gang.

"Let me see," ordered Ty.

The boy obediently reached into his coat and showed Ty the freezer bag filled with what Beth believed to be smaller baggies of weed.

"You make any money?" asked Ty.

"Some."

"Give it to me."

Was he actually shaking down a child?

"I'm supposed to give it to Chino."

"Did I ask you what you were supposed to do?"

The boy held out an envelope. Ty snatched it from him, took the weed and then took his cap. "This bag is light, Randy."

"No. I swear."

"Light," he repeated. "I'm telling Faras that you're a thief."

"No." Randy was crying now. "He'll kill me."

"He doesn't kill children. Run home, Randy, and don't come back or I'll put a cap in your ass."

Randy wiped his nose and Ty took one menacing step toward the boy, grabbing the handlebars of the new bike. "I said *run*."

The boy sprang from the seat and ran as fast as his sticklike legs would carry him. He was too young to be hanging around a bar. But not too young to have his services bought for a ball cap and a new bike. Ty might have done the boy a favor.

Beth pushed aside that thought.

Jake shifted in his seat. Yeah, she'd be uncomfortable, too, if this gem of humanity was her big brother. Luckily, she had no siblings and was free as a bird. She could pack everything she needed in the saddlebags of her bike and head to LA, DC or NY. But first she had to make a big case. Would her mother even notice she was gone?

Ty let the bike fall and headed for the door of the bar, carrying the weed in his leather bomber jacket, which was black, of course. Jake insisted that his brother operated on the fringes of the gang. Jake said that Ty's responsibility was only to keep the gang's cars running. All evidence pointed to the contrary.

He had enough weed on him right now for her to get a conviction, but since he was on the rez, arresting him would just get her in hot water with Lieutenant Luke Forrest, who headed this operation. She reported to him, for now. So she watched Ty walk away and ignored the bad taste in her mouth. If she got a break, she'd catch Ty Redhorse with something far more serious than a bag of weed. She didn't expect to get that lucky. Most of her luck came from hard work and taking the occasional risk.

She reached for the door release.

"Wait," she ordered Redhorse. "Don't leave unless you see me leave with your brother. Then follow us."

Beth had dressed in clothing that showed she was a woman but also concealed her high-performance liquid chromatography, abbreviated as HPLC and commonly known as pepper spray, her service weapon and handcuffs. On her right hand she wore a series of carefully selected rings designed to inflict maximum damage and lacerate skin should she have to throw a punch.

What she intended was to charm and pick up Ty Redhorse in front of all his buddies on his home turf. Tomorrow, well after all the customers in this watering hole had assumed that he'd made a successful score, Beth would let him know who and what she actually was. She suspected that Ty did not want Faras Pike, the leader of the posse, to know what he had done to help his older brother, Kee, and that he was on less than stable ground with the gang. A little more shaking might just get him on their side.

Risk and reward, she thought, and slid from the truck and onto the packed dirt parking area.

"Help me get my sled down," she said.

Jake lowered the back gate and set the metal ramp.

Because of the intentionally disabled starter motor, Beth needed to bump-start her motorcycle. She released the straps holding her bike and mounted the seat, then rolled it down the ramp in second, using the incline to get it going fast enough to allow the engine to engage.

She roared across the street, anticipating Ty's face tomorrow morning at eight, when he saw her walk into the interrogation room. Between now and then, she intended to find out everything she could about the second-oldest Redhorse brother.

Chapter Three

Ty walked into the roadhouse and glanced about. The mix of the usual patrons filled the stools surrounding the rectangular bar, which had seating all the way around except for the hinged portion that allowed the help in and out.

Beyond the center altar to drinking was the stage, which rose a good sixteen inches above the floor level but was dark because the musical entertainment didn't begin until nine. By then most of these men—working men—would be home with their families. They just needed a short transition between one and the other.

There were exceptions—men who were not drinking after work because they were still on the job. The first, Quinton Ford, sat on a bar stool. Quinton was lanky with close-cropped black hair and a hawkish face that bore acne scars on his gaunt cheeks. One hand rested in his open jacket as he used the half-lowered zipper like a sling. Ty knew his hand was on the grip of a pistol. Quinton faced the door with the other hand on his untouched beer. His eyes met Ty's, and Ty nodded to Faras Pike's man. Quinton raised his chin in acknowledgment and then his gaze flicked back to the door.

Ty was no threat to Faras Pike.

There were tables to the left and everyone knew the

ones under the wall of highway signs, stolen from all
over the state, were reserved for Wolf Posse members.
There at his usual spot was Faras Pike, the leader of
the tribe's gang. Perched on his knee was his current
favorite, Jewell Tasa.

Jewell wore a glittery sequined gold crop top that
featured an unobstructed view of her midriff, which was
tight and toned. Jewell's skinny jeans and biker boots
made her a shimmering billboard of gang colors. Her
makeup was thick, ringing her eyes like a raccoon, and
her long black hair had been bleached blond at the tips.

Faras spotted Ty before Jewell did, and lifted her
from his lap. Then he gave her rump an affectionate
pat to send her off to the group of women at the nearby
table. She spotted Ty and sauntered past him, hips swaying as if advertising what he could not have.

The unattached women at the table gave Ty encouraging smiles. He was not interested in more entangle-
ments with the gang, no matter how tight they wore their
clothing. So he turned his attention to Faras.

The head of the Wolf Posse was small with a face
that had been handsome once, but the smoking, drinking and responsibilities of his position weighed heavily
on that face and Faras now looked like a man nearing
forty, instead of twenty-eight. His hair was drawn back
in a single braid and he wore a hoodie, jeans, cowboy
boots that were all black and several thick gold chains
around his neck. His take on the black-and-gold color
scheme. His ears were pierced and he wore diamond
studs in each that Ty very much feared were real.

Seated between him and the bar was his second man,
Chino Aria, his newest favored muscle. Chino could
handle most situations if he didn't have to think or make
any decision on his feet. Chino's appeal came from his

size and bulk. The tattoos on his neck and bald head helped discourage trouble.

Ty cut a direct path for the two men.

"S'up, bro?" said Faras as he came to a stop before the circular booth and table.

"That little shit, Randy Tasa, is stealing your stash, is what's up," said Ty. He slid into the vinyl seat beside Faras. Chasing off Randy was a risk, because his big sister, Jewell, was already in the Wolf Posse and becoming Faras's favorite.

Chino looked none too happy at Ty's appearance, judging from the way his mouth tugged down on his broad jowly face.

"Randy Tasa? He don't work for me." Faras snapped his fingers before Chino's face, redirecting his stare from Ty to Faras. "Chino, we recruit Tasa?"

"Yeah," said Chino.

"When were you going to mention it?"

"First night, boss. Wanted to see how he worked out."

Ty scowled. You didn't earn a bike like that in one night. Chino was lying and Ty wondered why. It occurred to him that Randy would make a very good spy, keeping an eye on his big sister's business. But that was the sort of thing he'd expect Faras to pull. Perhaps he'd underestimated Chino?

Chino laid his beefy fists on the table, challenging Ty with his stare. Ty set the bag of weed on the padded bench between him and Faras.

"Yo, don't bring that in here," said Faras, sliding away.

"He was smoking the product instead of making sales. You get him that bike?"

Faras lifted a brow at Chino, who nodded. Faras glared. He knew how to recruit kids into the gang. Up until this minute, Ty thought the decision of when and who was recruited had rested solely with Faras. From the way he was glaring at Chino, perhaps Faras did as well.

"You picked it?" asked Faras.

Chino nodded.

Ty broke in. "Well, he tried to sell it to me for fifty bucks."

"That little puke," said Chino, coming awake. Unfortunately, he forgot he was sitting in a booth and so, when he stood, the bench did not move back and he collided with the table, sending their beer bottles sloshing to their sides.

Faras swore.

"Sorry, boss."

Chino used his sleeve to prevent the river of beer from reaching Faras's lap.

Ty tossed Randy's cap onto the puddle of beer. "I took his bike. It's out front."

Faras sighed and lifted a finger to Sancho, the head barkeeper, who was always very attentive to Faras, met his gaze and pointed to the spilled beer. One of the bartenders was out from behind the hinged counter and mopping up before Chino had even sat his big fat butt back down.

"I'll need to find a replacement," said Faras. "Deliveries, you know."

Ty knew there was no stopping that. But Randy had a future. He was a runner. A good one. If he was smart and lucky, he might just run out of Turquoise Canyon and make a life that did not involve allegiances to the posse. One little minnow, escaping the net. Ty felt a longing for a freedom from such allegiances, or at least to become something other than the family poster boy for wasted potential. He wasn't the only one who thought so.

Kee had been asked to join the Turquoise Guardians right out of med school, as if it was a foregone conclusion. Gaining admission to the tribe's medicine society was a coup that Ty coveted. But to be asked to join Tribal Thunder, the warrior sect of that medicine society, well, that was an honor above all others. Last month, they'd asked Jake to join.

"Chino, get rid of this and get me another beer," said Faras.

His man grabbed the baggie Faras pushed at him under the table, tucked it into his jacket and slid out of the booth. Then he hurried to the bar.

Faras waited until Chino and the bartender both retreated.

"You can't keep doing this," said Faras.

Ty said nothing.

"It costs me money and time."

Ty met his gaze and read the warning there. Things were serious now. With the pressure of the Russians and the tribal police bringing in the FBI, Faras was in a difficult spot. He could not afford to bring his suppliers less, to even let one little fish swim out of the net.

"That's the last one. You feel me?" said Faras.

Ty nodded.

"And where you been? I've been trying to reach you since Tuesday. You don't answer your phone or return my calls."

Ty told himself not to move his healing shoulder. Not to give away that he'd been injured, running for his life in the woods, trying to reach the reservation and home before the Feds caught him and locked him up beside his dad. Because if Faras knew, he'd also know that Ty followed his brother to the holding house that was stop one in the surrogate operation.

"I had a delivery in Phoenix. That '78 Nova. Matte-black."

"Phoenix and back takes six hours."

Ty met his gaze without shifting in his seat or offering further explanation.

Faras dragged his hand down his braid, tugged and then tossed it over his shoulder. "Listen, you asked me for a favor. You asked me to lie to my suppliers about a certain baby girl dying. I did that."

"And you already called that favor. Sent me on a pickup. I drove Kacey Doka at your request and I delivered her, didn't I?"

"And both those guys are dead."

"How you figure that's my fault?"

"It's your brother's fault. Colt killed them."

"He's not a dog on a leash. He loves Kacey."

"Love? Don't make me laugh. How did Colt know where to find those Russian dudes?"

"Dunno. Followed me?"

"You better hope that's how it went. If you tipped him…" Faras sat back in the booth and looked at the ceiling. Then dragged in a long breath and exhaled.

Ty read the signs. Now he was already in the danger zone. He regretted chasing off Randy. The timing had been bad.

Faras met his gaze across the table, his eyes flat and cold. "You still owe me for the baby. I'm calling it in. Moving you to transport."

"I delivered Kacey. That covers it."

"Not hardly. Two more of Vitoli's guys were killed in Antelope Lake."

"Too bad." Ty tried and failed to look sorry. The bastards had nearly killed Kee.

"And you were there."

"No."

"Says you."

Faras didn't know. He was fishing, putting together the pieces.

"No way," said Ty.

"Just making a three-day delivery of a Chevy Nova. Yeah, I heard. You want that baby to stay dead?"

Ty felt trapped. His entire life he'd been trapped. By his father, by the Marine Corps, by the gang. All he wanted in this shitty world was to have the chance, like Kee and Jake and Colt, to make something of himself. But he'd made his bed at eighteen. He didn't regret what he had done. But he never anticipated that by accepting Faras's help back then he would be tied to the man forever and painted with the same broad brush.

He wanted out. But if he left, just got on his bike and rode, who would protect his family from these predators that lived inside their rez like a nest of vipers?

The police couldn't do it, because they had laws to follow and they were outmatched in numbers and finances. The Feds couldn't do it. They didn't operate here unless invited and they flitted in and out like migrating birds while he wallowed down here in the mud.

"You hear me, Ty?" said Faras.

Ty nodded.

Faras leaned in. "I got a new operation. We're cookin' now. Ice."

Ty frowned, hating crystal meth and hating even more that the posse would be in production on his rez. "That so?"

"Yeah. First lab is in production up on Deer Kill Meadow Road. Old hay barn up there."

"Won't someone see the smoke?"

"Nights only. You gonna start transport next week."

The hell he was. "Sure."

Chino returned with the beer. Ty left his on the table, went to the bar and sat beside Quinton. Ty was sitting facing the taps when Quinton's foot dropped heavily off the bar stool as he sat forward. He did not reach for his gun, but his eyes widened and he looked as if someone had thrown a bucket of cold water in his face.

Ty spun on the swivel stool toward the door. A woman paused on the Budweiser floor runner and glanced about. Ty thought her attention paused on him, but that might have been wishful thinking.

"Damn," said Quinton. "Why I have to be working when something like that shows up?"

Ty thought it was a *someone*, not a *something*. But he agreed with Quinton that the woman was spectacular. She was tall with a confident stride and an economy of movement that spoke of power. Ty waited a beat for her partner to arrive and then it settled over him that this woman had come by herself to an unfamiliar watering hole, one with at least eight Harleys parked out front, and she had walked in with a self-assurance that showed either foolishness or strength.

Strength, he decided. That to him was more appealing than beauty because it took grit to survive up here. Both fortitude and compromise.

The tilt of her head and the way she scanned her surroundings gave her the air of a woman who knew what she was doing. There was no hesitation or wariness as she took in her surroundings. If he didn't know better, he'd say she owned the place.

The conversation lulled as one after another of both the single and married men considered their chances. Several of the men turned back to their beers, taking themselves out of the race by fidelity to their mates, or just by judging themselves to be farm-league players in a major league game.

Ty leaned forward and drank her in like water. High brown suede boots, with silver studs around each ankle, hugged her well-defined calves. Her jeans were dark, new-looking and tight, showing legs that went on and on. The cropped leather jacket seemed to have lived a long, interesting life as a favorite garment, and Ty resented the way it hugged her upper body and breasts. Below the bottom of the jacket was a wide silver rodeo buckle, the kind that was won, not purchased. From here, it looked like the lady was a world-class barrel racer. Oh, how he would love to see her ride.

Her fawn-brown skin held the luster of gold undertones, catching the light on her high cheekbones. She seemed multiracial. He thought he recognized the Native American lineage in her distinctive facial structure. Her pale eyes hinted at European roots, and she had full lips, light brown skin and a curl of her brown shoulder-length hair. A natural beauty.

Women, sitting beside their men, placed proprietary hands on their companions, claiming them as she again swept the room with a slow scan. Her gaze fell on him. Her mouth quirked and he saw trouble coming his way, again. Only this time he felt like walking out to meet it.

She raised her voice to be heard above the jukebox as she kept her eyes fixed on his. "I'm looking for Ty Redhorse."

Chapter Four

In Beth's opinion, the photos of Ty Redhorse did not do him justice. They didn't capture his roguish grin or his speculative stare. His mug shot, taken when he was just seventeen, showed a scared kid, and the one furnished by his brother pictured a man posing with his family as if he was uncomfortable in his own skin.

Maybe he was just uncomfortable with his family. Must be awkward at Sunday supper with his two remaining brothers. Comparisons were inevitable.

This man was broad-shouldered with a slim athletic frame. He also had the devil-may-care smile of a pirate. His forehead was broad and smooth, making him look more like twenty-one instead of twenty-eight. There was a slight, shallow cleft in his chin. One of his eyebrows lifted in conjecture. Dark eyes met hers and set off a flutter low and deep inside her.

She ignored the warning and continued on. Nerves, she told herself as she moved toward him. She might find Ty physically attractive, but he was just her admission ticket to the Wolf Posse, a means to an end. So it didn't matter how appealing she found his face and body. Beth liked bad boys, just not this one.

Still, there was something about him that made her regret the missed opportunity he presented. In another time and place she might have acted on impulse. But not now with so much on the line.

Beth had met his brother, Jake Redhorse, a rookie tribal officer, and had none of this immediate attraction. His younger brother had a look that she would describe as brooding. From the family photo, she thought the oldest brother, Kee, radiated the stability of a professional man with none of the indescribable edge of danger she found tempting. Unlike his oldest brother, this Redhorse man had none of that serious, stable aura. She knew of his youngest brother, Colt, only via computer records. Colt shared some of the defiant disregard she read in Ty's expression. But he also had PTSD and had given up speaking for months. That was way too much for her to ever want to take on. She met Ty's inquisitive stare. Everything about Ty seemed to broadcast mischief and the invitation to forget the rules and play.

"I'm Ty," he said.

All heads turned in his direction and then boomeranged back to her.

Beth had not anticipated the relaxed confidence of his physical self. He sat neither at attention nor slumped. Instead, he looked like he knew she was a problem heading toward him and he welcomed the diversion.

She used her thumb to adjust one of the rings on her right hand, breaking the steady stare. The man to his left was Quinton Ford, one of the Wolf Posse's higher-ups. Ty sat right beside the gang's right-hand man.

How cozy, she thought.

He rose to his feet in an easy glide, his movements as relaxed as his expression. But his eyes glittered a warning that belied the ready smile. "What can I do for you?"

"I've got bike trouble. The owner of the diner said

you were the man to see and he told me that I would find you here." She extended her hand. "I'm Beth."

He looked at her hand as if inspecting it and then his gaze flicked to her left hand. Was he searching for a ring on that all-important finger? Or the indentation and lighter skin that showed there had been one there recently? She wasn't sure, but there was a hesitation before his palm slid along hers in a sensual glide that made her skin pucker all over. His hand was clean, calloused. His nails showed the stain of stubborn motor oil. He gripped her hand and did not shake so much as stroke, his thumb caressing the sensitive skin on the back of her hand. Her heartbeat kicked up a notch and her lungs suddenly demanded more oxygen.

"Nice to meet you, Beth."

She drew back her hand, but it continued to tingle as if she'd just touched an electrified livestock fence.

"If you need a bike fixed," said Quinton Ford, interrupting, "you should ask Chino." He thumbed at the mountainous man sitting with the leader of the Wolf Posse.

"That so?" said Beth. "Why's that?"

"It's his specialty. Ty's is cars."

"A motor is a motor," said Beth. "And I don't think that Nathan would steer me wrong. What do *you* say, Ty?"

His smile relayed anticipation and mischief. "Let's have a look."

The whole point of coming here was to have everyone on his home turf see her leave with Ty and make the obvious conclusions. Her story to her supervisor, Luke Forrest, about getting a read on Ty was nonsense. She didn't need a read. All she ever wanted or needed to know about Ty Redhorse she'd found in his FBI file. What she desired was traction, an inescapable hook to get him on board, because he'd already turned down the Bureau's offer presented by his tribe.

If tomorrow morning, he discovered that he'd been seen leaving the roadside bar with an FBI field agent? Well, that was the sort of thing he might be inclined to want to keep to himself.

But Chino was on his way over. "I'll fix your bike," he said.

Beth had not anticipated a war over her sled. She definitely didn't want this mountainous wall of muscle to help her.

Ty stepped to intercept Chino Aria. "Lady asked for me."

"Because she doesn't know me," he said.

"And you're working," Ty reminded him.

Chino's expression went blank for a moment as his eyes lifted toward the ceiling. Then he glanced back at his boss, Faras Pike, who motioned to his muscle with two fingers.

"Master's calling," said Ty, just having to get a dig in, it seemed.

Not smart, thought Beth. If she wasn't undercover, she'd already have her hand on the grip of her pistol.

Chino shot Ty a glare that should have given him pause. Instead, it gave rise to a cocksure crooked smile that Beth admitted made her lips curl upward, as well. There was something satisfying about seeing the big man forced into retreat.

Chino pointed at Ty as if his finger was a gun. "Later," he said, and pulled the imaginary trigger.

Ty said nothing but scratched beside his mouth with his middle finger. Chino frowned and gave Ty one last angry look before he stalked away.

Ty motioned to the door. "Shall we?"

Beth swung her hips for all she was worth as she sauntered toward the exit. Just before leaving she grabbed Ty by the front of his black T-shirt and tugged. The kiss came naturally.

That surprised her. She'd thought it would feel forced. Unfortunately, they fit together all too well. Ty's mouth was hungry. His hands moved down her arms to capture her waist and tug. She did not resist, falling against him as he deepened the kiss.

She barely registered the hoots and banging from the customers, who all had ringside seats, as she'd intended. Beth closed her eyes and savored the velvety contact of his mouth and the sandy stubble of his cheek. She hadn't been really kissed in so long she had forgotten what it felt like.

As his tongue slid along hers and her body began to tingle in all the right places, she realized that she'd never been kissed like this. The warning bells sounded too late. She'd made a mistake, a costly one, because her body did not understand that this was work.

Beth broke away and saw that she'd wiped the crooked smile off Ty's face. He was now looking at her with a mixture of anticipation and healthy wariness. All large predators had that instinct—the ability to judge if he was facing an opportunity or a threat.

Ty reached past her and pushed open the door. The roar of the customers mixed with shouts of encouragement.

Someone shouted after them. "Fix that bike, Ty!"

Beth turned but not before she saw Ty wave to the crowd like the victor of some sporting competition. Beth smiled. He thought he'd won, but she believed that, in the interrogation room of his tribe's police station, when she flashed her badge, he might see things differently.

Chapter Five

Outside, the world was dark except for the single spot-light fixed above the bar, illuminating the rutted dirt parking area before the roadhouse. In the windows, the neon glow of beer advertising sent beams of bright color reflecting off the windshields of dusty pickup trucks.

"I'm this way," she said, leading him to the darkest portion of the lot.

Ty dragged her between two trucks and kissed her again. This time she did not kiss him for show. Oh, no, this time she let herself enjoy each nerve-tingling second. But when his hand moved from her lower back to her backside, she stepped away.

"The bike?" she reminded him.

"Yeah, but I'm figuring that if I fix it, you might use it to get away."

She smiled at him. He really was a handsome man. Such a shame he'd chosen so poorly in life. Those dark eyes gleamed with the promise of pleasure, and his mouth turned up in a way that offered a challenge she was tempted to accept. It was a winning combination. Especially when coupled with the hard jawline, straight nose and dark, slashing eyebrows. His hair was a wind-blown mess, as if he didn't care how it looked or, per-haps, understood that his mop of hair begged a woman to comb her fingers through the tangles. She indulged herself in the impulse as her eyes feasted on the quint-essential bad boy.

The tribe should make warning posters about this one. Still, she was tempted. So tempted to see what he had.

"You need a shave," she said. His hair was as thick as a horse's tail. She drew her hand back and touched her own cheek. "You're giving me razor burn."

"I have a razor at my place," he said.

The man did not waste time.

"Unfortunately, I can't ride there. My bike…" She offered him a regretful look, but her eyes offered something else.

"Let's go see."

She led the way across the rutted, dusty lot. He fell into step just behind her left shoulder.

"What kind of sled you have?"

"It's a BMW F800GT."

He whistled as his hand stroked her bike, starting at the leather saddle and gliding all the way up to the instruments until his long fingers finally wrapped around one grip.

Beth shivered in response to that sensual glide, and he hadn't even touched her.

"Rich," he said. He stretched out his fingers and then wiped his hand across his flat stomach.

Beth's skin flushed and she found she needed a long intake of air. "I got it used off a guy who…well, he gave me a good price." She let him wonder about that. The bike was truly hers. She had purchased it at a police auction and knew it had been owned by a man who liked to gamble with his clients' money. The way she figured it, a bike like this deserved a better owner.

She'd parked it at an angle so no one parked too close and so she could push it out, if necessary.

"You rode in here?" asked Ty, turning his attention to the bike.

"Yeah. It died at the diner. So I checked what I could and then did a push-start. Lucky the diner is on a hill. Got it going all right."

Ty looked at the bike. "Battery, maybe."

"It's fine. Nearly new."

"You might have left the headlight on when you were in the diner."

She flipped on the headlight, which glowed brightly.

She pointed to the console. "Says it's good, plus I flipped back the saddle and tested one of the terminals to ground. It arced just fine."

"Gas?" he asked.

She cut her gaze away. "Please."

"So I won't ask if the kickstand was up and the sled in Neutral."

"You try and start it," she said.

He straddled the bike. She couldn't believe it, but he looked even more handsome. The neon glow from the beer signs illuminated his high cheekbones, and a lock of hair fell over his forehead as he tried and failed to get the bike started.

"How are the plugs?" he asked.

"Good, I think."

"Well, then I'd say you have gunk in the fuel lines. Maybe the clutch starter. Bike needs air, fuel and spark. We know you have spark and fuel, so…"

She swore as if surprised it was not a quick repair.

"Did the guy at the diner mention that I have a garage?"

Beth nodded.

"I live above my garage."

Which she knew, but it was obvious he wanted her to know where the closest bed might be.

"You want me to bring it tomorrow morning?"

"Now is good." He gestured with his thumb over his shoulder. "Only thing, you'll have to drive. I already had too much to drink."

Which was interesting because she knew from Jake that Ty Redhorse did not drink.

"I don't think I want a drunk working on my bike."

"I could fix a carburetor drunk or asleep."

"Nobody drives my bike."

He slid back on the seat. "You want me to bump-start the bike with you on the back?"

He wiggled his eyebrows and she accepted the challenge.

"What about your bike?" she asked.

"In good hands."

No one would touch his bike. He had the protection of the Wolf Posse and tribal police, since his brother was on the force.

"Just out of curiosity, how were you planning to get home?"

"I never plan that far ahead," said Ty.

"You don't look or act or smell drunk," said Beth.

"Maybe I just can't resist lying flat across your back or maybe I want to see what an eight-hundred-cc in-line engine feels like. It's a tour bike. Plenty of room."

"If you fix my bike, I'm paying for the repair and I'm not sleeping with you."

"If you say so."

Had she anticipated an argument? She didn't expect him to give up so easily. But maybe he figured, wrongly, that he could change her mind. He was too charming and too good with that sexy mouth. She imagined he wouldn't disappoint in the bedroom. But her plan involved trapping him, not the other way around. Sleeping with him would give him power, and she was not going into that meeting tomorrow in a position of weakness.

"You got a helmet?" she asked, retrieving hers.

"Never wear one."

Of course he didn't. Another bad decision, she thought.

"Then let's go." She lifted her leg and slipped it neatly over the saddle, then knocked back the kickstand. Once she had the bike in Neutral and the clutch in, she rocked them forward and turned the wheel away from the line of trucks. It took a moment for gravity to grab hold, but by the time they reached the road they were gliding at five miles an hour. She shifted with her foot to second, waited until they hit fifteen miles an hour and then popped the clutch. The engine turned over and she gave it some gas. A moment later, they were ripping down the road.

"Where's your shop?"

He called directions as he slipped his hands around her waist. It felt good, riding with him. She loved the bike, despite what her mother thought, and knew that in this, at least, they would find common ground.

His body warmed her back as they raced in the direction of Koun'nde, one of three settlements here on the Turquoise Canyon Apache Indian Reservation.

After a few minutes he pointed out his place. The two-story building was mostly dark except for the floodlight over the double-bay doors. She could see a row of windows above the shop and knew that was where he lived.

She rolled up to the bay doors and cut the engine.

Something moved to her left, an animal, big and black. Beth startled.

"That's just my dog, Hemi."

She glanced back at him. "Like the motor?"

His smile showed a kind of appreciation that warmed her far more than it should have. "That's right."

He slid off the bike and she removed her helmet, leaving it on the seat.

"Nice ride," he said, and then he turned to Hemi and scratched her behind the ears. "Hemi, this is Beth."

She dropped the kickstand and straddled the bike, offering her hand to the canine, who had a definite wolfish look to her.

"Hey there, Hemi," said Beth.

Hemi took two steps in her direction and then dropped to the ground, her head between her front paws. Beth's brow wrinkled as she watched the dog, trying to interpret this odd behavior.

"What's with that?" she asked, lifting her gaze to Ty, who was now scowling at her.

"You packing?"

"What?"

"Hemi says you're carrying a gun."

Beth eyed the dog. Likely his brother would have warned her about the gunpowder-sniffing dog if she'd told anyone what she had in mind. She hadn't because the chances were too great that Jake would tip off his big brother.

Forrest had agreed, but she had only one shot, because every agent he put on the abduction case was one less on the eco-extremist investigation.

Beth set her jaw and glared at the dog.

"So what is it?" asked Ty.

She opened her jacket and showed him the holster

and her service weapon. She did not show him the FBI shield she had around her neck and under her blouse.

Ty's expression went grim and all anticipation left his eyes. They went flat and lifeless. He looked at her as if she had disappointed him. That would be ironic.

"I don't allow weapons in my place."

"Girl's got a right to protect herself."

"Deal breaker," he said.

"You act like you're on parole."

That made him glare. So he didn't like being painted as a criminal, even if that was just what he was.

"Not on parole," he said, raking a hand through his hair. "Tell you what. I'll get you started again. Take it to Piñon Forks. Spend the night at the casino and call Ron in the morning." He grabbed a pen from his shop and extended his hand for hers. She gave it to him and he wrote a number on the palm of her hand.

Was he actually sending her off? Beth couldn't believe it and she really couldn't believe that her disappointment was way more physical than emotional. Damn him and that kiss.

"He's good with bikes," said Ty.

"Where's his shop?"

"Across from the police station. You know where that is, right?"

He didn't wait for her to answer, just positioned himself behind her bike. She didn't even have her helmet on when he started to push as if he could not wait to be rid of her.

But he wasn't. Not by a long shot.

Chapter Six

On Sunday mornings, Ty worked on his own projects.
Today it was body repair on the 1978 Pontiac Trans
Am that he'd saved from the scrap yard. But his en-
thusiasm for muscle cars did not generally get him up
at 5:00 a.m. Still, that was what had happened the last
two mornings and he knew exactly who to blame for
that. The woman—Beth.

She captivated him. Not just the way she looked but
the way she handled that bike and how she knew things,
like that his dog was named after his favorite engine
and how to bump-start a bike. Who was he kidding?
It had been their kisses that had kept him from sleep.

Beth was too good to be true. Women like that did
not just show up in your life. Someone had sent her. And
that was the other reason he could not sleep. It wasn't
the Wolf Posse. She didn't have the look of Russian
mob. That left cop.

"Damn." He threw aside the rag he used to wipe
his hands.

The phone rang, echoing in the empty space. He
glanced at the clock on the wall to see it was already
eight in the morning. Ty reached for the greasy hand-
set. Jake was on the line, telling him that they needed
him to come into the station.

Ty's stomach dropped. Had the tribe reversed their decision about not turning him over to the Feds? As much as Ty wanted to be free of the Wolf Posse, a prison cell was not his chosen route. He had driven Kacey to the Russians, but her statement corroborated his. She had known where he was taking her and gotten into his vehicle voluntarily.

Maybe they matched his blood from the window at Antelope Lake. Some trumped-up charge on B&E? he wondered. The coffee he'd had for breakfast now clung to his stomach lining like motor oil.

"I'll be there," he said. He thought about his go-bag, the one under his bed. He'd added to it bit by bit, knowing that someday he'd have to use it.

Was today that day?

You could only dance with the devil for so long. Eventually the devil had to be paid. What kept him here was his mother and his brothers and the looming threat of his father's return.

They were all worried about what would happen upon Colton Redhorse's return. Ty wasn't worried because he knew how it would go—badly. Because people didn't change except to get worse.

He'd have to leave in forty minutes because the ride from Koun'nde to Piñon Forks took twenty. Ty removed his welding helmet and hung it back on the wall. Then he turned off the tanks. Friday, he'd spoken to tribal police and he'd made his position very clear. He didn't imagine that Detective Bear Den was going to have a second round of asking for his cooperation. So that meant they were going to charge him.

It was his own stupid fault. He must be losing his edge because he did not make that incredibly sexy woman as a cop. The way she hugged those curves on her bike, the woman could ride. And that kiss. Ty growled and headed upstairs with Hemi at his heels.

He showered and packed a duffel in case they kept him. Ty dragged out the go-bag from beneath his bed and unzipped it. Inside was survival gear, camping gear, first-aid supplies, ready-to-eat food, tools, money, a horse bridle and the keys to one car and one bike. Was today the day he'd need to run?

Ty carried both duffels to the GTO. Then he fed Hemi. After they'd both eaten, he took his dog to his mother's place. His mother, May, lived on the high ground outside Piñon Forks. Redhorse was busy getting his sister, Abbie, and the foster girls ready for church. She tried to feed him, of course, and accepted a kiss on the cheek. He asked Burt Rope, her new husband, to look after Hemi.

Burt knew exactly what that meant. "You in trouble, son?"

"Maybe. Tribal police want to talk to me again."

"Three times, isn't it?"

"Four." Four times and each time they had more pieces of the puzzle. Maybe they'd just take a blood sample today and let him go.

"We'll look after your dog, Ty." Burt laid a hand on Ty's shoulder and gave him a little pat.

Burt was a good man. Not like his rotten of a father. He felt relieved that his mother had found a man who, though not very industrious, was as reliable and kind as any he'd ever met.

Ty drove to tribal headquarters in his '67 Pontiac GTO because he didn't want to leave his bike outside the station. Burt could pick up his car. But no one drove his Harley but him.

Way he figured, tribal was done asking for his help.

So they would either charge him or turn him over to the Feds. The only good thing about the attention of the police was it had kept Faras Pike from pulling him all the way back into the Wolf Posse.

Ty rolled his shoulder, wondering if Kee would be willing to take the stitches out a few days early. If the Feds took his clothing and saw him without his shirt, they might just wonder how he sliced his shoulder open and then remember the blood they'd found on the shattered picture window at the house on Antelope Lake where two women had been held.

Neither Kee nor his girlfriend, the tribe's new dispatcher, had mentioned that Ty had been there. Kee thought Ty should get some credit for helping them get away from the Russian mobsters. Ty knew that the questions as to how he knew where to find them would make him vastly less heroic and possibly culpable for some serious jail time.

Ty knew about the capture because Faras told him that Ty was on call as a driver. That meant that the Russians had sent someone after Kee's girl and he was the backup if there was trouble. Ty had been on hand when the Russian, Yury Churkin, captured Ava Hood. The rest of the job was just shadowing them to the location where the women were being held. Faras's order to Ty to drive the Russian to safety if he ran into trouble would be enough to connect Ty to the criminal organization, and down the toilet he would go with the rest of them.

He drove to the station in Piñon Forks, which had been relocated now that the dam had been reinforced by the US Army Corps of Engineers. The state of Arizona had already begun repairs to the compromised Skeleton Cliff dam above their rez.

Ty parked at the health clinic, right next door to tribal

headquarters, where the police station was housed. Kee was likely up to his eyeballs in patients, since he was now the only physician on the rez. The other, Hector Hauser, was dead and Ty could not muster a drop of regret over that. Ty wondered if they'd lock him up today or just tell him not to flee. Where would he go?

Alaska, he thought. He could follow his youngest brother, Colt, up there to a wide-open state where his reputation would not dog him. More likely he'd be relocating to a cell next to his father in the federal prison down in Phoenix.

Ty made the long walk across the formal courtyard between the buildings into tribal headquarters. Once inside, he turned toward the police station. Jake greeted him in the squad room.

"I need a lawyer?" Ty asked his little brother.

Jake did not smile or make a joke. The look he cast back was deadly serious. "Don't think that will do it."

"Am I getting arrested?" he asked, glancing toward the chief's office and making eye contact with Wallace Tinnin, who rose from behind his old battered desk and collected his aluminum crutches.

"It's one of the possibilities. Ty, I think you should cooperate."

Jake didn't understand. How could he? Jake had never been on the wrong side of anything. Yet Ty's younger brother had understood how things worked well enough to ask Ty to get Faras to report to his associates that the baby Jake wanted to adopt had died. Ty had done it and hoped Jake never learned what the favor had cost him. How would his brother feel if he knew that Ty had been pulled into service driving the Russians off the rez because of that little favor?

Tinnin clicked his way to them on his crutches. The

foot, broken in the blast after the dam collapse, was in a black plastic boot.

"Thanks for coming in, Ty," said the chief. "If you'll follow me, please."

Damn, they were taking him to the interrogation room. He wondered if he still had the card with his attorney's phone number in his wallet.

They locked Ty in the room for twenty minutes. Enough time for him to consider exactly what evidence they had turned up. He'd heard that the tribe had voted to turn Kacey Doka's mother over to the Feds after she was connected to the surrogate ring. And they voted to turn over the former tribal health clinic's administrator, Betty Mills, after she broke the conditions of her agreement for cooperation by failing to tell them that Ava Hood's cover had been blown. That nearly got Ava killed, which was no skin off his nose except that Kee was in love with her. So he'd followed Churkin and waited for Kee and Hauser. Then when the shooting started he'd busted through that plate glass window and bled all over the place.

They were probably looking at him through the one-way mirror right now. He forced his bouncing knee to stillness.

The door latch turned and in stepped Detective Jack Bear Den, one of Ty's least favorite people. Bear Den held the door for Tinnin, who thumped in on his crutches, and behind him came...

Ty sat back in his chair. He did not keep his jaw from dropping as his mouth opened like a trapdoor as she strode in—Beth. There she was, the woman on the BMW sled whose kisses rocked his world. But today her eyelids did not shimmer and the liner around her eyes was not black, but was an earth tone. She was more beautiful today, with a burgundy-colored lipstick that added to her aura of authority. She wore blue slacks, practical shoes, a blazer and a white cotton blouse. The outfit made it easy for him to see her pistol, holstered at her hip, and the FBI shield and plastic ID on a lanyard about her neck. Today she radiated a different kind of power, the kind that came with the full weight of the system. Ty had run against that system often enough to know that it didn't work. At least not for him.

FB freakin' I.

Ty closed his mouth and narrowed his eyes on her.

Beth's crazy, curly beautiful wild hair was tugged back in a scalp-hugging bun and gleamed with some kind of hair product. She stood there with a triumphant glint in her lovely pale green eyes and the hint of a wicked smile curling her wide lips. The woman had counted coup on him, defeating him with a touch of the metaphorical crooked coup stick, like the plains Apache of old. And she knew it.

Ty pressed a hand to his forehead as it sank in. Faras had seen him kissing Beth. So had Chino and Quinton and at least four other members of the Wolf Posse. Everyone in the roadhouse saw him leave with her, this two-faced woman who was on the opposite side of the law. His problems just got bigger than Antelope Lake. If the posse knew who and what she was, he was a dead man.

"Good morning, Ty," she said, taking a seat across from him and laying a file folder on the table between them. "How was your weekend?"

Chapter Seven

Ty faced the FBI field agent and realized that his dream girl had just become a nightmare. How could he be so stupid? And he was double stupid because he was staring at her mouth again while hot and cold flashes rippled over his skin. Even knowing she'd used him by making everyone in that bar think they spent the night together, she still made his senses buzz like a high-voltage electric line. But not enough to get himself killed.

"What do you want?" he asked.

He'd never pegged her as FBI. She was too sleek and sexy, with none of that stiff upright bearing or penchant for following rules. That kiss had definitely been against the rules, hadn't it? If it wasn't, it sure should have been. Memories of that kiss flashed, making his skin pucker and forming a cold knot in his stomach. He didn't like being used, and that was what she had done. Played him like a harp.

Their gazes met and locked. He expected a triumphant smile. Instead she narrowed her lovely green eyes and angled her head, studying him and waiting. For what? The explosion she expected? The tantrum of a criminal pressed against the bars of his cell?

Sorry to disappoint.

There was a power about her that still called to him

and he wondered how his instincts had been so thoroughly foxed. Beth had slipped right under his radar because he'd only seen a strong, confident woman who walked on the wild side. Only Hemi had seen through her mask. His dog had smelled the gunpowder and machine oil that clung to her skin when Ty had smelled only orchids and spice.

Worse still, she'd succeeded in connecting herself to him in front of everyone in that bar. Faras would be curious about her and he'd look into her background. Ty sure hoped her cover was tight or they were both dead.

Bear Den cleared his throat. Ty didn't look at him. The tribal police detective stood to the FBI agent's left, and Tinnin moved to her right, resting his armpits on his crutches. Ty could hear him working his gum. All three blocked his path to the door that he knew was locked.

He was the only one sitting. They'd placed him in a position of weakness. But he knew the game and kept his attention on this new threat.

"I'm agent Beth Hoosay. I'm a member of the Apache tribe of Oklahoma and a field agent for the FBI assigned to a special task force here in Arizona."

"How's the sled?" he asked, feeling off balance, but forcing himself to relax past the buzzing that was now in his ears. "Get it going?"

"Just a starter motor, loose wire. Easy fix."

No doubt because she'd been the one to loosen it to begin with, he thought.

"Your boss know the company you been keeping?" he asked. If he thought to embarrass her, he failed. Her smile widened and she looked pleased with herself.

"A better question is, do you want your boss to know the company *you've* been keeping?"

Ty shifted in his seat and then told himself to sit still.

"Okay, points for you. Counting coup? You have coup sticks up there in Oklahoma, right?"

"It's on our great seal." Beth opened the file she carried. "But that's not all I've got."

She drew out a sheet of paper, laid it on the table and turned it toward him. "This is a transcript of a conversation recorded by Agent Luke Forrest on his phone. It is from the phone of Colt Redhorse, your brother, a phone given to him by Agent Forrest. It was used by Kacey Doka to call for help during her abduction."

He knew that because he'd been the one to tell her to call the FBI. That had been one of his stupider moves. But one that did help save her life.

"The pertinent portion is right here." She stretched out her arm and pointed with one well-manicured nail. "Do you recognize this conversation?"

He glanced at the page and read:

Kacey Doka: "They aren't here yet."
Driver: "Look again."
Pause.
Driver: "Exactly."
Kacey Doka: "Where's Colt?"
Driver: "Don't know. High ground, I hope. He's a hell of a good shot. But so are they."

TY PUSHED THE page back. They had proof he'd driven Kacey. But he'd admitted that already and they had both his and Kacey Doka's statements. They wouldn't hang him on that, he hoped. But they might.

"What am I looking at?"

"Don't you know?" asked Beth.

He did not reply.

"Well, then." Agent Hoosay retrieved the page and

substituted another. "This one might interest you." She pointed. "Blood results from the shoot-out involving your brother Dr. Kee Redhorse at Antelope Lake five days ago. Somehow Dr. Redhorse managed to get two kidnap victims out of that house past two armed men, yet he was unarmed and both captors had handguns. This blood was found in the living room on broken glass. On the dock behind the house. On the boat that your brother used to escape and on the shore at the northeastern shore of the lake."

Ty did not look at the page. He preferred looking at Beth. She was so sure she had him boxed. Did she remember that a trapped animal is the most dangerous kind?

"It's your blood. We don't need a sample because we obtained one with a warrant from your clinic. Perfect match. So we don't need your brother Kee or Louisa Tah or former detective Ava Hood to verify your presence at Antelope Lake."

Ty propped an elbow on the table and splayed his hand over his jaw, studying her. He'd known she was beautiful at first sight. Her entrance at the roadhouse showed she had a confidence bordering on recklessness. She also knew how to ride a motorcycle, a beauty of a bike. He added smarts to her list of attributes and wondered what she'd do if he put his hand over the one beside the damning evidence.

He wouldn't, of course. They were adversaries from now on and he'd do well to remember it instead of noticing the way her eyes bordered on gray under the fluorescent lights.

Bear Den spoke up. "You assisted Dr. Redhorse in rescuing Ava Hood and Louisa Tah."

"You here to give me my medal?"

Bear Den's smile showed how much he was enjoying this. Ty had been a burr under Bear Den's saddle for years.

"You were there and that is no crime. But how you knew where to find your brother and Dr. Hauser might be," said Beth, the threat veiled in her soft, honeyed voice.

"Yet I'm not under arrest," he said.

The FBI agent glanced to Tinnin. "Because you encouraged Kacey to call for backup and stayed to help her escape and you came to your brother Kee's aid on Antelope Lake. Other circumstances, you'd be a hero, son."

Ty made a face and sat back in his chair. "My whole life has been other circumstances."

"Distinguished yourself in the US Marines," added Tinnin.

"After accepting a deal to serve in lieu of facing charges for armed robbery at eighteen," Bear Den said.

Jeez. Did the detective have his file memorized?

Tinnin ignored Bear Den's comment. "We know you've helped your brothers. We want you to help your tribe the same way."

"How exactly do you expect me to do that?"

"First off, if you have any information on any criminal activity on this rez, you need to tell us now."

Ty thought of the meth lab operating on Deer Kill Meadow and kept his mouth shut.

"Nothing?" said Bear Den.

"You didn't call me in here to be a snitch. Tell me what you really want."

They told him and he laughed. "So. Take the deal or my tribe will turn me over to face federal charges.

Question is, how likely is it that this deal of yours is going to get me killed?"

Agent Hoosay sat back, draping an arm over the back of her chair. Now there was the woman he had met the other night, all danger and promise.

"Now, I figured you for a risk-taker, Ty. I'm willing to take a chance on you if you're willing to give us certain assurances."

"Be your trained monkey, you mean."

Her voice was almost a purr. "I prefer to think of you as a lapdog. *My* lapdog."

"The posse has tribal police outmanned and outgunned. And I know they drive better cars because I fix them. Plus they currently have very powerful friends."

"Victor Vitoli, Leonard Usov and the Kuznetsov crime organization."

"Ding, ding. Someone has been doing her homework."

"We aim to break up the posse for good, son," said Tinnin. "And see that the Russian mob finds it too hot to continue operations up here."

Bear Den leaned in. "And we want the four remaining missing girls back."

Ty wanted that, too. But it was on the list of impossible things, like wanting to stay out of the gang or be invited to join Tribal Thunder, the warrior sect of the tribe's medicine society. He'd thought he'd put that one to bed years ago, but here it was, popping up in his mind like burned toast. He added the even more far-fetched possibility of recovering his smashed and ruined reputation to the list. Impossible. Yeah. Sometimes you were just doomed to be disappointed.

"What's the deal?" asked Ty.

"Your full cooperation in our investigation," said

Beth. "And in exchange we forgo pursuit of you in connection with our investigation."

Ty nodded. "What do you expect me to do, exactly?"

"Introduce me to the Wolf Posse as your new girlfriend and give me your continued efforts to get me on the inside."

"No way." Was she crazy? Did she even know what she'd have to do to join the posse?

Bear Den smiled. Ty could see the pleasure he got in just imagining turning Ty over for federal prosecution.

"I need to get on the inside," said Beth.

"Not by joining the posse, you don't."

Tinnin interjected then. "What about just having you pose as Ty's girlfriend? That will get you into the roadhouse and access to members of the posse."

Beth rolled her lips between her teeth and drummed her fingers. She didn't seem like the kind of gal who would compromise.

"We'll start with that," she said. Her eyes offered both challenge and promise. "So, Mr. Redhorse. Do you accept this arrangement?"

Ty wondered just how realistic she wanted their relationship to be. Anticipation made his heart race. Attraction to this Fed was the most stupid reason of all to take the deal. "I accept."

Chapter Eight

It was not until he breathed fresh air that Ty had a chance to wonder whether he had accepted their deal to prevent federal prosecution, or because accepting was the only way to get near Beth. He hoped it wasn't the latter, because he liked to believe he was smarter than that.

He spotted a vehicle as he drove out of the parking lot by the tribe's headquarters with FBI agent Beth Hoosay. His eyes narrowed at the familiar black RAM pickup with the pencil-thin gold detailing. It was a truck with which he was acquainted because he'd had to do the detailing twice. Chino Aria hadn't liked the first gold Ty used because he wanted the paint to sparkle. Pain in the ass, that was what he was. Chino was also dangerous, especially to women.

Ty could think of only one reason that Chino would park his truck across the street from the police station and not be in it. The Feds had themselves another snitch. What did they have on Chino? Ty didn't know but knew that the man was one of Faras's enforcers. Ty's list of sins was black, but Chino's was blacker, as he inflicted pain and enjoyed it.

"Hedging your bets?" he asked.

"What?" asked the agent.

"If I can figure it out, so can Faras. Chino is a nit-wit, a dangerous one. Parking over there, at the diner, it's a bad move. Any of the gang could see his truck."

"Chino wasn't driving it," said Beth.

Ty frowned. Who would dare drive Chino's truck? he wondered. Faras was the only answer he could come up with, but he would never come into the station. Faras was deadly and suspicious, but he would never cooper-ate with the police. Ty was certain.

"Who, then?" Ty asked.

Beth ignored the question.

"You don't have to worry about being spotted. Tin-nin assigned an officer to watch for any of the known vehicles," said Beth. "Besides, you parked at the clinic. Very smart."

She knew where he parked his GTO. He didn't like that.

"Where my brother Kee works," said Ty.

"Your younger brother, Jake, works at for the tribal police. It gives you a reason to park in their lot."

"That's one of the things Faras likes about me—my family connections." He didn't say the rest, that Faras was a master at using those connections to keep Ty in line. "So, where to?"

"Your place. I'm moving in."

Ty smiled and gave her the kind of predatory look that made most women adjust their clothing to cover up. Beth met his stare with one of her own, cold and dan-gerous. The woman gave him the chills in all the right and wrong places and both at the same time.

"I don't think Hemi will like having another female around the place."

"She'll get used to me. I'm good with animals."

"Ought to make things easier on us both, then," he said.

She laughed and then glanced out the window. The music of her mirth made him want to hear it again.

"You grow up on the rez up there in Oklahoma?" he asked.

"No. I'm just on the tribal rolls. My mother's a member, so I'm entitled to membership, too." She pressed her lips together and her eyes shifted and narrowed. What was making her angry? A memory of the tribe, her mother? Ty's instincts said there was something back there that nettled.

"They have a blood requirement?"

She shot him a glance that seemed laced with poison. Was it because his question implied she would not meet most tribal requirements? If so, perhaps he had just found a chink in her armor.

"The requirement is one sixteenth Oklahoma Apache unless you have a parent enrolled. I meet either prerequisite."

Yup, she was prickly as a cholla cactus and all signs of humor had fled from her features.

"I've never lived anywhere but here," said Ty.

"You've been out there, though. US Marines."

She could read, he thought, and realized that she also would know why he joined. Some of the reasons anyway. Now he was frowning, too. Back then, he had tried going to the police. But his mother would not press charges and he was too young to do it. All he'd managed was to get protective services out to their place, which scared Jake and Colt so much he'd never done it again. He didn't want his father hitting his mother, but he also didn't want his brothers separated through the foster-care system. Jake had called soon afterward, though, still believing in the system that had let them down. That had been one particularly bad night after

Ty had tried and failed to defeat his father. It had been satisfying seeing his father loaded into Tinnin's patrol car. But he'd been out in less than twenty-four hours. Ty had learned an important lesson that day. He'd learned that bones took longer to heal than it took to get out of jail after assaulting your wife.

Beth spoke again, prompting confirmation. "Distinguished yourself in Iraq. Isn't that right?"

"Yeah, I was a jarhead," said Ty. Back then he'd considered reenlistment. But he couldn't because his family needed him here. Ty had come back home when Colt received his psych discharge.

"Ever think of leaving the rez?" she asked.

"Sometimes."

She cast him a puzzled look. Had she ever felt trapped?

"Why the FBI?" he asked as they left the main community and the river behind and headed toward Koun'nde.

"Oh, well, I'll give you the official version first." She cleared her throat and raised her chin a notch. "Growing up in Oklahoma after the bombing that put us on the map, I felt a need to protect our nation from threats both domestic and foreign."

Now he was even more curious. Was she really trying to save the world? Her smile seemed to challenge, as if asking if he swallowed that tale.

"The unofficial version?" he asked.

She faced forward again, gazing out the windshield as they passed the river and the ongoing reconstruction of the destroyed dam.

No answer, he thought, was still an answer. What part of her past dogged her?

"I have to stop and get my dog."

"At your mother's?"

She knew his mother. Likely knew more about him than he did. He didn't like it, the advantage she had over him. He wondered if Jake could find out anything about her with his databases. Did his brother have anyone up there in Oklahoma who he could ask for information on Beth? But the Oklahoma Apache tribe was not like this rez. The tribe was huge and a conglomeration of many Apache people. Oklahoma City was huge as well. If Ty was going to learn anything about his opponent, he'd have to get the information from the source.

Ty never liked handling explosives, and Beth seemed more dangerous than the IEDs back in the sandbox. If she blew their cover, he'd be dead. If she blew the arrest, he'd be dead. That didn't scare him as much as knowing that when a bomb detonates, it was indiscriminate with collateral damage. Jake and Kee were here, in close range. His mother and her new husband and his little sister, Abbie, were all so very close. And each one was a weapon to use against him. He'd stayed as long as his presence served to keep them safe. When that changed, he'd take off.

Ty adjusted his hands on the wheel and stepped on the gas. In a few minutes, they arrived at his mother's place. Burt Rope was out in the yard watering down the dusty driveway and greeted them with a wave.

"Well, what a nice surprise. You missed Sunday supper," said Burt.

The largest meal of the week was served at noon, after church. His brothers Jake and Kee were now bringing their significant others. Ty was almost happy he'd been in the interrogation room, because the idea of joining his family for the Sunday meal with this woman posing as his girlfriend did not sit well.

They were all gone, thank goodness. He knew this because their trucks weren't there.

He asked in any case. "They gone?"

"Yup. Jake took the girls, too. Off to visit their younger brothers," said Burt.

Jeffery and Hewett were fostering with one of the tribal council members, Hazel Tran, because Ty's mother just couldn't house two more children.

"Abbie, too?" he asked, getting out of the car.

"Abbie, too." Burt turned to Beth, who now stood on the drive beside the passenger side of the GTO. "Who's this?"

Ty made introductions. Beth shook hands. Neither her weapon nor her shield was in evidence and she seemed as if she'd just come from church, instead of his funeral.

"I didn't know that Ty had sisters," said Beth.

Like hell, he thought. She thought she knew everything about him. But that was impossible.

"Oh, he has one, plus three more now. We've taken them in."

The Doka girls included sixteen-year-old Jackie, thirteen-year-old Winnie and eleven-year-old Shirley. Three girls, four including his sister, and all the right age for the Russians to pluck like flowers. Ty knew that his cooperation was what kept them from entering the rolls of removal. Faras had said as much and as head of the Wolf Posse, he made the selections. But now, with the doctor killed at Antelope Lake, operations had ceased. For now. He feared that this was a temporary respite.

And the FBI was so concerned about their problems that they had allocated one single agent. Now he must decide if he would add her to his growing list of those he must protect, or throw her to the wolves.

BETH ENJOYED MEETING his mother and Burt Rope. She knew all about them on paper, but she appreciated meeting the real version. His mother's life had been difficult. She'd married young to a violent man who had been in and out of jail until the felonies piled high enough to make him serve real time. Despite that, May Redhorse had managed to get all four of her boys raised and each had graduated from high school. Two had additional higher education. May had a big heart, obviously, because she was fostering the Doka girls, though she had neither the room nor the resources to do so. The girls were lucky. They would likely have a chance now, Beth decided, all because of May.

Ty introduced Beth as his girlfriend, as arranged. Beth felt a twinge of guilt at the joy on May's face. Did his mother see the promise of grandchildren when she looked at Beth? Beth had been undercover for up to six months at a time. But somehow fooling this woman made her feel dirty.

She was relieved when they finally left, having been fed lunch, of course, from the leftovers of the Sunday supper they had missed.

The stop to pick up his dog had lasted over an hour. Hemi now sat in the rear seat, her eyes half-closed and her tongue lolling.

"She's a great cook," said Beth as they returned to the car. "And quite a woman."

"Yes."

"She's strong like her sons."

But not her body, thought Beth. Her body was dying bit by bit because of the diabetes and the diet she had not altered. Fry bread and sugary baked goods were abundant in the house.

"I don't want you to see her again," Ty said.

"Why?"

"Because I don't bring my women here. Coming here makes you special to her. I don't want you to be special."

He was right, of course. So she couldn't understand why it hurt her that he wanted distance between her and his mom. Under other circumstances, they might have been friends.

"It's good that you look out for her," she said.

He snorted but said nothing.

"Lucky she didn't lose you and your dad both after that robbery."

Ty's laugh held little humor. "Yeah. Lucky."

"Your age, I mean. Protecting you."

"You could see it that way."

Now he had her attention. "How do you see it?"

"Hey, I'm just glad he's gone."

"But he's up for parole again."

His grim expression showed that he knew that all too well. Ty pulled into the drive in front of his shop in the golden light of late afternoon. The landscape was lovely here and changed by the mile. The river rushed along beside the road in places and there were vistas of rocky bluffs and mountains. She had yet to see the ridges of turquoise from which the tribe derived its name. The territory was so different than the city where she lived and the flat plains that surrounded it. Hemi stood in the backseat and stretched. Ty let her out first, leaving Beth to collect her gear and follow them into his place.

"Apartment is up that way." Ty pointed to the stairs that ran up the outside of the building. "It's unlocked."

He left her, returning to his shop and the rusty Ford Impala in the second bay.

She settled into the upstairs apartment that Ty called home, dropping her bag beside the couch before going to explore. The main area was divided into a tiled kitchen-dining combo and a carpeted living room. Anchored to one wall was a long couch, draped in a brightly colored Navajo blanket. Above the couch was a framed vintage poster of a Model 101 Indian motorcycle.

She smiled. "Can't argue with that."

That bike was a classic.

In front of the couch, there was a square maple coffee table with a stack of *Popular Mechanics* magazines on it, along with the motorcycle auction news. Between the table and kitchen, a worn leather recliner faced a modest-size flat-screen TV. Before the television was a large padded circular dog bed, the faux-sheepskin inner lining liberally sprinkled with dark hair.

A window flanked one side of the television. Bookshelves lined the other side. He had a good collection of mysteries and thrillers, plus some biographies. But most of the shelving was filled with framed photographs.

His brothers at all stages of life grinned at her. His sister as a toddler, on Ty's skinny knee. His mother in full regalia. Kee in a cast sitting in a hospital bed surrounded by his family. There was one person noticeable in his absence from Ty's collection. He had no photos of his father, Colton Redhorse, on display.

The only actual photo Beth owned was in her wallet. It was of her mom and dad and her, back when they were happy and whole. The rest of her photographic memories of her family were at her mother's home in boxes.

The remainder of the upstairs consisted of a short hallway. On one side was a full bathroom with white porcelain tub, sink and toilet and a small study. On the other side of the hall sat the master bedroom with a queen-sized bed, reading chair and bureau. The bed was also covered in a Navajo-style wool blanket, this one in red, black and yellow.

She had not expected his inner sanctum to be so scrupulously clean and Spartan. He lived like a man in a monastery. All the flash of his bike and the style and character of the cars he restored did not transfer to his apartment.

Beth headed to Ty's bedroom and poked around. His clothing was also utilitarian. Jeans, not too tight or loose. Worn, but not worn out. T-shirts in muted colors. She found no jewelry, no rings or necklaces, no earrings or hair adornments. He liked leather for his jackets, boots and belts. She found no drugs or weapons of any sort. Why didn't he carry a weapon?

She wondered how Ty had survived so long without one or if, perhaps, his unwillingness to carry a weapon had kept him alive. She liked a puzzle, and Ty was that. In spades.

There was nothing of interest under his bed but a stuffed squeaky toy squirrel that she guessed, from the teeth marks, belonged to Hemi. Beside that was an old baseball glove cupped around a tennis ball. In his bedside table he had batteries, a lighter, a candle in a glass jar. She sniffed, inhaling the scent of balsa wood and pine. The drawer also held a flashlight and condoms.

Her search of his bureau and bathroom turned up no drugs, legal or otherwise except for extra strength BC Powder. Ty did not take drugs, apparently, and suffered from no more than an occasional headache. Meanwhile she carried a roll of antacid tablets perpetually in her pocket and chewed them like breath mints. The acidic condition of her belly being a result of stress, according to her doctor.

"What gives you headaches, Ty?" she asked her reflection in the medicine cabinet. "Your family? The gang? The police? Your conscience?"

Beth returned the packets to their place.

Where were the clues to a man whom she had not yet placed in his proper box? Chief Tinnin believed Ty was a tragic hero. Bear Den believed he was a criminal who had slipped from the noose.

Who was right?

As it got later in the afternoon, Beth joined Ty in his garage, hoping she would gain more insights from him there.

He lifted his head at her arrival.

"Find anything interesting?" he asked.

"Nice selection of condoms," she said, hoping to wipe that smug smile from his mouth.

"I aim to please," he replied, and returned to his work.

Now she was the one blushing. She perched on a stool beside his workbench with her laptop on a clean rag spread upon the surface. Hemi appeared from beyond the bay doors and settled into her dog bed at Beth's feet. She stared at the dog, who regarded her with one open eye. It was a neat trick, spotting weapons. She wondered if it was the scent of gunpowder or the gun oil that alerted the canine. And she wondered if Hemi knew any more tricks.

Tonight Ty would be introducing her as his new woman at the bar. She had been right to meet him there first. It gave her a much-needed advantage and the leverage necessary to gain his help.

At 5:00 p.m., Ty finished work and used some goop to clean the grease off his forearms and hands. The process was a sensual glide of skin on skin. Beth tried not to be mesmerized, but failed. She liked tattoos and appreciated the US Marine Corps insignia on his arm. It was, unfortunately, beneath the one near his elbow that marked him as a member of the tribe's gang.

Upstairs Ty left her to shower. Beth dressed in her costume and carefully applied the makeup that said she was trouble. She liked this mask. It gave her a different kind of power and the edge she needed to take on the role. The best kind of power came from military rank and now her FBI shield. She still had both, but now she also had red lipstick. She let down her hair and worked in the product until it coiled in wild ringlets. Then she popped an antacid as a preemptive strike against nerves.

Ty appeared in black jeans, a white T-shirt and a brown bomber jacket that looked vintage. His feet were covered with motorcycle boots, of course, and he radiated danger. Nearly irresistible, she thought.

What he didn't wear were gang colors. Ty somehow operated on the gang's periphery, and she didn't understand why.

On the drive to the roadhouse, she tried and failed to ignore the spicy scent of his aftershave. He spoke first.

"You work gangs before?"

"No."

"No gangs?" He was frowning now, as if he had already decided she was not the woman for the job.

"It won't be a problem. I've been briefed by our experts."

"Any of those experts actually been in a gang?" Ty asked.

"No. Of course not."

"If you have no experience with gangs, Agent Hoosay, why are you here?"

"You should start calling me Beth."

"Sure."

"I was asked to join the task force because I have specialized knowledge regarding organized crime."

"And because you're Apache," he said, his words accusatory.

She did not quite keep herself from making a face. "It's not a factor."

He actually laughed. "You think they could have sent a male agent to do what you're about to do?"

She didn't.

"They picked you because you're hot, young, enrolled in an Apache tribe and stupid enough, or hungry enough, to take some monster risks. What is it you're after, exactly? Promotion? Accolades? Make Mama proud?"

She pressed her lips together and watched him. Finally she gave him something. "I wanted out of Oklahoma City."

"You have a bike. Easy to get out."

"Is it? So why are you still here?"

"Touché," he said.

She turned to watch him as she spoke, his strong jaw illuminated by the dashboard light. He certainly was easy on the eyes.

"I was stationed in DC. Worked at Quantico and I got interested in the FBI."

"Stationed?"

"US Army."

Ty groaned.

She ignored it. "I applied to the Bureau and they took me."

"And assigned you back to Oklahoma?" he asked, guessing correctly.

"Exactly. Plunked me right back where I started because I was familiar with the territory."

"Ironic. And reassignment to a bigger field office requires you to make a case—a big one. Isn't that right?"

Now, how did he know that? She was constantly reassessing him and still she'd underestimated him again.

"What you work on up there?"

"Organized crime for the last five years. I know this group. We know every player."

"Yet they're still walking around."

"Hopefully, you can help change that."

"I'm just going to get you proximity. That was the deal I signed."

Beth smiled, but said nothing to reassure him.

"You don't want them gone?" she asked.

"Depends on the cost." He changed the subject. "Why do you want out of Oklahoma?"

She snorted. No way was she answering that. "The Midwest is too flat."

"What about Arizona?"

"It's not flat."

"Is that what you're leaving behind?" he asked. "The landscape?"

She didn't answer. His questions had turned too personal. "You have my cover story down?"

"Yes, ma'am."

He pulled into the lot, already half-full with a variety of pickups and bikes. It did not escape her that most of the vehicles were some variety of the gang's colors, black and gold.

Ty cut the engine of the GTO, and the world went quiet for just a moment before the sounds of music from within the roadhouse reached her. Beth's heartbeat pulsed and her skin prickled a warning as she faced the lion's den with only Ty Redhorse as her backup.

He grinned. "Ready to meet my friends?"

Chapter Nine

Ty tried not to admire the way that Beth had dressed for success in tight blue jeans and a hip-length brown suede jacket that tied at the waist and hid the pistol she now had in the inner pocket. The jacket gaped open to show a tight V-necked top in cherry-red that revealed enough cleavage to make a man want more and to take his attention away from her face. The red matched the color of her lipstick. Ty loved a woman in high boots, and hers were high and laced up the front.

Inside the bar the Sunday football game still blared on the television and patrons at the bar cheered as the Houston Texans' kicker sent the ball through the uprights for a field goal.

Ty kept an arm about her as they entered, staking a claim. But at the bar, Beth chatted up several of the customers, zeroing in on any wearing gold and black. Ty beat her at pool because she let him and they drew a crowd. Faras claimed winner, but he didn't want to play Ty, so he stepped aside and let Beth do her job.

She was good. Just the right amount of charm and allure. Not overdone, but when Faras invited her to the Wolf Den, Ty stepped in and told them the two of them had plans. He cast Beth a warning look that you would have to be blind not to see.

She ignored it. Was he responsible for her safety if she did stupid things that might get her seriously messed up? He growled as he realized that, even if she deserved it, he could not let her go to the Wolf Den alone.

He was prepared to advise her on what a bad idea going into their crib could be for a woman, but she turned down the invitation, looping her arm in Ty's as she chatted with Faras.

Ty scanned the occupants of the bar. There were the usual characters and a large number of the posse, who were watching the game on the large-screen television. Eight men plus the one outside. Just the ones he could see outnumbered the tribal police force by two, and there were more, Ty knew. Five women, all longtime members of the posse, watched Beth from their usual table. None were exclusive except for Jewell. She'd risen in the ranks to become a favorite with Faras. Ty knew why. Jewell was young, only twenty, but she was cunning and beautiful, the female version of an alpha.

The last true couple in the Wolf Posse had been Minnie and Trey. But Trey got clipped and Minnie switched horses, going with Earle. Now they were both awaiting trial. Ty smiled as he thought of his small part in their capture. Hemi had done most of it. Luckily, Hemi wasn't talking and the FBI kept anyone from seeing those two so they had no chance to spill the beans to Faras that Ty had been there watching over Jake and his new baby girl.

He saw Jewell speaking to Chino and sensed trouble. Faras was paying too much attention to Beth for Jewell to do nothing, and Ty's claim on Beth meant nothing because all here knew that Faras took what and whom he wanted.

Jewell ambled over and took Ty's other arm, giving

Chino the chance he needed to drag Beth from his side. Jewell clung tight as Chino propositioned Beth.

"Maybe you'd like to stay up here on Turquoise Canyon. Join our group," said Chino, drawing Beth before him and moving in way too close.

Beth shifted away and Chino tugged her back. Ty realized she was trying to prevent him from feeling the gun in her jacket pocket.

Uh-oh, Ty thought, unfolding his arms as he reached the coffee table and Beth, trapped between Faras and Chino. Time to go.

Beth was FBI, but she'd worked organized crime. Did she know what was involved with a woman joining a gang?

"Just a small initiation," said Chino, unable to keep the smile of anticipation from curling his lips.

"No," said Ty, extracting himself from Jewell's ferocious grip. Her job done, Jewell moved beside Faras.

Chino kept a hold on Beth and faced Ty. "Why not let the lady decide?"

Ty looked to Faras to settle the argument. He didn't. Instead, he lifted his hands from his beer bottle and offered them palms up.

"Settle it outside," said Faras.

Chino rose to his feet and bumped Ty with his shoulder on the way past. Ty grabbed Beth and muscled her toward the rear exit.

"What are you doing?" she asked.

"Getting you out of here."

"I'm not going without you," she said.

"Only way out for me is through Chino," he said.

Ty watched the big man head through the door, followed by several of the men and all the women.

"Don't go out there," said Beth.

"You want to be my girl? This is how it's done. If you plan to hang on the posse's turf, I have to establish my singular claim."

"That's barbaric."

"So are they."

Beth hesitated, looking toward the back of the road-house.

"We won't make it," said Ty.

"Well, I can't let him kill you."

Ty nodded. Beth had assessed their chances, pictured the encounter and decided Ty would not only lose, but also be killed. Her confidence was touching.

"If I help you, I have to blow my cover."

"Who asked you to help me?" said Ty, and headed for the door.

She grabbed him before he went outside. There in the entrance, between the roadhouse and the lot, he faced her.

"Do you know what the initiation involves?" His words came as a rasp, like a file on metal.

She looked at the dirty rug advertising Coors beer. Her words where flat, as if she was just reciting them. "Crime is a standard initiation for males. For a female, it's sex."

She lifted her gaze and their eyes met.

"Exactly." Ty wiped his face with both hands. "I don't like you, Agent Hoosay, but I'll protect you if I can."

Now he saw the worry in her eyes, and her hand went into her jacket pocket, reaching for the pistol he knew was secreted there.

He grabbed her wrist and pulled her close, speaking against her temple. "No."

She clung to his shirt with her free hand. "It's a last resort."

"You can run, but you cannot draw that pistol. If you do, I'm a dead man because I brought you here. Do you understand?"

"But what if—"

"Do you understand?" he growled.

"Yes." Her voice was breathless.

"While I'm fighting, you're backing up until you get to my car and then you are out of here." He held up the key fob.

She took it.

Ty pressed his lips to the top of her head and closed his eyes.

"You don't have to do this," she said again.

"Either you're mine or you're not. No middle ground."

Then he let her go and stepped out to the lot, where the circle of spectators waited. There in the center stood Chino.

"Thought you snuck out the back," said Chino.

"Had to take a piss," he said.

"When I'm done with you, you'll piss yourself again," snarled Chino.

Several in the gathering laughed at this.

The man looked positively delighted, though whether at the prospect of fighting Ty or sleeping with Beth, Ty did not know.

Faras arrived behind Ty with Quinton at his side.

"Come on!" Chino was already flexing and snorting like a bull preparing to charge.

Ty looked to Faras, who sighed. Then he gave Ty a slow shake of his head.

"She worth it?" asked Faras.

Ty did not hesitate and nodded once.

"Then you got to prove it."

"You won't blame me if I damage your man," he said, thumbing toward Chino.

That caused many of the watching Wolf Posse members to laugh out loud. Faras didn't laugh because Faras had seen Ty fight.

Chino roared and charged without waiting for Faras to answer the question.

He came at Ty with his shoulders back and chest out. Most fights started with shoving and jostling, sometimes with a chest or belly bump. Ty never wasted time or effort with posturing. Chino was bigger. But he wouldn't win.

Ty glanced to Beth. She wasn't backing up. Worse still, she clearly thought Chino would win, because she had her hand in her jacket pocket again.

Chapter Ten

Beth wrapped her hand around her service pistol and used one finger to flick off the safety while keeping her eyes on Ty and Chino.

She'd been undercover before and thought she knew what she was doing, but somehow in less than twelve hours she had managed to put both herself and her contact in jeopardy.

Chino lifted a hand to shove Ty. It was a sloppy first move.

His hand never made contact. Ty grasped his wrist and spun him so fast the entire thing was a blur. Chino folded at the waist as Ty forced his wrist up behind his back, using only his thumb as leverage. Then Ty ran him across the circle. The members in the gathering marked Chino's course and moved aside a moment before Chino's head hit the door of the pickup parked in the handicapped spot. The car door was dented on impact.

Ty let him go, which Beth thought was an incredibly stupid thing to do.

Chino rose from the ground, roaring as he turned like a Kodiak bear preparing to charge.

Ty looked to Faras and lifted his hands as if asking for directions or perhaps hoping Faras would call this off. Faras nodded his consent and Ty's shoulders sank and he turned his attention back to Chino. Beth thought Faras had just given Ty the okay to continue. Ty would have to finish this fight. But what were the rules? Did they fight until someone conceded, or what?

Ty rolled his shoulder. Chino fixed on the movement, sensing weakness like a shark senses blood.

Speaking of which, was that blood on the front of Ty's T-shirt? His bomber jacket was unzipped and the shirt beneath glistened in a way she associated with blood. Beth knew that Ty had been injured at Antelope Lake and that he had lost a significant amount of blood because of the samples collected. She'd seen the photos, but she did not know where exactly Ty had been injured while crashing through the picture window. She also could not get her mind around how a man with that much blood loss could manage to make it twenty-three miles over rough ground back to his rez, on foot and alone.

Chino's eyes narrowed as he shook out his arm and rubbed his sore thumb. She knew Chino had an eighth-grade education, had been expelled for bringing a weapon to his middle school and had been arrested twice for shoplifting and drug possession. Meanwhile, Ty Redhorse had served in the US Marine Corps. Had distinguished himself in several combat engagements and had left with an honorable discharge.

Size aside, she now had her money on the warrior. Quinton wandered over to stand beside her.

Beth rested her free hand on her hip as her sweaty hand gripped the pistol. Quinton folded his arms and leaned against the truck bed behind them as Chino took his first swing.

"Wish I had the guts to challenge Chino sometimes,

but he'd break me in two pieces like a dry stick," said Quinton, and then pantomimed the break. "Snap!"

Beth cut her gaze away from Quinton and back to the fight.

"I'm Quinton."

She knew who he was. Quinton had finished high school. Barely. He'd been in the tribe's jail for three months after a bar fight that tribal suspected was gang-related. He'd lost the fight, which was how the police picked him up, bleeding all over himself.

"Beth," she said, and was forced to release her pistol to shake his hand.

"This has been coming for a while. Chino hates Ty."

"Why's that?"

Beth hoped she would not have to draw her weapon to keep one male from killing the other. She did not want to blow her cover, but she was not going to watch this gorilla kill Ty. Especially when Ty was defending her.

"Chino resents that Ty gets to come and go as he likes. That Faras shows him a kind of respect he doesn't give the rest of us. But those two got a long history. Back to high school. Almost like Faras owes Ty or something."

Chino's second swing was clumsy and Ty ducked under it.

"Brewing for a while is all." Quinton motioned to the women, all sitting on the open gate of a pickup across the circle, glaring daggers at her. "Looks like you haven't made any friends here yet but Faras."

Ty glided under Chino's flailing arm, punched him in the kidney and watched the big man sink to his knees.

"Down goes Frazier," said Quinton, imitating Howard Cosell's famous words. "You a fight fan?"

"No."

"Got a favorite?" asked Quinton.

"I like the horse I rode in on."

Ty cast her a look and motioned his head toward his car. He'd given her plenty of time to escape. But she wasn't leaving him here wrestling that gorilla.

"I'd love to see Chino land just one punch," said Quinton.

"Why's that?"

Quinton shrugged. "Pretty boy. Teacher's pet."

It seemed Ty did not have many friends among the gang, either, except perhaps Faras Pike himself.

Chino started to rise and Ty kicked him in the head with his booted foot. Chino fell facedown, hard. Ty was on Chino's back an instant later. Ty had the man's beefy arm up over his head and bent his arm back toward his shoulder blade until his wrist nearly met his shoulder.

Chino cried out and kicked.

Beth took a step forward. Ty increased the pressure on Chino's shoulder, and the man stopped struggling.

Ty had won and chosen to spare Chino's life, which was great because it kept Beth from having to arrest him for manslaughter.

"Yield," demanded Ty.

Chino's eyes were bloodshot and his mouth screwed up like that of a man who ate limes for a living. Finally he nodded.

"Yield," Chino said.

Ty rose and his opponent rolled to his back. Ty offered his hand. Chino hesitated, then looked at Faras, who inclined his chin by the slightest measure. Chino snorted but accepted Ty's help to his feet.

Beth slipped her hand from her jacket and glanced to Faras, who pinned her with a steady stare. Did he suspect she had a weapon or, worse, did he suspect who and what she was?

Ty remained where he was as Chino shuffled back toward Faras; then he turned to Beth.

"You're still here," he said through clenched teeth.

"Didn't want to miss your win."

"Win? All I did was make Chino even more determined to kill me."

She looped her arm in the crook of his elbow, casting a glance around at the crowd, who would all watch Ty Redhorse leave with her.

"You are both welcome at the crib anytime," Faras called after them.

Beth lifted her hands and wiggled her fingers in farewell. Ty's breathing was heavy and his face was pale. She glanced at his shoulder. His black T-shirt was definitely wet and she suspected it was wet with blood. His blood. She needed to get him home and find out what was wrong with him.

She lifted the keys. "I'll drive."

"Thank God," he said.

"Hospital?"

"No."

Beth clenched her jaw and didn't argue, ignoring the flutter of worry in her chest. He was a contact. Not her man. Though he had just fought as if he was. It was a level of commitment you couldn't get with threats or bribes. She knew that, but she didn't want to think about it or what it meant.

She did admit, to herself at least, that Ty was not what she had expected.

"Did you know that might happen when you agreed to this?" she asked.

"I knew it was likely."

"How?"

"Because Chino has challenged me before. Any excuse."

"Has he ever bested you?"

"No. But sooner or later he's going to stop playing fair."

She'd put him in danger and he'd fought to protect her. It required acknowledgment.

"Thank you for getting him off me," she said.

He turned to stare for a long moment. Then he said, "Bet that wasn't easy to say."

That made her smile. "You're not what I expected, Ty."

He turned back to look out the window. His words seemed spoken more to himself. "That's because no one expects much."

Beth got him back to his place. She walked behind him as they mounted the outside steps, keeping one hand on his lower back. She ignored the flexing of the strong muscles that rippled beneath the thin fabric of his shirt and concentrated on supporting him. Ty unlocked the door. Hemi charged at them and then skidded to a halt, her toenails scraping on the tile floor. Then she dropped to the ground and whined.

"I know she's got a gun, Hemi." Ty extended his hand and Hemi rose, still whining. His dog knew something was wrong. Ty motioned her outside, but she wouldn't go. Beth admired the canine's loyalty. Hemi was staying right where she was until she knew that her master was all right.

Beth drew out a kitchen chair.

"Sit," said Beth to Ty. He did. Hemi did not.

She removed her jacket and slipped her pistol into the waistband of her jeans, in the center of her back.

Then she got his jacket off. The sticky black T-shirt left a smear of blood when she dragged it up and over his head. Now Beth saw what Hemi smelled. Blood coated the strong muscles of his chest and torso, painting them crimson. Across the top of one shoulder was the cause of the torrent. A six-inch wound cut a jagged course across his flesh. Someone with skill had sutured the laceration, his oldest brother, she suspected, but a one-inch section had torn open.

"Call Kee," said Ty. Then he closed his eyes.

"Do you feel sick?"

"Tired. Tired of fighting and lying and…" His words fell off.

"Is this wound from Antelope Lake?" she asked.

Someone had helped Kee overpower Yury Churkin, the Russian crime family's hired assassin, and taken on the other man on guard in the house. Kee had managed to get to two missing women with the help of his mentor, Hector Hauser, who turned out to be up to his eyeballs in the entire mess. Both captives were rescued, Kee escaped, Hauser was shot and killed along with one of the Russian guards. Yury Churkin had shot himself to avoid arrest. And Ty had been there. The blood evidence said so.

Beth wadded his shirt and used it as a compression bandage, pressing it tight to the wound.

Beth suspected that Ty's arrival had saved his brother Kee and two women. The fact that Ty knew where to find his brother could mean he was involved or that he followed Kee. Instead of wanting the truth, Beth was disturbed to learn she hoped he had tracked his brother to the holding house.

"How did you know where to find Kee and Hauser?" she asked.

"Call him and then you can ask him yourself."

Ty took possession of the shirt. Beth did not remove her hand, and his fell on top of hers. He met her eyes and his expression held a warning as if he knew what would happen if she didn't move away. That attraction was there again, despite his pallor and tight-lipped expression. His eyes flamed and his gaze dropped to her lips.

"You've got my cooperation, Beth. You can't convict me of helping Kee. You want the story, he'll tell you, but call him before I bleed all over my clean floor."

Droplets of blood had already landed, spattering outward evenly in all directions, looking like one of the many crime scenes she had investigated.

She lifted her phone from her back pocket and called Kee Redhorse, identified herself as Ty's new girlfriend and relayed the situation before disconnecting. "He's on his way."

The compression bandage seemed to be doing its job. No more blood ran in rivulets down his smooth ochre skin.

"Do you want me to wash off some of that blood?" she asked.

"Is that code for taking a blood sample?"

He was quick, she'd give him that.

"That ship has sailed."

"Then knock yourself out."

She went to his sink, got a dish towel and returned with a basin of warm soapy water. She dipped the cloth and wrung away the excess water before beginning at the farthest rivulets of blood. His stomach muscles twitched at the first contact and then braced. As a result, his abdomen turned to ridges of taut muscle. His jaw muscles bunched as his eyes met hers and she read the heat. Her body responded and her hand shook as she continued to wash away the blood.

"Am I hurting you?"

"More than you can ever imagine." His voice trembled.

Her smile was part grimace. He was not hers. She needed to keep reminding herself of that. But as the cloth moved over his warm skin, she ignored what was and imagined what might be. Beth took the time and trouble to memorize the patterns on his skin, the tiny mole under his armpit and the scar on his rib cage. The water in the basin turned pink as she worked. The cloth offered little barrier because she let her fingertips graze his torso, stomach and chest. The pads of her fingers relayed the electric excitement that snapped and arced like a power line ripped from its anchors by a violent storm. The storm in Ty's eyes raged as he watched her, one hand clenched to the wadded T-shirt at his shoulder. His free hand rested on his knee, fingers clamping down as if struggling not to touch her.

She worked up his arm, noting again the stylized *W* of inked feathers as she wiped the body art clean. Lower on that arm was the familiar tattoo of the US Marines Corps. As a former army captain, she had her prejudices against his branch of the armed services. But he had her respect because he'd served in Iraq and earned a rank equal to hers in half the time.

"Why didn't you stay?" she said, fingering the tattoo.

"In the marines?" He blew out a breath. "Needed at home."

"Your mother had remarried. Kee was in his residency. Colt was in the service. How where you needed?"

"Discharged."

"What?"

"Colt was discharged."

Oh, now she understood. Colt's records indicated that he had been in Walter Reed with PTSD after capture by Afghanistan insurgents.

"You left the service to bring Colt home?"

He nodded.

Again, an honorable thing to do.

"And you dove through a window for Kee." She shook her head, not wanting to change her assumptions, even when faced with new information. "And you fought Chino for me."

"Didn't do it for you," he said, and looked away, turning his attention to Hemi, who poked at his free hand until he rested it on his dog's square head. Hemi pressed her jaw to Ty's leg and looked up at him with soulful eyes.

"No?" she asked, moving to his back.

Ty glanced over his shoulder at her. "If you're blown, I'd have to do a lot more than bash Chino in the head."

"You'd have to leave."

"Only I can't because if they find out who and what you are, it's not just me. It's my whole family. You understand? It's why I didn't want this deal."

And she thought he'd been reluctant because he didn't want to risk his own neck or because it would endanger his pals. Now she understood that those men weren't his friends. They were using him and Ty was trapped. Ty had plenty of skin in this game. She was going for accolades and position. He was trying to keep his family safe. Beth wondered if she'd be able to get him free.

"I do understand," she said.

Ty was getting under her skin. She was starting to admire him, and that was just bad all around. He was her informant, and his help allowed her access to members of the Wolf Posse. Any relationship between them was impossible.

Still, she brushed his loose straight black hair away, exposing the nape of his neck. She didn't need to touch his hair but took advantage of the excuse. He did not object as she washed the juncture of his neck and shoulder, around the compression bandage and down his back. She took her time, smiling as she watched his skin pucker.

It was the last week in October and fall had arrived in the mountains, turning the leaves yellow. But it was warm in his upstairs apartment. Still, he shivered at her touch.

"You going to kiss me or just tease me?" he asked.

She dropped the dishcloth into the basin as irritation flared. He'd called her bluff.

"Is that what you want?" she asked.

She threaded her damp fingers in his hair.

"What I want you can't give me," he said.

"What's that?"

"A way out that doesn't get me or anyone I love killed."

"I'll keep you safe," she purred.

"Beth, you are the exact opposite of safe," he said.

The temptation was nearly irresistible. He reached with one hand and captured her behind the neck, drawing her in for a kiss.

"You going to stop me or kiss me again?" he asked. Was that hope in his voice, the slight strain and breathlessness?

She pressed her free hand to his chest, feeling his heartbeat pounding too fast and too hard.

"The last kiss was business."

He held her gaze. "Keep telling yourself that."

"I can control myself if you can."

His smile was all challenge. Beth's hands slid around his neck until she splayed them at the base of his skull, tilting his head back and angling it to receive her kiss. He offered no resistance as her mouth moved over his. This time their kiss was a slow sensual exploration. The heat was there, burning like a wildfire, just over the ridge, the smoke visible as the flames approached. His tongue slid against hers, and her breathing and pulse went haywire.

She was in trouble. Beth recognized that a moment before she closed her eyes and gave herself over to his sensual assault.

Hemi scrambled to her feet, toenails scraping on the tile. She growled, hackles going up. Beth drew away and reached for her pistol. The sound of an engine reached them and then silence.

Chapter Eleven

"Kee," said Ty, guessing at the identity of their guest.

Beth moved to the side of the kitchen window, peering out at the wide driveway, weapon drawn. There was a dark pickup truck parked there. The cab light flicked on and the driver disembarked.

"How do you know?"

"I rebuilt that engine and haven't had a chance to fix the hole in his muffler. Blue 2004 RAM pickup, right?"

That looked right, she thought, eyes on the man standing beside his truck. He was the right size and build for Dr. Kee Redhorse.

The visitor turned back to his truck and withdrew a nylon bag. He looped the wide strap over his shoulder.

"Medical bag," she said. The man looked up toward the house, illuminated now by both the cab light and the automatic sensor spotlight that tripped upon his arrival.

It was Kee Redhorse. He waved and headed for the stairs. Beth tucked away her sidearm. "Remember, I'm your new girl."

"New? You sound like I have a lot of them."

"Don't you?" A man as handsome as Ty could have many.

"I'm selective."

Ty's phone rang and he lifted the mobile from his

back pocket. Beth saw the caller ID. It was his younger brother, Jake Redhorse, the tribal police officer.

His voice was loud and animated enough for her to be able to hear him clearly.

"Where are you?" asked Jake.

"Home. Why? What's up?"

"Nothing. Just on a call."

"Where?" Two vertical lines etched Ty's forehead.

Jake did not answer.

"I've got to go."

"Jake?" Ty's voice held a warning as his scowl deepened and he rose to his feet, holding both the phone and the compression bandage. "Jake?" he barked, and then stared at the phone, which indicated the call had ended. Ty swore at the same time Kee knocked on Ty's kitchen door.

Beth moved to admit Dr. Redhorse, but now she was frowning, too. It seemed clear that Officer Redhorse thought his brother might be somewhere he was not supposed to be. But where?

"Responding to the fight at the roadhouse?" she asked as she turned the knob, admitting Kee.

"They'd never call the police after a simple fight like that. Chino wasn't even unconscious."

"You kicked him kind of hard."

Ty smiled as if savoring the memory. Beth frowned and opened his kitchen door to Ty's brother.

Kee looked from Ty to her. Ty's older brother was shorter and his build was leaner than Ty's and his brow was thicker. Their jawlines matched but not their noses because Kee's was longer. Kee dressed like a professional in loafers, Dockers and a blazer worn over a collared button-down shirt. Ty sat topless in jeans and biker boots with a bloody shirt pressed to his injury.

"Kee, this is Beth. She's a new friend of mine."

Kee offered her a nod but then hurried toward his brother.

"Girlfriend, according to Ma," he said to Ty.

"She called you?"

"I don't think you were even out of the drive."

Kee rummaged in his medical bag, which opened at the top like an oversize nylon cooler.

"Let's see," he said, and Ty lifted the sticky T-shirt to reveal the clotting blood and gaping wound.

"You tore out my stitches." Kee sounded put out.

"How did he do that?" Kee asked Beth.

She glanced to Ty, who shook his head.

"I'm not his keeper," she said.

"He needs one," said Kee.

Kee readied his supplies, taking out bottles and packets. Very quickly, he wiped down the injured flesh with a yellow-brown wash that Beth knew was a Betadine solution.

"You want Novocain?" he asked Ty.

"No. That stuff hurts worse than the stitches."

Kee shrugged and then, grim-faced, pulled together the ragged torn flesh and sutured the wound. When he finished he bandaged his shoulder and gave Ty a prescription for antibiotics. "Take some acetaminophen."

Ty rose as Kee packed up. "Some what?"

"Tylenol." Kee handed over several square sample packets of pills.

Ty walked Kee to the door and down the stairs, preceded by Hemi. Beth watched them speaking beside Kee's truck for several minutes before Kee left. She heard the noise caused by the hole in the muffler as he pulled out.

When Ty returned to the kitchen, she had the basin

cleaned and set to dry in the empty dish rack. "You remembered our agreement includes telling no one who I am."

Ty pinched each side of his nose and then dropped his arm to his side. "Why would I do anything to drag my brother into the mess he's just gotten clear of?"

Kee Redhorse had been one of two prime suspects in the abduction cases. It turned out to be the work of his mentor, Hector Hauser, and his administrative assistant and mistress, Betty Mills. Hector had left a mess, which included a community whose trust was shaken, a wife with three grown daughters overshadowed by the shame of their father's actions and a tribe still trying to find the four women who were still missing. Elsie Weaver was the first taken, last November, though the two recovered kidnap victims had never seen her. Kacey Doka had escaped and reported that she had been held with Marta Garcia, Brenda Espinoza and Maggie Kesselman.

Beth knew that finding those surrogates would be the break she needed to get a promotion and her ticket out of the Oklahoma office forever. Ty had been right about why they picked her. It had been her good luck that they'd needed a woman with membership in an Apache tribe. It might have taken her five or six more years to make the kind of case that had been handed to her.

Now if she could just ignore the crackle of fire between herself and Ty Redhorse, she might get through this with a commendation, promotion and transfer orders.

Sleeping with Ty was tempting, but she wasn't going to jeopardize all that she had worked for to have him. No man was worth that. He seemed to know she would be watching, because he turned to look up at her and cast her a wicked smile that made her breath catch just as it would in the instant between when you realize you have triggered a trip wire and the moment it explodes.

He stood without his shirt, the elastic of his white underwear pressed against the flat skin of his stomach.

"I'm going to grab a shirt." He thumbed toward the hall. "You ready to turn in?"

Ty FELT MANY things at that moment, his shoulder throbbing from the stitches, his skin tingling from where Beth had washed him, the restriction of his jeans against the erection that he hoped she didn't notice and the dryness in his throat when he thought of sleeping with her. Most of all he felt his heart jumping around in his chest as if on a trampoline.

"I only have the one bedroom," he said.

She thumbed toward his lopsided couch. "I'll take that."

He frowned. That would be better, easier for him, surely. But she was supposed to be his girl.

"I've never had a woman over here who slept on the couch," he said.

She smiled. "First time for everything."

He shook his head. She didn't understand.

"I'll wager you never had an FBI field agent sleep over, either," she joked.

"Exactly. My girlfriend, my *real* girlfriend, would sleep in my bedroom. A narc would sleep on that." He pointed to the sofa.

"Who's going to see me?" she asked.

He shrugged and instantly regretted it. "Anyone who comes up those stairs."

Beth glanced to the curtainless front door and frowned. The line between her eyebrows and the slight thrust of her bottom lip, paired with the look of concentration, made his skin itch. Were those goose bumps? He glanced at the hairs lifting up on his forearms and then rubbed them back down.

"That happen a lot? Folks at your door?" she asked, still facing the door.

"Folks break down. They show up here. Sometimes it's the posse. I never know."

"So why don't you have a curtain?"

"Never needed that kind of privacy before. Nothing to hide means no reason to break in."

Why did his body act as if he was about to perform a bungee jump instead of fall into bed? She wasn't going to sleep with him. He knew it. His brain knew it. His body was irrationally hopeful.

She turned to him, meeting him with those sage green eyes. "Can't we tack up a curtain?"

"Go ahead." He turned toward the hallway. "Just never did that before."

She had a hand on the back of her neck now and was frowning at the door.

"What's wrong?" he asked.

"It's the small stuff that gives away undercover operations, tips off the criminals. Like an unfamiliar car or an uncharacteristic unease in a colleague. Somebody sweating that shouldn't be."

"Or a curtain?" he asked.

"Yes. Or a darn curtain." She lowered her chin. "Your bed's big enough for two."

She'd seen it, he was sure, because he'd given her ample time to snoop around his place.

"I've always thought so."

She met his teasing smile with a glare. Agent Hoosay was not happy.

"I'll sleep on the floor," she said.

"Hemi sleeps on the floor. Or at least she starts on the floor."

He motioned to the room, then followed her as she carried her duffel down the hall that had his bathroom, small bedroom and linen closet on one side and his bedroom on the other. He waited behind her as she stood in the doorway. He knew what she saw. The queen-sized bed pushed up between the window on the back wall with a small table and lamp on one side. A reading chair with floor lamp and, opposite, the dresser drawers.

Beth's hands went to her hips. "Great."

Hemi nudged past her, dragging her living-room dog bed in her jaws. She laid it by the side of the bed where the other end table would have been. Then she abandoned her bed and claimed her spot in the center of Ty's.

"Fabulous," said Beth.

Hemi could act as a living barrier between them. In the past, when Ty had company, Hemi stayed in the living room, but tonight, he thought her presence was just the reminder Ty needed to stay on his own side of the bed.

"You take window side," said Beth, as if it was her bedroom.

"Yes, ma'am."

Beth retrieved her duffel bag and headed to the bathroom across the hall. He heard the sound of water running in the sink and wondered if she'd know where to find the fresh towels. When the shower clicked on he sat on the bed beside Hemi and pictured Beth naked, with rivulets of hot water gliding over her taut, slim body. Hemi laid her head on his thigh and sighed. Ty felt the same way.

The door across the hall finally opened and steam

billowed into the hall. It brought to him hot, wet air with the earthy scent of ginger and the fragrance of orchids.

She stepped into view. Hemi lifted her head and stared with Ty. If he had a tail it would have been thumping, as well. Beth wore a loose-fitting pink T-shirt with a scooped neck and black cotton yoga pants that stretched over her hips and her long legs, ending below the knee. From there on it was all rich golden-brown skin and slender feet. Her toes curled at his inspection, gripping the floorboards in the hall. Her toenails were painted an unexpected shocking hot pink. The color was so different from the cool, confident agent and hinted at a whimsy he had not seen. He lifted his gaze to meet hers. Her eyes held challenge.

"You don't like pink?" she asked.

"I love pink, especially on you."

She smiled. "Your turn. I set the shower temperature to cold."

So much for hoping she didn't notice his excitement. His mouth twisted downward and he wiped his sweating palms on the cotton covering his thighs. The movement made his shoulder twinge and he flinched.

Her expression changed to one of concern. The look made his heart twist. This was what it would be like to have a woman like this care what happened to him. So many choices he'd made in his life had led him here, to this place and time. He knew a confident, self-sufficient woman like Beth would not be interested in him or would be interested for all the wrong reasons. But that look almost seemed as if she cared.

"Do you need help removing that bandage?"

"I'll manage. Can't get it wet for a day or two anyway."

"Did you take anything for the pain?" she asked.

"Not yet." He didn't say that his favored medication was in the bathroom.

"It's in there, isn't it? The BC Powder?" she asked, thumbing back toward the hall. Her movement made it clear that she wore nothing beneath that T-shirt.

His gaze strayed and he watched her nipples tighten to buds beneath the thin fabric.

"You didn't take the medication your brother gave you?"

"It doesn't do anything for me."

He rose from the bed. Their eyes met. Heat flared between them, and his skin began to itch.

"I'll get them for you," she offered.

"I can do it." He didn't want to be babied. He just wanted to get through this unlikely partnership without doing something stupid, like forgetting he was a job to her.

Beth turned back at the same time he tried to step past. Her elbow collided with his biceps and he gave a hiss of pain through his teeth.

"Oh, I'm sorry!" She had a hold of his opposite arm now, helping him straighten as she looked up at him with that adorable worried expression. Now Ty's stomach hurt worse than his shoulder. Beth was killing him. She hurried to the bathroom medicine cabinet, her scent filling his nostrils as she went. Her wet hair was a riot of curls and he wanted to press his mouth to her neck and thread his fingers in her thick wonderful hair as he breathed her in.

Instead, he clenched his teeth and headed with Hemi to the kitchen, for a glass of water. She arrived with the BC Powder, his go-to for all body pain, as he was letting Hemi out.

"Extra-strength okay?" She held up the package.

"Fine."

She offered him a papery envelope of ground pain reliever in her open palm. His fingers swept over her hand, and Beth's hand trembled. His eyes lifted to hers and she lowered her lashes as green eyes darted away. He unfolded one end of the packet and poured the bitter powder to the back of his throat, then chased it with cold water.

Her upper teeth clamped over her plump bottom lip and dragged over the tender flesh. He took another long swallow of water and his throat still felt dry. There was a definite lump lodged there.

"Wow," he said. "You are something because I can't think about anything but kissing you again."

Her eyes rounded and she backed toward the hall.

"Shower," she said. "Because I am sleeping with you, but we are not having sex."

"Tonight," he said, qualifying.

"Ever. It's a job. After I bust up this surrogate ring, I am moving on and you're staying where you have always been, here on Turquoise Canyon with your family."

"Between my family and the Wolf Posse, you mean."

"What?"

"It's why I've stayed."

"You saying you are here to protect them?"

He did not reply, just walked past her down the hall. He'd already said too much. He thought about the information that Faras had given him about the location of the first ever meth lab on tribal land. He didn't like it, but it wasn't his business and it wasn't Beth's, either, because despite their agreement, this was not part of the surrogate kidnapping ring. Faras was hedging his bets, because it was very possible that the Russians would find their little fertile field of young surrogates ruined by the increasing attention of the police and federal authorities.

Ty was angry over the fact that the Russian crime organization supposed that no one would miss the girls that disappeared and even more furious that they were right. Up until Jake and his new wife, Lori, made the connection between the disappearances and the tribe's clinic, no one had thought these missing girls were anything more than runaways.

Ty hit the shower, careful not to soak the bandage Kee had fixed to his shoulder. The stitches tugged, but he managed to get himself clean and ready for bed. He dragged on a pair of loose sweatpants and shuffled like an old man across the hall. Beth was in bed under the sheets and blanket. Hemi stretched out on top of the blanket beside her like a living partition. Ty no longer cared. He was too tired to do anything more than imagine having a woman as smart and beautiful as Beth pressed up beside him in his bed. He realized that living above his garage was not likely what she pictured when she closed her eyes and that conjecture took some of the spark from him. Hemi fell asleep first, snoring as usual. Beth fell asleep next, likely with her hand on her service pistol.

Ty waited for the medication to take the sharpest notes of pain from his shoulder and then he closed his eyes, drifting away to sleep. His dreams were filled with a sense of looming menace that woke him in a sweat during the night. He wondered if he had a fever. Hemi lifted her head and then dropped it on his stomach. He rested a hand on her shoulder and noticed that Beth was lying on her side facing him. One of her hands was on the dog's rib cage, just inches from his. In sleep, her skin glowed ethereal, like a fairy queen's, and her face was as serene and calm as the clear night sky. He resisted the urge to touch his fingers to hers and closed his eyes. The beat of his heart echoed in his healing shoulder.

The next thing he knew he was startled awake a few hours later by an unfamiliar ringtone. He threw himself to a seated position as Beth scrambled off the bed and retrieved her mobile phone, which she had plugged into a charger on his dresser. He scooped up his mobile from the nightstand and saw that it wasn't even 6:00 a.m. He'd been asleep less than five hours.

Ty sank back to the pillows and groaned, covering his eyes with his arm against the pale gray light that filtered through the slats of the blinds. His shoulder pulsed to life, sending a dull ache down his arm with each heartbeat.

Beth was speaking to her supervisor. She was telling him she could be there in twenty minutes. When she finished the call she was scrambling through her duffel.

"Be where in twenty?" he asked.

"Go back to sleep," she said.

"Yeah, right. Am I going?"

She shook her head, her arms now full of clothing and her bathroom bag. "I'll see you later today. Just carry on as you normally would do."

"So fix the carburetor. Is that your suggestion?"

But she was already gone.

He was still in bed when she returned. She was dressed as a civilian, her brown leather coat hiding her shoulder harness and her black turtleneck sweater hiding the FBI shield he suspected she wore. "Call me if you hear anything from Faras."

"Yes, Agent Hoosay."

Hemi stood before Beth, tail wagging.

"Let her out?" she asked.

"If you wouldn't mind."

Beth and Hemi disappeared down the hall and Ty rose to meet the day. He was on his second cup of coffee when Hemi demanded readmission and breakfast. Ty spent Monday morning in the shop and the afternoon took Hemi over to his mother's place. Ty fixed her bathroom sink drain, which was choking under the strain of hair shed by the three foster girls, Lori's sisters, and his own sister, Abbie. He pulled a wad of wet black hair the size of a drowned rat from the drain, solving the problem.

His mother thanked him in the usual way by fixing him a sandwich. But she sat with him, waiting until he finished to bring up whatever it was that was troubling her. Then she pushed a folded sheet of paper at him with the warning to not get upset.

He unfolded the page and noted the prison insignia at the top of the letterhead. His heart rate doubled as he scowled. He was already upset.

When she spoke, his mother's voice held a familiar tightness he had not heard in a long time. "He's been paroled."

Chapter Twelve

There was no need to ask who Ty's mother meant. His father had served seven years on a ten-year sentence. They'd all been bracing for this. Seven years ago, Ty had thought he had everything settled. Addie would be in college, hopefully, and Ty would have his brothers to help protect their mother.

But Colt was gone. And Kee and Jake both had their own families to protect.

"When?" asked Ty.

"Soon. I don't know exactly. I put in a postconviction request form so they'll notify me fifteen days before release, but you know, the mail up here is slow. Might not know right away."

Ty glanced down at the letter again and realized that it was over a month old. "You just got this?"

His mother flushed. "No. A while ago."

"And you didn't tell me until now?"

"I knew you'd be upset."

That didn't even begin to cover it. Ty had been to see his father only once after he was incarcerated because he wanted to see him locked up. Only after the visit did Ty realize the vanity of that meeting and the danger it brought. Colton Redhorse had figured it out at first glance. His father was a brutal man with a hairpin trigger. He'd raged and the guards had come. Ty had not gone back. He didn't need to. The damage was already done.

His father was as unpredictable as a tornado. And just like with a tornado, Ty knew he would cause destruction, but there was really no way to predict where or when. "Do Jake and Kee know?"

"I didn't know how to tell them. I haven't even told Burt yet." She'd told Ty before her own husband.

Ty's intake of breath was sharp. Both Jake and Kee visited their father on occasion. It had been Kee who had related to Ty that Colton had discovered that May had remarried, and his father had not taken the news well. Burt was in serious danger.

"But he won't come here," said May, her head bobbing as she tried to convince herself.

Ty met her gaze, offering no reassurance. He knew that his father would strive not to get caught. But he highly doubted he would resist the urge to hurt Burt and the woman he still considered his wife, divorce papers aside.

"Your father isn't stupid, Ty," said his mother. "He doesn't want to go back there."

"That doesn't mean he won't hurt you, Mom. He knows you won't press charges."

"It only makes things worse," she said, defending her position.

And here he was, right back where he'd been when he was eighteen, trying to protect his mother, brothers and sister from his father. Only this time, his father would see Ty coming.

Going to the police would do nothing. His father had served his time and Ty knew that tribal could act only after his father committed a crime. By then it would be too late.

He needed to speak to Faras. Again. Damn.

Ty made his excuses to his mother and broke the news to Burt about the firestorm heading their way. Burt went pale. He was a good-hearted man, but not a fighter. Ty cautioned Burt to contact him if they received any more information on his father's imminent parole. Then he whistled for Hemi, who crawled out from under his mother's front porch and stretched. Ty opened the passenger door and folded back the seat, waiting for his dog to climb in. Then they drove directly to the Wolf Posse's headquarters.

The gang had moved up in the world since their affiliation with the Russian crime syndicate. They no longer lived in a hollowed-out shell of a building. Faras had purchased a ranch outside the town of Koun'nde with cash. The outfit was fenced with an electric gate entry. The only one on the reservation, as far as Ty knew. Once beyond this first security barrier, Ty passed two checkpoints, although only one would have been visible to outsiders. When he was within sight of the barn and house, he was greeted by the first sentry. Today it was Henry Lavender, who stepped off the porch and raised a hand at Ty in greeting, waiting for the dust to settle before approaching his car. Ty lowered his front window with the crank.

"Hey, Ty. Heard about the fight with Chino. Man! You messed up his face. He had to go to the dentist in Darabee. He been gone for hours." Henry offered Hemi his hand and then scratched behind the dog's ears while Hemi lifted her chin and let her eyes roll back in her head. "She likes that," said Lavender, grinning.

Ty stuck with the topic of conversation—Chino and

the dentist. "Maybe we'll get lucky and they'll wire Chino's jaw shut."

Henry snorted with laughter, holding his fist to his mouth to stifle his mirth. He glanced over his shoulder at the closed door as if checking to see if anyone had noticed his hilarity. Then he shifted his gaze back to Ty.

Ty stepped from the '67 GTO and signaled Hemi to stay put.

"Faras here?" Ty asked.

"Yeah, but he's in some kind of meeting. Something's happening, bro. I heard them mention Quinton. They didn't sound happy."

"What about him?"

"Dunno. Something bad, you ask me."

"Tell him I'm here. I'll wait."

Henry nodded and ducked into the house. Ty glanced about at the trucks and cars parked along the drive. He had worked on most of them. He recognized Faras's second car, a new black Mustang. He studied the cars he did not know. He wondered if any belonged to the Russian connection.

Today he was here about his own business. Business that concerned Faras as much as himself. Dangerous business. But if the opportunity arose to learn some information about the missing women from his tribe, he was not above taking advantage.

Henry returned after a few minutes and ushered him in through the living room, where Norleena Caddo and Autumn Tay lounged on the overstuffed sofa watching a reality TV show involving women as overly primped and made up as the two of them. Ty paused to issue a greeting in Tonto, which they both returned without shifting their eyes from the large-screen plasma TV. Both women were in their early twenties, pretty if you wiped off the paint smearing their faces, and both had joined the gang during high school. They reminded him of Japanese geisha, here to entertain and attend to the men and, equally, to stay out of their way when unwanted. Ty compared their vapid expressions to the purpose he saw glimmering in Beth Hoosay's bright eyes. Were there gangs where she lived in Oklahoma? Did she have a solid home life that helped her avoid such land mines and trapdoors?

As he entered the dining room, he made a mental note to find out more about her past. She interested him and he thought it would be to his benefit to know more about where she came from.

Faras sat at the head of the rectangular wooden table. He motioned for Andre Napualani to move over and make room for Ty. Also at the table were two other members of his posse, Deoma Quintero and Eldon Kahn. Noticeable in his absence was Quinton Ford. And Chino Aria, of course, though Ty knew where he was today and the knowledge that Chino was in a dentist's chair gave him some measure of satisfaction.

Ty took the seat vacated by Andre. Despite what his brothers, his mother, his father and tribal police believed, Ty was not a member of the Wolf Posse. Perhaps he was in a worse position because he owed Faras. But Faras also owed Ty. Friends since high school, the two had a sort of symbiotic relationship forged by need, mutual respect and common history.

"You want something to drink, Ty?" asked Faras.

"Dr Pepper."

Faras called to Norleena Caddo to fetch the drink. A moment later Norleena clicked through the dining room on ridiculously high heels that were as impractical as her short shorts and halter top. The men watched as she opened the refrigerator and then leaned over as if knowing all eyes were upon her. She retrieved the soft drink and used the edge of the counter to pop off the cap with practiced expertise. Then she returned, swaying her hips, and slid the drink before Ty. Her mission completed, she rested a hand on Faras and asked if he needed anything else. Ty always felt nauseated at the displays of submission required by the females in the gang. Their compliance was mandatory. However, he noted that the pecking order between females was much less civilized. Some of the battles for dominance were epic. Most recently, the removal of the alpha female, Minnie Cobb, had left a power vacuum. Much as Noreen would like the spot, Ty knew that it was Jewell Tasa who seemed to be stepping into Minnie's expensive shoes.

Faras gave Noreen a pat on the posterior and pushed her back toward the living room. Then he watched her go. Only when she was out of sight did they return to business.

"Happy to see you, bro," said Faras.

"I'm sorry about Chino," said Ty.

"Had it coming. She wasn't one of ours and you told him she was your girl. Listen, we've had some trouble. I need to finish up with my council. You got any business for me?" asked Faras.

Ty appreciated Faras seeing him without notice and interrupting his own business for Ty. It was the kind of respect he did not afford anyone else, except his bosses, the drug distribution network and now the Russians. Ty got right to the point.

"My dad's parole came through." Ty watched as some of the color drained from Faras's face.

"That so?"

Ty nodded, holding his friend's gaze and seeing the worry there. Faras understood that his father's release threatened them both.

"Yeah, we need to talk. Meet you out by the fire pit in ten."

Dismissed, Ty left the council table.

"You want company?" asked Faras, motioning his head to the living room.

Ty swallowed back his disdain. "Naw. Not today."

Or any day. Ty didn't want a woman who was obliged to service him like he was some John. The entire practice sickened him almost as much as knowing that Faras chose who would be initiated each year, just as he picked which girls would disappear. Faras knew the tribe in a way that even their own tribal council didn't. He knew who was vulnerable and who was not, who would be missed and who would not. He'd chosen well, but he hadn't counted on the resourcefulness of two of his victims.

Zella Colelay had evaded capture by his posse for long enough to deliver the baby forced upon her. And a second victim, Kacey Doka, had escaped capture to prove she had not been a runaway. And that had been a problem that could not be erased.

Ty sat under the newly erected pergola beside the circular masonry fire pit. He did not attend the Wolf Posse parties. He avoided this house whenever possible and met Faras only in the relatively neutral ground of the roadhouse. But today he made the exception because his father would be coming home to Turquoise Canyon.

It was another twenty minutes before Faras appeared carrying an open beer bottle. He sat in the shade beside Ty.

It was a common way in his culture to speak around issues. The proper way to address a concern was to sneak up on it casually after some degree of small talk. But Faras was a businessman and rarely had time for custom.

"Before we get to your dad, I want to tell you about Quinton."

"What about him?"

Faras leaned forward, gripping the neck of the bottle with both hands as he stared at the dirt before his boots. Then he shook his head, his lips a tight line.

Ty leaned forward as well, though the action hurt his shoulder. "Faras? Did something happen?"

"Yeah." His voice was hushed. "Well, it hasn't happened yet. But it will." Faras shook his head. He was not usually this obtuse. Then without warning Faras lifted the full beer bottle and threw it with all his might. The bottle sailed in a graceful arc, spinning end over end as it expelled its contents before smashing on the masonry.

Ty sat back, waiting.

"There was a raid on our meth lab."

"Deer Kill Meadow?" asked Ty, repeating the location of the lab that Faras had mentioned to him previously. Faras had also told Ty that he would be responsible for making deliveries from that meth lab. Ty had been thinking of ways to get out of that. Now, however, with his father's imminent release, his bargaining position was greatly compromised.

"No, no, man. That's the point. Ain't no lab on Deer Kill Meadow. Just like there ain't no lab down on Canyon Ridge Road."

"What?" Ty didn't understand.

Faras turned in his seat to face Ty. "We ain't got a meth lab, bro. Neither place. Made it up."

Ty felt his skin tingling as he recalled how close he had come to telling Beth about the lab. But it wasn't related to their case and he hadn't made an agreement to help with anything but the surrogate ring. Then he remembered the early morning phone call and Beth's hasty departure. Was that the tip from Quinton reaching the FBI here on Turquoise Canyon? Ty clenched his fists and forced himself to remain still as his muscles twitched and his skin prickled.

Was she all right?

"Why?"

"A test," said Faras. Finally, he met Ty's gaze. "I should have known it wasn't you. But I had to be sure. You've been different since Jake found that baby. Distant. I knew you didn't like our association with the Russians and I knew we had a leak. Someone told the FBI where to find Kacey. You delivered her and she was your brother's girl, so you seemed the obvious choice. And then someone told the FBI where to find the two girls they were keeping at Antelope Lake. Your brother Kee was there with Dr. Hauser. I thought it likely that Kee had told your brother Jake about the location of the house. But I know your brother Kee and, no offense, he could not have overtaken those Russian soldiers. I still don't know what happened except that Hauser and the two watching over our goods all died."

Ty did not like hearing the captured women being referred to as goods. He had a sister about the same age as the missing girls and it burned him up inside to think of someone doing that to Addie.

"So I set up you and Quinton," continued Faras. "Fed you each a different location. Today the FBI raided the house on Canyon Ridge."

Ty needed to speak to Beth. To warn her. Was it just

a test or also a trap? What if Faras's men saw her and remembered her?

If Faras knew Beth's identity, then she was dead and he would follow soon after.

Suddenly, it was hard to sit still. He longed to reach for his phone and call her. Hear her voice and be certain she was safe. Instead he laced his hands before him and told himself not to let Faras see that he was nervous or that his shoulder was injured. He was grateful for the leather jacket he wore over the injury earned while helping Kee rescue Ava Hood at Antelope Lake.

"Quinton?" asked Ty.

"Yeah. My second. Can you believe that? I hope they paid him well and he put something away for his woman and kid because he's not coming home to them."

Ty's heart hammered. "No?"

"Minute I got the call about the raid, I sent out Chino."

Chino was not at the dentist's. He was assigned to murder Quinton. Ty's ears buzzed. He liked Quinton. He'd almost been Quinton.

"I'm sorry," said Ty. His throat felt as hard and dry as a canyon wall.

"I need a new second."

"Chino wants that job," said Ty.

"And you don't. But the Russians are pulling out and when they go, so does the money. They're used to it now, my guys. Food, booze, nice wheels, you know? It won't be easy replacing that kind of income. We need to prepare for that. Besides, Chino don't want to be my second. He wants to be alpha wolf."

"They're pulling out?" Ty tried to keep the elation from his voice. The scourge among them was leaving. Jake and the FBI had done it, put enough pressure on the organized crime bosses that the Russians were leaving their rez. His brother Colt could come back home. Ty could have danced, he was so happy. "What about the ones they still have?"

"They own them. Use them again or send them into service some other way." He shrugged. "Dunno."

Human trafficking, Ty realized. That was what Faras was saying. "They're our women."

"They're like Peter Pan's lost boys. The ones that fell out of their strollers and no one noticed or cared. Remember you read me that story?" Faras grinned.

Ty had a sickening feeling that the very sad and lost boy he'd read that story to had grown up to be a pirate himself and used that tale to influence his selection of victims.

"We should demand them back," said Ty.

"You don't ask those guys for nothing. They'll hand you your ass and make you wear it as a hat. Besides, we got our own troubles. Your dad is coming back. We have to be strong because sure as hell, he'll challenge me. I need you as my second, Ty. I want you to join us again."

Chapter Thirteen

Beth returned to Ty's place after sundown on Monday night to find the bay doors of the shop open and Hemi trotting out to meet her. The dog escorted her down the drive, barking joyfully but not getting too close to her motorcycle. She cut the engine as Ty stepped out of the garage, using a rag to wipe his greasy hands.

The day had been terrible. The tip was bad, the location wrong and the result was that fifteen heavily armed FBI agents had startled a very nice older couple from their bed. The rest of the day had been spent making apologies and trying and failing to bring in their informant, Quinton Ford.

There had also been a break in the surrogacy case. Police in Santa Fe, New Mexico, had picked up Elsie Weaver, the first of the women to go missing. Beth's supervisor had flown out there and discovered that Elsie had never been abducted. According to the sixteen-year-old, she had been to the clinic in November of last year but that visit had nothing to do with her decision to run away with her twenty-three-year-old boyfriend, now being held in the Santa Fe jail on a growing list of charges.

Beth had gone back to Betty Mills, the former health clinic administrator and Dr. Hauser's accomplice there.

Mills had been transferred to the larger facility in the neighboring city of Darabee. Betty had been less than cooperative. Her plea deal had gone out the window when she failed to mention that tribal police detective Ava Hood's cover had been blown. Mills had let Hood walk right into a trap that nearly got her killed. Eventually, Mills verified for Beth that Elsie Weaver had never been one of their girls, as Mills called her, simply the inspiration, because when Elsie disappeared, no one cared. No one looked. She was listed in a database and forgotten. That gave Hector the idea of a simple way to raise the funds he needed to bring their facility into the twenty-first century.

Hector had approached a colleague in Phoenix who ran a fertility clinic. Then a contact was made with Kuznetsov's representative. The tribe's gang was enlisted to capture and deliver, and just like that, they were in business.

Beth rolled the bike onto its kickstand and slid off the seat. Beth still did not wholly understand Ty's role in all this. He was an enigma. May Redhorse's second son was not at all what she had expected. He had clearly moved to protect his brother Kee's fiancée from her captivity and, if Officer Redhorse was to be believed, to save Jake and the infant he and his wife adopted from attack. Yet they had him on driving the recaptured Kacey Doka back to the Russians. She suspected there was more to that story than what she had read in the deposition, but they didn't need it because his blood at the crime scene was the hook that guaranteed Ty's compliance, as much as that was possible.

Ty stepped into the circle of the floodlight fixed above the bay doors. The bright light reflected off his brow, cheeks and chin. His biceps bunched as he worked the rag, and her stomach pitched and something lower thrummed. Seeing him momentarily chased away the weariness that had settled between her shoulders.

She cast him a lazy smile. He didn't return it. In fact, there was a new tension in his face and a ticking beneath his eye.

"Where's Quinton?" he asked, his voice calm, but he bunched the rag at his side. Hemi came to him, sitting at his feet. She whined, as if sensing his upset.

"How do you know about that?"

"Canyon Ridge Road. Meth lab. Right?"

Beth faced him, now completely on alert. She needed to know how Ty knew about this.

"Did anyone see you?"

"What?"

"Were you there?" He moved forward, his gaze sweeping her as if searching for injury.

Her skin tingled a warning. "I can't tell you that. Now tell me, how did you know about this?"

"They told me it was Deer Kill Meadow Road," said Ty.

"Who did?"

Ty explained it to her. Beth felt her chest squeeze. They'd thought their informant had run out on them. Intentionally fed them bad intel for his payout and then fled. The truth was much worse.

"But you signed an agreement to reveal such information," said Beth.

"No. My agreement was specific to the surrogate-ring case."

He was right and his intelligence now irritated her. She wasn't used to informants who had this kind of smarts.

"Beth, if they saw you, you're blown."

That made her pause as she thought back over her day.

"I never left the vehicle. Tinted glass," she said as much to herself as to Ty.

His shoulders sagged. "You sure?"

She nodded. That was relief in his expression and not for his own skin. Ty was concerned for hers.

"Tell me all you know about this," she said.

"They fed us each different locations to see which way you moved. Canyon Ridge Road was the location they told Quinton. You understand? Now Faras has his snitch. It's Quinton and he's sent Chino to kill him."

Beth wheeled back to the bike, pausing only to make a call. Then she was racing back to the command center they had set up in Koun'nde. They had to find Quinton before Chino Aria did.

BETH DID NOT return that night. On Tuesday, Ty tried to get Kee and Jake out for supper but only managed to get them to come for a drink. They met in the casino's sports bar. The waitress wore an elaborate purple wig, a plastic tiara and fairy wings. She took their drink orders and left them three small candy bars with the menus.

"What's up with that?" asked Ty.

"It's Halloween," said Kee. "I promised Mom I'd be home in time to take Abbie, Shirley and Shirley's brothers out trick-or-treating."

Halloween. Ty had completely forgotten. Lately, his entire life seemed a sort of trick. Ty glanced at the waitress and wondered if he should know what she was dressed as.

"What about Jackie and Winnie?" he asked, mentioning the other two foster girls staying with their mother.

Kee ticked off the children on his fingers. "Winnie is manning the door for Mom, Jackie has a party and Ava is taking the girls out." He was referring to Ava Hood's nieces, Olivia, Alexandra and Margarita, all under five. It looked very much as if Kee and Ava would take temporary custody of her nieces while Ava's sister sorted out her drinking at a six-week rehab program.

"What are they dressing as?" asked Jake.

"Princesses for the twins and Olivia is going as blue."

"Blue what?"

"I have no idea. She likes blue."

That three-year-old had ideas all her own, admitted Ty.

He waited until the waitress delivered their drinks before dropping the bombshell about their father's parole.

"Well, he won't do anything stupid, like threaten Mom, because he'll be on parole," said Kee, ever the rational and optimistic one. "If he even sets foot on her property, she can have him arrested."

"She never had him arrested before," Ty reminded him.

"I'll start the paperwork on an order of protection," said Jake.

Ty groaned. "That won't stop him."

Jake still believed in the law, even after all he'd seen. Admirable and naive, Ty thought.

Jake had once called the police on their father, assuming, wrongly, that they could help. Neighbors had called, as well. But May had, without exception, failed to press charges at every opportunity. Afraid, he now knew, of what would happen when he got out.

Jake lifted his chin and glared at Ty. "It won't stop him, but it will give me the right to arrest him if he goes near her."

Ty hissed between his teeth, letting the frustration

escape like steam from an engine. "You can't be there twenty-four-seven. Eventually he'll come after her and Burt. And what about Addie? What if our sister gets between Colton and Ma?" Ty had stopped calling their father Dad the day he saw his father bounce a beer bottle off his mother's head. He'd called the police that time and paid the price.

Jake's mouth flattened and his eyes went steely.

Ty hadn't been there when his father broke their mother's arm. But Addie and Colt had been. Colt had called Jake, who was then fourteen and at basketball practice. Ty had been off with Faras somewhere causing trouble and Kee had been in his second year of medical school.

"Restraining orders only work on people who follow the law," said Ty.

"What do you suggest?" asked Kee.

Ty's reply was immediate. "One of us needs to be out there with her."

Jake's face was grim. He had a new wife and baby girl to look after. He had a full-time job that required him to be away long dangerous hours.

"Prison might have changed him," said Kee, looking for the good in people even where there was none.

"I'm sure it has," said Ty. "Made him meaner, tougher and more dangerous."

"We don't need to do anything yet," said Jake. "I'll call the parole office and ask to be contacted when his release is scheduled. In the meantime, I'll get Mom to file the paperwork."

"Good luck with that," said Ty.

"Just let me handle this," said Jake. He rubbed his neck. "Maybe I'll go pick him up. Better way to keep an eye on him. Find out what his plans are. You don't know for certain that he's coming here."

Ty did know because his father had a score to settle with Faras and with him. "He'll be back."

"Well," said Jake, "we'll see." Then he turned to Kee. "Did I hear that Ava is going back to school?"

Ava Hood, Kee's intended, had been a tribal police detective down on the rez in Salt River, but she'd broken one too many rules and lost her shield. Woman after Ty's own heart. Ava had done what it took to get her niece back. Now she and Kee had custody of Louisa Tah and her other three nieces while her sister struggled with some addiction problems. Both his brothers had full plates.

"Yes," said Kee. "Forensic fire investigator."

Sounded hard to Ty.

"Knew we wouldn't keep her in dispatch for long," said Jake. "Oh, and I heard from Bear Den that we found Elsie Weaver."

Elsie was the first to go missing and, according to what Beth had told him, the inspiration for Hector's plan to use certain women from their tribe as surrogates.

"Where?" asked Ty.

"Flagstaff. She's working down there, living with her boyfriend."

"She's okay?" asked Ty.

"Completely. She wasn't taken by anyone. She's a runaway. When they picked up her boyfriend on shoplifting, Elsie came to get him and was detained. She just wants nothing to do with her family."

"Can you blame her?" asked Ty.

Jake made a face and continued, knowing as well as anyone what went on in the Weaver family. "They've been contacted nonetheless. She's told the police down there that she didn't know about the others."

"She coming home?" asked Kee.

Jake sighed. "She's a minor, so yes. Don't think they'll keep her long, though."

"So that leaves just three missing?" said Ty.

"Marta Garcia, Brenda Espinoza and Maggie Kesselman," said Jake.

Kee glanced at his watch. The gathering had reached its conclusion. Ty had failed to get either brother to recognize the magnitude of the threat their father posed. But that was because he had been unwilling to share one critical piece of information, the reason Colton Redhorse would be coming back looking for blood.

Chapter Fourteen

Quinton Ford's body was found on the southern bank of the Hakathi River between the Red Rock Dam and Antelope Lake sometime on the morning of Tuesday, October 31, by two kayakers. Beth had not learned this until late that afternoon when someone from the Arizona Highway Patrol notified tribal police that they'd found a body, possibly Native American. Photos had been sent and the identification made.

In other words, the body was found off the rez, making it a matter for the Arizona Highway Patrol. By the time Beth discovered that they had a body, Ford's remains had already been moved to the morgue in Darabee Hospital. Beth met with the medical examiner, who had made only a preliminary check. The ME had experience with several suicides from each of the series of four dams and told her that, based on the visible injuries, he believed the death was caused by a fall and not drowning. He said the autopsy would determine if the deceased had water in his lungs or if he survived the plunge, only to drown. Beth took charge of the records and the body, waiting until after 9:00 p.m. for someone from the Phoenix office to arrive to take custody of Quinton Ford's remains.

Beth suspected the manner of death would be listed

as homicide, not suicide. The worst part, aside from
having one of their informants killed, was that there
was no one to notify. Quinton Ford's mother was dead.
No father was listed on his birth records and he had no
siblings. It seemed Ford had only the Wolf Posse, and
his betrayal of that family had come with swift retribu-
tion. Now she needed to prove it.

For now, she would concentrate on the case that
would get her noticed—breaking up the surrogate ring.

When she returned to Ty's home, it was after midnight. She had expected to be locked out, but saw the
bay door open and the lights on.

Hemi sprinted out to meet her and escorted her in,
her barking muted by the sound of Beth's bike. The dog
waited until Beth cut the engine and dismounted before
jumping up on her hind legs to wave her front paws in
the air as if to say hello. Beth laughed and gave Hemi
a scratch as she fell back to all fours.

Beth walked with Hemi to the open bay door to find
Ty working in his garage. He wore jeans and a tight gray
muscle shirt that revealed the white gauze now covering his shoulder injury. Sweat and grease mingled on
his defined muscles, his arms raised as he worked beneath a car he had driven up onto a lift using ramps.

The mobile light, complete with cage and hook, was
fixed to the undercarriage of an automobile she recognized as belonging to his mother.

"You're going to pull out those stitches again," she
said by way of greeting.

He ignored the warning and spoke without looking
at her. "Busy day?"

"Yes."

"Hungry?" he asked.

She hadn't realized just how hungry she was but now recalled she completely missed dinner. "Yes."

"I've got steaks, steak fries and mini Snickers."

She lifted her brows in confusion, thinking chocolate an odd choice as a side dish.

"It's Halloween," said Ty, and glanced at the wall clock. "Or it was."

She'd been reminded by the medical examiner's necktie, which had been covered in skeletons. She really thought he could wear that any day. Beth glanced toward the road.

"You get any trick-or-treaters out here?" She looked back at the highway that threaded down the lonesome stretch between Koun'nde and Piñon Forks, thinking a kid would have to be crazy to come down this drive.

"I got them for you. Trick-or-treat," he said.

She managed a weary smile. "Have you eaten?"

He should have, hours ago, but he shook his head. "Not yet."

Had he been waiting for her? That thought pleased her far more than it should have because it made them seem like a real couple. The disturbing feeling of intertwining her work and her personal life wiped away her smile. Ty had become much more than a way in to the Wolf Posse, a way to make her case.

"Been busy," he said by way of an excuse, and headed for the stairs with Hemi at his heels.

Ty flipped on the oven to preheat it, then returned several minutes later, after showering and putting on a clean shirt. She'd managed to set the table in his absence. She offered to make a salad, but Ty had opted to just slice a head of lettuce into quarters and drizzle blue-cheese dressing over the wedges, then sprinkle bacon crumbles on top. It was all she could do to keep from scooping it off her plate and into her mouth as he dropped the frozen potato wedges onto a cookie sheet and tucked them into the oven.

She told herself that steak did not take long to cook and she could wait, as she followed him downstairs on weary legs. He turned on the gas grill, which sat tucked under the stairs. Beth rested in a lawn chair feeling like a pencil worn down to the nub. The steaks hit the hot grill with a satisfying sizzle. The smell of cooking beef made her mouth water. When she next trudged up the stairs, the kitchen was filled with the homey aroma of roasting potatoes. She sighed with pleasure.

"Beer or water?" he asked.

Beer sounded good, but she was still on duty. "Water is fine."

Ty stopped at the open refrigerator. "I have one ice tea."

"Sold," she said, raising a finger as if at an auction.

Hemi curled in her bed by the door. Clearly she did not subsist on table scraps, which was good because Beth doubted there would be any left, at least from her plate.

Ty handed over the bottle of tea and set a glass of water beside his own plate. Then he served the steak, medium rare, with Worcestershire sauce and ketchup for the fries. For the next few minutes Beth was completely occupied with the meal. She paused when she noticed Ty was not moving. She glanced up and found him smiling at her.

"Good?" he asked.

"Great. This is the best steak I've ever had."

His head tilted to the side and his eyebrows lifted in a look of skepticism.

"No. Really."

"Well, hunger makes the best spice." He lifted his fork and stared down at his plate. "I think I see why my mom still likes having us all over for Sunday dinner. There's something satisfying about feeding someone…" He seemed like he was about to say more, but his mouth snapped shut.

Someone…you cared about? Beth wondered, silently finishing the sentence. She gave him a wary smile. In another time and place he would be exactly the sort of man she would find appealing. He clearly loved his family. He worked hard. Was a risk-taker and took excellent care of his other female companion, Hemi. But the list of problems could not be overlooked. Ty had committed armed robbery at only eighteen. His father was a career criminal and abused his wife. Such things ran in families, didn't they?

"Well, it's excellent. Thank you for dinner." She returned her attention to her plate to finish the last bite of steak and the three remaining fries.

He waited until she set aside her fork and knife before speaking again.

"Snickers?" he asked.

She smiled, hands on her stomach. "No room."

Beth finished the last of her ice tea.

"Did you find Quinton?" he asked.

She lowered the bottle to the tabletop and nodded, her smile gone. "We did."

He didn't ask her if he was alive. It seemed to her that he already knew. He tucked his chin and was silent for a long time.

Finally he spoke without meeting her gaze. "Where?"

"Below Red Rock Dam."

His steady gaze seemed to accuse her of something. "You're a witness." She stretched her hand across the table. "You can testify that Faras fed you false information."

His eyes rounded. "You didn't go to Deer Kill Meadow?"

"No. After the intel you supplied, we felt going there would compromise you."

She didn't say aloud that Quinton's death was on their hands. They had moved on the intelligence Quinton had provided, even though it had no bearing on the case they were supposed to be up here investigating, exposing him as their informant. Ty had held the information and she was so glad.

"I'm sorry about your friend," said Beth.

"He wasn't my friend. None of them are my friends."

"But…" Her words trailed off. She didn't know what to say. It seemed clear that he had chosen to join the gang at some point. He had acted on Faras's order. And he had branded himself with their sign. She glanced at the four eagle feathers forming the letter *W* on Ty's forearm. She lifted her attention to find Ty's gaze sharp and intent.

"You're a member of the posse," she said.

He did not argue. "I joined when I was eighteen. When I came back from Iraq, I partially severed that relationship. But we're still connected."

"I've never heard of anyone leaving the gang. I don't think it's possible."

"It is."

"How?"

"If I tell you something about that day I drove the getaway car with my father, can you use it against me?"

"Not on that one. Statute of limitations is up and you were offered a deal. Right?"

"Yes."

"So I can't use anything you say against you unless it is related to a crime without limitations, like murder."

Ty nodded his understanding, still not meeting her gaze. She waited, praying that whatever he might tell her would not incriminate him, that he had never killed someone. She realized with a sinking feeling she did not want him to put her in the position to have to arrest him.

Gangs had entrance rituals. For boys it was usually crime. For girls it was sex. What crime had Ty committed to join?

His chin lifted and his eyes narrowed. The expression made him look dangerous. "I joined the Wolf Posse because of him."

"Your father?"

He nodded, sending his hair over his forehead, where it hung across his eyes.

"Why?"

"My father was the next in line to head the Wolf Posse back then. He was thirty-nine and second in command. Then Gerome Hessay was shot in a drug deal gone wrong. They lost their leader and the product. So nothing to sell. After Gerome died, my father moved to take his place. So did Faras Pike, but he was young, only twenty. The members were leaning toward my dad."

"Faras was a classmate of yours back then." Beth sat forward, interested in what he would tell her.

"Yes and no. Faras was a classmate of Kee's, but he'd been left back. He was in my grade for a year or so. Then he dropped out. Encouraged me to do the same. Almost did."

"So what happened between Faras and your dad?" she asked.

"Gang was short on funds because of the drug deal falling through. A robbery was a way for my dad to establish dominance, be the hero and fix the problem with our distributors. They don't care if we sell the drugs or lose them or smoke them, just so long as they get paid on time. I offered to drive my dad, and then I called Faras."

She sat back as the implication of what he was saying sank in. Beth met his intent stare and saw that her suspicions were correct. But she had to hear him say it. "You set up your father?"

Ty did not answer the question at first. Finally, he inclined his head, admitting it. Hard to blame him. His father was a petty crook, a known gang member, and by all reports, a brutal man.

"Faras had the police there waiting," said Ty. "Tipped them before my dad even cleared the doors of that liquor store."

"And you made sure he didn't escape. Crashed the getaway car." She should have known if for no other reason than that Ty did not crash cars. He was a good driver. No, a great one. "But you were arrested as well."

"Worth it. He broke my mother's arm that January and still she wouldn't press charges. Jake called the cops, but my dad was back the next day. So I went to Faras. Two months later my father went to prison. They blamed him for picking me. Young kid. Stupid choice for a getaway driver. And Faras became the gang's new leader."

Ty gained respect in her eyes. He'd been dealt a hard hand and done what he could.

"Why wouldn't your mom press charges?" she asked.

He rested his forehead in his hand, elbow on the table, and peered up at her as if talking about this gave him a headache. But he answered her.

"Because he said it would only be worse if she did.

He threatened us, his kids, used us as collateral to keep her from leaving him."

"And you made him go away without killing him."

"For that, I would have gone to jail."

"But instead you went free."

"They let me join the US Marines."

"And you distinguished yourself."

She recognized the look of sorrow as his eyes changed the direction of their focus, drifting off to some unknown place.

So many of the pieces of the puzzle that were Ty Redhorse fell into place. Ty had used his Big Money, the portion of the tribe's revenue from the casino profits distributed to members on their 18th birthday, for Kee's education. He had provided Colt with a vintage Chevy pickup truck that was distinctive, in that the colors he chose were not the ones favored by the Wolf Posse. In fact, the only one he had not provided transportation for was his brother Jake.

"Did you want to stay away, Ty?"

His gaze drifted back to her. His jaw was set tight. She reached across the table and took his free hand.

"What difference does it make?"

"It matters to me."

His fingers curled around hers, and his thumb stroked the skin on the top of her index finger. She ignored the stirring of desire, but it was there, banked but burning brighter each time he touched her.

"Everybody over there in the sandbox talks about coming home. About the girl they left, about the family they left. I just wanted to stay there. Stay so far away that they could never get to me."

"The gang?"

"Yeah." Ty drew back his hands back and sat straight

in his chair, both palms now flat on the table. His shoulders sagged and he looked like a man defeated. "I stayed away as long as I could, but Colt joined the service. Wanted to be like me. If I'd been here I could've stopped him."

Beth knew what had happened during Colt's tour of duty in Afghanistan. He had been taken prisoner and tortured and was the only survivor among his unit. Was that burden also on Ty's shoulders?

"Jake called me. Told me that Colt was in Walter Reed. They released him on the psych discharge. I picked them up in Phoenix. What a mess. He couldn't drive in the car. Stopped talking. Walked all the way from Phoenix to the rez. I helped him get situated in the mining cabin that belongs to my family."

"You came back to take care of your little brother."

"Yeah, that's about it." Ty put his hand on the top of his head and ruffled his hair. "But I made a mistake. Stopped by to see my dad down there in Phoenix. Couldn't resist."

"Why was that a mistake?" she asked.

He cast her a look filled with pain and she felt a stab of grief cut across her middle. Understanding struck.

Beth's eyes rounded. "You told him?"

"No, but he knows." Ty's answer was just above a whisper. "Figured it out. Just needed to see him behind bars and…" His words trailed off. He pushed his plate out of the way.

"He guessed."

Ty met her stare. "At first glance. Don't know how. But he knew. No one in the gang guessed."

"He can't get to you."

"I'm not worried about me. I'm worried about my

mom because he knows the best way to hurt me is through her."

"He can't touch her from prison," Beth assured him.

"He's scheduled to be paroled."

Chapter Fifteen

Beth sat back in alarm. Ty's father would be paroled and his father knew that Faras had used his son to snatch the gang's leadership and his freedom. Ty was right to be worried. She needed to speak to Forrest about this. "When does he get out?"

"I don't know. Soon."

"I'll find out and I'll speak to Forrest about this. We'll come up with something to keep your family safe."

Ty heaved a heavy sigh. "Already lost Colt. He can't come back until you take down that Russian organization."

"We're making good progress on that. The Antelope Lake house where they held Ava Hood and Louisa Tah has yielded good evidence. We've identified all the men recovered and connected them to the Kuznetsov crime organization." She used the word *recovered* because all the men found at the temporary holding facility, where Ava Hood had been held, were all dead. They'd had a chance to capture Yury Churkin, a hired killer sent to murder Kee's fiancée, Ava Hood. Unfortunately, Churkin had put a bullet through his brain before they got to him. Still, Churkin's presence on the rez had been connected to at least one death here, Dr. Richard Day, a FEMA physician. Now they needed to connect Churkin's actions to Usov's orders. The head of the southwestern region, Leonard Usov, was Beth's target. If she could implicate him, she'd have a chance to shut down the western arm of the surrogate ring.

They had only one suspect in custody, Anton Igoshin, the man who had fallen chasing Kacey Doka and broken his back. He was now a wheelchair user facing multiple charges, including kidnapping.

Ty laced his hands before him on the table.

"Faras wants me back in the gang. Seems I passed the test. He found his snitch and he requests me as his second." He lifted his chin. "Congratulations, Agent Hoosay. You've got your informer."

This was what she had wanted, wasn't it? The bureau finally had a man inside the Wolf Posse. Unfortunately, that man was Ty and she no longer saw him as just her informant. She'd read about agents who went undercover and got all mixed up with the people they worked with and lived with. They lost objectivity and began to see the people who trusted them as friends and confidants. She saw that happening to herself right now and did not know how to stop it. If she was honest with herself, she'd admit she had feelings for Ty. It hurt her to use him and endanger him.

"Maybe we can make my case, break the back of the gang and make sure your father doesn't ever hurt your family again."

Ty's smug smile was back and he lolled back in his seat. "Great. How, exactly, do we do that?"

Now it was her turn to press a hand to her forehead. "I don't know. But we need to do all of it."

Ty stood and retrieved the dinner plates. "I helped Faras take power and in exchange he's left me out of the worst of the gang activities. But now that he's facing another power struggle, all that has changed." He carried the dishes to the sink and she cleared the rest of the table.

Beth knew Ty was smart, and his understanding of how things worked here was far better than hers. Informants provided information. But Beth had a real desire to include Ty in strategic planning.

"I think you could be more than an informant," she said, picking up a dish towel to dry the dishes he set in the strainer.

He quirked an eyebrow, mildly interested. "That so?"

"You have every reason to be suspicious. But you know as well as I do that if we remove Faras, whoever is challenging him will take over and things will soon be right back where they started."

"Chino Aria. He's the most likely challenger. Very territorial around Faras, but he's got some things going on that I'm not sure Faras condoned."

"What exactly?"

"I heard something from one of the newer recruits, Randy Tasa."

"The kid on the bike," said Beth.

Ty lowered his hands and turned to face her. "How do you know about him?"

"You were under surveillance. I saw you hassle him outside the roadhouse the night we met."

Ty shook the water and suds off his hands and shut off the tap. "Hassling? That what you saw?"

She felt the same doubt as when she had watched the interaction. It had occurred to her vaguely that Ty might be running him off.

"Randy is a smart kid with no father and a big sister already in the gang. He's got potential. Faras sees it and so do I. But Faras sees another member of the posse and I see a rabbit that might just escape the snare. I just gave him a shove in the right direction."

"They recruit kids that young?"

Randy was only fourteen.

"They do, but the interesting thing is that Faras didn't know Randy was working for him. Chino had him out there selling weed and Faras didn't know."

"So?" asked Beth.

"Faras used to know everything. Maybe the surrogate ring is taking all his attention or maybe Chino is working something on the side."

Beth leaned a hip against the counter and folded her arms beneath her breasts. "What do you think?"

"Chino is preparing a takeover. I'm sure."

"Because of one kid?"

Ty angled his head to the side and then righted it. The gesture reminded her of a shrug.

"If you are right we could work those two against each other," she said.

And just like that, they were talking strategy. Beth set up scenarios and Ty poked holes in them. They moved to the sofa, sat facing each other, each with a leg tucked up on the cushions. Beth scrawled notes on a pad on each member of the gang. Ty provided so much intelligence, it would have taken FBI months to get even close to this kind of inside information.

He also told her exactly why he had helped Faras recover Kacey Doka and the reason he'd done it.

"So you made a deal with Faras and so he reported to the Russians that the baby delivered by Zella Colelay had died?"

"Yes."

"Because Jake and his wife had decided to adopt that baby?"

"Zella escaped capture and delivered a baby. The Russians still wanted it because somewhere out there is a couple waiting for their biological offspring."

"Do the parents know? Do they understand where their surrogates come from?" asked Beth.

"I doubt it. But I don't know. All I know is that Faras found out that Zella's baby had arrived and sent two of the posse after her. I was watching Jake and when I saw that the ones that were after the infant were members of the Wolf Posse I knew they wouldn't stop, ever, unless I went to Faras."

"What did he say?"

"He agreed to report the infant deceased."

Beth was impressed. Ty had gotten Faras to give false information to his contacts.

Ty did not look smug over his coup. Instead he looked worried as he continued. "But Faras doesn't give something for nothing. He wanted my word that I'd start driving again. Up until then I just repaired the cars. Kept them moving faster than the competition and the authorities."

"Driving?"

"Pick-ups, escapes, deliveries."

"And he called and told you to pick up your younger brother's girlfriend, Kacey Doka."

"Exactly. I couldn't refuse without endangering Jake's baby."

"You could have come to the police."

Ty gave a mirthless laugh. "Right."

"Instead, you collected Kacey from in front of the clinic and drove her to her captors."

"Only after I called Colt and reported the drop location."

"Again, you could have called the police."

"Yes. And then I'd be dead. Kacey would be recaptured and Jake's new baby would be back with the Russians."

"You don't have very much confidence in us."

"We called the police on my father again and again. He went in and came back like a boomerang."

She understood his point. Without May's willingness to press charges, there was little to be done.

"You can't protect us," said Ty. "You guys come in after a crime is committed. I was trying to keep the crimes from happening."

"You were trying to protect your family."

Ty looked away and she knew that she understood. He'd defended his brother's baby. He had told Colt where the drop was. And in telling her, he had just given Beth the information that could destroy him. She could use it to ensure his compliance, and she knew that she never would.

"You kept them all safe, Ty. But you have to let us help you or it won't stop. Sooner or later you'll fail or they'll figure out what you did."

"I know that. I was certain they'd figure it out after Kacey's escape. But Faras didn't hear what I did there to help her get clear of them, and the one survivor is in custody."

"Sequestered. He is out of general population for as long as it takes to close this case."

"What does that look like to you? A closed case?"

"We get the remaining girls back and shut down the operation, not just up here but all over the southwest.

We make a case against Leonard Usov and possibly tie him to Kostya Kuznetsov in Atlanta."

"Who?"

"Usov runs all human trafficking operations here. He reports to the Kuznetsov crime family, and Kostya is their head."

"That's a big case."

"We have Betty Mills as a witness. The health care administrator made the calls to Faras. She's a treasure trove of information, but her attorney is smart. He wants some concessions to ensure her full cooperation. Once she's on board, we arrest Faras and every other member of the posse involved. Your tribal police has been outnumbered over two to one by this gang. Not anymore. Once I have evidence, I get resources and we end this."

"We?" he asked.

"Yes, we." She took his hand and squeezed. The gesture was intended to demonstrate they were a team. Instead, something happened. Her breath caught at the tingling awareness that blossomed over her skin. Their eyes met and hunger surged as powerful as a waterfall. The hairs on her neck lifted and her skin puckered. His breathing accelerated, making his nostrils flare.

"Ty?"

He was inching closer, his gaze now on her mouth.

Beth could have stopped him. She knew that just a word, a gesture, and Ty would retreat. But she said nothing because in her heart she wanted this. Her soul yearned for the connection and her body ached with need.

His mouth melted to hers, touching off a series of tantalizing shocks that rippled over her skin and settled low in her belly. She did not know why her body sang at his touch. It had been this way since she first laid eyes on him. Back then she had thought him a trickster. A man with two faces who showed her exactly what she wanted to see. She thought she knew the truth of him. She thought a man as uncomplicated as Ty could be summed up in the contents of a manila folder.

He couldn't be. Ty was so much more.

His fingers grazed her neck, caressed her cheek and threaded into her hair. He tipped her back, trapping her between the sofa headrest and his hungry mouth. She reached for him with greedy fingers, dragging her nails up the skin of his back beneath his T-shirt. When she reached his shoulder blades, she tugged him against her. They fell together to the sofa, Ty on top. The weight of his chest against her torso was sweet torture. His hips pressed to hers and she raked her hands back down the long muscles beside his spine until she gripped him by the seat and rocked him forward.

Her tongue delved, dancing with his inner rhythmic thrusting that electrified her senses. She was surprised that it was Ty who halted their kiss. He lifted himself up on his forearms to peer down at her. He cast her a look of surprise and concern. "Do you know what you're doing?"

"I'm through with thinking for a while," she replied.

"Bad things happen when you stop thinking."

"And great things."

His smile was devilish. His dark eyes glittered. She brushed back the hair that fell forward over his forehead, her fingers gliding over the satin strand before tucking it behind his ear.

"I want to sleep with you, Ty."

"Have you thought about the consequences?"

"I'm on birth control and I have a feeling you have condoms close at hand."

"That's not the consequences I was talking about. As far as the Bureau is concerned, I'm your informant and you're undercover. I appreciate you wanting to appear to be my new girl, but I don't want you regretting this or getting into trouble because of something we do here."

"Break in professional ethics."

"Yup."

"Ty, it occurs to me that you don't often get what you want. You put your family's needs ahead of your own needs and even ahead of your own safety. You're a man who takes risks. I admire that."

"Tell me that if your boss finds out about this, you won't get fired."

She said nothing. At the very least she would receive a reprimand. Ty pulled away, sitting beside her hip on the sofa. She drew her legs from behind him and sat next to him a little too close.

"Only way they find out is if I tell them or you tell them," she said as he turned to meet her gaze and stared a long while. Then he stood and offered his hand.

Chapter Sixteen

She wasn't sure exactly how she got to the bedroom. All she knew for certain was that she had hopped out of her boots, dragged off her socks and shed her slacks, all while kissing Ty. She had removed her personal weapon and holster, which had been clipped to her belt, before stepping from her slacks. Hemi had risen from her dog bed to follow them and Ty had issued a command to stay that had sent his dog back to the living room. Then Ty had carried her, half-dressed, to his bed. She had set her holstered weapon and badge on his bedside table beside her handcuffs. Then she had torn his shirt over his head as he slipped her panties over her thighs.

The danger and the need mingled within her. She knew it was a misstep and that the consequences could be enormous. But some part of her didn't care. Having Ty was worth it all. When he stretched her out on his bed, they were naked. Nothing shielded her from the luscious slide of his heated flesh on hers. His rough calloused hands stroked her, each touch feeding her desire.

"I need you," he said.

She lifted her feet to the bed and splayed her thighs. Ty's eyes widened and his expression turned hungry. His mouth descended to her earlobe, sucking and nipping her sensitive flesh as he descended from her neck to the blade of her collarbone and below.

They came together in a rush of need and madness. He laced his fingers through hers and trapped her hands beside her head. Ty gazed down at her with dark soulful eyes, his expression one of pleasure marred by pain. She watched him move as she felt the velvety glide of his body connecting with hers. Perfection, she thought. Just as she'd known it would be.

And then the whirlwind of sensation took her. She gasped and lifted herself at the pleasure arcing her spine. His mouth found hers and he followed her a moment later. He held her as the bliss rolled through her. The pleasure was bone-deep and raw. She closed her eyes, knowing that this was the man she had always dreamed of and he had appeared in her life in the worst form imaginable. She knew there would be regret and that this relationship was doomed from the start. But she had started it and she was not sorry. Time enough for regrets tomorrow. Tonight she would hold him in her arms and pretend that she could keep this man who had so unexpectedly crept into her heart.

Ty fell beside her on the mattress, panting. He rolled to his side and gathered her close as the sweat glistened on their spent bodies. Gradually, their breathing came back to normal and their skin dried. She snuggled close, trying to escape the chilly air that disturbed her doze. Tendrils of cold air wafted through his bedroom from the open window beside the bedside table. Beth shivered. Ty roused enough to draw her closer.

She fought the cold, not the cold of the room but the one creeping back inside her. This time with Ty was right—so right and so good. It made her wonder what they could be like together and how they could make that happen. But to have him she'd have to give up her dream or take him from his family. It was impossible, but her mind would not give up and continued to throw what-ifs at her as her heart ached with need.

Ty peered at her.

"Cold?" he asked, his voice lethargic and deep.

"Mmm," she murmured, and inclined her head.

He tugged the bedding from beneath them and slipped them under the blankets. They nestled together, her forehead on his cheek, his arm about her shoulder, her hand over his heart.

He toyed with her curly hair, winding a strand around his index finger.

"Beth, I know the scent of your hair—" he inhaled "—is orchids and I know the soft feel of your body." He stroked his palm up her ribs. "But you haven't told me anything about yourself except the bullet points of your resume."

She stiffened and his hand slipped away.

"What do you want to know?" she asked, feeling the walls rising around her.

"Everything."

She said nothing as she struggled against the need to unlock her past to him. It wasn't professional, so why did she have to fight to keep silent?

"Anything," he whispered.

The silence stretched and the tension in her mounted.

He nuzzled her head with his cheek. "You were wearing a rodeo buckle the night I first saw you. Was that yours or part of your cover?"

She could not help smiling at the memories. "Both. I used to ride when I was a teenager. My mother allowed me to compete because horses are so closely tied to our culture."

"You must have been good."

Back then barrel racing was an acceptable risk. One that her mother allowed, and there were few enough of those. Beth was not even permitted to ride in a friend's car in high school. The smothering sensation returned to her. "That buckle was for barrel racing at our annual rodeo."

Her answer must have encouraged him because he asked another more personal question. "Did you grow up on the reservation up there in Oklahoma?"

"I lived there when I was young. Registered member. They dropped the blood quota a while ago, so if your parent is a member, you're eligible. My dad didn't like Oklahoma because it's so cold and rural on the rez. He missed Miami. But my mom's family was there." She stopped talking because she already felt she'd said too much.

Ty lifted himself up on an elbow to stare at her. "He was?"

"My father is from the Caribbean. So I'm brown, but not the same sort of brown as most of the kids there." She tugged at a tight curl in emphasis.

"So you felt different."

"Yeah. The kids were okay. The rez was okay, too, but…" She threw up a hand. "It made my dad unhappy to be there. It was like he couldn't wait to get back to the army and away from us."

"You blame your mom for that?" he asked.

"She could have gone with him instead of making a life without him there."

"What did she do there on the rez?"

"She's a neurosurgeon."

Ty's eyebrows lifted; he was clearly impressed. "Really?"

She nodded. "Anyway, they met when he was stationed there and they might have loved each other but not enough for him to stay or her to go." She hated talking about this next part and counseled herself not to cry. "My dad was an army ranger, but he died when I was thirteen."

"KIA?" asked Ty, meaning "killed in action."

"No. Traffic accident. He was riding his motorcycle and was hit by the driver of a pickup truck who never saw him. The impact threw him from the bike and he was hit again by a car traveling in the opposite direction. He died of his injuries at the scene." She got the whole thing out and only then did her throat close up. She made an involuntary high whining sound.

Ty gathered her in his arms.

"I'm so sorry, Beth." He held her and rubbed her back as she struggled with her tears. "I'm surprised you ride."

"He used to take me with him on his bike. After he died I missed it. Riding is like being with him. My mom flipped when she found out, of course. She always called people who ride bikes 'organ donors.' Then my dad died and he actually was one. She doesn't say that anymore. When I came home with my first bike, a Suzuki, she ordered me to sell it. But I wouldn't. My act of defiance, I suppose. I was so mad at her after Dad died. It was like she caused it. I know that sounds crazy. I know it's not fair or even rational, but it's how I felt. If we'd gone with him, he wouldn't have been on that bike in Oklahoma. Anyway, I'm glad I kept riding, because I love my bike."

"I understand that. Did you join the service because of him?"

"Yes. And the Bureau. Dad had been accepted…" She hesitated and took two deep breaths, then plunged back in. "Before the accident, he joined the FBI. It was his next move after the army. Got his dream placement, too, in DC."

And that placement would have taken him away from them permanently.

Ty's eyes rounded and his expression went wary. He wasn't stupid. But she wasn't doing this for her father. She wanted to make a difference, too. Was that so wrong? Her mother thought so. It was why Beth stopped calling home.

"But I also joined…" She shook her head, still not believing she'd told him about her father or that she was even considering bringing up her mom.

"Also joined…" he coaxed.

She'd had enough. Her stomach ached from talking about this and she needed an antacid.

"So," he said, "you'll sleep with me. But you won't tell me the other reason why you joined the army?"

She could feel him drawing away. It made her mad, too, his withdrawal, because she wouldn't give him what he wanted.

"I joined to get away from her." She spat the words.

His face registered surprise, but he didn't speak.

She blew out a breath and reined in her anger. "After he died, my mom got weird. She drove me everywhere and wouldn't let me in anyone's car but hers. I was going crazy."

"Protecting you." Ty's voice was just above a whisper as if he understood and was taking her side.

Beth doubled down, getting it all out. "Suffocating me. After he died she forbade me to ride horses. I wasn't allowed to play soccer. She said that was too dangerous because of the possibility of head injuries. So when I turned eighteen, I bought a bike. I knew she'd go crazy. That's exactly why I bought it. And she did. Ultimatums, the whole thing. I joined the army to get away from her, but I stayed because I fit there. They promote you on merit. You succeed or fail because of what you do, not who your parents might be or if you look a certain way."

"I remember," he said. "No history or past mistakes, just what they can see."

"The Bureau is different but also the same. You rise based on what you produce, what convictions you make. Merit, like in the army. They don't have many agents who look like me. The demographics are still mostly men and mostly white. I'm different there in a good way. It makes me stand out and it got me this assignment."

"Your mom still in Oklahoma?"

"Yes. She lives and works in the city and keeps a place on the rez."

"And you took this case because you could help our people," said Ty.

She hadn't. They'd picked her because the database said she was Apache and she'd been happy to let that distinction help her along.

She lifted her gaze to meet his and felt small as she admitted the truth. "I took the assignment to make a big case."

"Why is that so important?"

She didn't know how to explain it or if she really wanted to explain it.

"Because I can make more of a difference in a bigger field office," she said.

"Oklahoma is not a small place," he reminded her.

"I hate Oklahoma."

"Because your dad hated it."

She dropped her gaze. "The best agents are in New York and DC."

"Ambition, then. I understand that."

But he didn't approve. She could tell by the way he rolled to his back and folded his uninjured arm behind his head to stare up at the ceiling.

"I was ambitious once," he said. "Then I realized that I was one small fish in a big ocean. You know what little fish do, right?" He turned to her.

"What?" she asked.

"They try to stay alive."

She made a sound in her throat that acknowledged the truth in that. Then she curled against him. He didn't stop her, but neither did he take her in his arms again. There was a barrier rising between them again.

"Big world. I can't save it. But I try to save the ones I can."

Their goals were different. Was he thinking that she didn't need him or wouldn't need him for long? He planned to stay here with his family and she was leaving as soon as they let her. She wanted to take back what she'd told him. Take it all back. She had position and authority already. But he had something more valuable, he had people he cared about and who cared about him, real living people, while she was still trying to make her father proud.

She fell asleep to the rhythm of their heartbeats.

The ringing of Beth's phone woke her from a deep sleep. She glanced at the phone's display and saw it was three in the morning and that the call was from her supervisor, Agent Luke Forrest.

"Hoosay here."

"Get to the tribal police station," said Forrest. "Mills

committed suicide tonight and someone set the clinic on fire."

Beth threw herself to a seated position. Beside her, Ty sat up against the headboard, his body a dark silhouette in the bedroom. It had come too soon, the crash of reality that ripped her from his embrace.

The records! The Bureau had removed what they deemed significant, but there was always the chance they could unearth more.

"How bad is the fire?"

"Bad enough."

"Maybe kids. A Halloween prank?" she asked.

"Started in the records room. When the firefighters are done, we'll sort through what's left. Meet me there."

"En route," said Beth, but Forrest had already hung up. She slipped from the bed. "I have to go."

He captured her wrist. "It's a trap."

She hesitated. He wore no shirt and she could clearly see the stitches that ran across his shoulder, the wound he had suffered at Antelope Lake. Why hadn't she remembered that during their lovemaking? They could have torn the stitches. "What?"

"It's just like the nonexistent meth lab on Canyon Ridge Road. Set a fire and see who shows up. My girlfriend shouldn't be there. I know that much."

She mulled it over. What he said was smart. "I'll be careful. But I have to go."

Ty released her wrist and she snatched her pistol and badge from the bedside table. She recovered her underthings on the way to the living room, gathering her slacks and shirt along the way. She sat on the couch and flicked on a side lamp to draw on her ankle-high boots. Hemi came out to keep her company.

Ty stepped into the hall a moment later, leaning

against the wall. He now wore a pair of gym shorts and nothing else. The red scars on his shoulder marred the perfection of his skin. His arms and face were tanned, a workingman's tan, she realized.

"Beth, you're undercover. Here with me."

"They won't see me at the fire."

"What if they see you leaving here right now?"

She glanced toward the windows and the darkness looming all around them. Then she gathered her courage. "It's my job."

"What am I supposed to do?"

She cast him an impatient look. Hemi moved to stand by the door, glancing back at them.

"Everything you do doesn't have to involve risk."

He was psychoanalyzing her based on a five-minute conversation that they never should have had. She stood and grabbed an antacid, popping it into her mouth.

"Stay here and wait for me to come back."

She holstered her weapon and looped the lanyard over her neck. She couldn't stay. This was her case, her chance.

He snorted and his chin dipped. "Yeah, right. Play time's over and you're back on the clock."

He turned and retreated toward the bedroom, snapping his fingers to call his dog. Hemi trotted after him. She stood and considered going after him. But what could she say? She did have a job to do and it did matter what they had shared but not enough to change anything. As she had feared. Ty was the man she wanted and could not have, at least not for long.

Beth shrugged into her leather jacket and retrieved her motorcycle helmet on her way out the door.

TY HAD GONE back to bed, but he didn't sleep. Instead he lay on his back with his arm across his forehead and watched the light rise until he could see all the objects in the room, including the pair of handcuffs she had left behind on his bedside table. She'd been gone for hours. Was she safe? Did she need him? Ty threw back the covers and sat on the edge of his bed.

Hemi groaned and lifted her head. She had slept on the dog bed she must have dragged in here sometime in the night. Usually he brought her dog bed into this room at night, but she could do it herself and he had been distracted.

She came to sit beside him, resting her enormous head on his thigh while staring up at him with soulful eyes. He stroked the thick fur on her ruff with distraction. Hemi sighed. When his hand stilled, she stretched and walked to the door, her toenails clicking on the wood floor. She paused in the doorway, looking back at him as if asking if he was coming along.

"Need to go out, girl?"

Hemi's reaction—hurrying toward the front door as she wagged her tail—was answer enough. Ty let her out and then retreated to the bathroom. He was half-dressed and shaving when his cell phone rang. He snatched it up, hoping it was Beth. His shoulders sagged as he realized it was Faras calling at 6:05 a.m.

"Not good."

Chapter Seventeen

When Faras called, you didn't ask him why. Ty fed Hemi and took her along, fixing the carrier to the back of his Harley. He reached the clubhouse, as Faras called the Wolf Posse's headquarters.

Ty was surprised to be greeted by Chino, an unlikely guard, at the entrance to the property. Ordinarily, his second in command would not be given the menial task of sitting in his automobile and checking in arrivals. Something was going on.

Chino cast him a glare and waved him on. Ty was happy for the roaring engine of his motorcycle, which made speech between them difficult. He rolled up to the ranch property, noticing again the number of new trucks. Once upon a time he was all that kept the posse's old fleet of battered high-mileage vehicles moving. That time had come and gone, and Ty's usefulness dwindled as the number of autos under warranty grew.

Ty released Hemi from the crate and they were ushered in by the guard at the door. Once inside, he found Faras sitting alone at a large dining room table. Before him was his open laptop, a cigarette smoldering in an ashtray and, at his elbow, a full cup of coffee.

Faras pinned his weary gaze on Ty.

"About time," he grumbled. Then he lifted his cigarette and took a long drag, exhaling smoke toward the ceiling, where it swirled, forming a blue-gray haze.

Ty pointed to the couch, and Hemi hopped to the cushions, stretching out for a nap. Ty continued through the living room to stand before Faras on the opposite side of the rectangular table.

"What's up?" asked Ty.

"You see Chino outside?"

Ty inclined his head and glanced toward the door. The house was uncharacteristically empty. Some of that could be blamed on the earliness of the hour. But Faras usually had a guard inside the premises.

"Found out the Russians called him. Believe that?"

"Who? Chino?"

Faras took a drag on the cigarette and nodded.

"What does that mean?"

"It means he's trying to take over. Doing an end-run. He knows that Usov is ticked at me. Knows Quinton narced on me and that the guys are getting restless because tribal arrested Hauser and Mills. Perfect timing. Remember when I took over?"

"That was different. The posse had lost its leader."

"Yeah, but I was a long shot. Only reason I'm sitting here is you, bro. Don't think I forget it, either."

Ty wondered if Faras was appreciative enough to let him go free and clear. But he knew Faras well enough to understand that he had not called Ty to his side at this hour to release him from his obligation or to offer thanks. Faras had helped him entrap his father. Ty had owed him, though that debt should now be more than paid.

"I want you here full-time starting right now," said Faras.

That was definitely not going to work. Ty drew up a chair and sat down. He folded his open hands before him on the top of the table, partly to show he was getting down to business, but also to show Faras where his hands were.

"I just don't know who to trust. Time to fall back on the ones who were there from the start. You know?" asked Faras.

"Yeah. Understandable. So the Russians... How's that going to work with Dr. Hauser dead and the clinic closed?" Ty did not mention that the clinic had been set on fire, but wondered if Faras might already know.

"They don't need the clinic or Hauser. They just want the posse to pick up candidates."

Ty had never asked how this part of the operation worked. Up until three weeks ago, when Kacey Doka arrived after escaping captivity by the Russians, he didn't even know it was happening. But it was like driving by a horrific accident. You couldn't unsee that.

"How does that happen, exactly?" asked Ty.

"I used to pick rejects from our recruitment. Girls we didn't want because they were too messed up or their families were. Easy to find the ones that no one would miss. But now tribal police are on to us and they're going to take note of every girl who 'runs away.'" Faras used air quotes around the words *runs away*.

"So what are you going to do?"

"I don't know, man. This is bad. I have to deliver four girls, so I got bigger problems than Chino trying to take the reins."

Ty thumped his hands on the table. "Hate to add to your troubles, but my dad will be out soon."

Faras took another long drag on his cigarette, then stubbed it out. He lifted his coffee mug and took a sip. For a moment Ty thought Faras was weighing his options or brainstorming a plan. But then he slammed his laptop shut, leaving his hands splayed upon the black plastic casing as he glared at Ty. "You take care of him. You hear? This time you do like I said and kill the bastard."

Ty understood. Faras would be of no help where his dad was concerned. Ty was on his own on that one.

But by ordering him to take care of his father, Faras had presented him with the opportunity to escape Faras's demand to move in permanently.

"All right. I'll take care of it."

Ty stood and exited the Wolf Posse's headquarters. Hemi roused as Ty strode through the living room and hopped down from the couch to fall in step beside him as he cleared the front door.

He almost made it out, but Faras called after him.

"I was thinking of taking girls that are passing through. You know?" He drew out a new cigarette from the pack and lit it. The tip flared orange for the intake of his breath. "Take them from outside the boundaries of the rez or take them at drinking parties. We always get outsiders at parties."

"Outsiders?" Ty asked. Faras was getting desperate.

"Yeah. You know, any women from outside the rez?" Faras set the cigarette in the ashtray and quirked an eyebrow. "I just need four more and those bastards will move on and I'll be back to business as usual."

Which meant drug sales, protection and money laundering. Ty had never seen Faras look so frazzled. If he didn't know what Faras had done and what he was capable of doing, he'd almost feel sorry for him. But Ty knew that a cornered animal was the most dangerous sort.

Faras drew out a cigarette from the pack on the table and then realized he had one smoldering in the ashtray. He slipped the tube of tobacco back into the pack and turned his attention on Ty. "You know any women who don't belong here?"

Did he mean Beth? Did he actually think he'd turn over his girlfriend? Or did Faras know who and what Beth really was? He schooled himself to hold a blank expression.

"No," said Ty.

Faras slipped the open pack of cigarettes back into his shirt pocket. "Think about it, bro. You ain't known her that long. Then it'd be one down and three to go."

Ty's jaw tightened.

Faras's smile was cold as winter frost. "You take care of this trouble with your dad. Permanently. Then get back here. If he ain't out yet, come back. I need four girls in their hands by Friday or Chino won't have to challenge me."

Ty headed out with Hemi trailing beside him. His canine needed no assistance in hopping up to her traveling crate and sat with tongue lolling as he fixed the harness about her. He needed to find Beth and warn her that she was on the capture list.

Ty stopped at the top of the drive for the rolling gate to open and permit his exit. Chino made him wait. Finally, the barrier rolled back and Chino flipped him the bird as he roared away on his sled. He made sure he was out of sight and earshot before pulling over. His cell phone offered him no service. Ty swore. Hemi rested her large chin upon his shoulder. He lifted his hand to give her an absent scratch on the cheek. Then they were off again, heading for Piñon Forks.

He was careful to park at the clinic because he couldn't very well pull in to the parking lot of tribal headquarters. His bike was too distinctive to be seen right in front of the building that housed the police station. Luckily, the tribe's clinic was a separate building and his big brother worked there, giving him all the reason he needed to visit. Plus, Beth might be here because of the fire.

He saw none of the posse's vehicles as he pulled in. It didn't mean they were not here.

Despite the damage to the reception area and medical records, the clinic was open. Ty entered through the main doors to find the waiting room half-full. A desk and computer had been set up in the waiting area before a blue plastic tarp that covered the fire-damaged section beyond. The burned smell permeated the chilly air despite the fan set to high in the open window.

Ty asked the new receptionist if he could speak to his brother. Kee appeared a few minutes later. Ty explained that he wanted Kee to take him through the clinic and out the back door, where he could cross between the buildings and into tribal headquarters.

They walked side by side past the exam rooms and into the women's health clinic in the back of the building.

"Any word on Dad?" asked Kee.

"Not yet."

Kee grimaced. "Maybe I should go out and see Mom after work today."

Ty left him at the back door and headed for the station, where he met with Officer Wetselline, who was manning the squad room with Kee's fiancé, Ava Hood, the former Yavapai detective turned dispatcher.

Ava used the radio to call Wallace Tinnin, their police chief, who was at home this morning. Ty waited in his office for the five minutes it took the chief to drive from his home to headquarters. Once Tinnin was in his office, Ty relayed everything that Faras had told him.

"Be too much to ask, I suppose, to have Chino and Faras kill each other in a power struggle," said Tinnin.

"Any word from the prison on when my father will be released?"

"Not yet. Paperwork is pending." Tinnin offered Ty some coffee, but he declined.

"Beth is not answering her phone. Can you get word to her?"

"I'll sure give it my best shot."

He was referring to Luke Forrest, the agent in charge of the Russian trafficking case.

"You get cell-phone service out at your place?" asked the chief.

"Sure do."

"So go home and I'll call when I make contact."

Ty did as he was told and spent the rest of a very restless day working on replacing the head gasket on the '76 Cadillac Eldorado and waiting for Beth to return or Tinnin to get word from his…what? Girlfriend? Supervisor? FBI contact? He was her informer and despite the night they had spent together, Beth had not included him in her plans. Ty had a good long time to think about the limitations of their arrangement, and the fact that just because he wanted something did not mean he would have it. His life had been full of many such dreams brought to dust by the heel of reality. He knew who he was and what he was. He had just forgotten for a moment.

On the bright side, the Eldorado was now running and, man, that engine purred.

When his phone rang at four that afternoon, he snatched it from his pocket on the first ring. The display announced that the phone call was from Kee.

"Hey, Kee. What's up?" asked Ty.

"Abbie is missing."

Chapter Eighteen

Ty straightened as his entire body flashed hot and cold. He swallowed, wondering if Faras would have dared to snatch his little sister.

Beth and Abbie. That would leave him only two more girls needed. This was why Ty didn't own a gun. He knew the limits of his temper, and his marines training ensured that he was a deadly shot.

"Repeat that," he said.

Kee did and Ty felt his world tilting off its axis. He didn't know how or why, but he was certain that this was his fault.

Kee gave him the details. Abbie had been taken from their yard twenty minutes earlier. The police were there. Winnie Doka, one of the three girls fostering with his mother, had witnessed the abduction. But they hadn't taken Winnie. To Ty that meant the attack was specific—his sister, and just his sister.

"She said the guy was big, bald."

Chino, Ty thought. "What color was he?"

"Brown. She thinks he was Apache."

"I'm on my way." But first he would speak to Faras. He knew Faras would tell him nothing on the phone. He'd need to show up in person at the Wolf Posse headquarters if he had any hope of getting answers. He left

Hemi at the garage and called Beth again before departing. His call was flipped over to voice mail. This time he left a message.

Why would Faras take Abbie? Or had Chino acted on his own? Was it possible that Abbie's abduction was unrelated to the Russian surrogate ring?

He roared down the road to the Wolf Posse's crib and slowed only long enough for the gate to gape enough to permit his Harley.

Faras met him on the front step.

"She's not here," he said, hands raised.

But he knew she was missing. Ty rolled the bike onto its kickstand and dismounted.

"You have her?" asked Ty.

"Insurance. Your new girl, she isn't a drifter. Is she? She's a narc. So you got a decision to make. Either she dies or your sister does."

The rage poured through Ty and he took a step toward Faras. Chino lifted a double-barreled shotgun with a smile.

"Go for it," he challenged.

"Beth or Abbie," repeated Faras. "You pick."

Ty forced himself to breathe past the panic swirling with the rage.

"What do you want, exactly?" he asked.

"I'm sending you to settle up with the Russians, get our final payout and make the last delivery. You need four women. Get them any way you like. Take your narc as one, but one way or another, she disappears. Meanwhile, I hold your sister safe and sound until I hear from Usov that you've made the drop."

"How am I supposed to deliver four women?"

"Apply yourself." Faras glared. "Drop is tomorrow." He tossed a piece of paper at him. "There's the address. Four girls including your narc girlfriend. You could take those kids fostering with your mom. Three of them, right?"

There were. Jackie, Winnie and Shirley Doka, Kacey's sisters. Shirley was eleven. Ty felt something in his middle harden to glass. Had he really once counted Faras as a friend?

"They expect you in a single auto. Take the Caddy you're working on. That one has a four-body trunk."

Ty turned to go, but Faras issued a last warning.

"If I hear you are looking for Abbie, I'll be so disappointed and something bad will happen."

For the first time, Ty wondered if he had made the right choice by helping Faras take over the Wolf Posse. Ty's father was vicious and volatile. But he did not have Faras's capacity for manipulation. His father used his fists to keep order. Faras used the ones you loved.

Ty paused and then spoke over his shoulder. "Understood."

He left Faras and drove toward Koun'nde. Long ago, he had handled his father without telling anyone in his family what he had done. They all thought that it was just good luck and his bad driving that had finally eliminated the dangerous tyrant from their midst. Ty didn't believe in luck. But despite his attempts to keep his family safe, Colt was in witness protection, Kee and Jake had almost been killed by members of the Wolf Posse and Russian mob and his sister was now a captive.

Ty's back was to the wall. For far too long he had walked the fine line between the posse and the law. He was sick of it. Sick of trying to find opportunities to undermine the posse while still protecting his family and keeping himself out of the morgue. He was sure it had not been Faras's intention, but in taking his little sister, he had flipped some switch inside Ty. He was no longer an ally or an attack dog or a turncoat, snitch or bystander. He was in this, and Faras was the enemy.

Ty would not stop until he had his sister back and had destroyed every last member of this gang.

His first call was to Jake and his second was to Detective Jack Bear Den. They were meeting him at his mother's house in Koun'nde. Beth and her FBI supervisor could catch up when they became available. He wasn't waiting.

He had twenty-four hours to destroy the Wolf Posse, capture the Russians and get his sister back.

Jake was already there when Ty arrived and he had a police unit stationed across the end of the drive. Officer Wetselline moved to allow Ty access. Bear Den arrived shortly afterward. Jake had called Kee, who had uncharacteristically left the tribe's health care clinic with Jake's wife, Lori, in charge. Kee started talking to Ty before the dust from Ty's bike had even settled.

The men gathered in the circular dirt driveway in front of his mother's home. Ty rocked his bike to the kickstand.

Having four boys raised here in this modest home meant that May Redhorse had given up having a front yard years ago in favor of extra parking for her sons' trucks, so there was plenty of room for the extra vehicles.

"We need the help of Tribal Thunder," said Jake.

Tribal Thunder was the warrior sect of their medicine society, the elite group Ty had once foolishly wished to be asked to join. Stupid to think such a group would ever want him. But today, he sure needed them. Tribal Thunder was called into action whenever there was a threat to the tribe. They had protected Kacey Doka for a time after she escaped her captors. Ty knew that both Jake's wife, Lori, and Jake were members of this elite band of protectors. Their entry only made his shortfall more painful.

Kee interjected his opinion. "I'd call Kenshaw. He has connections outside the tribe."

Jake said, "Kenshaw has been working with the FBI on the dam collapse. He is the only one who managed to infiltrate the eco-extremists' operation, and his cover has never been blown."

Bear Den scowled, thrusting his fists onto his hips as he narrowed his eyes at Jake. Ty got the feeling that this information was classified.

Jake faced Bear Den. "She's my sister, Jack."

Bear Den's hands dropped to his sides and he nodded, then faced Ty. "Jake's right. Kenshaw has connections all over the state. I agree to bringing him in. But we must also involve the FBI. The chief is getting to both Forrest and Hoosay."

Ty's mouth twitched and his stomach squeezed in irritation. "Beth got a call last night about the fire and I haven't been able to get a hold of her since."

Kee took that one. "The fire at the health care clinic damaged our medical records. We suspect it was a clumsy attempt to destroy evidence. Our firefighters made short work of the blaze. It will take a while to sort through the soggy mass of paperwork."

"There's good reason to suspect that the paper records will not jibe with what Betty Mills entered into the computer system," said Bear Den.

"Why weren't they removed already?"

Bear Den shrugged. "Oversight."

"And Betty's dead?" asked Ty.

"Suicide," said Bear Den. "Tore up her skirt for a noose."

Ty shook his head as he pictured Betty swinging from her designer skirt in her cell.

"You didn't have her on suicide watch?" asked Ty.

"No, we did not," answered Bear Den. "Because she was working with us, filling in the pieces. The FBI was building a case against the Russians, and Betty was hopeful because her attorney was working on a deal to arrange a reduced sentence and preferential placement. But something happened, because her death and the clinic's fire on the same night is just too much of a coincidence for my liking."

"What?" asked Jake.

"You ask me," said Ty, "someone got to her. Yesterday she had one visitor, her youngest boy, Clinton."

Boy was a stretch, thought Ty, as Clinton was in his midtwenties.

"Until yesterday not one of her three sons would see her. She had no visits from them or their children. But then Clinton shows up and his mother kills herself the same day."

Kee scratched his chin. Jake rested a hand on the grip of his service weapon, and Ty spoke up.

"Someone threatened her family," said Ty. "Clinton came to tell her they were in danger."

Bear Den met his gaze and Ty thought he saw respect in the big man's expression.

"My thoughts exactly. Now we have no witness."

"Wolf Posse or the Russians?" asked Ty.

Jack shook his head. "Not sure. FBI is questioning Clinton now."

"Great. But how are we getting Abbie back?" asked Kee.

Bear Den's and Jake's radios both came alive in unison as Officer Wetselline called from the end of the drive.

"I've got Agents Forrest and Hoosay here."

"Let them up," said Bear Den.

"Tinnin is coming in behind them," said Wetselline.

His car moved from the driveway entrance and a black Escalade rolled past. Behind him, slowing down to make the turn, was Tinnin's official SUV. The stencil on the back fender was the tribal seal. The front door panel carried the police emblem and the word *Chief* below in bold black letters. The police chief drove all the way up to the gathering and opened his door, swinging himself around to face them. His leg, broken in the dam collapse last month, was now in a black plastic boot that made walking awkward, but he was finally done with the crutches.

Bear Den caught them up.

"Seems we have two operations," said Agent Forrest when Bear Den had finished. "Ty needs to make contact with the Russians tomorrow and simultaneously extract Abigail Redhorse from her captors in the Wolf Posse."

"The Russians are expecting Ty," said Tinnin.

"Anyone else shows up and we lose the possibility of locating our missing women and we lose Abbie," said Jake.

"We need to find Abbie," said Ty.

"And the missing," said Beth.

"I want Leonard Usov," said Forrest.

"You look a lot like Ty," said Tinnin to Jake.

Ty and Jake looked at each other. Jake's hair reached past his shoulders and he wore it back with a black elastic tie threaded with red cloth, while Ty clipped his hair chin-length and wore it loose. Jake's mouth often tipped down and Ty's naturally lifted up at the corners, making it seem as if he was perpetually up to something. But their facial features were very similar, their eyes a near match and their builds close enough to be, well, brothers.

"Yeah?" said Ty, inviting Tinnin to continue with a motion of his hand.

"So we need Ty in two places," said Tinnin. "He needs to make contact with the Russians. But honestly I would much rather have a police officer there to make that contact. And we need him to get past the Wolf Posse members who are likely holding his sister."

"You want Jake to pretend to be me?" asked Ty.

"Yes. And I want you to bluff your way past the posse to get to Abbie."

"Don't we have to find her first?" asked Bear Den.

"I'll take the kidnapping operation," said Beth, calling dibs on Abbie's abduction case and Ty all in one.

"I'll oversee the operation to make contact with the Russians," said Agent Forrest.

"What about the women? The Russians will be expecting me to be transporting four women, one of which is supposed to be Beth," Ty reminded them.

"Well, they are just doomed to disappointment."

Tinnin looked at Ty. "You know every member of the Wolf Posse."

Ty inclined his head.

"So find out where they are, each one, because one or more of them has your sister."

"I'm supposed to be kidnapping women."

"Jake and I will handle that. You find your sister, and when you have her, you call me so I can arrest Faras." Forrest glanced at the paper Ty held. "What's that?"

"Address of the meet," said Ty.

Tinnin held out his hand. Ty extended the page and Beth clasped his wrist, bringing his hand between them.

"If he does this," Beth interjected, "he does so in exchange for both the Bureau and tribal dropping any and all pending charges against him."

All the men stared at her. Forrest and Bear Den glared. Jake gaped and Tinnin smiled. Was she really negotiating an agreement for him?

"Tribal will take that deal," said Tinnin.

All gazes turned to Forrest. Beth had made a play that clearly annoyed her supervisor. He was the one who could put forth her name for promotion. The way he was staring daggers at her, Ty realized the chance of that ever happening had just gone up in flames and she'd done that for him. Why would she do that?

"What are you doing?" he whispered.

"Just wait," she replied out of the side of her mouth.

"Whose side are you on, Agent Hoosay?" asked Bear Den.

"Ty's," she answered.

Forrest tucked his chin and glared at Beth. Ty held his breath. What had she done? Beth had publicly advocated for him in a time when Forrest needed the information he held in his hand.

Forrest spat his answer. "Done."

"He gets the deal in writing today," she said.

Forrest nodded and motioned for the information with an impatient hand. Ty handed over the address.

Bear Den lifted his chin toward Ty. "Faras underestimated you. Never figured you'd come to us."

"Don't make me sorry," said Ty.

Jake pulled the elastic tie from his long hair. "Looks like I need a haircut." He turned toward the house, and shouted, "Ma!"

Ty smiled. Their mother had given them each their haircuts throughout their childhood, beginning with bangs and shoulder-length clips. Only Kee, who preferred short hair, went elsewhere for his grooming. Ty, Jake and even Colt, until he had left, all continued to

have their mother cut their hair. If anyone could repli-
cate Ty's style, it was their mom.

"What about Colt?" Ty asked Forrest.

"You lost me," said the agent.

"If you get him—Usov, I mean—can Colt and Kacey
come home?"

Tinnin inhaled and glanced toward the sky, as he
processed the question and implications. Finally he met
Ty's gaze. "If that's what they want. But Colt is doing
well where he is. He and Kacey are both working and
Colt sees a counselor about the trauma he endured and
his PTSD. He's talking now."

"He can do all that here," said Ty.

"Yes. But it is up to them. You'd understand if after
being abducted by a member of her tribe and held captive for months, Kacey was not anxious to come home."

"I'd disagree," said Kee. "I saw her leaving her brothers and sisters. She wants to come home."

"All right. First things first. Okay?" said Forrest.

Yes, thought Ty. First he'd find his baby sister while
Jake helped the Feds close down the Russian surrogate
ring. Then they'd get their little brother to come home.

He shook his head at the chances of all that going
right. Worry pressed down on him. His head began a
dull ache at his temples.

Jake appeared on the front porch carrying a battered
kitchen chair. May appeared behind him, a comb and
her sewing scissors in her hand. This pair of shears
was used solely for fabric and hair and woe to any of
her children caught using them for any other purpose.

Jake sat and May pulled the elastic from his hair.
Jake's expression was stoic and May's pained. She
combed out the strands until they sat across Jake's back
in perfect order. Then came the snip of the scissors.

Chapter Nineteen

Beth sucked the last antacid in the pack, the minty flavor ruined by the taste of chalk, as Ty drove them in Jake's Silver F-150 pickup back from Turquoise Ridge. They'd been up all night checking each member of the posse. Ty now wore Jake's clothing and his hair was tugged back in an elastic band, smoothed with hair gel to keep the short strands in place. The red cloth tie hid most of the evidence that his hair was nowhere near as long as Jake's had been.

It hadn't taken him long to figure out what she had done.

"You came here to make a big case," he said.

Her stomach tightened as she anticipated where this conversation might lead.

"Yet you chose to look for my sister, a simple kidnapping, instead of overseeing Jake's contact with the Russian mob."

"This operation might lead to the apprehension of Faras Pike." Her throat was also coated with chalk and she had to clear it to continue. "And furnish necessary information to tie this gang to the Russian crime organization."

"Yeah, yeah. It will get you assigned back to your desk in Oklahoma."

His skin glowed blue in the turquoise light from the truck's dashboard. "Why did you do that, Beth?"

She couldn't look at him. "I don't know."

"Bad move," he said.

"You don't want me here?"

"Forrest has more experience." That didn't exactly answer her question. But, then again, she had not really answered his. She couldn't. The answer was too complicated and too close to that part of her she protected.

"Well, I'm the best you got," she said.

"Fine, then let's get to work."

Beth had never seen Ty so focused. It had taken the evening and much of the night, but together they had tracked down and set up surveillance on eleven members of the Wolf Posse and their vehicles. From their efforts they had determined only three were in a position to be holding a captive.

When they pulled to a stop behind the only gas station in Koun'nde, it was officially Thursday morning, but so early even the roosters were still in bed. They parked here because there were other cars parked around and because it gave an excellent view of Oliver Boehm's residence. The posse member lived here alone. He was inside with Vernon Dent, and all the window coverings were closed. That could mean they were sleeping or just smoking weed. But it could also mean they had Abbie.

Beth consulted her list of the remaining gang members, furnished by Ty.

"Chino's too obvious," said Ty.

"So that leaves—" Beth consulted her pad of notes "—Oliver Boehm, Eric Goseyun and Geoffrey Corrales."

"Eric has been moving up in Faras's favor. He'd expect me to have Eric on my list. Oliver is reliable, but not the brightest of his men. Geoffrey, I don't know. He's young. Maybe twenty-one or so. But he's already impressed Faras with his ruthlessness. He's the one Faras sends to hurt people when Chino isn't available. His understudy." Ty swallowed. Of all the three remaining possibilities, Geoffrey Corrales was the man he most hoped Abbie was not with.

"We have to eliminate each one," said Beth. "That means getting into their places."

Her phone rang and she lifted it from her pocket.

"It's Forrest," she told him, and took the call. "Hoosay." She listened. "Good. Yes. All right. Let us know." She disconnected and turned her attention from Boehm's residence to him. "Your tribal council gave us permission to track the phones and conversations of all the names you provided."

"That's a lot of phones," he said.

"We might get something."

Ty shook his head. "I don't think so. Faras was too damn smart."

"Why do you think he is using you instead of Chino?" asked Beth.

"He needs Chino for protection."

"But he suspected Chino was out to take his place. Now he trusts him? And why you? Any one of his men would make a delivery, if asked."

"You've got a theory?"

She nodded. "I think he's going to let you make the delivery and then tip the police, throw you under the bus and make the whole mess go away."

"Handing me over to the police is stupid because I could turn on him."

"Not if you're dead."

Ty was silent as if letting that sink in. "Yeah, maybe."

"I have to admit, I was certain you were tied up in this."

"I *am* tied up in this."

"Yes, but not the way I expected. I believe I've convinced Forrest of your efforts to remain neutral, but there's a reason my boss isn't letting you make the delivery."

"He doesn't trust me."

"And he wants Usov. Your sister is secondary. He wouldn't have taken this operation if I had chosen the other. He's the boss and he goes where the action is."

"You get the leavings," said Ty.

"Exactly."

"But you didn't wait to have him assign you. You volunteered."

"Looks better. Don't you think?"

His expression showed he was unconvinced with her line of logic. Well, that was the best she could do.

Ty focused on Oliver Boehm's current residence, such as it was. The tilting double-wide had once belonged to Oliver's mother, who had died long ago, and it seemed very much as if neither she nor Oliver nor the tribe's HUD offices had done anything in the way of upkeep. The yellow grass grew high enough to cover the dirty, faded paint but not the torn screens or broken windows patched with cardboard.

"So, do you want me to try the front door to get a look inside one of those windows?"

Beth lifted her binoculars and stared toward Oliver's trailer. "I believe I can get inside through that back window."

"You mean the one covered with cardboard?" he asked.

She smiled. "Yeah, that's the one."

"I'll be outside the door. You holler if you find her or if you need me."

She handed him a radio. Then she clicked the side button. His radio relayed the sound. "You hear that and I need you to break in."

"Got it." He clipped the radio on his belt.

Next she offered him a pistol. He shook his head. He still carried no gun.

"I need you armed," she said.

He gave her a sad look. "I turned in my rifle when I got stateside, Beth, and I don't ever plan to aim a firearm at a human being again. Each one you kill takes part of your soul."

She motioned her head toward the trailer. "These men don't have souls."

"Everyone does."

They made their way to the trailer. Ty boosted Beth through the window and then moved to the door, standing off to the side.

The light was coming up and time was flying by. She returned her backup weapon to her coat pocket and left him.

Ty waited for what seemed like a week outside that door. The fact that he heard nothing was all that kept him waiting. His gaze was on the window, but he was alert to the sound of the front door click. The door cracked open and Beth stared back at him. She lifted a finger to her full lips and then stepped out.

"Oliver is there, passed out in the room I entered. The trailer is filthy, but empty."

"Cross him off the list."

Beth glanced up at the sky. "Jake should be making the drop soon."

They exchanged worried glances. Ty knew the danger of Jake's mission. He prayed that his brother came home safe and that Forrest succeeded in striking a blow at the Russian crime organization.

"Who next?" she asked. The clock was ticking. If any one of the Russians alerted Faras to trouble, Abbie's situation would only become more perilous.

"Eric Goseyun or Geoffrey Corrales?" she asked.

"I'd choose Corrales. He's more trustworthy and he's been with Faras longer."

But as it turned out they watched Geoffrey leave his home and they followed him to the Wolf Posse headquarters. He could not be watching Abbie.

"Goseyun," said Ty, turning Jake's truck back toward Piñon Forks. In a few minutes they reached his place, on a circular dirt road with five other single-family homes, all built in the 1970s, of cinder block and painted beige. The yards were littered with broken plastic toys, grills and faded lawn chairs.

Ty slowed before making the circle. "No way to creep up on Goseyun."

"Also no way for his neighbors not to see him come or go."

"Front door?" asked Ty.

"Fastest way in." She drew out her badge.

"Don't use that. If we're wrong, word will get out."

She tucked the badge beneath her shirt as Ty parked in Goseyun's driveway behind a van. Had he taken Abbie in that vehicle? Ty's mouth went grim and his breathing increased.

Beth looked through the back window and then to him, shaking her head. Abbie was not inside the van.

She remained where she was, with a clear view of the main entrance, as Ty mounted the stairs and knocked.

Eric Goseyun appeared at the front door in a pair of sweatpants slung low on his narrow hips and a white tank top. He smiled at seeing Ty and looked completely at ease. His eyes were dull and bloodshot. There was a definite odor of weed clinging to him. His long hair hung limp and the yellowish color of his skin seemed to be the harbinger of illness.

"Yo, bro. What's happening?"

"Delivering a message from Faras." Ty did not wait to be asked in but stepped past Eric into his house. Before entering he waved Beth away. It was her turn to wait outside and wonder.

"Why don't he just call me, bro?" Goseyun offered his joint, thus far held behind his back.

Ty waved away the offer. "You know that Fed, Forrest? The one supposed to be looking in to the dam collapse?"

"Yeah, I heard about him," said Goseyun.

"He's looking at Faras for the missing girls."

"Wow. That's bad."

"So don't call him. You got something to say, say it in person."

"Yeah, sure thing."

Ty thumbed toward the bedrooms. "Mind if I use the can?"

"No, go on. Sorry about the smell. Got a broken pipe or something."

Ty headed off and turned to see Goseyun reach his sagging couch and drop into the cushions, completely at ease. Then Ty searched the place.

As he had suspected, Goseyun's place was filthy, but Abbie was not here. Ty went back outside and, with Beth, returned to his vehicle, slipping into the driver's seat.

"That's all of them," he said, in confusion. The Wolf Posse had more members than tribal police and he had checked each one. Time was ticking away. As soon as the Russians failed to contact Faras about a successful drop, Faras would know Ty had failed. Then he would hurt Abbie. His heart now ached in his chest and his throat was tight.

Ty grabbed his hair at each side of his temple, feeling the sticky gel as he clenched his fists.

"What about the women?" Beth asked.

He straightened as the fog of panic lifted from his brain. He turned to face her. Her expression was open, thoughtful. No panic, all business.

"What?" he asked.

"Women," she repeated. "Female members of the gang."

Ty gripped the wheel and gave it a shake, bringing himself forward and then back against the seat.

"Yes! I know where she is," she said.

Ty met her gaze with one of wonder. She was so smart. He'd been lost, sinking as he faced failure, and she'd just turned them in a new direction. The right direction. He knew it and now his heart pounded in anticipation.

Ty set them in motion toward the alpha female of the Wolf Posse, certain that his sister was in the care of Jewell Tasa.

Chapter Twenty

Jewell had a private place between Koun'nde and Turquoise Ridge. She liked horses and Faras made sure she had several. But he couldn't buy her what she most coveted. Jewell wanted the title of Miss Indian Rodeo Queen. She could qualify, being from a federally recognized tribe and being over the age of eighteen. She'd have no trouble raising the money to compete because Faras would hand it to her. But that did not mean she would win. She'd have to enroll in college and she'd have to impress the judges with her horsemanship, among other things.

Ty pulled the silver pickup off the road and pointed to the ranch house with a small horse barn and new fencing corralling four fine horses. A large satellite dish on the western side of the house ensured that Jewell had internet, phone and cable.

"That livestock belong to Jewell?" asked Beth.

"Her pride and joy," he answered.

"Looks like great collateral."

He liked the way she thought. "You'd have to catch them first. The chestnut is her favorite. She calls him Big Red."

"I've been around horses most of my life. I can get that horse haltered and ready."

They discussed strategy as precious seconds leaked away. The dashboard clock told him that Jake and Forrest should be making contact with the Russians. It was going down right now.

"We better be right," said Ty.

Beth gazed at the house with her binoculars. "She's got a look-out."

"Where?"

She offered the glasses and pointed. He spotted Randy, her kid brother, throwing a ball against the side of the barn. Ty glanced at the clock on the dash. It was almost nine in the morning. He should be in school. Beth was right. He already knew that Randy was a solid worker and just the right age to be inconspicuous.

"I'll get him clear before I go in," said Ty. He had no interest in hurting children, but he knew how effective they were as members of the gang.

Ty stared at the house. He no longer just wanted to rescue Abbie. He wanted the Wolf Posse eliminated. He wanted to take out those who sold their children and kidnapped his sister. Ty was done walking the line because that was not what lines were for. They were for crossing.

"Ready?" he asked.

Beth checked her pistol and then nodded. Then she crouched down out of sight as Ty drove them the short distance to the house, parking out of view on the side of the barn. Before they were completely stopped, Beth was out of the truck and running along the side of the building. She disappeared before Randy's reflection appeared in his side mirror.

"Jake?" Randy called. "That you?"

Ty's phone rang. It was Jake. He took the call as Randy approached from the back of the truck.

"Yeah," Ty said.

It was Jake's voice. Just hearing him caused Ty to squeeze his eyes shut and blow out a breath of sweet relief.

"We're done. Got four members of the crime organization, all alive, and they didn't have time to destroy their computers or cell phones. We got it all, Ty."

Ty couldn't speak past the lump.

"Do you have her? Did you find Abbie?"

"Jake?" Randy spoke from beside Ty's open window.

"Not yet. I'll call soon." He ended the call and turned to Randy, whose eyes were now widening.

"Ty!" he said, and backed away from the door.

Ty slipped out to stand before him in the tall grass. Randy looked back toward the house. He'd misjudged the situation and the distance, finding himself out of sight of the house and facing Ty instead of a tribal police officer.

"Your sister home?" he asked.

From somewhere in the pasture, he heard the sound of a tin can being shaken with what sounded like oats. Ty was certain that Beth would soon have her pick of the horses.

Randy redirected his attention to Ty.

"She's got her period. Ma sent me over to take care of her."

"That right?" Ty closed the distance.

"She don't want to see no one," said Randy, backing up as he spoke.

"Not smart to come up to the truck, Randy. It's a Trojan horse."

"A what?"

"See, if you were in school, you'd learn about stuff like this. Didn't I tell you to stay in school?"

"Yeah." He glanced toward the house, no longer in sight. "Listen, I gotta go. My sister…"

With his head turned, he never saw Ty strike. Before Randy could call out, Ty had him against his chest with one hand over his mouth. The boy's struggles were ineffective.

"I'm not going to hurt you, Randy. But you aren't warning Jewell."

In short order, he had Randy tied hand and foot and secured to a sturdy fence post. His mouth was gagged with the cloth Ty had worn in his hair.

"Quit wiggling. It only tightens the knots, and that post will give you slivers."

Ty left Randy and headed for the house. The front door was unlocked, owing to the fact that Jewell did not expect company and was confident that Randy would alert her if there was any.

He found her lying on the couch watching afternoon soaps.

"Ty! What a nice surprise." She glanced behind him toward the door. "You see my brother outside?"

"He's tied up."

Jewell rose from the couch, assessing him now with her large intelligent eyes.

"Where is she?" Ty asked.

"I don't know what you're talking about." Her eyes shifted, telling him otherwise.

"My sister. Get her," said Ty.

Jewell's laugh was forced. "She's not here."

"That so?"

Jewell lifted her chin in a gesture that some women used as a display of arrogance and disdain. "Get out of here."

"My sister?"

She waved an impatient hand and Ty saw her nail polish was black. "Search the place if you want."

"I don't have time for that."

"Faras finds out you've been bothering me and he'll take you out. I don't know why he lets you hang with us anyway. You're not one of us and your brother's a cop."

Ty was done talking. He grabbed Jewell by the upper arm and forced her to the door.

"Hey! Let go of me." She struggled but still hurried along beside him. "Faras's gonna kill you for this."

He took her through the open door and to the yard, where she had a clear view of her barn and pasture.

"Where's my brother?" she asked, her voice losing the fury and taking on notes of panic.

Ty did not answer.

"Beth!" he called.

FBI Agent Hoosay stepped from the barn wearing her body armor, looking tough and oh, so sexy to Ty. He tucked that image away for another time, hoping they both lived long enough for him to enjoy it.

Beth had her pistol drawn. In her opposite hand, she held the red nylon rope of a lead. She made a clicking sound and came out leading Big Red.

Jewell gasped and lifted her free hand to her heart. Beth raised her pistol and pressed it at the horse's head just below the ear.

"All right." Jewell threw up her hands. "She's here. I'll get her. Where's my brother?"

"Abbie first," said Ty.

Jewell turned toward the house and he walked with her. A glance showed Beth's pistol holstered. She held the horse, by a loose lead, and gently stroked his cheek.

Ty allowed Jewell to take him upstairs. She moved the large wooden linen cabinet, which was on rollers.

He released her so she could move the rack of towels and makeup to reveal a small door cut in the wall. It was closed with a bolt.

Jewell motioned with her head. "She's in there."

"Get her." Ty held his breath as he worried what he would find. If she'd hurt Abbie, he didn't know if he could control himself.

Jewell threw back the bolt and tugged open the door. There was no sound from within the dark crawl space. She reached and tugged a beaded pull chain, snapping on the single lightbulb.

Ty crouched and saw a large dog crate on the dusty floor. Inside, Abbie lay on her side on a blanket, facing away from them, unmoving.

"What's wrong with her?" asked Ty.

"I give her some cough medicine, the kind with codeine and alcohol. It keeps her quiet."

"Get her," he ordered, pushing Jewell toward the cubby.

She crawled to his sister, opened the crate and rolled Abbie to her back. Ty gasped at the gray pallor of her face.

Was she breathing?

"Wakey, wakey, Abbie. You've got company."

Abbie's eyes blinked open and Ty let his head drop back. He could breathe again.

He heard a light tread on the stairs. A glance to the hall showed Beth on the stairs, gun drawn.

"It's me," said Beth, coming to the landing and heading for him. "You okay?"

He nodded and turned his attention back to the bathroom.

Jewell was yanking a very groggy Abbie from her prison. Ty stooped and gathered Abbie to him. She smelled of sweat and tears and alcohol. Ty kicked the small door shut.

"Hey!" shouted Jewell.

Beth threw the bolt shut. "She have her phone?"

"No. It's downstairs on the coffee table."

Ty raised his voice. "Jewell, when you see Faras, remember that I have Randy."

The pounding ceased.

"I have to bring her in as well," said Beth.

Ty spoke to Jewell, cautioning her. Then he let her out. Beth took it from there and in short order Jewell's hands were cuffed behind her back. Ty preceded her down the stairs, carrying his little sister in his arms. She stopped in the living room to take Jewell's phone.

Once outside, Ty set Abbie carefully in the truck cab as Beth ordered Jewell to lie down on the ground. Then Beth saw to Randy. She took off his gag, replaced the ropes with zip ties on his wrists and delivered him to the truck cab.

Ty was in the cab trying to get Abbie to stay awake when Beth ordered the boy into the cab. Randy hesitated.

"Is that Abbie?" asked Randy, the shock evident in his voice. Ty realized that Randy and Abbie were likely in the same grade at school.

"Didn't you know?" asked Ty.

Randy shook his head and began to cry.

"Get in, Randy. Hold Abbie up," said Ty.

Beth spoke from the open passenger door. "I'm putting Jewell in the back."

"She might jump."

"I'll cuff her to your brother's tool kit."

Jake's tool kit was stainless steel, bolted down and

went from one side of the bed to the other. Jewell would not be able to escape it.

Ty exited the vehicle to help Beth secure Jewell. Then they returned to the truck cab. Abbie sprawled across Randy's lap.

He gave Ty an apologetic look. "I can't hold her on account of the cuffs."

Beth climbed in and pulled Abbie across her lap, then secured the seat belt around Randy. Then Ty set them in motion.

"We have to get them to tribal before Faras finds out that his whole world just went sideways."

Ty set them in motion. Randy sat sullen beside Ty sniffing occasionally and Abbie slumped against Beth.

"Call Kee," said Ty. "Tell him I have Abbie and that she's on something."

Beth lifted her phone at the same time Jewell's mobile played a popular rap song about the boss.

"Faras," she said, looking at the screen.

They didn't answer and the call cut out, followed by a text that displayed on the lock screen.

No word from R. Bring her.

"R? Is that Russians?" asked Beth.

"Possibly."

"He knows. And we got him," said Beth, lifting Jewell's phone. She called Kee first. Ty listened as she gave him the important details. She disconnected and turned to him. "He'll meet us at your tribal health clinic." She made a call to her field office, reporting the successful recovery of Abigail Redhorse and listening while Ty wondered what she knew. He didn't have long to wait, but the call seemed endless. They flew through

Koun'nde under stormy gray skies and were heading for Piñon Forks when she disconnected.

"Jake is safe. They have the Russians in custody, including Victor Vitoli. He's the one Mills called when they had issues. Forrest was hoping to bag him because Vitoli answers directly to Usov." Beth blew through pursed lips, a sound of relief.

"Where are they?" asked Ty.

"Still in Darabee, but Forrest is sending all available agents to the Wolf Posse's headquarters to make arrests."

"The missing? Garcia, Espinoza and Kesselman?" asked Ty.

"Not there."

Ty knew that Marta Garcia was a close friend of Kacey. She had risked her life to get Marta free.

"Maybe we'll get something from the Russians' tech. We have very good people. They could still find them," said Beth.

Ty wanted more. He wanted that organization shut down for good and all the girls that they had taken to be returned to their families.

They reached the clinic to find Kee waiting on the sidewalk, pacing beside Lori. Kee had Beth's door open the instant Ty put the truck in Park.

"Jake back yet?" he asked Lori.

Lori cast him a worried gaze. "All en route to the posse according to Ava."

As the tribe's new dispatcher, Ava knew where all the officers were at all times.

Beth passed Abbie to Kee. He took her to the waiting stretcher, removing his coat to place it around his little sister. Then he began checking her vitals as Lori pushed them toward the side entrance on the women's health care side of the clinic.

Beth left Randy, who sat with head bowed as tears splashed the denim of his jeans, leaving dark spots. Ty paused beside Beth to speak to Randy.

"Ask for Bear Den," said Ty. "He'll help you, Randy, if you let him. You hear me?"

Randy sniffed and nodded.

With all the tribal police on their way to Wolf Posse headquarters, Beth had to bring Jewell to the tribal police herself. Ty hesitated as Beth took the driver's seat, torn between following Kee and following her.

"Call your mother. Tell her we have your sister," said Beth. "I'll be right back."

"Okay," answered Ty, and he followed Kee and his sister.

Beth drove Jewell and Randy from the clinic lot to the one before headquarters. Randy waited beside the truck as she released his sister from the toolbox, then neatly snapped the cuffs back together behind her back. She assisted Jewell down and found Ava Hood taking charge of Randy. Beth walked Jewell into the station, stopping at the dispatch desk while Ava retrieved the keys to the only cell on the premises.

Ava lifted the headset to report Beth's arrival to Tinnin. Beth deposited Randy in the squad room beside Ava's desk. Beth knew the woman had been a detective in Salt River and would know how to process a prisoner, even a minor one.

Beth escorted Jewell down the hall and happily deposited her in the cell, loving that satisfying click of the lock engaging. Then she returned to dispatch.

"I called protective services," said Ava. "They're sending someone for Randy."

Beth nodded and then kneeled before Randy. "You aren't your sister, kiddo. You can make choices. The gang is gone. You're not."

Ava used a tissue to wipe Randy's running nose.

Beth was already on her way out and Ty had to jog over to catch her.

"You going to the clinic?" she asked.

"I did. Abbie is doing all right. Kee's got her, so I'm going with you," he said.

"Your mom?"

"On her way. I want to see Faras arrested."

Beth cast Ty a winning smile. "Just what I was thinking."

Unfortunately, they arrived too late to be of much use, but just in time to see Faras led to Jake's police cruiser in handcuffs. Ty met his gaze as Faras did a double take at Ty's clothing and appearance. Ty felt satisfaction at seeing his former friend in handcuffs and he found gratification in knowing that Faras would no longer be preying on their people.

It took the rest of the day for the FBI and tribal police to round up all the Wolf Posse members.

Beth was back in her element as she and Forrest began the process of interrogating the suspects, starting with the Russians.

Ty felt like a fifth wheel. Beth no longer needed him. The creeping realization dawned that she would never need him. He had served his purpose, helped her make the kind of case that would bring her notice, accolades and the transfer to a major field office that she so coveted. In helping her reach her dreams, he would lose her forever. It was in that moment of crystallizing awareness that he admitted to himself that he loved Beth and that, as usual, his life choices stank. Just once he'd like to make a move that didn't end up kicking him back in the...teeth.

Ty left Jake's truck at tribal headquarters and walked to the clinic alone. Not that anyone noticed he was missing. Once inside, he found Kee. It was now after hours and Abbie was the only patient still here.

"How's she doing?" he asked.

"She's good. Whatever they gave her is wearing off. She's tired, bruised and hungry."

"Hungry is good," said Ty, the gratitude at his sister's recovery warming him.

Ty looked around. "Where's Mom?"

"Did you call her?" asked Kee.

"I did. But that was a while ago." Confusion morphed into a cold panic. It was hours ago.

Kee's voice held a note of concern. "I was going to call, but it got crazy busy here and..."

Ty phoned the house and got no answer. He disconnected and met Kee's worried gaze.

"Call Jake. Send him to Mom," said Ty, running back toward the door.

"What? Why?" called Kee.

He paused to look back at his brother's worried face. "Dad. His parole."

"Oh, no!" said Kee.

Chapter Twenty-One

Ty reached his childhood home in Jake's pickup and immediately spotted a problem with Burt's truck. The driver's side door gaped and Ty's worry solidified into certainty. His father was here. Ty narrowed his eyes, finding no unfamiliar vehicle. The absence did not reassure him. His father didn't have a truck of his own. In fact, he would have only what possessions had been returned to him upon release. Likely he got here by bus or caught a ride.

Ty thought back to that day when he was convicted, picturing the sports jacket, shirt and jeans. His father's appearances in court had been the only time he'd ever seen his father dressed like that.

He took his foot off the gas and the truck glided past his mother's place. His dad did not know Jake's truck, and if Ty didn't stop, he might not realize he had company. He glanced at the dashboard clock, which read 6:00 p.m. The Doka girls, fostering with his mom, should all be home from school. As if having their mother arrested for drug trafficking was not enough, now his father had broken into their life.

Ty fumed as he acknowledged that in one way he and his father were alike. They were both dangerous when angry. But unlike his father, Ty preferred to settle scores without the other party knowing Ty had done anything at all. He'd pulled that off once with his father. He'd never do it again. But he didn't need to broadcast his arrival.

Ty parked behind the neighbors' place and crept through the backyard, past the fire pit and the circle of mismatched lawn chairs. He reached the rear door and paused, squatting below the level of the windows. The daylight had faded, and in the twilight it would be difficult for anyone inside to see out. But if the lights were on, it would be perfect for him to see in.

He lifted himself up high enough to peer inside. He knew his mother did not lock the doors except at night, so it was likely still open. Nothing moved inside the kitchen. At this hour, his mother should be preparing supper, but the room was empty. Her absence here was as worrisome as her absence from Abbie's bedside.

The knob was cold in his hand as he slowly turned it. A moment later he was inside.

"Leave him be, Colton!" That was his mother's voice and Colton was what she had always called Ty's father. The idea of fighting his father turned his stomach as much as the belief that he might very well lose. Like him, Colton Redhorse did not fight fair.

Ty continued through the empty kitchen toward the sound of his mother's voice. He'd forgotten the way her voice went high and quavered when she confronted her ex-husband's rages.

"I got your message. Divorce papers, order of protection. Funny, but no one asked me if I wanted a divorce."

Where was Burt? Ty wondered as he tried to push back the terrible possibilities that rose in his mind. His father would not tolerate a rival.

"This sack of turd is my replacement?" asked his father. There was the thumping sound of something striking something hollow, followed by a groan.

Burt, Ty suspected, was down.

There was a cry from one of the Doka girls, followed by his father's shout.

"Shut up!"

How often had his father told him the same thing?

Ty stepped into plain view, his gaze sweeping the living room. His mother sat on the very edge of her chair beside her cane, her damaged foot wrapped in its special stocking with gauze covering the place where her amputated toes should have been. His mother's diabetes made her dizzy and weak at times and the surgeries decreased her mobility.

On the floor between the coffee table and his mother's chair was Burt Rope. Burt was motionless, bleeding from a head wound, and seemed to be only semiconscious.

The three Doka girls, Jackie, Shirley and Winnie, were all huddled together on the floor before the muted television. Behind them, the evening news flashed video of other tragedies. Ty focused on the one unfolding before him.

His father had not seen him yet, as his back was to Ty and he was concentrating on winding up to kick Burt again.

"Welcome home, Pop," said Ty, leaning indolently on the door frame.

Colton Redhorse spun about.

"Kee?" he asked.

Ty smirked. "Nope."

"Ty. Should have known from that grin. I'll get to you in a minute." He turned back to Burt.

"No. You'll get to me now."

Colton turned, his expression filled with anticipation. His dark eyes glittered and a smile lifted his mouth. He was looking forward to this. Ty managed not to take a step backward as he met his father's cold stare, but it was hard.

"Figured it out. Took a while because you're so slick. But I finally worked it through." Colton turned to May, who had slipped off the chair and kneeled beside Burt. "Get away from him."

His father pulled a gun from his waistband and pointed it at Burt. May complied, dragging herself up and back to her chair. When Ty's father turned back, Ty was three steps closer.

Ty lifted a finger at the pistol and then pointed to Burt. "Got three parole violations that I see. B and E, weapon and assault. Not your best start."

"Shut up," said Colton, and turned the gun on Ty as he spoke to May. "You know what your son did? He set me up. Crashed on purpose so we'd all get caught. What they call that? Cut off his nose despite his face."

"To spite his face," Ty said, correcting him.

"Shut up," said Colton. That was his favorite expression, his easy go-to.

Ty spoke to the Doka children. "Girls, I want you to walk behind me and out the back door."

They rose, but Colton turned his pistol in their direction.

"Abbie stays," he said.

He'd last seen Abbie when she was eight years old. It was no surprise that he could not recognize her.

"Like I've been telling you," said his mother.

"Shut up," barked Colton.

"Those are foster kids. None of them is Abbie," said Ty.

His father glared at him. "Why should I believe anything you say?"

Ty motioned to the girls to come to him with one hand. Jackie pushed her younger siblings ahead of her. They rushed past Ty and out the back door a moment later.

"Fine, go on," said Colton, closing the door after the cow was out of the barn.

Ty had hoped that he wouldn't shoot children, but his father's temper had not improved with his incarceration and he had never looked more fit. Ty, on the other hand, was still recovering from the lacerations on his shoulder.

"Where's Abbie?" Colton raged. "I want to see my little girl."

"Faras Pike kidnapped her to get my cooperation."

May cried out and then began to weep.

"Faras? That little turd. He's next on my list."

His father would have to stand in line behind the FBI, thought Ty.

"You want to call him?" Ty offered his phone.

Colton grinned. "My message needs to be delivered in person."

Ty slipped his phone into his back pocket.

"How about you and I settle this outside?" asked Ty.

"You're my son, but you betrayed me. Betrayed your own father. So I'm going to return the favor, make 'em open those closed records." He turned the grip of the pistol toward Burt. Then he wiped the trigger and grip with his shirttails. Ty had an inkling of what Colton planned as his father crouched beside Burt's still form and pressed the pistol into his limp fingers.

"That won't fool anyone," said Ty.

"Shut up."

Ty had been told that just one too many times. He kicked his father's arm, sending the gun thumping across the carpet, but Colton grabbed Ty's leg and twisted, sending Ty sprawling to the floor.

His father roared and dove onto Ty. During the wrestling match, Ty only once had his father in a headlock, but was quickly tossed by the man who outweighed him by fifty pounds of muscle.

His mother struggled to get Burt to his feet. Ty wished she'd leave Burt and run, but she didn't. When Colton reached for her, Ty landed a body blow to his exposed ribs. His father expelled the air from his lungs and caved toward the blow. His mother was up and Burt gained his feet as the two shuffled out the front door. Ty blocked his father's pursuit with his body and his father changed direction, retrieving the pistol.

Colton aimed the weapon at Ty and ordered him to move. Ty didn't. Colton roared as he holstered the weapon in the front of his jeans. Then he charged Ty, the tackle sending them both out the door, Ty flying backward. Ty caught a glimpse of his mother on the hard ground first beside Burt, who was on his hands and knees, retching.

His father twisted and grabbed something at his hip. Ty saw the flash of steel. His father had a knife. He needed to keep his father from hurting his mother. Sending him to prison had worked but only for a while. He was back, he was a wild animal and he needed to be put down. But Ty did not know if he could do it. A primal part of him resisted until Colton's gaze locked on his mother. Then something broke inside him.

Ty lunged for the blade, capturing his father's wrist in both hands. His father released the weapon. They rolled over and over, out into the yard. Colton came up on top, straddling him and tugging the pistol from the front of his jeans.

Colton's eyes blazed with triumph. "Still the better man," he growled, and then lifted the pistol, pressing the barrel to the center of Ty's forehead.

Ty kept his eyes wide open. The gunshot made him jump.

There was another shot, followed by another.

He shouldn't have heard that, not if the bullet passed through his skull. He stared up at his father, at first thinking his dad had shot wide just to scare him.

Colton's arms hung at his sides and he gaped at Ty with a look of confusion etched on his brow. Ty's attention moved to the red stains blooming by the second on the front of his father's blue denim shirt. Colton tipped sideways and fell beside Ty. Behind his father stood FBI Special Agent Beth Hoosay, her gold badge swinging before her and her arms outstretched, holding her pistol.

BETH STARED IN shock at Colton Redhorse's inert form. She'd discharged three rounds, fearing all the while that she might hit Ty. The cold panic still froze her from the inside out and she stood motionless, pistol still aimed at Colton Redhorse's body.

Neither man had heard her approach or her order for Colton to drop his weapon. Only May Redhorse had looked in her direction, seen her run across the lawn and draw her sidearm, shouting that she was FBI.

Kee had phoned her, told her what had happened. During that drive, racing from Darabee to his mother's home, all she could think of was that she'd be too late. Too late to save Ty. Too late to reach the conclusion that she didn't want a promotion if it meant losing him. Too late to understand what was really important in her life...who was really important. And too late to have a chance to tell him that she loved him with all her ambitious imperfect self.

Beth stood staring at Colton Redhorse, waiting for him to move or groan or try to hurt Ty again. Her finger began to cramp upon the trigger. If he moved, she'd shoot him again right in the back.

Colton Redhorse didn't move because her training was too good and her reflexes too programmed not to hit center mass. Now there would be an inquiry into this shooting, as there was with all cases when an agent used deadly force. But instead of considering the implications to her career, she could think only of how close she had come to losing Ty forever.

Would he forgive her for killing his father or would he thank her? Ty understood about protecting his family, and they were a wonderful family. Getting to know them all made her long for what she had missed being an only child. Every one of his family had treated her with the respect and acceptance she thought could only be found in her career. What was a career set against the potential of the man before her?

Ty had shown her his capacity to love. He loved his mother and his sister. He'd protected everyone in his family at great personal expense. He was a shining example of brains and heart. And she knew she'd never find another man like him.

Ty shoved his father the rest of the way off him. There was the sound of sirens heading toward them. His brother Jake was coming. The whole tribal police was coming, but they'd all been out between Turquoise Ridge and Koun'nde. Darabee had been closer and she'd driven like a madwoman. Her backup pulled in, Agent Forrest exiting his vehicle with his service weapon drawn.

Ty checked his father's pulse and then left him to move to his mother and Mr. Rope. Ty never looked at Beth or even acknowledged her presence. His shoulder was bleeding again, but he didn't seem to notice that, either, as he gathered his weeping mother in his arms.

Beth kept her weapon on Colton Redhorse as Forrest placed a foot on the perp's weapon and then stooped to retrieve it. He also checked the man's pulse and shook his head, eyes on her.

"Clear," he said.

She holstered her pistol and expelled a long breath. The next one came fast and rasping. The adrenaline, previously contained to the narrow focus of her suspect, now released into her nervous system, giving her a trembling, disjointed feeling that surged through her with increasing ferocity.

"Is he...?" Her voice had lifted an octave. Nothing in her training had prepared her for the moment she took a life.

Forrest nodded.

The yard filled up with law enforcement vehicles, headlights shone across the yellow grass, casting long shadows before her. Ty and May's faces turned blue and red as the lights from the police vehicles flashed. Officer Redhorse jogged past her to his mother while Ty saw to Burt Rope, getting him to his seat to await the incoming ambulance. Beth just stood there watching the chaos as her ears buzzed.

Forrest approached, touching her elbow. "You all right?"

"Never shot anyone before," she said.

It didn't feel good, and even knowing it was necessary and that Colton Redhorse was a dangerous man, she felt ill. Suddenly Beth understood Ty's insistence to never hold a firearm.

"Feel sick."

"Yeah. I know," said Forrest.

He ushered her to his vehicle and opened the passenger side door, pressing her into the seat. "Going to need you to make a statement. Man, you got here fast. Never seen anyone drive like that. I lost you on the switchbacks between here and Darabee."

Switchbacks? She didn't even remember them. She lifted a trembling hand, extending her fingers to show him.

"That normal?" she asked.

"It hits everyone differently. But always after the danger is past. You did your job, Agent Hoosay."

That was a nice way of saying it. But she hadn't been doing her job. Her flight here and the shooting had been personal. Only her training had ensured that she announced herself and followed the rules of engagement. But she would have shot Colton Redhorse regardless and the fact that she shot him in the back mattered to her not at all.

"Listen, I'm going to have the EMTs have a look at you."

"Is Ty all right?" She tried to see past Forrest, who squatted before her. There were so many people here now and Ty was lost in the crowd.

"He's with his brother Jake. I have to set up the perimeter."

Perimeter? Yes, that was what needed to be done.

"His mom and the girls?"

"The girls are all scared but safe. Burt will need a trip to the ER. But I'm sure he'll recover."

"Can I see Ty?"

"Not now. We need his statement first. You wait here a while, okay?"

No. Not okay. She put her head in her hands and took some deep breaths. She just needed a minute.

Chapter Twenty-Two

What a car wreck, thought Ty. Two hours after the shooting, he waited in the interrogation room, the only one in the small tribal police headquarters. The walls were white and the floor a scuffed gray tile. Furniture consisted of two chairs, one with a student-style, flip-up desk. He sat in the other, the one where the occupant was not required to take notes. A glance at the mirror showed only his reflection. His hair was disheveled, his cheek bruised and his T-shirt bloody from the wound that just would not stay closed. Kee would be mad at him about that again, no doubt.

Ty had been here before, once too often. This time he was not handcuffed…yet.

He'd wanted to help Beth make her case, her career and gain her ticket out of the field office where she had reached as far as she could. FBI agents advanced by making a big case. But he sure had never intended to have his dysfunctional family as the center of her investigation.

His father was dead and his overwhelming emotion was relief. The man who had terrorized his family and beaten his mother would never hurt them again. But the scars he left behind would take time to heal. His mother and Burt had gone by ambulance to the tribe's clinic, where Kee would be seeing to their injuries. Abbie was already there. Kee's family had become some of his best customers, and that was no coveted position.

He wondered if Shirley, Jackie and Winnie were all right and he wondered how many nightmares would follow from this evening's events. Had they seen Ty's father shot down like the rabid animal that he was?

The door opened and Ty shifted, lifting his chin in a weary acceptance that things would get worse before they got better. Three men stepped into the small room, Kenshaw Little Falcon, their medicine man and a certified therapist, Police Chief Wallace Tinnin, chewing gum and rocking awkwardly on his booted foot, and FBI Agent Luke Forrest. Ty looked toward the hall but Beth did not appear, and Forrest closed the door.

They wanted his statement. He wanted some answers. They indulged him. He learned that Abbie was dehydrated but otherwise healthy…physically, that is. Jewell Tasa had been charged with kidnapping and currently occupied the tribe's only jail cell right down the hall. Ty's mother was being treated for a spike in her blood pressure and Burt was recovering from a head wound and broken ribs. The Doka girls had been seen by Kee and released to Hazel Tran, one of their tribal council members and the retired teacher who had been fostering their younger brothers, Hewett and Jeffery. The Doka family was together again, except for their big sister Kacey, still in witness protection with Ty's brother Colt.

Forrest answered all of Ty's questions. Except the one he didn't ask—where was Beth?

Tinnin took over. "We got Faras and all members of the Wolf Posse under arrest. They've been transported to the Darabee jail under Detective Bear Den's supervision."

Ty had no doubt that the posse would not be seen by visitors of any sort while Bear Den was in charge. "Randy Tasa?"

"Protective services picked him up. He'll be placed with a family on the rez in a day or two," said Kenshaw.

"So," said Tinnin. "We need to take your statement."

"Starting where?" asked Ty.

"Go through your day, searching for your sister with Agent Hoosay."

"Where is she?" he asked.

"Debriefing. Statements," said Forrest. "Same as you."

"Can I see her?"

Forest shook his head.

Ty sighed and then gave them what they came for, going through the events of the day and their search for his sister, ending with their successful recovery of Abbie from a dog crate. He wondered if he'd ever be able to think about that without the scalding fury filling his stomach like boiling sap.

They released him a little before 10:00 p.m. with instructions to return in the morning for a second round of questioning. Jake took him over to the clinic for treatment. Kee scolded him as he opted for Steri-Strips instead of stitches or staples.

"If you're just going to keep tearing them out, this will work best. That cut will leave a scar. Don't blame me. It's your fault."

"Most things are," he muttered, the weariness settling between his shoulders.

Kee looked at him with wide eyes. Ty cocked his head in confusion and then watched in surprise as

Kee's dark eyes filled with tears. Despite his injury, Kee hugged him, holding him tight as the sobs came.

Ty looked to Jake, who stood with his hands on his utility belt, his own eyes swimming.

"You saved Abbie," Jake said. "You found her and brought her home safe and you saved Mom."

Jake stepped forward to join the hug. Ty lifted his free hand to pat his older and younger brothers in turn.

Kee drew back first and yanked a tissue from the stainless-steel cart beside the examining table.

Jake pulled back and dropped his gaze to the floor as he spoke. "We just found out what you did."

The myriad of possibilities filled Ty's mind, but he kept mute, unsure as to what Jake referred to.

"Dad," clarified Jake, meeting his gaze. "Driving Dad and hitting that pole. You did it on purpose to get him out of our life."

Ty's eyes rounded, but he inclined his chin.

"And you helped me protect my baby girl," said Jake, "when the posse came after my baby."

"I couldn't have gotten Ava out of the hands of those Russian mobsters without you," added Kee.

"And he made sure Colt was in place to save Kacey," Jake said to Kee. Then he turned to Ty. "I'm sorry I didn't understand. That all this time I thought you were one of them."

"He's always been one of us," said Kee. "Always."

Ty's throat tightened. They were seeing him as if for the first time, recognizing his value, and their gratitude tore him up inside. He didn't know what to say.

"Does Mom know?" asked Ty at last.

"She said she knew all along. Suspected, at least, that you were the reason our dad was locked up," said Jake. "I don't know why she didn't tell me."

"Is she here?" Ty asked.

"Spending the night in the clinic with Abbie," said Kee. "Burt, too."

"Her house is still an active crime scene," added Jake. He rested a hand on Ty's uninjured shoulder. "They're gone now, the posse. Finished."

Ty let that soak in. All his life they had been there, this dark black hole that swallowed up their youth and from which they could not escape. But he and the tribe had done what couldn't be managed before. The Wolf Posse was no more.

"We have to make sure they aren't replaced by another gang," said Ty.

Jake smiled. "Might be a good job for you."

Ty shook his head, not understanding what he could do.

"All this time," said Jake, "I was looking up to Wallace Tinnin and Jack Bear Den, when you were right there in front of me. I feel so stupid."

"He was behind you," said Kee. "Behind all of us. That's why we couldn't see him."

Ty placed a hand over his mouth to keep them from seeing his trembling lower lip.

"Can I see Abbie and Ma?" he asked.

Ty was back at tribal headquarters the next morning and greeted by Kee's girl, Ava Hood.

"They're waiting for you in the chief's office," she said.

A step up from the interrogation room, he thought.

"Good work, Ty," said Ava, and gave him a warm smile.

This feeling of pride was so new to him he didn't know what to do with it.

"Thanks," he said, and ducked his head, making his way across the squad room.

On the way he was congratulated by Officer Harold Shay and thanked by Officer Daniel Wetselline. Detective Jack Bear Den stood at the chief's office and extended his hand. Ty took it and accepted both the handshake and Bear Den's sincere thanks to him for coming in.

Ty felt as if he'd stepped into some alternate universe, where he was no longer a "known associate of the Wolf Posse" and a potential threat to the tribe. It felt so odd and he was uncomfortable in his own skin.

One glance told him that Beth Hoosay was still not here. It seemed they were intentionally keeping them apart. Or perhaps Beth knew better than to buy the hometown-hero bit. Perhaps she did not wish to see him again, not even to say goodbye.

Tinnin waited for Ty to be seated in front of the large wooden desk that seemed to have survived from another century.

"It's possible that Chino Aria might testify in exchange for a deal. He would be tried here in our court system. What's your opinion on that?" Tinnin asked.

Ty tried to think of the last time anyone had asked his opinion on anything other than auto paint color and came up short. "He's dangerous. Wanted to take over the posse. If he's out, he'll try to build it again."

Bear Den met the chief's gaze and there was a silent exchange. Ty surmised that this was the opinion of at least one of them.

"What about the others?" asked Ty.

"The rest will be turned over to the DA for federal prosecution."

It was a break from past practices. The tribal leadership tried very diligently to take care of all violations of law. But they had never faced an organization that preyed on their women and worked with a notorious criminal organization.

"That's a good move," said Ty.

They reviewed his statement with him and he signed it.

"Anything else?" asked Tinnin.

"Randy Tasa?" asked Ty.

"Yeah, he's in some trouble. But we'll handle it within the tribe."

Ty approved of that. Even considered taking Randy under his wing. The boy reminded Ty of himself at times, trying to please and fit in and look out for his sister even when she was a mess and far beyond his help.

The last question was hardest. "Will I be seeing Beth Hoosay again?"

"Not officially," said Forrest. "She's been retrieved by the Oklahoma field office. She'll complete her work on this case from there."

Ty thought he did not succeed in keeping the emotions from showing in his expression. What did you do with a broken heart when it fell into your lap before a roomful of tough, seasoned lawmen?

"Doesn't stop you from seeing her unofficially," said Tinnin.

Ty met his gaze and then let it slip away. He was not going to chase after Beth unless she made it known that the partnership that he had taken all the way to his heart had affected her in some way.

Tinnin's sigh was audible and he lifted his spur, the one that perpetually sat on his desk, and spun the rowel absently. "When this is all settled, the tribe would like to offer you a position."

"Auto pool?" he asked, trying not to feel insulted. It was considerate of them to think at all about his future because the market for fast cars by the Wolf Posse had just dried up.

Thank goodness and heck, yeah, he thought.

"No," said Bear Den. "With the tribal council and in conjunction with our school system. They want you as a youth counselor."

"A what?" His head snapped up and he looked from one man to the next. They did not smirk and nothing in their expressions indicated that they were pulling his leg.

"I don't have any qualifications for that," he said.

"We disagree. You are overqualified to work with troubled kids and we have more than most," said Tinnin. "We'd consider it an honor to have you. And if you want some letters after your name, Kenshaw Little Falcon has offered to help you apply to the correct programs. Though I doubt they'll teach you anything you don't already know about human nature."

Ty stammered, "I—I don't know what to say."

It was a position of merit and respect. The very last sort of job he ever expected to be offered.

"Say yes," said Tinnin.

Chapter Twenty-Three

Beth waited with Hemi on the bottom step of Ty's place. She'd missed him this morning. Her black Escalade waited in his drive before the closed bay doors, packed and ready to go. Forrest had assured her that once this case was settled she'd have her pick of any field office in the country.

She was considering Phoenix. It wasn't New York, but it was a larger office than Oklahoma, though that no longer seemed to matter. She began to wonder if the real reason that she had wanted out of Oklahoma was that it was where her father had died. Perhaps some distance would help her come to terms with her mother's anger and allow them both to mend their relationship.

She'd called her mother today for the first time in she didn't know when. The conversation had been awkward, but it was a start.

Strange that, accidentally, while she was trying to solve a case, she had fallen in with a tribe and a family and a man who had all reminded her that family was worth fighting for. Ty had shown her what it felt like to be a part of something, and she wanted that. She loved it here. Turquoise Canyon was beautiful and, with all its flaws and troubles, it had people of character who loved this land and this tribe with the sort of selfless hearts she admired.

And Ty was here. If this was where he intended to be, then this was where she would stay, if he'd let her. He was worth losing a placement over. Why did she need to go to New York? The job here was no less valuable and neither the size of the field office nor the prestige of the placement made any difference to her now. She knew that because she'd finally gotten what she'd wanted and it didn't make her feel more important or more valuable.

She accepted in her heart that trying to be placed in an office of ex-army rangers and special ops agents would not bring her closer to her father any more than riding her bike or joining the army had done.

The offices in New York and DC handled big problems—global problems—and they were important. But so was this corner of the Southwest, so close to the Mexican border with all that that entailed.

The question remained, would Ty let her in?

The sound of the GTO's engine was unmistakable. Beth stood to greet Ty. Hemi rose and stretched, glancing back at her before trotting out to the road to escort Ty's gold Pontiac into his drive. He parked beside her Escalade, hands gripping the wheel as he glanced to her, and cut the engine. His expression was grim and his movements were slow as he exited the vehicle. Everything about him said he dreaded this meeting. Beth's heart sank and her smile dropped away.

He greeted Hemi with a pat and the dog trotted off to circle his Pontiac, sniffing as she went.

"Hey," Ty said.

"Hi there," she replied, forcing her hands into her

back pockets, which caused her blazer to gape in the front so her shoulder holster and pistol showed.

She'd killed his father. The scene flashed before her, and her smile went brittle. What did he think of that?

Ty approached with a slow, measured tread.

"So, you all packed?" he asked, thumbing toward her vehicle. She was but not for the reasons he suspected.

She began to wonder what Forrest had told him. Did he know about her being called back to Oklahoma?

Ty continued without waiting for an answer. "You did it. Made a big case. Broke up the surrogate ring and took down our gang. Well done, Agent Hoosay."

"We don't have all your girls back yet. Still working on that."

"You think you'll find them?" he asked.

His gaze slipped over her and she felt her body responding to just his glance. She held herself back, not wanting to make a mistake. This was too important. "I have confidence that their location will come to light. I'm not going to give up."

"That's good."

He wasn't looking at her now and it seemed he was trying not to look at her.

"Ty?" she asked. She drew her hands from her pockets and intended for them to hang at her sides but found herself reaching for him. "I have to go to Oklahoma for a while. But it's temporary."

"Before you get your promotion?"

"Yes, but I'd call it a choice of placements."

"I remember. DC or NYC. All the important initials." Ty's shoulder throbbed. His heart ached and he could not keep himself from staring at her. She was going without him, onward and upward, to take on the world.

And he would stay here and protect his tiny corner of it. "Congratulations, Agent Hoosay. I'm happy for you."

How had he even managed to say that? *Happy for her?* He needed to get away before he did something unforgivable, like begging her to stay here. He glanced at his garage and the tiny apartment above, feeling all his insecurities roiling up like the river after the monsoon.

She reached and took hold of him by each hand, her cold palms sliding into his warmer ones. "Are you? I was hoping you'd want me to stay."

He blinked at her. "Stay? Stay where?"

Hemi returned and nosed at their joined hands. Beth laughed and released one hand to pet Hemi's blockish head.

"Ty, I don't want to leave you. If you let me, I'll transfer to the office in Phoenix or Flagstaff so this would be my territory." She motioned to the world around them.

"Here? You want to stay here? That doesn't make any sense," he said, but his heart was hammering now, crashing against his ribs like a fist. "Why would you do that?"

"To be with you."

He withdrew his hand from hers and stepped back. "No. You are not giving up everything you've worked for to stay here."

"Why not?"

"Because you'll resent me for it, for making you lose your chance."

"First, I wouldn't have a chance if you hadn't helped me because we both know I had exactly zero likelihood to make this case alone. Second, I love it here. Your tribe is special, Ty. You're special."

"You're making a mistake," he said.

"No mistake. I love you, Ty, and I will do anything and everything to prove it."

"I don't want you here."

She gave him a knowing smile. "Yeah, right. Not this time, buddy."

He shook his head, not understanding what she meant.

"You think love is selfless. You sacrificed for your family, to keep your brothers safe, to give them families of their own, and you did all that at your own expense. How about I show you the kind of love that does not require loss? My love for you will make us stronger and it won't hurt."

He swallowed past the lump.

"Are you sure?" he whispered.

Beth stepped into his arms and wrapped her hands about his neck, kissing him on the lips. When she drew back, he was certain that he wondered if she might really mean it.

"I'm yours, Ty Redhorse. I've found the best man for me and you know I am not letting you go. I love you, Ty."

He gathered her against his chest, resting his cheek on the top of her head.

"Thank God," he whispered.

Epilogue

Two months passed, and January arrived with a cold, constant rain. Here in Atlanta, Georgia, the winter was wet and gray. The raid had been successful. Ty and Beth stood together outside the adults-only establishment in FBI rain slickers. The puddles and wet pavement reflected the flashing neon pink of the sign that read: *Girls All Nude* and the red and blue lights of the police cruisers.

The local FBI field agents brought out the entertainers one by one. Beside Ty stood his brother Colt and Colt's wife, Kacey. The arrest of Victor Vitoli and his crew had led to the capture of Leonard Usov himself. Usov was the head of the western territory for the Kuznetsov crime organization. Kostya Kuznetsov himself was in custody and Ty trusted Beth's assessment that the crime boss would not be wriggling out of the charges against him.

Both Maggie Kesselman and Brenda Espinoza had been recovered in December from a surrogate house outside Tucson, both pregnant. They were two of many recovered just days after a raid spearheaded by Luke Forrest based on intel from the materials and files recovered during the Turquoise Canyon rez case.

Forrest had given Beth a courtesy call so Kacey

Doka Redhorse and Colt could be on hand for the recovery of Kacey's best friend. With Usov and Vitoli behind bars, there was no need to continue their witness protection. The young couple had elected to come home immediately with their son, Charlie.

Chief Wallace Tinnin had come with them along with their tribe's psychologist and medicine man, Kenshaw Little Falcon. Tinnin wore a tribal police jacket and Kenshaw stood in a saturated sheepskin jacket, more appropriate for the mountains of Arizona. The wide brims of their cowboy hats kept the rain from their faces.

The back door of the building banged open. A group of three more women emerged, their eyes wide and frightened. Some of the employees here were legitimate, but many were human slaves, sold to this establishment by the Kuznetsov organization. Here they worked as servers, dancers and prostitutes, never leaving the property. Ty wondered how Faras would feel at seeing them at the moment of their release, thin, hunched and defeated. The shame wafted from them like a living thing. Ty grieved at witnessing their suffering.

Beside him, Kacey gave a shout. Then she called out, "Marta!"

The last girl in the group turned. Her once lovely brown skin had taken on yellowish undertones and there were dark circles beneath her eyes. But Ty knew her. That was Marta Garcia, Kacey's dearest friend and the last of their women to be recovered.

Marta's eyes widened and her hands came to her mouth. Tears sprang from her eyes. Kacey ran the distance to her friend. The two embraced, sobbing, as they dropped to their knees in the parking lot in the rain.

Ty swallowed down the lump in his throat at witnessing their reunion. He hoped that the tribe would follow through with their decision to turn all members of the Wolf Posse over to state authorities for prosecution with the exception of Randy Tasa. He was glad that Detective Bear Den had agreed to foster Randy. With that sort of role model in his life, the boy would have a chance.

Forrest stepped up beside Ty.

"What will happen to Marta's baby?" asked Ty.

He knew from Beth that they had found the names of all the birth parents who had donated sperm and paid exorbitant fees for the care of their surrogates without knowing that the photos and reports they received were all bogus. Their surrogates were not happy, smart college grad students funding their education through surrogacy. They were slaves.

"Courts will have to decide. There will be repercussions."

"You mean fines?"

"Definitely. Perhaps criminal charges. They've broken the law by not using the legitimate options available to them. I don't know if the state will take away their children. They're the genetic parents, but…" Forrest rubbed his neck. "I'm glad I don't have to sort that all out."

Colt left them to go to his wife and her friend. He wrapped a blanket about Marta's shoulders and Kacey helped her rise.

"You're going home with us, Marta. It's over now," said Kacey.

Marta clung and nodded. Ty thought it would not be over for the victims for quite some time. Such abuse left damage. But he knew that Kenshaw had put together a mental health team to help the returned deal with their emotional trauma. Just as he had helped his mom in the aftermath of the shooting.

Perhaps the women who had been taken would find

some comfort in knowing that no other among them would suffer what they had gone through because of the work of the good people of their tribe.

"You ready to go home, Ty?" Beth asked.

Her transfer had been approved and she now worked out of the FBI field office in Phoenix, Arizona. He nodded and took her hand and they headed back toward the waiting vehicles, getting out of the way and letting the locals take care of business.

THE WOLF POSSE was crushed. Ty and Beth would be two of many who would make sure that it would not rise from the dust. But first they had a wedding to plan and a house to build.

"I've been thinking of buying some horses," she said.

"Barrel racing?" he asked.

"Yeah. For a start."

"Sounds good."

What a joy to be able to do what she loved with the man she adored, a man who knew better than most about risk and reward.

They walked together, arm in arm.

"I'm glad you feel that way," she said.

"Beth, I love riding horses and our bikes, but more than anything, I love you."

She smiled. "Don't let Hemi hear you say that."

"No." He laughed. "I won't."

Beth paused before him and then leaned in to kiss him on the lips. When she drew back she rested her hands on his chest.

"I love you, Ty."

* * * * *

COMING SOON!

We really hope you enjoyed reading this book. If you're looking for more romance, be sure to head to the shops when new books are available on

Thursday
14th June

To see which titles are coming soon, please visit
millsandboon.co.uk